Lucy King spent her ado
glamorous and exciting w
when she really ought to l
attention to her teachers. As she couldn't live in a dream world for ever, she eventually acquired a degree in languages and an eclectic collection of jobs. After a decade in southwest Spain, Lucy now lives with her young family in Wiltshire, England. When not writing, or trying to think up new and innovative things to do with mince, she spends her time reading, failing to finish cryptic crosswords and dreaming of the golden beaches of Andalusia.

Tara Pammi can't remember a moment when she wasn't lost in a book—especially a romance, which was much more exciting than a mathematics textbook at school. Years later, Tara's wild imagination and love for the written word revealed what she really wanted to do. Now she pairs alpha males who think they know everything with strong women who knock that theory *and* them off their feet!

Also by Lucy King

Passionately Ever After… collection

Undone by Her Ultra-Rich Boss

Heirs to a Greek Empire miniseries

Virgin's Night with the Greek
A Christmas Consequence for the Greek
The Flaw in His Rio Revenge

Also by Tara Pammi

Billion-Dollar Fairy Tales miniseries

Marriage Bargain with Her Brazilian Boss
The Reason for His Wife's Return
An Innocent's Deal with the Devil

The Powerful Skalas Twins miniseries

Saying 'I Do' to the Wrong Greek
Twins to Tame Him

Discover more at millsandboon.co.uk.

AFTER HOURS

LUCY KING

TARA PAMMI

MILLS & BOON

First published in Great Britain 2024
by Mills & Boon, an imprint of HarperCollins*Publishers* Ltd,
1 London Bridge Street, London, SE1 9GF

www.harpercollins.co.uk

HarperCollins*Publishers*, Macken House, 39/40 Mayor Street Upper, Dublin 1, D01 C9W8, Ireland

ISBN: 978-0-263-32025-1

09/24

This book contains FSC™ certified paper
and other controlled sources to ensure responsible forest management.

For more information visit www.harpercollins.co.uk/green.

Printed and Bound in the UK using 100% Renewable Electricity
at CPI Group (UK) Ltd, Croydon, CR0 4YY

BOSS WITH BENEFITS

LUCY KING

MILLS & BOON

For Heidi and Natalie,
my fellow billionaire bachelor bet babes.

CHAPTER ONE

'Do I know you? Because you look a lot like my next girlfriend.'

Sitting at the bar of Manhattan's newest and buzziest cocktail lounge, Ella Green winced. The chat-up line delivered by the guy on her left was as repellent as the malodorous combination of alcohol, sweat and cologne that was emanating from him and catching her at the back of her throat. It was the twenty-first century. Could a woman *still* not drown her sorrows in public on her own on a Friday night in June in peace?

'You don't know me, I'm afraid,' she said politely, as she ramped up the *back off* vibes and edged away.

'But I'd like to,' said the guy, leaning a little more heavily on the bar, his smile presumably aiming for seductive but resulting in somewhere between dribbling and lecherous. 'I'm Pete. Do you have a name or should I just call you "mine"?'

Ugh. 'Never do that.'

'You know, if I could rearrange the alphabet, I'd put "U" and "I" together.'

Ella sighed. 'It's "you" and "me."'

'What?'

'If you're going to try and pick me up with terrible lines, at least be grammatically correct about it.'

Utter befuddlement met that remark. '"U" and "me" doesn't work,' said Pete with a frown.

'Well, there you go then. Take the hint.'

He didn't. Instead, he doubled down. 'Would you at least stroke my arm so I can tell my friends I've been touched by an angel?'

'No.'

'Then how about I stroke yours?'

He reached out and put his hand on her bare upper arm, and in the blink of an eye she'd spun round, her knee had connected with his groin and the contents of her glass had landed on his shirt.

Pete gave a yowl and clutched his genitals, his face contorted in pain, but Ella refused to feel guilty. She had given him every opportunity to go away and leave her alone. It was his own fault he hadn't taken it.

'Sorry,' she said, not sorry at all. 'Dodgy stool.'

Gasping and spluttering, Pete plucked at the vodka-soaked cotton, puce with humiliation and evidently furious. 'Frigid bitch.'

'Inebriated jerk.'

With a filthy glare, he limped off and Ella swung back to the bar. She wasn't frigid. Or a bitch. She just valued her personal space and didn't appreciate being groped against her will. Like most people, she imagined. Although most people probably hadn't grown up in a dangerous, deprived backwater of a neighbourhood where it was sensible to learn self-defence at an early age.

'Nice moves.'

This dry remark came from the guy on her right, who was a different kettle of fish entirely.

She'd been bitterly contemplating her drink when he'd sat down beside her ten minutes earlier. An odd sort of charge had electrified the displaced air. An exquisitely woodsy scent had wafted towards her. Her skin prickling in the most peculiar way, she'd instinctively glanced over and out of habit had catalogued what she'd been able to see from the side.

A man of around her age, maybe a few years older. Thick dark hair. Straight nose. Square jaw with the hint of a five-o'clock shadow. Pale blue Oxford shirt, sleeves rolled up. Tanned, muscled forearms. An expensive-looking gold-faced and tan-leather-strapped watch on his left wrist. Big hands, long fingers, short, neat nails.

Very attractive in profile, she'd concluded as a hot shiver had rippled down her spine. Possibly even more so from the front.

She'd reluctantly averted her gaze before he could catch her ogling. He'd summoned the bartender and given the order for a large Scotch, his cut glass accent indicating that he came from the other side of the Atlantic. Parking her curiosity and leaving him to whatever had him also studying his drink, Ella had resumed her acidic ruminations on the gross unfairness of life that meant her unspeakable ex was up for an industry award while she was still trying to repair her career after their short yet illicit workplace affair blew up a year ago. But she'd nevertheless remained acutely aware of her neighbour's size, stillness and his intriguing sense of contained power—until her attention had been claimed in the other direction.

Now, however, with that deep deliciously sexy voice aimed straight at her, the timbre of it vibrating through her body and igniting her nerve endings, she turned. Her gaze met his, and for one breathtaking moment the world slammed to a halt. The dimly lit bar with its glittering opulence and sultry vibe vanished. The bottom fell out of her stomach. Her heart skipped a beat and then began to race.

She'd been right, she thought dazedly, her head spinning and her temperature rocketing. He *was* even more attractive from the front. His eyes were like the ocean. As blue and as deep as the Pacific. And suddenly she felt a stab of empathy for Pete, because as cringeworthy as the thought was, she wanted to dive right into them.

After what felt like an hour but could only have been a second, Ella blinked, snapping the sizzling connection. Her surroundings swam into focus and the world cranked back into gear.

'I don't know what you mean,' she said, still a little breathless from the impact he was having on her. 'It was an accident.'

His mesmerising eyes glinted with wry amusement. 'Of course it was.'

'The perils of an uneven floor.'

'A dodgy stool, I thought you said.'

'It's a dangerous combination.'

'And there was me deliberating over whether to intervene.'

'How would you have done that?' she asked, immediately envisaging him stripping off his shirt and squaring up to her former admirer, all rippling muscles and simmering outrage on her behalf. Which was bizarre when, firstly, she was a financial auditor with a keen eye for numerical detail but next to no imagination and, secondly, she had never *ever* needed rescuing.

'I hadn't thought that far.'

That was a shame. 'Lucky, then, that I can take care of myself.'

'Not so lucky for Pete.'

'I gave him fair warning.'

'More than enough,' he agreed. 'His lines were appalling. He needs to learn to take no for an answer.' He ran his gaze over her face, her hair, her body, scorching her like a laser where it lingered. Then he added, with the glimmer of a devastating smile, 'But I can't blame him for trying.'

In response to his appreciative scrutiny—*so* much more welcome than the leery Pete's—Ella flushed from head to toe and fizzed with pleasure. 'Thank you. I think.'

'I'm Adam.'

Swinging round, he held out his hand and she automatically took it. 'Ella,' she said, just about able to recall her name even though tiny shocks were shooting up her arm into her head and short-circuiting her brain.

'May I replenish your drink?'

He could do anything he wanted with that voice and those eyes. If he reached out and peeled off her dress, right here, right now, she'd be helpless to stop him. In fact, she'd probably tell him to hurry up. And that was concerning for a single-minded control freak who made decisions with her head, not her heart. But she couldn't remember the last time she'd been so instantly and comprehensively attracted to a man. Ever.

'That's very straightforward of you,' she said, boldly checking out the perfection of his masculine features and the impressive breadth of his shoulders while the heat whipping around inside her coalesced into a puddle of lust that settled low in her abdomen. 'Don't you want to tell me that even though you're not a photographer you can picture us together?'

'No,' he said, his voice dropping an octave. 'Although I can.'

'How?'

'You don't want to know.'

'I do.'

He leaned in and murmured, 'It involves a large bed and no clothes.'

God. He didn't beat about the bush. If she'd had any doubt about the mutuality of the attraction, it had just been pulverised. Her mouth dried. Her entire body throbbed. This man could invade her personal space any day of the week, she thought as she exhaled slowly and swallowed hard. 'Tell me more.'

'I'm still working on the details,' he said, drawing back just enough for her to be able to see that his pupils were so dilated little of the blue remained. 'But if you're after a line, I'm more than happy to admit that I was feeling a little off today until you just turned me on. Perverse, I know, but there it is. You're beautiful and fierce. It's another dangerous combination.'

If anything was dangerous, it was him. She'd always enjoyed this dance, the flirty back and forth and the heavy looks—until the lousy experience with her ex had meant that she'd had to focus on rebuilding her career to the exclusion of all else. But what was going on here was on a whole other level.

This man, who was gazing at her with such heat that she felt as though she could catch fire any moment now, was unleashing that reined-in power she'd sensed earlier. He wasn't bothering with a slow-burning build-up. He was pouring petrol on the bonfire and setting it alight. Deliberately or not, he was killing her brain cells, one by one, and unravelling the control she'd always considered rock solid.

They'd only been talking for five minutes, but already she could visualise them writhing around together in that bed. Her breasts were tingling. White-hot desire was pouring through her with such strength that her inhibitions were fast becoming history. She wanted to leap onto his lap and seal her mouth to his while yanking his shirt aside and putting her hands on his bare chest.

It was insane. Incomprehensible. And to someone who'd had to forswear fun for the last twelve months to concentrate on her career and had sorely missed intimacy of the steamy, sweaty kind, it was absolutely thrilling.

'What were you drinking?'

That was an excellent question. Liquid dopamine? Dynamite? 'Martini.'

'How do you like it?'

'The dirtier the better.'

A faint smile curved his gorgeous mouth and detonated tiny bombs of excitement inside her. 'A woman after my own heart.'

'I'm not after anyone's heart,' she countered with an imperceptible shudder. Never had been, never would be. Even the thought of giving up her hard-won independence brought her out in a cold sweat. Compromise? Sacrifice? No, thank you very much. She'd had to climb countless ladders to get out of the impoverished, fetid and perilous trailer park in which she'd grown up and make something of herself. Conquering the world of auditing was her number one priority and she needed no distractions.

But the pure unadulterated lust currently ravaging her system? That she could indulge.

'Neither am I,' he said with equal intensity.

'Single?'

'Always.'

'You could not be more perfect,' she breathed on a sigh.

'Nor could you.'

For one long hot moment, they just stared at each other, the air between them humming with energy, her drink forgotten. His hand found her bare knee, and her skin first shivered then sizzled when it inched up her thigh. She leaned in as if magnetised and touched her fingers to those of his other hand, which rested on the bar. The buzzing electricity that flowed through the circuit they formed was so powerful she wouldn't be surprised if the effects could be felt in Brooklyn.

His gaze dropped to her mouth and her heart thundered. The desire radiating off him was almost palpable. She'd never experienced such instant and blistering chemistry or felt so...*carnal.*

The sensible, rational voice in her head—to which she usually paid avid attention—insisted that this was no simple flirtation, that she was way out of her depth, that she really should not do what it suspected she was going to do. She must not lose focus, it demanded. Rebuilding her career had been her primary goal for the last twelve months and she had to stick to that.

But it didn't stand a chance.

Nothing mattered except satisfying the primal urge to act on the need rampaging through her. Like a train thundering along the tracks, she was heading in one direction only, her destination flashing at her like a beacon from the moment their gazes had collided. It wasn't as if she'd be there for long, she assured herself. She'd be back to reality soon enough.

'Would you like to take this conversation somewhere a bit more private?' she said, so desperate to assuage the throbbing ache between her legs that she was incapable of thinking about anything else.

He didn't hesitate. He didn't even blink. 'Yes,' he said, sounding as though he'd swallowed gravel. 'I very much would.'

What the hell he thought was doing as he closed the bathroom door behind him and flipped the lock, Adam Courtney had no idea. He didn't pick women up in bars, no matter how powerfully sexy and beautiful they were. He'd given up that sort of selfish, reckless behaviour fourteen years ago at the age of eighteen, when his mother had died because he'd been too busy screwing around to save her, and Charley, his then eight-year-old sister, had been left rudderless.

At no point since had he relapsed. These days, his ultra-brief relationships were infrequent and discreet. He would not turn into his callous, philandering father, he'd reminded himself over the years on the rare occasion his control threatened to slip. His reputation for steadiness and integrity was inextricably linked to that of the Courtney Collection, the luxury goods empire that had been in his family for over a century and which he now headed up, and he would do nothing to jeopardise it.

Yet he hadn't hesitated for even a moment when Ella had suggested he give her a couple of minutes and then join her in here. His reputation hadn't crossed his mind. For the first time in years, he wasn't thinking with his brain. From the moment he'd looked into her gorgeous brown eyes, he'd been driven entirely by the clamouring needs of his body, and he was far too battered by recent events to resist the power of the desire that had surged through him.

He'd noticed her the minute he'd reached the bar at which he'd intended to rid himself of the tension that had been dogging him for weeks by consuming large quantities of single malt. It had been impossible not to. Her hair flowed down her back in long golden waves that gleamed in the low lighting and looked as though they would feel like silk. Her sleeveless dress, the colour of buttermilk, clung to generous curves and revealed toned tanned arms. A brief glance to his left as he'd taken possession of the stool to her right had told him that her profile was exquisite, her complexion flawless. And judging by the looks she'd attracted, he wasn't the only one to think so.

But although his interest had been piqued, he hadn't planned on speaking to her. She'd appeared preoccupied and he'd had plenty else to dwell on. Such as Helberg Holdings, the global conglomerate that had been in his sights for over a decade, which was in serious financial trouble and therefore ripe for a takeover.

The minute he'd heard seven months ago that the cantankerous owner had died, he'd started buying up the dirt-cheap shares, and victory, he'd thought with grim satisfaction as his stake steadily grew, would soon be his. Once in his possession, he'd sell off everything except Montague's, the jewellery business that had been beloved of his mother and used to belong to the Courtney Collection until his father had sold it to Reed Helberg for a dollar out of spite. That, he'd welcome back into the fold and restore to its former glory, and then, perhaps, the crushing guilt that had weighed on him so heavily and for so long might lift a little.

Lately, however, the availability of the stock had plummeted, and the share price was rocketing to a level that was beginning to challenge even his exceedingly deep pockets. He faced the very real possibility that the company could slip through his fingers, and that simply could not happen. Whatever the threat—rivals, internal machinations, *anything*—he needed to neutralise it.

Adam had been contemplating hiring a private investigator to dig into what was going on when the idiotic

Pete had made his move and then the coolly magnificent Ella had made hers. He hadn't been able to resist checking she was all right under the guise of expressing his admiration at her handling of the situation, but never in a million years could he have anticipated feeling as though he'd been struck by lightning when their eyes had met.

Yet that was precisely what had happened.

In the space of a millisecond, his pulse rate had shot through the roof and his head had emptied of everything but the need to get her naked. Every drop of his blood had rushed to his groin and the erection he'd sprung had been so hard it had ached.

They'd talked—about what he could hardly recall—and all he'd been able to focus on was her mouth. He'd wanted it on his, on his skin, taking him in as deeply as she could. She'd stared at him hungrily, obliterating years of ironclad control and stripping away millennia of civility, and if she hadn't suggested this, he had no doubt that he would have.

Now she was standing at the black marble-and-gilt vanity unit with her back to him, feet apart, her hands gripping the edges. Her warm brown eyes connected with his in the Art Deco mirror, glittering with excitement and invitation. Any lingering doubt he might have had about the wisdom of what he was about to do was swept away by a thundering tsunami of desire.

'We have to be quick,' she said raggedly, her cheeks flushed, her chest heaving.

'That's not going to be problem.' Thanks to his recent fixation with Helberg Holdings, he hadn't had sex in months and was wound so tightly he was about to explode.

Stepping forwards and pressing up against her, he swept her hair to one side and set his mouth to her neck. Her skin tasted faintly salty. The coconut scent of her shampoo wafted into his head. He briefly thought of the many holidays that gruelling sixteen-hour days hadn't allowed him to take, but then she shivered and moaned, grinding her bottom into his groin, and he stopped thinking about anything at all.

Compelled by the primitive need to be inside her slick welcoming heat, Adam unbuckled his belt and unzipped his trousers. He pushed down the clothing that was in the way and, gritting his teeth, rolled on the condom he'd fished out of his wallet. He wanted to touch her everywhere, slowly and thoroughly, savouring the experience, but that wasn't an option under the circumstances. So he put his hands on her bare upper arms and then ran them down her body, over her soft curves, until he reached the hem of her dress. They shook as he lifted it and stilled completely when he found her naked where he'd expected underwear.

'I thought I'd save some time,' she murmured in response to the hiss of his breath through his teeth.

'I'm impressed,' he said, his blood pumping through his veins even faster as he slid one hand round between her legs, feeling the dampness there, and pressed his fingers to her core. 'I'm way beyond thought.'

Ella groaned and bent forwards, shifting her feet wider apart to allow him better access. 'Hurry,' she breathed unnecessarily, because he was already there, the blunt head of him pushing at her entrance. She gave her bottom a quick wiggle of encouragement—not that he needed it—and with one smooth hard thrust he lodged thickly inside her.

His heart lurched and then began to pound. She swore softly, closed her eyes and threw her head back, her golden hair shimmering in the low light. Bewitched by the sight of it as much as the ferocious desire thundering through him, he was barely aware of his hand gliding up her back and into the glorious tresses as he began to move in and out of her with long steady strokes.

'Yes,' she breathed on a ragged pant, granting him the permission he hadn't even known he was seeking to close his fist around the silky strands close to her scalp and tug on them lightly.

Gasping, instinctively arching her back, she took him in further, the penetration at this angle so deep he saw stars. She opened her eyes and their gazes once again connected in the mirror, with an unexpected intimacy that tightened his chest. But he didn't have the wherewithal to wonder why that should be. His control was fast disintegrating. The exquisite tension inside him was intensifying, the muscles in his stomach, his back and his chest contracting. His fingers were tightening around her hair and his thrusts were quickening.

Her breathing was harsh and the look in her eyes was wild, desperate, and he didn't know how much longer he could hold on, when suddenly she tensed and clapped a hand over her mouth, muffling her cry as she shattered around him. Everything inside him spiralled in, sucking into a single point, a black hole in the pit of his groin. He thrust one last time, hard and deep, and the whole universe collapsed into nothingness before suddenly exploding out the other side into colour and light.

When feeling eventually returned to his limbs and his head had stopped spinning, Adam carefully withdrew and dealt with the condom, his body still spasming with tiny darts of lingering pleasure. As he put himself back together and regained control, Ella slowly straightened, smoothed her dress and her hair, then turned to face him, flushed, glowing, still slightly tousled.

'That was…' She shook her head, looking dumbstruck. 'I don't even know what that was.'

Neither did he. He'd never experienced anything like it. He usually deployed far more finesse, although he usually had far more time and these days he favoured a bed. All he *did* know was that he wanted to take her home and do what they'd just done over and over again in every position under the sun all night long—and not just because it would obliterate thoughts of difficult boards and troubling share prices. 'How about that martini?'

For a moment, she looked torn and his pulse spiked. But then she gave her head a regretful shake and picked up her bag.

'Some other time,' she said, hooking the strap onto her shoulder while a wrecking ball of disappointment thumped him in the gut. 'But thank you.'

With the faintest of smiles, she dropped a quick kiss on his cheek as she brushed past him, then unlocked the door and slipped out.

CHAPTER TWO

Four weeks later

ADAM ARRIVED AT the office at 8:00 a.m. after a Fourth of July holiday weekend that had very much *not* been a holiday. In fact, the last forty-eight hours had been so frustrating and stressful they had given him a full-on tension headache that still nagged at his temples.

The trouble had started bright and early on Saturday, following a round of squash that he'd arranged with Zane deMarco and Cade Landry in response to the report he'd received from the private investigators he'd hired to dig into the Helberg Holdings conundrum.

Zane was a deceptively laid-back corporate raider from the poorer part of the Hamptons, who he knew from his Cambridge rowing days and considered a friend. Cade, a hard-edged lone wolf from Louisiana who'd worked his way up from construction worker to big-shot property developer in just over a decade, he'd become acquainted with since arriving in New York.

The three of them crossed paths at functions and met up occasionally to shoot the breeze or thrash the living daylights out of each other on the squash court. They were equally driven, equally competitive and had always operated in different spheres of business.

Until now.

Because both men, the report had revealed, were behind the Helberg Holdings share price surge. And neither, Adam had learned to his annoyance when he'd confronted them in the sauna to which they'd headed after the match, was prepared to step aside.

'No can do,' Zane had drawled at the same time as Cade had given his head a sharp shake and declared, 'Not happening. It's a once-in-a-lifetime opportunity, y'all.'

Of course it was, and with hindsight, Adam didn't know why he hadn't considered their involvement sooner. The portfolio of heritage enterprises owned by Reed Helberg was vast and varied, and in business his so-called friends were sharks. But he'd had no time to process the implications of this unbreakable three-way dead lock because Cade had then delivered yet more bad news, the trouble this time brewing in the offices of *Blush*, the women's glamour magazine.

'Did y'all know we're the star players in their latest dumb article?' he'd practically snarled, having just received a text from his PR consultant on the subject. 'The Billionaire Bachelors Least Likely to Marry. Apparently, we three have been tagged as the One-Date Wonders—the guys with the longest odds—and they've already started a tally of how many dates we'll have racked up by Labor Day… My PR team are freaking out about it. Personally, I don't give a damn what a bunch of click-bait junkies and their enablers think of my dating habits.

But no way in hell am I letting anyone make me look like a jerk who can't keep his junk in his pants.'

Although he wouldn't have put it in those terms, Adam had shared Cade's sentiment. His integrity was everything, and this article, with both its inaccurate, unsavoury slant and the traction it was gaining, had sounded as though it had reputational damage written all over it. He, the board and the women he was regularly photographed with knew that his dating record wasn't what it seemed—ninety-five percent of them were strategically selected by him to promote the company, and there weren't even that many of them—but of what use was that? The optics were disastrous and the fallout could be catastrophic. At the height of his father's philandering, which by that point had become legally as well as morally questionable and therefore even greater fodder for the merciless tabloids, sales had plummeted by seventy-five percent.

That wasn't happening again on *his* watch, he'd thought, his temperature soaring in a way that had had nothing to do with the heat of the sauna. He'd worked himself to the bone building up both his reputation and that of the Courtney Collection, and he was not having four years of blood, sweat and tears put at risk simply to fill gossipy column inches and collect social media likes.

They'd all agreed that the interest in them needed to be nixed asap. But it was Zane who'd come up with the idea they take themselves off the market by dating one woman—and one woman only—for the duration of the summer.

At the time, that suggestion had made no sense to

Adam at all. How on earth would *that* reduce the rampant interest in them? he'd asked himself while wondering whether the ruthless corporate raider had actually lost his mind. Wouldn't the sudden shift from multiple dates to one only increase it? Wouldn't the women in question attract attention of their own? And then there was the subterfuge and manipulation that such a response would involve. The lying, deception and the complete absence of integrity—everything he strove to avoid.

Given that the three of them were at the top of their game with infinite resources at their disposal, he'd racked his brains for a more mature, less complicated way to protect their reputations. But before he'd been able to come up with anything, Zane's absurd proposal had somehow evolved into a bet, with their Helberg shares as the stake.

'We meet back here on Labor Day,' the man had drawled with a languid smile, as if acquiring the ailing conglomerate was nothing more to him than a game. 'Winner takes all accumulated shares and has an unimpeded run at Helberg. Two birds. One stone.'

While Cade had gone along with the mad idea, Adam had reeled, scarcely been able to believe his ears. This solution to the twin problems of the reputational impact of the article and the stalemate surrounding the company they all wanted had felt farcical. Surreal. Ill thought out at the very least, and he'd protested these points. But ultimately he hadn't been able to see how else they were to keep the share price down and determine who got Helberg. As Zane had coolly pointed out, the likelihood of them stepping out of each other's way just because he—Adam—had asked nicely was zero.

So he'd accepted the bet. He'd had no choice. No matter how important his principles, he was not forfeiting Helberg. He needed it to right the wrong that had been a festering thorn in his side for years. Only when he'd reclaimed Montague's would he find some kind of peace from the torment of knowing that because he'd declined his mother's call the night she'd overdosed he was responsible for her death. Only then would he be free of the guilt that was preventing him from exploring a proper relationship with his sister, Charley. Vengeance and justice would appease his conscience, he was sure. Therefore, he had to play the game and play to win.

After leaving the gym on Saturday morning, he'd checked out the *Blush* article, which had been just as inaccurate yet as salacious as he'd feared, and the 'one-date wonders' hashtag, which had been worse.

Realising he needed to nip any fallout in the bud, he'd immediately called an extraordinary pre-emptive board meeting. He'd spent an hour soothing the ruffled feathers of those who'd caught wind of the story and had then moved on to reassurances that his standing—and that of the company—would remain intact.

That evening, he'd attended the event that had prevented him from insisting to Cade and Zane that the terms of the bet required celibacy and involved no unwitting women in it at all. He couldn't have cried off the company's Fourth of July extravaganza when he was hosting the bloody thing. He hadn't even been able to ditch his date for the event because Annabel St James was the face of the Courtney Collection's leading cosmetics brand, which had just launched a new five-hundred-dollar face cream whose sales would benefit from as much publicity it could get.

Instead, he'd capitalised on the situation by asking her to do him a favour and, for the next couple of months, feed any speculation that they were dating. Annabel—an old friend he'd known since school—had recalled that he'd once done the same for her to deflect some tiresome speculation about her own sexual preferences and agreed.

At least she wouldn't get the wrong idea about the nature of their relationship, he thought darkly as he sat down at his desk and fired up his computer. There was no danger of her wanting more than he could ever give. He was never settling down for real. For that to happen, he imagined he'd have to embrace the chaos of desire and emotion, and even the *thought* of it turned his blood to ice.

Short discreet flings with women who posed no threat to his control were more than adequate for his needs. He had no wish to pursue the kind who tempted him into recklessness in the compact bathroom of a cocktail bar, who blew his mind and then left him there dazed and confused, and who subsequently stormed into his thoughts and dominated his dreams with alarming and unexpected regularity until he'd forced himself to shove her from his head once and for all. That had been a blip.

He wasn't cut out for love or family anyway. To him, that word didn't conjure up images of loud happy dinners round the table and warm cosy thoughts of unconditional love and support. It meant a father who'd preferred the company of much younger women to that of his wife and children and who'd liked to party hard even into middle age. A mother who'd been so miserable in her marriage that she'd wasted away in the castle in Northumberland before life had become too wretched to bear. A sister who, because he'd been away at school when she'd been born, he'd never really got to know but had let down nevertheless. It meant dysfunction so severe that if they hadn't had billions in the bank, they'd have been on the radar of social services.

So Annabel was perfect for the situation in which he now found himself. He'd secured one woman for the entirety of the summer, and though it pained him to admit it, Zane had been right about the effect of that tactic. The half dozen paparazzi that had gathered outside his Central Park West apartment block had gone by the time he'd left home at the crack of dawn this morning, which meant that he was no longer a one-date wonder. His reputation was safe.

All he had to do now was sit back and wait for Cade and Zane to knock themselves out of the contest, and Helberg Holdings would be his. He didn't imagine it would take long. There was no way on earth either man would be able to limit himself to one woman for the next nine weeks. Not only did they go through the opposite sex as if the human race were on the verge of extinction, but also, they weren't nearly as driven as he was.

Cade seemed more bothered by the article and its effect on his PR team, and Zane clearly considered the whole thing nothing more than a source of entertainment. The text message he'd sent ten minutes ago was evidence of that. It had contained a photo of him—Adam—and Annabel at the party, entwined in a deliberately intimate embrace. Zane had captioned the photo with Could do worse for the summer! and a winking emoji.

Adam had rolled his eyes at the puerility of the message, but it was gratifying to know that his efforts had produced the desired result, and so soon. Now he could look to the fortnight ahead and the annual financial audit, which, this year more than most, needed to go without a hitch because the battle for Helberg wouldn't be completely won on Labor Day. Even after taking possession of Cade's and Zane's shares, he'd still need to hoover up the rest. Unlike Zane, he wasn't in the business of hostile takeovers. He'd have to woo the remaining stakeholders, and they'd be more likely to greenlight the deal if the credentials of the Courtney Collection were as spotless as could be.

Therefore, he would be laying out the red carpet for the people his father had scathingly described as 'bean counters,' the auditors who were due to arrive any moment now. He would see that their every requirement was satisfied. He'd be available for consultation 24-7, on hand to deal with anything that arose personally, which was why he'd had his secretary relocate the team from the basement to his domain up here and cancel any imminent travel arrangements he had.

He could not afford another hit to his reputation or that of the company should something be amiss. Both needed to remain squeaky clean until the acquisition of Helberg was tied up. He would allow nothing to go wrong and jeopardise the absolution he'd been pursuing for months and was now within such close reach. Nothing.

There were more disagreeable places to be spending the next two weeks before going on some much-needed leave, Ella mused as she glanced around in appreciation, then headed for the lift to which she'd been directed. Such as the noisy, cold, out-of-town manufacturing plant, where she'd been scheduled to go right up until seven this morning when she'd received instructions to divert to this team instead.

The twenty-five-storey Courtney Collection tower had been constructed thirty years ago. Its highly complex postmodern Art Deco design was said to resemble the fall of a skirt over a bent knee. It was clad in glass that was green on the left and white on the right, lit with multicoloured neon at night and had won widespread praise from architectural critics.

Inside, the extravagantly airy lobby oozed controlled, refined elegance. A palate of soft creams and taupe exuded expensive and exquisite sophistication. In between acres of glass that granted a view of Madison Avenue, tastefully abstract art hung on the walls and pale Italian travertine tiles covered the floor. Even the air smelled divine.

She'd read briefly, in the blissfully air-conditioned cab on the way in, that the Courtney Collection was the world's largest luxury goods empire. It had one hundred offices on five continents. Vineyards in France and

Australia. Seven-star boutique hotels in London, Paris and Rome. And upmarket retail spaces selling clothes, jewellery, perfumes and cosmetics in every fashionable corner of the globe.

Far more importantly, however, it offered her the chance of a long-awaited, well-deserved promotion.

In the aftermath of her regrettable affair with Drew Taylor, her then boss's then boss, her career had stalled. She had not moved a rung up the ladder, as she'd previously expected. She'd continued as team leader on small, low-profile audits, and she had received neither a pay rise nor a bonus in a year.

A coincidence? When Drew had been transferred to the other side of the country to head up the office there? She didn't think so. But she'd had no solid evidence of discriminatory treatment, and even if she had, she doubted she'd have done anything with it. The moral high ground could be a lonely place. Word travelled. She'd have likely been eased out of the firm and might never have worked in the industry she loved again, and she'd fought too hard to risk everything.

It had taken an immense amount of courage and determination to finish high school and attend college when, on that front, expectations both at home and in the classroom had been virtually non-existent. She'd had to be incredibly strong to stay out of trouble in an environment that seethed with it and retain the belief that unlike her parents, she didn't have to deal drugs for a living. Once she'd decided at the age of fourteen that acquiring a profession was going to be her way out—accountancy, since she was good with numbers—she'd pursued it with dogged determination. She'd found the library. She'd researched and contacted charities that would help. She'd blagged her way into jobs in town to fund her studies and kept her endeavours quiet. Later on, she'd shed the visible stain of her upbringing by taking elocution and etiquette lessons and learned to network. She'd done whatever it took to graduate top of her class. She'd had her pick of jobs and she hadn't looked back.

Briefly, stupidly, she'd lost sight of her goals, but she would not double down on her mistake. So instead of filing a complaint, instead of risking unemployment by resigning, she'd shoved a lid on her anger and bitterness and kept her head down. She'd bided her time until memories had faded, although her own hadn't because she still couldn't believe she'd been so reckless.

What had she been thinking? was the question that had hammered her for days after the affair had come to light when she'd accidentally messaged her boss instead of her lover. How could she have lowered her guard the night her department had gone out to celebrate the end of a successful financial year? Sure, there'd been gallons of champagne, and after working flat out for months, everyone had been on a high, but that was no excuse for falling into conversation with Drew and flirting. For allowing herself to be flattered by the attentions of an older man. For succumbing to the spark of attraction and then investing far more in it than he had when he'd made her no promises.

Even now she couldn't work out what had been going on in her head. She'd lost focus. She'd let herself down badly. Because of the fallout, she'd ceded control of her career for the first time ever. She was still as furious with herself as she was with HR and Drew over what had happened. But playing the long game—however frustrating and unfair it had felt—finally seemed to be paying off.

Thanks to the previous incumbent coming down with a virus late last night, she was now leading this team of ten for the next two weeks on an audit that was anything but low key. It had been hinted that on the back of it, if all went well, she'd be awarded the promotion she should have received twelve months ago, together with a commensurate pay rise and bonus.

And it *would* go well. Because her year out in the cold was nearly over. Redemption was so imminent she could almost taste it. Soon she'd be able to let go of the rage and regret that consumed so much energy. And she would allow nothing to threaten any of it.

The doors of the lift opened with a soft swoosh. Ella pulled her shoulders and lifted her chin, then emerged into a vast space that was more penthouse apartment than office. It was triple height and had two adjacent walls made entirely of glass. Her gaze flickered around for a moment, taking in the laden bookshelves, the abstract art and more of the cream-and-taupe décor. The squishy sofas, the abundant flower arrangements and the conference table upon which had been placed a carafe of water, a glass and a platter of pastries.

But the contents of the room and the stunning view beyond disappeared the minute she clapped eyes on the man standing at the top of the staircase on the mezzanine, radiating power and authority as the master of all he surveyed, the man she'd known for twenty earth-shattering minutes four weeks ago and had never *ever* expected to see again.

For a moment, she stood frozen to the spot, staring up at him in utter shock. The world screeched to a halt. Her heart gave a great crash against her ribs and then accelerated until it was beating a thundering *Oh-God-Oh-God-Oh-God* tattoo. She had to be hallucinating. Because this could not be happening. It simply could not.

But as he set off down the stairs and the world started up again, she realised she *wasn't* hallucinating and this *was* happening. By some horrible coincidence, perfect, sexy smouldering Adam, who'd rocked her foundations and stolen her wits in the restroom of a cocktail bar, was evidently her brand-new client.

And, oh dear God, she thought as a hot clammy sweat broke out all over her skin and she began to hyperventilate, the implications of this for her redemption, for her career, for her future, were not good *at all.*

CHAPTER THREE

WHAT FRESH HELL was this?

Adam strode across the floor towards the woman he thought he'd consigned to the past weeks ago, his pulse thundering, his head spinning in an effort to contain the shock reeling through him. How much more chaos could he be expected to handle? First, the issues with Helberg. Then the mad bet that had had him abandoning his principles and faking a girlfriend. And now Ella from the bar—who'd forced him to take more cold showers in a week than he had in his entire life, who'd stolen his control so comprehensively he'd almost worn a hole in the carpet with all the frustrated early morning pacing he'd done—was no longer a forgettable moment of insanity but actually here, in his office, evidently none other than the lead auditor he'd been told was on her way up.

So much for having hauled everything back under his control, he thought grimly, forcing the breath from his lungs before he passed out. What, precisely, was he going to do about this latest development that had trouble written all over it?

Instinct was urging him to hustle her straight back into the lift and have her escorted off the premises because as he approached her, it was becoming appallingly apparent that her effect on him was as immediate and intense as he recalled. A month ago, she'd decimated fourteen years of steely control with one blink of her beautiful brown eyes, and he was in danger of allowing her to do it again now.

Today, in addition to a sleeveless cream silk top, she was wearing a knee-length fitted skirt the colour of raspberries. And despite the horrified disbelief rampaging through his system, all he could think was, what was she wearing beneath it, if anything? In a flash, it occurred to him then that the sofa to his right was large and accommodating. Within moments she could be sprawled across it while he found out. In his imagination, he saw her long golden hair spread out all over the butter-soft leather with his hands once again tangled in it. He heard the desperate sounds she'd make. He even felt her stiletto heels digging into his back.

But he couldn't get rid of her, dammit. Because, while he sent so much business her accountancy firm's way that he had ample leverage to do so, a response like that would cause a delay to the audit. Disruption. In some quarters—say, among the remaining Helberg Holdings shareholders—such ripples in the water might be seen as indicative of potential problems, which was not an outcome he could allow.

So there'd be no hustling her anywhere. No matter how much in this moment he might regret choosing that bar and that night to alleviate his colossal stress with whisky, she was staying put.

He could handle the attraction, he assured himself as he came to a stop in front of her and banked the response of his body to her intoxicating proximity. It wouldn't be the first time he'd denied his libido. Overwhelmed with guilt, he'd pretty much given up sex altogether in the aftermath of his mother's death and he'd survived. Once this job was underway, he would keep interaction to a minimum and maintain his distance unless strictly necessary. He had no reason to deliberately seek her out and more than enough work to be getting on with. He would focus on the endgame and keep a clear head. It was only for two weeks. It would pass in a flash.

'Adam Courtney, CEO,' he said, pasting a professional smile to his face and holding out his hand. 'Welcome to the Courtney Collection.'

Ella stared down at the hand that Adam was holding out, disbelief and pique spiralling through the shock that was still wreaking havoc on her system.

He hadn't recognised her.

While she'd spent weeks trying not to recall every single second of what they'd done together, he'd clearly forgotten all about it. He hadn't suffered sleepless nights and feverish flushes that attacked whenever they felt like it. Or experienced any pangs of regret that she'd walked out of that bathroom instead of joining him at the bar for the martini he'd proposed. He'd put her straight from his mind and moved on, as if for him that kind of thing wasn't a frenzied moment of madness but an everyday occurrence. Nothing out of the ordinary. Nothing special. And how unflattering *was* that?

But the blow to her pride was something to be analysed at a later date, if at all. Right now, she had to focus on the hammer that was smashing her hopes and dreams to bits and the nausea churning up her stomach as the reality of what was unfolding here hit.

Whether he recognised her or not, their shared history had serious ramifications. That promotion she so badly wanted? Gone. The career she'd worked so damned hard to repair? Back to where it was a year ago. Her future? Very much not mapped out. Because a smooth and successful audit with her in charge was now unthinkable.

How could she possibly stay in the role when there was such a massive and undeniable conflict of interest? Auditing was not a grey area. There were rules and she abided by them, because without integrity, without control, what was there? She wouldn't compromise the standards she'd clung to as she'd battled her way out of poverty and despair, no matter how much she wished right now she could. They were the framework on which she'd built her entire career. She lived, slept and breathed them.

So she couldn't pretend that she hadn't recognised him either, even though that would be so very convenient. She couldn't just sweep this under the carpet and carry on as if her world hadn't imploded. She had to do what was right.

Fighting back the hot fiery ball of frustration, injustice and hopelessness that was barrelling through her, Ella swallowed hard. She lifted her gaze to his, her heart pounding, her throat impossibly tight. 'I need to step aside,' she ground out, having to push every word through her teeth.

Adam dropped his hand and took a step back, his eyes on hers, his smile gone. 'Why?'

'We have a conflict of interest.'

A muscle jumped in his cheek. 'Because we had sex?'

Once again, the floor beneath her feet rocked and her heart practically stopped. A slew of vivid images slammed into her head and a rush of blistering heat propelled a flush to her cheeks.

'So you *do* recognise me,' she said with a breathlessness that appalled her, but at least she was spared the mortification of having to explain *why* there was a problem.

'Of course I do.'

'I thought you'd forgotten who I was.'

His gaze ran over her and she nearly went up in flames. 'On what planet would that be possible?'

'For all I know, you pick up women in bars on a regular basis.'

'I don't. That night was a one-off. And who picked who up is debatable. I may have made the first move, but you made the last.'

That was true. Wasn't it? She couldn't quite remember. Or think straight. Her restored ego might be cheering with relief, but she'd forgotten how mesmerising his eyes were, how easy it was to fall into them and how good he smelled. Despite the disastrous nature of this situation, tiny flashes of electricity were zinging through her. Heat was pooling between her legs. If she took a step in his direction, she would be within kissing distance. She could lift herself up, wind her arms around his neck and press her mouth to his. She hadn't dared do that the night they'd met. Suspecting she might well weaken and wind up agreeing to the martini and further madness, she'd limited herself to a brush of her lips against his cheek before disappearing. That now felt remiss.

'However, I was intending to forget all about it,' he said, jolting her out of her trance and bringing her back down to earth with a bump.

What? For a second, she just stared at him, her brow furrowing in confusion, the ferocious heat momentarily doused as if a bucket of iced water had been thrown at her. Surely he couldn't have said what she thought he just said.

'You can't mean that,' she said, as baffled as she was astonished.

'Why not?' he replied with cool self-assurance.

'It would be highly unethical.' Why wasn't he concerned? He should have frog-marched her out of this building five minutes ago. She would have if she were him. 'I could get fired. I'd never work again. And the risks would be substantial for you too. The integrity of the audit would be compromised. Your reputation might take a hit.'

That silenced him for a second. Something flared in the depths of his eyes, but it was gone before she could identify it. 'Are you good at your job?'

'Exceptionally.' Which made the situation all the more painful.

'Would what we did have any impact on your work?'

Was he questioning her commitment? Her professionalism? Or was he concerned that, once again unable to control herself in his presence, she might demand he ravish her over the photocopier? 'Absolutely not,' she said, determined to reassure him on all those fronts. 'Nothing gets in the way of that.'

'Do you *want* to stand down?'

The prospect of it cleaved her in two and drove a stake through her chest. 'I can't think of anything I want to do less.'

'Then don't.'

Oh, if only she weren't so principled. If only she'd chosen a different bar in which to drown her sorrows that night. But it was far too late for regrets. 'It's not that simple.'

'Have you told anyone about what we did?'

'No,' she said as a shudder ran through her. Why would she want anyone knowing how weak and impulsive she'd been when she'd told all her friends after the Drew affair that she was steering clear of men for the foreseeable future? 'I can barely believe it happened in the first place. It was so out of character.'

'Good. I haven't either.' His jaw lost some of its rigidity, and his expression relaxed a fraction. 'The way I see it is this. We hardly know each other. We're not going to have sex again. We don't even need to *refer* to it again. The conflict of interest is negligible. So negligible, in fact, that I don't believe there even is one. So why should you be made to suffer for something that is ultimately irrelevant, when no one knows about it but us?'

Well, when he put it like that, he made a good case, she thought, nibbling her lip as she considered the arguments he'd used to bulldoze her objections.

They *didn't* know each other and of *course* they weren't having sex again. She'd only ever intended it to be a one-time event. The reason she'd rejected his offer of a drink that night was because even though she'd instantly craved another hit of him, she'd sensed he was lethal. She'd suspected that if she ever found herself in an actual bed with him, she might never get out of it, and what impact would *that* have had on her career? So the disappointment that was surging through her could take a hike. It wasn't happening. Even if he hadn't made it clear he had no further designs on her, at which she should be feeling relieved and not insulted, she had absolutely no desire for history to repeat itself by her mixing business with pleasure again and potentially sacrificing another promotion.

And it *wasn't* fair that twenty minutes of madness a month ago should destroy all the progress she'd made and threaten her future. Especially since, this time, what had happened wasn't even her fault. What they'd done together *was* irrelevant. It *wouldn't* have any effect on her conduct or the outcome of the audit. Her impartiality and objectivity would *never* be at risk.

But what about her principles if she did decide to follow his lead and forget all about what they'd done? How could she treat them with such disrespect when they'd helped her to get where she was? When they'd been her guiding light for over a decade? It didn't bear thinking about. Although, she wouldn't be sacrificing them forever, observed the devil's advocate in her head. She'd merely be temporarily setting them aside for the duration of this one crucial audit, upon which the future of her career depended. She could reclaim them the minute she finished here.

The only fly in the ointment would be the chemistry that unfortunately hadn't diminished one little bit. Her every nerve ending was quivering in response to his proximity. Her temperature was sky high. She'd never considered a white shirt particularly sexy before, but right now she wanted to rip his open and get her hands on his skin.

However, it wasn't as if they'd be having any further contact. This unfortunate meeting was just a courtesy, and once she and her team were set up in the basement or at the end of some dark dingy corridor, liaising directly with the finance department as per usual, she need never lay eyes on him again.

She deserved the opportunity to correct the mistake she'd made a year ago, and ceding control of her career to external forces again wasn't the way to do that. Besides, if she didn't stick with it, there'd be repercussions. She'd have to explain her decision to her colleagues. Her boss. She'd have to confess that, once again, she'd messed up again because of a man. She'd lose the respect she'd been fighting so hard to restore, and this time her career wouldn't just be damaged, it would be over, because she wouldn't be given another chance. She'd be out in the cold for good, and after everything she'd worked for, she simply could not contemplate it. No, she had to see this job through to the end. And she *would* see this job through to the end.

'All right then,' she said, ruthlessly crushing the protest of her principles and channelling cool, clear-headed professionalism instead. 'Just tell me where to go and we'll get started.'

* * *

Having neutralised the risk of Ella stepping down and screwing up his plans for a trouble-free audit, Adam relaxed marginally and stalked over to the conference table that was to be her workspace for the next couple of weeks.

Thank God she'd seen the situation his way. Not that there was any other way he could have allowed her to see it. If she'd stuck to her guns and recused herself, she would have made life extremely tricky for the both of them. Then what would he have done? Bribed her? Resorted to threats?

Such underhanded tactics weren't his style, but this set of circumstances was unprecedented. There was no end to which he wouldn't go to get what he wanted, and if that meant taking advantage of the battle between integrity and a burning desire to see the audit through that had played out on her face, then so be it. Whatever the reason, it was clear she wanted this job with a determination that seemed to go beyond mere duty. Something else appeared to be at stake for her here, and he was not above weaponizing her desperation if necessary.

A part of him loathed that he had been forced to put any amount of trust in her when she was such an unknown quantity. The women he generally slept with he chose because they were safe. The attraction they shared caused him no trouble. When he was done, they were gone and he didn't look back. But he hadn't selected Ella. She'd selected him. If she decided to go to the press with details of what they'd got up to, she could obliterate four years of reputational reconstruction in a heartbeat. He'd instantly lose the respect and trust he'd worked so hard to earn. His authority would crumble to dust. He'd be labelled as his father's son.

When Adam had taken over as CEO—following the fatal aneurysm his father had suffered while in bed with a nubile blonde—he'd faced an uphill battle to remove the stain on the family name. There'd been many who'd feared business as usual. One or two who'd benefitted from the gravy train and had expected it to continue.

But he'd been determined to restore the plummeting fortunes of the company that had been in his family for over a century. So he'd fired those members of the board who'd repeatedly vetoed his father's dismissal and put a stop to the bottomless expense account. He'd implemented policies that encouraged reporting bad behaviour and transparency. He'd negotiated loans and trebled the marketing and PR budget.

With the rot gone, the climate—not just at this office but worldwide—had done a full one-eighty within six months. A year later, sales had risen by forty percent and the share price had doubled. Now, the Courtney name on a personal level was associated not with sleaze and corruption but integrity and trust.

Ella had the power destroy all the progress he'd made. She could blow his plans for Helberg Holdings right out of the water, because he well knew that shareholders could be funny about things like sex scandals. However, the conviction in her voice when she'd answered his question about whether she'd told anyone about that night in the bar, as well as her very visible shudder, had not been feigned, and that concern had been allayed. At least, for now.

Had his curiosity been piqued, he might have wondered why discretion seemed to matter as much to her as it did to him and why she was so determined to see the job through. Why she'd put aside her own integrity to do that.

But he wasn't remotely interested in the things they shared or what drove her. He wasn't intrigued by her at all. He certainly wasn't dwelling on the way she'd bitten her lip as she'd considered his arguments and imagining how incendiary kissing her would be. Or regretting that they wouldn't be having sex again. One monumentally reckless loss of control was enough to last a lifetime. Therefore, he would not be indulging the rogue urge to rile her up and get under her skin. Whether she was still as attracted to him as he was to her was utterly irrelevant. They had a job to do and that was all.

So why was she still standing where he'd left her instead of following him to the table she'd be working at for the next two weeks and getting started? Why was she still looking at him as if she couldn't figure out what was going on? Just in case it wasn't blindingly obvious, Adam pulled out a chair and gave it a pat. 'You're over here.'

CHAPTER FOUR

IT TOOK ELLA a good ten seconds to compute the implication of Adam's announcement, by which time he'd waved at her to come on over and poured her a glass of water.

What on earth was the meaning of this? she wondered in alarm, her gaze flicking between the table with the pastries and the man now heading for the stairs that rose to his office on the mezzanine. Why wasn't he directing her to the basement as she'd expected? To the finance department, perhaps? Or even to his secretary for further instructions?

Surely, he didn't intend the audit take place up here on his floor, did he? He had to be out of his mind. She could not work up here with him a matter of metres away. Her concentration would be wrecked. She'd never get anything done.

'Wait,' she said, needing to clarify the situation and fix it immediately if necessary.

Adam stopped in his tracks and whipped round. 'Is there a problem?'

'There could be.'

His brows drew together in a deep frown and she thought she caught a sigh of exasperation. 'What is it now?'

'Am I to understand you wish the audit to take place up here?'

'That is correct.'

She gave her head a sharp shake. 'It's out of the question.'

For a moment, there was utter silence. All Ella could hear was the pounding of her heart in her ears. Then his eyebrows shot up as if he wasn't used to being challenged, and he said, very coolly, 'I beg your pardon?'

His expression was darkening forbiddingly, she noticed, but she refused to be intimidated because he wasn't in charge here. She was. This was *her* audit—a vitally important one—and it was more crucial than usual that common protocol was followed. His ridiculous presumption needed to be corrected, so she lifted her chin, pulled her shoulders back.

'My audit will *not* be taking place up here,' she said, fixing him with a look that had once been called chilling. 'Firstly, from a practical point of view, there wouldn't be nearly enough space for eleven people and everything we require.'

'Which is why you will be up here with me and your team will be occupying the offices one floor down.'

Well, *that* was never going to happen. She and her team needed full and direct access to each other. She couldn't keep dashing up and down the stairs whenever face-to-face communication was required. It would be massively inconvenient and a complete waste of everyone's time. And then there was the stress of being completely alone with him, the possible intensifying of the attraction and the battle she'd have to fight it. Even hypothetically the thought of it made her feel quite weak.

'Secondly,' she continued, even more determined to prevail, 'a set-up such as the one you suggest could lead to accusations of undue influence. I mean, pastries? The best view in the city? When we're normally stashed away in a musty room at the end of a corridor with windows that look out onto a wall? Our impartiality would be compromised. Questions would be asked. I simply can't allow it.'

But if she'd expected Adam to take on board her undeniably valid point and surrender to her superior experience, she was to be disappointed.

'No questions will be asked,' he countered, folding his arms across his impossibly broad chest as his cool blue gaze bore into hers. 'No one would dare. Proximity is required because I will be overseeing this audit personally. I want to make sure that any problems are knocked on the head the second they arise. Every query you or your team have and every piece of information you require will go through me, so you and I will be liaising directly.'

Ella's stomach clenched. What? No. Absolutely not. 'That would be highly irregular,' she said, refusing to be distracted by the play of muscles she could see going on beneath the crisp white cotton of his shirt and instead mentally running through the consequences of such a strategy, the regulations surrounding neutrality and the headache of having to deal specifically with him.

'In what way?'

'Regardless of the questionable ethics of going through you for everything, your intended degree of involvement would not only add another layer of complication to an already complex investigation, but it would also make the process way more inefficient.'

'I disagree.'

That was his prerogative, but his opinion was irrelevant. 'You're not the expert here.'

'Do finance departments jump to attention the minute you tell them to?'

'Well, no, not always, but—'

'They will if it's me doing the telling,' he said bluntly. 'As will everyone else. They won't be able to work fast enough. I've cleared my diary for the next two weeks. I will be available to you and anyone else who needs me twenty-four-seven.'

In response to that, Ella's head began to throb. Once again, he was trampling over her every objection, only this time his counterarguments didn't make any sort of sense. 'Why?'

Up shot his eyebrows again. 'What do you mean, why?'

'Most CEOs don't take such a personal interest in something as prosaic as the annual financial audit.'

'I'm not most CEOs.'

That was certainly true. He was by far the sexiest CEO she'd ever come across. Tall, lean, powerful… And his forearms—long curves of hard muscle dusted with a smattering of dark masculine hair—really were something else. What would it feel like to be enveloped by all that strength? To have his strong hands on her body, his clever fingers coaxing her to the dizzy heights of pleasure? To be wrapped up once again in heat and passion and excitement?

'I don't see you as the enemy,' he said, bringing her back to the conversation with a bump. 'I believe in working together. Which we can, and will, do.' He tilted his head and regarded her coolly. 'You seem to be under the impression that you can influence what's going on here Ella. But you can't. This is my company and my audit. *I* make the rules, not you. So, if you have a problem with that, I'll just have to find someone to run it who doesn't.'

As his words hit their mark, Ella's blood chilled and her stomach fluttered. The heat whipping through her system fled. The heady desire vaporised. Adam looked calm enough, but there was a trace of steel behind his words. A glint of ruthlessness in his eyes. The ripple of tension in the air told her that he would stop at nothing to get what he wanted and that if she knew what was good for her, she'd surrender.

Suddenly simmering with outrage, she burned with the urge to march up to him and inform him that not only did he *not* make the rules that he was breaking left right and centre, despite his apparent wish to avoid trouble, but also that threatening the auditors was not a good move.

But she couldn't, dammit. Because, for one thing, when she got too close to him, her brain malfunctioned. And for another, whatever the reason for his stubborn insistence on the status quo, whether he saw this as some kind of a game or was simply a control freak, the truth was he held all the cards. She couldn't afford to antagonise him. If he acted on this power trip of his and got her thrown off the job, she could wind up unemployed, her career in ruins. She'd instantly lose everything. The condo she'd just bought would be repossessed. The security and empowerment that earning her own money gave her would disappear overnight. What would she do then? Where would she go? How would she survive?

She wasn't going to throw away everything she'd worked so hard for and jeopardise the future she deserved over a tussle for control. The late nights of study, the exhaustion, the doubts that she was good enough to make it weren't going to be for nothing. Like him, she would do whatever it took to get what she wanted, and right now it was clear that that meant keeping him onside until the audit was done and the financial records signed off.

So no matter how much she hated that he kept forcing her to make decisions that challenged her integrity, no matter how churned up he made her feel inside, she had no choice but to acquiesce. Somehow she would maintain the audit's independence. She would never let him see how bothered she was by the idea of the two of them working up here together alone. She could certainly contain the attraction she still felt for him. She had far too much at stake to let that get the better of her.

'Fine,' she said, with a cool smile and a deliberately casual shrug, as if she weren't bothered by the outcome of the conversation—or him—at all. 'You win.'

Once she'd wrestled her frustration at being thwarted under some sort of control and checked the regulations concerning impartiality, Ella headed downstairs to greet the team and make sure that everyone knew what they were doing—which they did because, unlike her, they'd had weeks to prepare. Then she returned to the penthouse, set herself up and turned her attention to work, determined to put her infuriating client firmly from her head.

Unfortunately, however, this turned out to be easier said than done.

By virtue of the fact that she'd been parachuted into this assignment at the last minute, she was going to have to work doubly hard and longer hours to keep on top of things. So she could not afford to waste even a second, let alone great chunks of time.

Yet that was precisely what happened. More calls than she cared to count went to voicemail. Files that should have been opened instantly weren't. And all because, whether he was at his desk or wandering around his office on the phone, the man up there on the mezzanine was just too darn distracting.

To her despair, the ruthlessness she'd witnessed earlier hadn't diminished his appeal in the slightest. On the contrary, every time she thought about it, shameful thrills of excitement shot through her.

In spite of her best efforts to stop it, her gaze slid in his direction with frustrating predictability. Her imagination, which had never troubled her before she'd met him, had gone into overdrive. She kept envisaging heading up the stairs and sidling into his office, where he'd invite her to come on over and make herself comfortable on his lap. Or perhaps he'd make his way down to her, clear the table with one sweep of his arm and lift her onto it. Either way, they ended up in a wholly unacceptable clinch.

This disruption to her concentration did not bode well for a trouble-free audit to be completed within the specified time frame, so after lunch Ella attempted to do something about it.

First, she shifted her position so that he wasn't in her direct vision, in the hope that out of sight would be out of mind. But that didn't work because, apparently, her awareness of him was all-encompassing. Then she tried loitering downstairs with her team, but the unproductivity of such a move was just too annoying to pursue.

She hated that controlling her response to him was proving such a challenge. She hated even more that he didn't appear to be remotely bothered by her, which was insane, because the last thing she needed was the added stress of the attraction turning out to be mutual.

But she would not allow another man she'd slept with to mess with her head and jeopardise her career, so she eventually figured she'd just have to double down on her efforts. If she was to stand any chance of not screwing this job up, she had to get a grip and focus. She had to keep what was at stake for her at the forefront of her mind and start acting like the professional she was.

So she stuck Post-it notes adorned with the word *PROMOTION!!!* to various items that surrounded her. She allowed herself to imagine in full dreadful detail how her life might fall apart should this audit go wrong—the humiliation, the uncertainty, the peril. Every time her gaze threatened to drift in his direction, she forced herself to recall her last performance review, during which she'd been told that she wasn't quite ready for the next step up, and that snapped it straight back to the laptop.

Although it took considerable effort, to her relief, these strategies worked. Largely managing to ignore Adam's existence, she soon found confidence in her spreadsheets and settled into the role. Being on a different floor to her team turned out not to be as problematic as she'd expected, and over the next couple of days they made excellent progress, aided, she had to admit, by the degree of his involvement, which—both annoyingly and pleasingly—*had* resulted in improved efficiency and ultra-quick results.

Ella wasn't prone to pettiness, but she couldn't deny that she'd relished bombarding him with emails, some of which didn't actually require his attention. She wanted to make him pay for effectively holding her ransom by spamming his inbox. She wanted him to sorely regret forcing her to bend to his will. However, she was thwarted in those endeavours too, because not once did he tell her to desist. No matter how trivial or important the request, each was handled promptly without either comment or complaint.

There were only two issues to which she was having trouble getting a response. One was an unaccounted-for trip to London in the company's private jet back in August last year. The other was the steady yet rapid purchase of millions of shares in a multinational called Helberg Holdings, whose portfolio was so sprawling yet in such trouble that no one could work out what he was doing with it.

Both anomalies had raised a flag with her team. Neither had yet been addressed, despite her repeated efforts to do so. Frustratingly, Adam had ignored the half dozen reminders she'd sent him, so on Wednesday afternoon she decided to tackle him directly.

Setting her jaw, practically vibrating with resolve, she picked up a notepad and pen and headed up the stairs to his office. 'Do you have a moment to go through some queries?' she said, trying not to notice how the sun streaming in through the acres of glass was giving him a corona that made him look like some sort of a god.

'Not right now, I'm afraid,' he replied as he pushed his chair back and got to his feet. 'I'm about to head off for a meeting.'

'When will you be back?'

'I'm not sure. It could go on for a while.'

'I thought you said you'd cleared your diary for the next two weeks.'

'This one's unavoidable.'

With a tight smile, he strode past her and out through the door before she could protest any further. And to her extreme irritation the meeting of his went on for so long that she didn't see him for the rest of the day.

Undeterred, however, she tried again the following morning. But on that occasion she didn't even manage to say a single word to him, because the minute she appeared at his door, he picked up his phone and said coolly, 'Do excuse me, I need to take this,' and that was that for the next two hours.

By Thursday evening, he'd left her with no choice but to take more drastic action. Determined to pin him down, she saw her opportunity when he left his office and headed for the lift. She slipped through the doors just before they closed, trapping them together, a move she regretted almost immediately when her lungs tightened and her head spun, as if all the oxygen had been sucked out of the space. How could she have forgotten what happened when she got too close to him? she wondered for one dizzying moment. Clearly, concentrating on work and being ignored by him these last few days had lulled her into a false sense of security.

But she would not be derailed from the plan, no matter what his effect on her, so halfway into the lift's descent she hit the alarm, causing it to judder to an abrupt halt.

'Why did you do that?'

Adam's vaguely amused tone belied the stony glare he gave her. She ignored the rash of goose bumps breaking out all over her skin, the flare of heat and the quivering of her nerve endings, and focused. 'We need to talk.'

'And what exactly do you need to say that couldn't have been said in my office?'

'That's the trouble. Nothing of significance *was* being said in your office. All I heard were excuses.'

He didn't even respond to that. He just let his glittering gaze drift over her before it settled on her mouth and lingered.

'You know what happens when you and I find ourselves trapped together in confined spaces,' he said, his voice seeming to drop an octave while her lips tingled and her mouth dried. 'I realise we weren't going to refer to that night again, but what else am I to read into this manoeuvre of yours other than invitation?'

In response to that, Ella's heart gave a great lurch and then began to race. He was right. What was she doing?

Instead of focusing on getting the answers she wanted, her head was clearing of everything but the urge to push him up against the polished walnut wall and kiss him the way she imagined in the early hours of the morning when she couldn't sleep. What would he do if she did? Fire her? Or would he bury one hand in her hair and lift her skirt with the other, then tackle his belt, his zip, his underwear, and within seconds be thrusting deep inside her, driving her to the dazzling heights of pleasure she'd only experienced with him?

The former seemed more likely, she thought, her head spinning like a top. He was so cool. So contained. He'd shown no sign of being troubled by their continuing attraction. So what did he mean by bringing up that night? Why the seductive tones? Was he messing with her, playing mind games to remind her who was in command?

Well, right now, that evidently wasn't her. In hindsight, this plan had been a terrible idea. So before her last few functioning brain cells disintegrated and she acted on the wild desire suddenly crashing through her, she pulled herself together and jabbed the button to restart the lift.

'You're right,' she said, consoling herself with the knowledge that she could try again tomorrow. With space. With air. Somehow. 'My mistake.'

And when they reached the ground floor—in a matter of seconds, although it felt like an hour—she didn't flee into the night as if the hounds of hell were snapping at her heels. Instead, she lifted her chin, gave him a cool smile and bade him a pleasant goodnight.

CHAPTER FIVE

INITIALLY, ELLA'S SUBMISSION to his will on Monday morning had given Adam one hell of a buzz. Yes, securing her compliance had been vital for a number of business-related reasons, so on that level it had been a much-needed win. But there'd been something else mixed up in it too. Regaining the sense of control that had rapidly started diminishing in her dangerously distracting presence had felt critical, and seeing her forced to accept his command, to play by *his* rules, had been not only deeply satisfying but also unexpectedly exhilarating.

However, the buzz had not lasted long. Nor had the plan he'd come up with the instant he'd realised that the past had collided with the present and his lead auditor was a woman with whom he'd shared one explosive encounter and to whom he was, inconveniently, still very much attracted.

Determined the audit would proceed without any further upset, he'd succeeded in staying out of her way as much as possible, in confining himself to his office and communicating entirely through email.

But as for keeping his eyes off her, well, in that he'd failed dismally. When she was on the phone, the throaty timbre of her voice wound through him, a ribbon of fire heating every inch of his body. Every time she sashayed across the carpet to the lift, to the coffee machine, to the photocopier, he found himself tracking the sway of her hips. At one point she'd stretched, lifting her arms above her head and arching her back as she eased out the kinks in her neck, and it had taken every drop of self-control that he possessed to contain his body's response to the sight of her breasts straining against the silky fabric of her top.

Even Maggie, his secretary, had noticed his discomfort. 'Is there something wrong with the way the audit's going?' she asked him when she popped up to run through his diary for August.

'No,' he muttered. 'Why?'

'You're staring at Miss Green as if you're trying to vaporise her with the power of your stare.'

Cursing the fact that it was turning out to be far more difficult than he'd expected to keep a grip on the disturbingly intense attraction, he instantly snapped his attention from the woman who was wreaking havoc on his equilibrium to the one who did her utmost to maintain it, and vowed to double down on his efforts to focus by immersing himself in the deluge of emails Ella had started sending him.

The first had dropped into his inbox on Tuesday morning, and thereafter he'd received one virtually every fifteen minutes. Frequently, they contained a single point. He could see no reason why, say, six could not be amalgamated into one, which meant she was doing it deliberately.

But if her aim had been to annoy him, she'd failed. In fact, he found her passive-aggressive attempt at control really rather amusing, and that was another reason he took great care to respond to each and every one with equal gravity.

With two notable exceptions.

Both of which were causing him grief.

First was the flight to London last August that apparently lacked the paperwork to match the log book.

The minute he'd heard that his sister, Charley, was buying a flat with the last of her savings from her ill-fated career as a model, he'd instantly felt compelled to check it out. He hadn't thought twice about dropping everything and commandeering the company plane to get him to her before she signed the contract. His sole concern had been that she was only twenty-one and had a tendency to be reckless—especially with money. She'd had a chequered adolescence, quitting school and getting spotted by an agency, and although she'd managed to pull herself back on track after leaving that world behind, he couldn't be certain she didn't still make impulsive decisions.

He'd had nothing except her best interests at heart, but to his astonishment, she had not been pleased when he'd turned up unannounced at the perfectly acceptable two-bedroom flat in an up-and-coming area of East London. In response to his offer of advice, she'd had a go at him about his need to control everything and everyone. She'd railed at his inability to trust her, insisting that she wasn't a kid any more, that she'd learned from her mistakes, and when the hell was he going to realise that? Would he *ever* let her forget the time he'd had to bail her out of a cell in Barcelona for swearing at a police officer? Or the occasion she'd run away from school and had wanted him to send her the train fare to get to London? When would he start taking her seriously and treat her like the savvy businesswoman she was?

He'd been more affected by the confrontation than he cared to admit. It had taken him weeks to get over the sharp sting of rejection. Even longer to accept that she'd made some very valid points.

Not that he considered his deep-seated need for control a problem. It was essential to contain the chaos he knew he was capable of. Without it, he feared being overrun with the personality traits he'd inherited from his father, with recklessness, and then everything he'd worked for going up in smoke.

As CEOs they were polar opposites. Adam hadn't generated tabloid headlines that crashed the company's share price. He'd never appeared in blurry photos indicating rampant drug use. And he'd certainly never indulged in the sort of inappropriate behaviour at the office that ended up in a lawsuit.

But in other respects, they were worryingly similar. He was the spitting image of his old man, a constant reminder every time he looked in the mirror of who he would turn into if he didn't keep himself in check. As an adolescent screwing around without a thought for anyone other than himself, he'd behaved like him too, and because of that selfishness, his mother had died. On the ultra-rare occasion his willpower failed these days—

such as five weeks ago in a cocktail bar bathroom—his true nature roared to the surface with no consideration of the consequences.

And as for controlling his environment and the people around him, well, he was responsible for the livelihoods of quarter of a million employees and revenue that ran into the tens of billions. How else was he to manage that?

But while he had no intention of apologising for his need to keep a tight grip on things, he did want to work on trusting Charley. He wanted to get to know her without the guilt he felt at robbing her of their mother getting in the way. Relationships of the romantic kind were out of the question. Indulging the sort of desire that led to impulsivity and left destruction in its wake turned his stomach. Envisaging the chaos caused by emotion made his head ache. And the thought of being responsible for someone else's happiness and well-being when he was so ill-equipped to care for such things brought him out in a cold sweat. But he hoped to attempt a familial one with his sister.

None of this was up for discussion, however. With Ella or anyone else. Nor was Helberg Holdings, the second item that she was so keen to quiz him about. Even if he had wanted to share details of why the company was so important to him—Montague's in particular—he wouldn't know where to start. With his father's philandering? With his mother's abject misery in her marriage and the one affair her unhappiness had driven her to? Would he tell her how, in retaliation, a hypocritical, vengeful Edward Courtney had sold the international jewellery business she'd worked for and loved so much to Helberg for a dollar? Would he then move on to his own role in his mother's suicide and confess to the guilt he still carried?

No.

All of that would remain strictly private. Only he knew the full story. Even Charley, who'd been just a kid when it had happened, was only aware of some of it.

He didn't particularly enjoy skulking around and disappearing whenever Ella hove into view, her jaw set with resolve. It smacked of cowardice and went against his confronting-problems-head-on approach. This evening's encounter in the lift had been particularly challenging. Her move had taken him by surprise. Once he'd got over his shock, with awareness suddenly ripping through him like wildfire, he'd been gripped by a ferocious surge of the rashness he fought so hard to contain. He'd wanted to back her up against the wall and kiss her until she couldn't think straight. To then strip her naked and sink into her, despite the security camera embedded in the ceiling.

How he'd stayed calm enough to de-escalate the situation, he had no idea. It was clear now that the only reason he'd been able to keep the desire he had for her under control was by maintaining his distance.

It was equally obvious that she was turning out to be unexpectedly tenacious, and he did not want her prodding around his psyche, because who knew what she might then get him to disclose in a moment of weakness? He couldn't stall her for much longer, however. At some point he would have to figure out how to give her the bare minimum of detail and shut these lines of enquiry down.

But for now, he had a stay of execution. Because he'd just received a call from the office in Madrid with news of potential strike action at a clothing factory outside Valencia, so he was on his way to Spain.

And when he returned, that would not be the only problem he'd have fixed. He'd also have shored up his defences so solidly that, come Monday, he'd be able to stand within a metre of Ella Green and not lose his head.

On Friday morning Ella arrived at the office unsure how to proceed, slightly nervous about seeing Adam again, and wondering how on earth she was going to keep the attraction under control after nearly assaulting him in the lift. Unfortunately, overnight, she'd been plagued by dreams about what had happened, but in them she hadn't backed down. She'd told him to take her up on her invitation instead and had woken up at four hot and shivery and unable to get back to sleep, which did not help her composure one little bit.

But it seemed she had nothing to worry about because Adam didn't show up to the office. She had no idea where he was. He replied to her email enquiring into his whereabouts with a vague, unsatisfying *Something's come up*. After that, radio silence. Even his secretary was cryptically obscure when she probed.

At first, she appreciated the chance to restore her self-possession in his absence. However, by 7:00 p.m. she'd come to the conclusion that none of what had happened in the past few days was a coincidence. In fact, she thought darkly as she pushed through the revolving door and out into the warm evening air, it felt like avoidance. For some reason Adam was stonewalling her, deflecting her—deliberately, she suspected when she thought of the extraordinary encounter in the lift—and now he was nowhere to be found.

It was pissing her off. Not because she was remotely interested in what exactly was problematic about these particular queries, or what he had to hide. She wasn't. All that mattered to her was that he was holding things up. He was jeopardising the time frame of the audit and it could not be allowed continue. The schedule was tight as it was, given the size and complexity of the job. It must not overrun. Her promotion depended on finishing on time. The leave she'd booked for the three weeks after—the first she'd taken in over a year—depended on finishing within the allotted fortnight. She was not having both her short-term and long-term future disrupted by him. She wasn't having anything disrupted at all.

So, having somehow managed to subtly wheedle out of Maggie, his secretary, that Adam would be at home tonight, Ella had come up with a plan. Not an entirely ethical one, admittedly, but he'd left her with no choice. Desperate means called for desperate measures. Enough was enough. He would avoid her no more. He would not wrong-foot her again. Or succeed with threats, because she was far too embedded in the process to be ousted from it now. She would get the answers she needed, and she would get them tonight.

* * *

Adam had spent all day containing the threat of strike action at his Valencia factory and ensuring there'd be no further trouble. Having accomplished that by late afternoon, and secure in the knowledge that the staff had been appeased—before anyone had gone to the press, thank God—he'd travelled back to New York satisfied that the impact on the company's reputation and the Helberg acquisition in particular was negligible.

Dropping his keys on the table in the hall and abandoning his suitcase, he strode into the white, minimalist living space, then headed for the bar. As a result of criss-crossing the Atlantic twice in less than twenty-four hours, he didn't know what time it was. He couldn't remember when he'd last slept. He was exhausted and stressed beyond belief. He couldn't shake a strange sense of foreboding, the feeling that everything he was trying to achieve balanced on a knife edge, and all he wanted to do was crack open a bottle of whisky and crash out for the next two days.

However, he'd barely had time to down half a glass of single malt when there was a knock at his door. Too spaced out to wonder who it could be when he'd had no warning of a visitor, he set his glass on the bar and went to investigate. Calling down to the concierge didn't occur to him. Neither did looking through the spyhole. So when he opened the door and came face to face with Ella, he was totally unprepared.

Reeling with shock, he wondered for a moment whether he could be hallucinating, the whisky stronger than he'd assumed, perhaps. But unfortunately, she was all too real. He could tell by the way the hairs at the back of his neck were standing on end and her scent, which was winding through him and scrambling his head.

'What the hell are you doing here?' he practically growled, thinking, *God, this week.* How much more could he be expected to endure?

'I could ask you the same thing,' she said, chin up, jaw set. 'Why aren't you at the office? Where have you been?'

'Spain.'

Her eyebrows shot up. 'Spain?'

'A business matter that required my attention. Strike action at one of my factories. How did you find out where I live?'

'Your address was at the top of an invoice,' she said without a trace of shame. 'I told the concierge I was bringing you a birthday surprise and he let me in. I must admit, I was expecting getting access to you to be a lot harder. Your security is terrible.'

Adam fought the urge to grind his teeth. 'This is a gross invasion of privacy.'

'You only have yourself to blame. You've been avoiding me all week.'

'A company the size of mine doesn't run itself.'

'What happened to being available twenty-four-seven?'

Right, he thought, thrown off balance for a moment. He had promised that. But he couldn't do this now. He was shattered and feeling more than a little unhinged. Combined with all that, her proximity was wreaking havoc on him. His hands itched to touch her. It was taking every drop of control he possessed not to move towards her. He had the unnerving feeling that he'd missed the edginess she drummed up in him these last twenty-four hours.

'You need to leave,' he said, a bead of sweat running down his spine, his pulse thudding heavily as he tightened his grip on the door-frame to his left and the door-knob to his right.

'Not until you tell me about the trip to London and Helberg Holdings.'

'I fail to see their relevance.'

'*I'll* assess their relevance.'

'You can wait until Monday.'

'No. I can't.'

'Why not?'

'Because the time frame is slipping, and I won't allow further delay.' She planted her hands on her hips, her eyes shimmering with determination and challenge. 'This audit *has* to finish on Friday, not least because I go on three weeks' leave immediately afterwards. You're holding things up. Deliberately, I suspect. And I don't get it. One minute you're striding about the place dictating how things are going to go and insisting that you be involved in every step of the process—although why you're taking such a close personal interest in things, I still have absolutely no idea—the next you're nowhere to be seen. What's going on?'

'Nothing's going on.'

'London, Adam,' she said, with the strength of will that in any other situation he'd admire, the strength of will that suggested that she wasn't going away and he couldn't just close the door on her because she'd simply bang on it until he opened it again.

He had to give her something, if only to get her to shut up and go away. He'd keep it brief. 'I went to see my sister.'

'Is she employed by the company?'

'No.'

'What does she do?'

'She has her own dress design business called Trouble Maker.'

'Is it, or was the trip in any way related to the Courtney Collection?'

'No.'

'The jet is a company asset. You should not be making personal use of it.'

'Crunch the numbers and tell me what I owe.'

The look she gave him suggested she didn't think much of that idea. 'And what about Helberg Holdings?'

No, that was too much. Explaining London was one thing, but he couldn't go into Helberg now. He didn't think he'd be able to stand having to deal with the memories that dredged up on top of everything else. Not with his composure so badly frayed. 'Quit while you're ahead, Ella.'

'I have no intention of quitting anything.'

He stifled a growl of frustration. 'You're driving me insane.'

'All I'm trying to do is my job, and I'm not going to apologise for being tenacious. I've had to work exceptionally hard to get where I am. I've faced obstacles virtually every step of the way. A decrepit trailer for a home in a park rife with danger. Dead-beat parents. Lousy high school. At one point I was working three jobs to earn the money I needed to study. Only once have I screwed up so badly my career nearly went down the drain. But I won't do it again. And I won't let you mess this up for me. So you *will* answer my questions. This audit *will* finish on Friday and I *will* get that promotion, even if it kills me.'

For a moment, Adam's head spun. The information she'd just hurled at him was too much to process. Obstacles? A trailer? When had she screwed up? What promotion was she talking about? 'That's not what I meant.'

'Then what did you mean?' she demanded, her cheeks flushed, the pulse at the base of her neck fluttering wildly.

'You've been causing me trouble since the minute you showed up on Monday,' he said, thinking that if scaring her off had worked in the lift yesterday, it would work again today. 'You're in my head all the damn time. You threaten my control and make me want to cross lines that I have sworn not to cross. I still want you badly, Ella, and I'm used to taking what I want. There's only so much pressure I can withstand, and my patience is about to snap. You have no idea how close you came to being ravished in the lift last night. Right now, I am seconds away from losing it completely and kissing you until neither of us can think straight. So if you have any sense at all, you'll go home this minute. Because if you don't, if you stay for even a second longer, I will pull you into my apartment and you will not leave until Monday morning. So *my* question to *you*, Ella, is do you want that? Do you want to spend the weekend in my bed?'

He stopped, his head nothing more than rushing white noise, his blood roaring in his ears. The silence thundered. Ella just stared at him, evidently rendered speechless by his words. Her eyes were wide and dark. Her breathing was shallow and ragged. The seconds ticked by like hours. Then, just when he thought she finally understood the danger she was in, she breathed a shuddery, 'God, *yes*,' and launched herself at him.

There was no time for shock. No time to wonder whether she had completely lost her mind. Or whether he had. The minute she was pressed up against him—her arms around his neck, her hands in his hair, her mouth on his like fire—pure instinct took over. He drew her into a crushing embrace, one hand clamped to the back of her head, the other on the small of her back. She moaned, immediately melting into him so that all he could feel was softness and warmth, and he took command, angling her head and deepening the kiss.

She tasted of heaven and he couldn't get enough. His exhaustion was history. Adrenaline was surging through him, zapping his nerve endings until they were on fire. He was on the point of doing as he'd promised, pulling her into his apartment and kicking the door shut when just as suddenly as the kiss had started, it stopped. Ella froze in his arms and jerked back. Her gorgeous brown eyes were glazed. Her hair was mussed and her cheeks flushed.

But right in front of him, the dazed passion on her face turned to distress. She clapped a hand to her mouth and shook her head, her eyes filling with horror and regret. And while he fought for breath, grappled to contain the rampaging need he had for her, tried and failed to make sense of what was going on, she wrenched herself out of his arms, spun on her heel and fled.

CHAPTER SIX

ELLA BURST OUT of Adam's building into the warm evening air, her breathing choppy, her heart banging frantically in her chest, while the only thought whipping round her head was, what had she done? What had she *done*?

How could she have lost control like that? What had she been thinking? She'd turned up at his door all professional guns blazing, on a mission from which she'd sworn she would not deviate. She'd ignored the flicker of concern she'd felt at how tired and drawn he'd looked. She'd noted that he hadn't seemed quite as in control of himself as usual but had immediately quashed the curiosity. With superhuman effort, she'd even managed to contain the surge of desire that had nearly taken out her knees. She'd kept to the plan and stuck determinedly to the script—until he'd told her that she drove him insane and all hell had let loose.

It was one thing giving him a potted version of her background to justify the persistence that annoyed him so much, she thought, hailing a cab with a hand that was still trembling, her head still whirling as if she were on a Waltzer. But she should never have told him that she'd once made a mistake that had messed up her career. She should never have revealed that she was dependent on this audit for a promotion when she'd already provided her upcoming leave as a perfectly valid reason for her desire to get things wrapped up on time. And she should never *ever* have kissed him.

Yet, once again, his nearness had destroyed her brain. With all that dark powerful energy swirling around them, all she'd been able to think with the one brain cell that hadn't been paralysed with shock was that despite his outward composure, he wanted her. As much as she wanted him. Her struggles with the electrifying attraction were also his. Contrary to what she'd thought, he wasn't unaffected by her at all.

That mind-blowing realisation, along with the heat that had burned in his gaze, had crushed what few defences she had against him to dust. The wave of need that had thundered through her had driven out all rational thought. She'd never craved a kiss so much. For days, she'd secretly wondered how it would be. Well, now she knew. He felt like strength and security and he tasted like fire and whisky.

But she'd crossed a line. For all the promises she'd made to herself not to mix business with pleasure, she just had. Even though her conscience had woken up in time to stop things going any further, she'd created a conflict of interest that was very much not negligible. As if she simply could not resist the lure of self-sabotage, she'd put everything she'd worked for into jeopardy. Again. She'd let herself down. Again.

This was so bad, she thought, breaking out in a cold

sweat as a cab pulled up and she climbed into it. So very, *very* bad. Maybe even terminal. Once more she'd indulged the chemistry that raged whenever they were close, but this time they were no longer two strangers in a bar with nothing to lose. They were colleagues. And she was halfway through a career-defining assignment with *everything* to lose.

But she was not going to go down without a fight. She wasn't going to go down at all if she could help it. She had the entire weekend to think of a way to fix the situation and reset the status quo, and that was precisely what she would do.

Adam did not have a good weekend. So much for the opportunity to recover from his knackering dash across the Atlantic. Despite working his way through the bottle of whisky in the aftermath of Ella's flight from his apartment, sleep eluded him. Every time he closed his eyes, the memory of the kiss crashed into his head. Such heat. Such eagerness. Then such distress and regret, no doubt caused by the fact that with his confession, he'd shifted their relationship from the professional to the personal.

This was why he fought so hard for control, he thought as he tossed and turned in the early hours of Saturday morning. Because without it he was wild and unpredictable, no better than his father, and he knew the devastation such conduct could cause. He'd behaved impulsively. Selfishly. He'd provoked Ella into doing something she'd never have done otherwise.

Extreme exhaustion, bitter resentment that she'd encountered him in such a febrile state and severe sexual frustration blackened his mood over the course of the day, and it did not go unnoticed.

'For God's sake, smile,' Annabel muttered to him at one point during the white-tie charity gala he'd escorted her to. 'No one's going to believe we're madly in love if you insist on looking like thunder.'

He snapped a smile to his face and forced the tension from his jaw, but his mood did not improve. Not even a Sunday spent pouring over a pile of Helberg Holdings data soothed the rumblings of deep unease.

The only moment of respite he had was a phone call from his sister that he received at 6:00 a.m. on Monday, by which time—having yet again woken early and been unable to get back to sleep—he was already showered, dressed and debating whether to wait for his driver to show up at seven or call a cab.

'I thought you'd like to know I was at tech billionaire Luke Broussard's fifth of July bash in Marin County last weekend,' Charley said, packing in the detail as if she thought it would impress him. 'The photos I posted of me wearing one of my designs are already going viral, which is going to be invaluable publicity for my business. Free publicity. Organic publicity. Plus, I picked up four new commissions while I was there. So I've decided to expand my operation.'

Expand her operation? Adam thought with a frown as, ditching the idea of a cab, he entered the kitchen and pressed yet another espresso capsule into the coffee machine. On the back of some pictures and a handful of new commissions? Was that wise? Should he tell her that? Perhaps she was calling for advice. 'Let me take a look.'

He stalked through the apartment to his study while the machine did its thing and sat down at his desk. After switching on his laptop, he pulled up one of the social media sites he knew she used. There were three photos in total, all showing his sister in a dress that was the colour of bronze and looked great, although he was no expert. But it wasn't the dress that had caught his eye. No. What caught his eye and set off great clanging alarm bells in his head was the man she appeared to be dancing with.

Who was none other than his squash buddy and Helberg rival, Cade Landry.

Adam nearly fell off his chair in shock. He hadn't even been aware they knew each other. But Charley was looking up at Cade with such adoration it was blatantly obvious that they now knew each other extremely well indeed, and a wholly unfamiliar protective instinct kicked in. Could the man have deliberately targeted his sister to win the bet? Had he been unable to resist the opportunity to needle Adam in the process?

As an older brother who'd failed his sister before, Adam felt it his duty to point out these facts. Unsurprisingly, Charley did not take the news well.

'Are you serious?' she said in response to the revelation that he, Cade and Zane had vowed to date one woman only for the summer in order to decide who won Helberg and that she was now part of it.

He told her that he didn't joke about Montague's and

tried to explain the situation again, even offering to fix it, but Charley didn't want his help.

'I'm sorry,' he said with a sigh. 'I didn't mean for you to get caught up in this.'

'I need you to release fifty thousand pounds from my trust fund,' she said coolly, ignoring his apology entirely.

Pinching the bridge of his nose and suppressing the guilt, Adam relented. 'I'll speak to the bank.'

The conversation provided distraction for a full half hour. Ruminating on the fact that this could be an excellent place to start trusting his sister—who might lack his commercial experience but, unlike him, had set up her own company, kept it going and sounded as though she knew what she was doing—mopped another ten minutes.

Then it occurred to him that with these photos going viral, Cade had effectively been knocked out of the competition for Helberg. The rules of the bet would force him to stick with Charley, and she'd made it clear that because of it, she didn't want him anywhere near her, and this was another brief but pleasing diversion.

But he refused to be blindsided like this again—by *anything* date or bet related—so he emailed Maggie with instructions to cultivate contacts at *Blush* magazine. He didn't care how she did it. Bribery using beauty products. The promise of a dozen full page adverts. It was all good to him. But he needed advance warning of any further updates to the site before they went live.

Now, as he sat in the back of his car on the way to his office, staring unseeingly through the blacked-out windows, Ella was back in his head. How was he going to handle seeing her today? The strength of his desire for her remained a concern. It was inappropriate on too many levels to count.

Could he trust himself to control it? Could he be certain that she would do the same? She'd clearly been as horrified as he was by what they'd done—which was encouraging if they were to forget it had happened—but what if she'd had a rethink over the weekend and decided to pursue the chemistry? What if she wanted more?

An icy chill ran down his spine and his chest tightened as if in a vice. More could not happen. It didn't even bear thinking about. For one thing, the recklessness she aroused in him must not be allowed to return. For another, to the world at large, he was still dating Annabel. If he were seen with Ella too—either two-timing both women or ditching one for another—not only would his reputation take a hit and interest in him spike, but he'd also be forfeiting everything that he'd worked so hard to achieve.

Losing Helberg and, by extension, Montague's wasn't an option. He'd waited too long and it meant too much. Who knew when he might get another chance for redemption? This might be his one shot. And as for the reaction of his rivals should he fail, he could virtually see the crowing now. Cade and Zane would be insufferable. He'd never hear the end of it.

Unless, of course, they didn't find out.

As that thought darted through Adam's head, every atom in his body froze. His pulse skipped a beat and his breath caught in his lungs. Was that even possible? It would be if he saw Ella in secret. She'd mentioned she had three weeks' leave coming up. He could match it. Business was winding down for the summer. He was the boss. Besides, he'd dedicated the last four years to restoring the fortunes of the company, working sixteen-hour days seven days a week, and he couldn't remember the last time he'd taken a break. He could take her to his private island in the Caribbean. They'd be unseen and undiscovered there. He could make the travel arrangements himself and ask Annabel to keep a lower profile for a while. Who else would ever need know?

But, no, he thought, shaking his head to rid it of the mad idea. It was out of the question. Secrecy wouldn't address the risk of his control unravelling and the fall-out that might ensue. Besides, such subterfuge would be insanely stressful, not to mention cheating. He'd sacrificed far too many of his principles recently to squander what few he had left. He wouldn't compromise his integrity any further. He just had to harness his formidable willpower and focus on the endgame for what was, after all, only another five days.

Although, would it *really* be cheating? *He* knew he wasn't genuinely dating Annabel and, with regards to his conscience, surely that was all that mattered. She'd set the public record straight if required, not that he would trust either Cade or Zane to believe her if it suited them better not to. But even if he *were* to cheat, the end would justify the means. Business could be brutal. Just look at how Cade had gone about targeting Charley. Had he had any qualms about her identity? Adam suspected not.

And how much damage could be done in three short

weeks? It wasn't as if Ella would develop expectations he couldn't meet. He could still recall the shudder with which she'd assured him in that bar that she'd never be after anyone's heart, and he didn't think she'd been lying.

So what exactly was he worrying about? If what went on the island stayed on the island, there'd be no repercussions. He had no reason to believe that succumbing to the physical chemistry might lead to anything deeper. It never had before. He would never be tempted to tell Ella the gory details of his journey to CEO. He would never share with her his ugly selfishness as a teen, his guilt, his self-loathing and his desperate need for absolution.

The details of his mother's overdose and his role in it were for his thoughts alone. Quite apart from the visceral horror of it, spilling his guts and leaving them exposed and bleeding for her to pick through would create a dangerous emotional connection that he'd sworn never to create with anyone in case he failed them and destroyed them too.

He couldn't rely on his desire for Ella suddenly disappearing the minute the audit was over. It might have taken him only days to recover from the incident in the cocktail bar bathroom, but she'd been a stranger to him then. This time round, he'd know where to find her. He'd get no peace. He needed to get her out of his system so he could focus on the takeover. He needed to sort it now so he could get through the next week without losing his mind.

It would mean having to come clean about the bet, of course. His integrity might never recover if he took her to the Caribbean under false pretences. There was also every chance he might be forced to talk about Helberg. But for the sake of the audit, he'd have to disclose his interest in the company at some point, so why not now? He wouldn't need to go into detail. He wouldn't be exposing parts of himself that had never seen the light of day. It would be fine.

The key point here was that he wanted her and he wanted Helberg, and with a little deception, some careful planning and a few tricks up his sleeve to neutralise any objections she may raise, he could have both.

CHAPTER SEVEN

ELLA WAS PACKING up her workstation when out of the corner of her eye she saw Adam exiting the lift and striding in her direction. But despite the leap of her pulse and a hot surge of desire, she didn't pause, not even for a second. She'd been preparing for this moment ever since she'd thought of it in the early hours of yesterday morning. They couldn't continue working together in the same space and breathing the same air, she'd concluded as she'd lain in bed, tossing and turning, so stressed by the memory of the kiss that her cortisol levels had to have been sky high. Not after what had happened. The chemistry that still arced between them was simply too dangerous, and she had to put a stop to the self-destruction upon which she appeared hell-bent.

Furthermore, she'd finally succumbed to curiosity and googled his name and had come across a photo of him wrapped round a stunning redheaded supermodel at some charity gala the night before—his *girlfriend* no less, according to one article she'd read yesterday evening, in which the luscious Annabel St James had gushed with excitement about the brand-new love of her life.

Evidently, Adam had lied about always being single that night in the bar, but what did she care? It wasn't as if she were jealous or anything. How dumb would that be? And what would she have to be jealous of anyway? Their relationship? No, thanks. Although it did explain why he'd been so keen to forget their one-night stand. And why he'd been so resolute it was never going to happen again. Why he'd kissed her so thrillingly on Friday night instead of pushing her off wasn't her problem.

It had briefly crossed her mind as she silenced the alarm at six and buried her head beneath her pillow that she could call in sick. She could work from home and avoid having to face the boss she'd thrown herself at so shamelessly. But she'd dismissed the thought virtually the instant it entered her head because she would not be doing any such thing. She was stronger and braver than that, and the success of this job meant far too much. She wouldn't put her promotion in jeopardy just because she felt uncomfortable and it wasn't as if this would be the first time she showed up to work riddled with embarrassment and shame.

When her secret affair with Drew had eventually become public knowledge, she'd run the gauntlet of sly comments and knowing looks. Her private life had suddenly been up for scrutiny, of far more interest than her work, and that had been a situation that no amount of career planning had prepared her for. The humiliation and loss of respect had been crushing. One of her colleagues, who'd previously openly admired her work ethic, had questioned her career progression, implying that she'd only achieved what she had by lying flat on her back. Another had asked with suspicion whether any indiscreet office banter could have been reported further up the chain.

She'd had to fight damn hard to get over the mortification and restore her colleagues trust in her. It had been months before they'd gossiped in front of her again. Longer still to get to the point where she could be assigned an audit as significant as this one and it didn't raise a single eyebrow. But she'd survived that and she'd survive this too.

'Where do you think you're going?' Adam said, his voice doing strange things to her insides.

'I'm moving downstairs,' she replied, stuffing some papers in a box and looking anywhere but at him because it was too mortifying, too risky, too everything.

'We've already had this discussion.'

Yes, well, a lot had happened since then. But despite the mess she'd made of things—would she *never* learn?—she wasn't going to resign any more than she was going to let him fire her and the plan she'd come up with was the only way forward.

'This arrangement is no longer workable.' She unplugged her laptop and stowed it in her briefcase. 'We clearly can't exist in the same space without some kind of chemical reaction going on. Distance is the only option. It worked last week. It'll work this week.'

'You're running away again.'

So what if she was? The only thing that mattered was completing the audit so she could reboot her career, and that wouldn't happen if she had a constant reminder of what they'd done. 'I'm trying to ensure success.'

'That means a lot to you, doesn't it?'

'What makes you say that?'

'You fight hard.'

'I do. I've had to fight for everything.'

'The three jobs, the trailer, the dead-beat parents, the promotion. I remember. So how did you screw up?'

She wasn't telling him *that*, she thought with a shudder, regretting even more that she'd been goaded into letting that slip on Friday night. Her last disaster of a relationship was not a topic of conversation. It was bad enough *her* knowing she'd made the same mistake twice. If Adam ever found out, he'd probably question her judgement. He might decide she was replaceable even at this late stage in the proceedings.

'Launching myself at you wasn't my wisest move,' she said, deliberately misunderstanding him. 'Please accept my apologies. It was deeply unprofessional. I can't think what came over me. But rest assured that it won't happen again.'

He perched on the edge of the table and folded his arms across the hard muscled chest, against which she'd been plastered for all too brief a moment. 'That's a shame.'

'Why?'

'I don't think much of your solution to our little problem.'

She frowned. 'If you have a better idea,' she said, pretty sure that their problem was anything but little, 'I'd be delighted to hear it.'

'I think we should have an affair.'

At that, Ella's eyes widened and her jaw dropped.

What? *What?* On the one hand, it was a huge relief to know that he wasn't planning on firing her for overstepping the line as thoughtlessly as she had, but on the other, what on earth made him think an affair would be a good idea? 'Have you gone stark raving mad?'

'On the contrary,' he said with enviably cool. 'I'm thinking clearly for the first time in a week.'

'Lucky you.'

'This chemistry we share isn't going to go away,' he said far too reasonably given the subject matter. 'The more we've denied it, the more it's returned with a vengeance. Do you really think that out of sight will mean out of mind?'

It had to. It was the only option. 'I'm willing to give it a try.'

'What we *ought* to try is getting it out of our systems.'

Her head began to pound. 'That's the most ridiculous thing I've ever heard of. What if it doesn't work? What if it gets worse?'

'If I remember correctly, you have three weeks' leave coming up,' he continued, completely ignoring her very valid point. 'So what I'm suggesting is that as soon as the audit is over, we spend your time off doing just that. No lines will be crossed. There will be no conflict of interest. Just sex. And lots of it. For a finite period of time.'

Her heart raced. Her mouth was bone dry. God, this *conversation*. He should not be talking about sex at work. Or anywhere. 'Or we could just say farewell on Friday and that would be that.'

'Is that what you really want to do?' he said with an assessing tilt of his head. 'Remember what we did in the bathroom of a bar, Ella? Imagine what we could do in a bed.'

That was the trouble, she thought a little desperately. She'd spent *hours* over the weekend imagining what they could do in a bed, and she *didn't* want to say farewell on Friday, which was why she was having to use every drop of willpower she possessed to bite back the desperate *yes* that was trying to escape. 'I might have plans.'

'Cancel them.'

If she had had any plans, she would have bristled in response to that diktat. But she didn't. Having bought her own place eighteen months ago and with a pay rise that hadn't materialised, she'd had to rule out travel of any sort this year. And she was bristling about something else anyway. 'And what would your girlfriend have to say about you embarking on a sizzling three-week affair with someone else?'

Adam's dark eyebrows rose for a moment, then lowered. 'Nothing,' he said with a shrug of his impossibly broad shoulders and the glimmer of a smile. 'Because I don't have a girlfriend.'

Ella stared at him. Was that really what he was going with? Denial? How dared he? She well knew how *that* played out for the woman concerned. When Drew had been confronted with the evidence of their affair, he'd blamed it all on her, the rat. How she'd ever believed herself in love with him when he'd just been in it for the sex she had *no* idea. At precisely what point had she forgotten that security came from her career, which she could control—as long as she paid attention—and not a relationship, which she couldn't? Truly, she did not know what she'd been thinking. 'Well, she and the press are under the impression you do.'

Adam's unwavering gaze bore into hers. The intensity of it seemed to be tinged with indecision, and she briefly wondered, was he about to spin her a story? Was he trying to work out whether or not she would believe it?

'The weekend before last, I featured in a magazine article that went viral,' he said with a wince that looked genuine enough, but who knew? 'It focused on the dating habits of myself and a couple of friends, implying that we're all one-date wonders. It wasn't very flattering. It presented a severe risk to my reputation, to the *company's* reputation, and it was generating some extremely inconvenient press and social media attention. Annabel agreed to act as my girlfriend for the summer in order to stop it.'

For a moment, Ella didn't know whether she believed what he'd just told her or not. What with the way this conversation had developed, her brain simply couldn't process it. And once it had—deciding in the end that it was too mad a story to have made up—all she could think to say, was, 'Are you *serious*?'

'Very much so,' he replied coolly. 'I've spent four years clearing out the rot caused by my father and rebuilding the Courtney Collection's brand. I won't let anything jeopardise the progress I've made. Certainly not some two-bit magazine that can't get its facts straight. That's not even who I am any more. If they'd bothered to do their research, they'd have discovered that almost all of the women I appear in public with are in some way involved with the company.'

Yes, well, whether or not he was actually a one-date wonder, she could certainly sympathise with not wanting to jeopardise progress. She'd read about the antics of Edward Courtney—who hadn't?—and occasionally she'd allowed herself to wonder how Adam felt about that, what it could have been like growing up the son of such a man. But what a way to go about it. It seemed like something out of a farce and very much not the behaviour of a controlled CEO of a Fortune 500 company.

Although his kiss hadn't been in the slightest bit controlled, now that she thought about it. It had been hot and wild and desperate, and not a betrayal of anyone, which was *such* a relief, because even though she'd been unaware of this Annabel St James at the time, she'd still felt sickened and ashamed when she'd found out about her, as though she'd trampled all over the sisterhood. 'How long are you planning to keep up the charade?'

'Until Labor Day.'

'That's very specific.'

'There's a bet,' he said easily, as if there was nothing outrageous at all about making such a thing. 'It involves Helberg Holdings. I imagine you've noted that I've been buying up the shares. I intend to take it over, but I'm not the only one after it. There are three of us. My fellow one-date wonders. We each now hold a large stake in it. None of us is prepared to back off. It was proposed that to break the dead lock and shut down the reputational damage caused by the article, we each date one woman between now and Labor Day. Anyone caught dating more than one woman in that time relinquishes their claim on Helberg.'

Once again, he'd rendered her speechless. Ella stood there, staring at him, not quite sure where to start with all that. Then she realised that she had the opportunity to get somewhere with her enquiries, and she was damned if she wasn't going to take it. 'What's your interest in Helberg?' she said, parking her many questions about the bet until later. 'I looked into the company. Its portfolio is huge and in trouble. It seems an odd fit.'

'I'm after Montague's.'

'The international jewellery business?'

How many times had she walked past the flagship store on Fifth Avenue? Only about a thousand. And how many times had she failed to stop and look at the eternally gorgeous window display? None. Even though, these days, the woodwork was peeling and the signage was rusting, the cases behind the glass were always so prettily filled. She had no interest in the engagement, wedding and eternity rings, of course, but she'd always thought a tennis bracelet or a pair of diamond stud earrings might be nice.

'That's the one,' he confirmed with a nod. 'It used to belong to the Courtney Collection. It's been allowed to decline and I want it back. I've waited ten years for the chance, and I won't let anything get in the way of it, whether that's a threat to my reputation, external competition or problems raised by an audit.'

Ah. So that was why he'd been so insistent on keeping such a close eye on things. And, presumably, why he'd been so willing to ignore a potentially pesky conflict of interest or two. But ten years? Buying an entire conglomerate just to acquire one relatively small company? A bet? 'It sounds as though Montague's is more than just business to you.'

Despite his outward languor, a muscle jumped in his cheek. 'It's all about the bottom line.'

'Are you sure it's not a game?'

'It's very much not a game.'

'Yet you've bet on it, which is not only unbelievably puerile but also fails to take into account the agency of the women involved. Plus, you've agreed to terms which make no sense, because what if you all win?'

'That won't happen,' he countered with absolute confidence. 'You don't know Cade Landry and Zane deMarco. They'll be out any time now, if they aren't already. And believe me, I am extremely aware of how puerile it is. And the questionable ethics of involving women. Which is why Annabel is fully appraised of the circumstances and why I'm telling you now. To lay all my cards on the table. So there are no misunderstandings.'

'You're cheating.'

'Not technically.'

Hmm. 'You want me to be your dirty little secret.'

'The dirtier the better.'

'That's shameless.'

'I go for what I want and I want you.' His gaze fixed on her mouth and heat flooded her body. 'Do you have any other objections?'

Well, she *ought* to, she thought, trying the stamp out the desire beginning to thud away inside her. She ought to have plenty. For one thing, she was *not* having another office affair. The last one had caused quite enough trouble. A second would sink her career for good if it came to light. Of course, if it started after Friday, with the audit signed off and Adam no longer her client, it wouldn't actually be an office affair.

But it wasn't a question of semantics. Or that simple. Nor was it just a matter of timing, despite what Adam evidently thought. It had been easy enough to part company five weeks ago, when she'd only known him for twenty minutes, but what if this time round she found it harder? What if once again she lost her head, got to know him and at the end of their time together wanted more? Or *he* did? How would she disentangle herself from that?

And if she *did* agree to an affair, would she really be all right with the subterfuge? She would be tinged with grubbiness—again—even if he had been open and transparent with her, which, come to think of it, perhaps made her feel slightly less grubby and maybe even a little bit flattered because he clearly wanted her enough to risk the company he'd been working so hard to get.

However, she'd been down that road before and she had too much self-respect to travel along it again. Although, she couldn't deny that the discretion would suit her as much him because it wouldn't do her reputation any good to be caught in the company of a man who had so recently been her client, however unlikely that might be.

But, no. Right now, she needed to focus one hundred percent on her career. She couldn't afford to be distracted. Of course, the sex would be dynamite. And the next five days would be a lot easier to handle with the promise of relief at the end of them. Furthermore, with the three-week time frame he'd specified, there'd be a definite end. There'd be no danger of entanglement. There simply wouldn't be time to lose her head. She would never want anything more, with Adam or anyone, and this limited the risk of that for everyone involved.

Commitment, which seemed to require constant sacrifice and compromise, did not appeal. Even the *thought* of 'settling down' sent chills darting through her and she certainly no intention of ever having children. She'd witnessed first hand how well *that* worked out for women occupying senior positions in her field. At her previous company, one associate director had married, and in the immediate aftermath, some jerk had opened a book on how long it would be before she announced she was pregnant. Ten months, as it happened. Three months after that the same colleague had gone on maternity leave and when she had come back a year later, she'd found that her job wasn't quite what it had been. Somehow she'd become…*lesser.* Respect for her and belief in her ability had plummeted. Eventually, she'd left and was last heard to be working part time at a third rate out-of-state firm.

Ella couldn't even contemplate the thought of unwillingly—or even willingly—giving up everything she'd worked so hard for, and if that made her selfish in the eyes of others, well, she could live with that. She would never want to resent a husband or kids for holding her back. That wouldn't be fair to anyone.

But a hot, purely physical summer fling with a man to whom she was wildly attracted *did* appeal to her.

Very much. Getting him out of her system would be a scorching, thrilling rollercoaster of a ride. She couldn't think of a better way to celebrate a successful audit, a promotion and a pay rise. After keeping her nose to the grindstone this last year, she deserved some fun. And so what if she was his dirty little secret? He was hers too.

'Three weeks?' she said, her pulse racing as the last of her resistance crumbled beneath the fizzling pressure of such hot heady desire.

'I don't have the time for anything more.'

'Just sex?'

'No strings. No complications. Just sex.'

'Then I'm all out of objections.'

'Excellent.' A gleam of triumphant satisfaction lit the gorgeous blue depths of his eyes. A devastatingly sexy smile curved his mouth, and as shivers ran up and down her spine, she wondered what on earth she was letting herself in for. 'How do you feel about the Caribbean?'

CHAPTER EIGHT

ELLA ARRIVED AT the exclusive out-of-town airport first thing on Saturday morning as instructed, practically quivering with anticipation. The excitement leaping about inside her was almost impossible to contain.

For one thing, she'd never been to the Caribbean. Generally, when she took a vacation, she went to Europe to improve her knowledge of geography, culture and history, only occasionally venturing farther afield, to India, Africa, Japan. Secondly, the heat in Manhattan in summer could be unbearably stifling, and a balmy private island which would ensure the discretion they both favoured sounded like a delightful alternative. Far more importantly, however, she was now mere hours away from allowing herself to give into the temptation that had plagued her since the moment she'd arrived at the Courtney Collection.

The last five days had not given either her patience or her nerves an easy ride. Evidently flush with success at having secured her agreement to an affair, Adam had persuaded her not to move downstairs. It hadn't taken much. He'd suggested treating the countdown to the end of the week as foreplay, and she was all unpacked three minutes later.

She'd half thought she'd regret the added distraction. But she hadn't, because she'd entered such a state of hyperawareness that the audit had kicked up a gear. Progress had steamed ahead as if on steroids. Long steamy looks across the divide had not derailed it. Nor had conversations that were ostensibly about the methodologies used to value inventory and the whereabouts of documents relating to revenue recognition but at the same time were laden with subtext. Somehow, she'd even managed to rise above the occasional steamy text message he sent.

Where were you at lunchtime?

That was how one such exchange had started.

I went shopping for Caribbean-friendly clothes.

That was a waste of time.

Why?

You won't be needing any.

The audit had wrapped up to her satisfaction, bang on time on Friday afternoon, and she hadn't stuck around to celebrate for long. She'd gone for one quick drink with her team, but she'd been too distracted by her own scorching thoughts to stay.

Now, the car that Adam had sent for her was drawing up to the jet that stood on the tarmac and shone bright white in the early morning sun. The driver opened the rear passenger door and Ella climbed out. Her entire body thrumming with adrenaline, she thanked him and then walked up the steps as if she did this sort of thing all the time. She ducked her head and entered the cabin to find Adam had beaten her to it. He was sitting on a buttoned sofa in a space that—with the low lighting, sumptuous furnishings and highly polished wood décor—looked more like the cocktail bar in which they'd met than any plane she'd ever been on.

Watching her with an intensity that ramped up the thrills whizzing through her to an almost intolerable level, he got to his feet, and immediately the cabin seemed to shrink in size and run out of air.

'Good morning,' she said breathlessly while trying to keep it cool because a crew member was flitting about, so they weren't alone.

'Good morning,' he said, his voice deep, low and tinged with a roughness that made her shiver. 'Come and join me.'

Giddy with the realisation that there was no longer any need to keep her distance, Ella did as he suggested. She walked towards him, feeling as though she were tied to the end of a rope he was slowly hauling in, and when he sat, so did she. The cream leather sofa was comfortable but small. Her knee was inches from his. His intoxicatingly masculine scent instantly enveloped her, and she fizzed so badly with the need to touch him that she had to sit on her hands.

'Coffee?'

'Thank you.'

He turned a fraction and leaned forward to pour her a cup. His shoulder brushed hers as he moved, and she nearly leapt out of her skin. She was never going to last the flight if she carried on like this, she thought despairingly, letting out a long slow breath and willing her heart rate to slow. She had to calm down. She really did. And what was there to be jittery about anyway? She was being ridiculous.

Mentally giving herself a firm shake, Ella accepted the cup he offered her with a hand that she was pleased to see was now as steady as a rock and took a fortifying sip.

'How was the show?' she asked, referring to the Broadway play he'd attended last night with Annabel and stamping out the voice that was whispering *dirty little secret* in her ear, because this was nothing like the illicit affair she'd had with Drew. Adam had been very clear about what he wanted from her. Exactly why he too was interested in no strings or complications was irrelevant. They were on the same page. That was the main thing. And this time round, she had herself under control. Mostly.

'Interminable,' he replied. 'How were the drinks?'

'Short.'

Even though she could look at him forever, to do so was sorely testing her resolve. So as the engines fired, she glanced around, her curiosity piqued, her auditing antennae quivering despite being on leave. 'Is this the company jet?'

'I wouldn't dare.'

Her gaze swung back to his. A gleam lit the blue

depths of his eyes. The ghost of a smile played at his mouth, and she wanted to kiss him so badly she ached with it. 'You hired one just for me?'

'I *bought* one just for you.'

For a moment, Ella didn't know what to say. Her brain had completely stalled. She'd never had anyone go to such lengths to address her concerns or want her so much that they bought a plane to facilitate a three-week fling. Drew, who, mortifyingly, had not had to woo her at all because somehow she'd thrown her self-respect out of the window along with her sanity and slept with him the night he'd chatted her up, hadn't even bought her dinner. 'I'm flattered.'

'I'm regretting it doesn't have a bed.'

That was indeed a shame, she thought, swallowing hard in response to the smoulder with which he was looking at her. 'How long is the flight?'

'It's five hours to Aruba. From there, fifteen minutes in a seaplane.'

'I believe it's called delayed gratification,' she said, wondering how on earth she was going to stand it.

'I believe it's called torture.'

'What shall we do to occupy the time?'

'How about I tell you everything I intend to do to you when we land?'

A flush hit her cheeks. Her pulse rate rocketed. Her lungs seemed to have collapsed. 'Will that take five hours?'

'More.'

Oh dear God. 'We have company.'

'Then come closer.'

Helpless to resist, Ella put down her cup and did so. Adam was as good as his word, his level of detail as impressive as it was mind-blowing, and by the time they arrived at the island mid-afternoon, she could barely stand. Her limbs were liquid. Her heart was beating so hard she was surprised she hadn't cracked a rib.

She'd never experienced anything like the intensity of his focus, she thought as she disembarked from the seaplane they'd transferred to in Aruba and he'd piloted himself. For as long as she could remember, she'd been her number one priority. Now she appeared to be someone else's, albeit temporarily, and it was a bit bewildering.

However, she must not let it overwhelm her. She must not allow herself to be swept up in the attention. It would do her no good at all to get carried away by the fairytale romance of it all. She was an auditor with a fondness for spreadsheets. Practicality and realism were in her DNA. For all she knew, Adam treated all the women he slept with like this. And what they were doing was about getting him out of her system, not allowing him to work his way even further into it.

While he removed their luggage from the seaplane, Ella stood on the jetty and surveyed the landscape. To her left, the rocky coastline disappeared around a curve. To her right stretched a band of dazzling pristine white sand upon which lapped tiny crystal-clear waves. Beyond the idyllic beach, nestled among the palm trees, stood the house, a sprawling white two-storey building with a wraparound veranda on the ground floor and balconies on the second supported by elegant white columns.

It was stunning, classy, everything she'd expect from a luxury goods magnate and nothing like what she was used to, and suddenly an unexpected flurry of nerves swooped into her stomach, because what was she doing? This wasn't her world. She wasn't a private-jet-private-island-billionaire's-plaything sort of a person. She ought to be back in New York, man-free, drycleaning her suits and clearing her inbox. This was reckless, rash and—

'Are you all right?'

His voice cut through the rising panic, and she blinked and blew out a breath as her pulse began to slow. There was no need to overthink this. It was a fling. That was all. And hadn't she just told herself not to get carried away? She had to ease up. Focus on the facts. Chill out, as they said, even though she couldn't recall the last time she'd actually done that. 'I'm just taking a moment.'

'Having second thoughts?'

'No.'

'Sure?'

'Yes.'

'Then stop dawdling.'

He slung his bag over his shoulder and picked up her case. With his free hand he took her elbow, then led her along the jetty and up some steps. He propelled her along a wide sandy path that led to the house and in through the front door. He dropped the case and the bag and kicked the door shut.

But she didn't get a chance to check out the light airy space, because in the blink of an eye he'd pushed her up against the wall and slammed his mouth down on hers, instantly wiping her head of the doubts and the nerves, because *this* was what they were about. Chemistry. Sex. Nothing else.

So it didn't matter what he was or what she was. All that mattered was that this was a kiss she'd waited over week for, a kiss that had kept her awake at night, twisting and turning in torment, and it was everything she'd been anticipating. More. It was hot. Wild. Electric. Days of pent-up desire exploding in a clash of teeth and a tangle of tongues.

Dizzy with longing, as tiny bombs of excitement detonating inside her, Ella lifted her hands to his shoulders, tracing the contours of his muscles that bunched and flexed beneath the black cotton of his polo shirt. She dug her fingers in his hair. He held her hips and pulled her pelvis to his so she could feel exactly how badly he wanted her.

His erection pressed hard against her and liquid heat pooled between her legs. Fire rushed through her veins. He tasted and felt better than she remembered and her entire world shrank to him, this dominating, punishing, utterly magnificent kiss and the ferocious need that pulsated between them.

He eventually tore his mouth from hers and she dragged in a much-needed breath, only to lose it again when he turned his attention to her jaw, her earlobe, her neck and the pulse that throbbed wildly at the base of it. When he slid a hand up her side to her breast, cupping it and brushing a thumb over her tight, aching nipple, she gasped in response to the lightning bolt of ecstasy that shot through her. Her knees buckled, and if he hadn't been pinning her to the wall, she'd have collapsed to the floor.

Desperate to arouse the same sensations in him, she disentangled her fingers from his hair and ran them over his hard, muscled chest, down, down, down to the waistband of his jeans—at which point he stilled, lifted his head from her neck and jerked back.

She opened her eyes, suddenly wracked with confusion. 'Why are you stopping?' she panted, gazing helplessly into his darkly glittering eyes.

'I promised you a bed.'

He scooped her up, and before she could protest that she wasn't some faint-hearted damsel in distress, he was carrying her across the hall and up the stairs. He barged into a room and dropped her onto the vast bed. Thinking that, actually, she would play the damsel in distress any day of the week if it meant being enveloped in all that heat and strength, Ella took the opportunity to whip off her sundress and tossed it aside.

Adam came straight down on top of her, and within moments, her bra had joined her dress on the floor. His mouth landed first on one breast, then the other, and as he began to lavish attention on her, she lost all track of time and place. Her head spun and her breath stuck in her lungs. The sensations sizzling through her were so devastatingly powerful, she had to bite her lip to stop herself from crying out.

'There's no one to hear you but me,' he muttered, his hot breath tickling her feverish skin as he began to inch his way down her body. 'Make as much noise as you want.'

When he reached the juncture of her thighs, he deftly removed her underwear. Then he put his mouth on her and she did as he suggested. She couldn't help it. She was beyond reason and he was just too good at this. Gasping, groaning, parting her legs even further, she clutched at the sheet with one hand and kept his head in place with the other. She tried to writhe to alleviate the throbbing ache, but he held her still. He removed her hand from his head, trapping her wrist on the bed, and took full command, dictating the pace, ignoring her pleas and increasing the torment until she was sobbing and begging for release.

She'd never felt desperation like it, never wanted something so badly, and when her orgasm finally hit, it struck with the force of tsunami, drenching her in such pleasure so intense she felt as though she might drown in it.

With stars still exploding in her head, her breathing still ragged and shallow, Adam reared up. He stripped off his clothes and rolled on a condom, and then he was back between her legs, angling her hips and sliding his gloriously thick length into her. And although it did not seem possible—surely her body couldn't recover from something so exceptional so quicky—a fresh wave of desire surged through her.

He kissed her deeply, fiercely, the taste of her on him scattering what few wits she'd managed to gather. When he began to move, she clung to his broad shoulders and wrapped her legs around his waist. His skin was hot and slick. The friction of his hair-roughened chest against hers was sensational. With every slow, controlled thrust, she lost a little bit more of her mind.

And she could tell that he was losing his too. He'd wrenched his mouth from hers and buried his head in her neck. His thrusts were becoming less measured and increasingly frantic. Astonishingly, the exquisite pressure was building inside her again, like a bonfire that had merely been doused, not wholly put out.

She tightened her legs around his hips and dug her fingers into his back, her blood on fire, her breathing rough. Then somehow, he slipped his hand between them, skilfully finding the spot where she pulsed and burned, and she shattered, gasping, panting, crying out his name. A second later, with a muffled roar, he buried himself deep inside her one last time and collapsed.

'Well, that was worth waiting for,' she murmured once she'd regained her breath and he'd lifted his weight off her.

'That's just the start of it,' he muttered raggedly, staring down at her, his glittering gaze filled with promise. 'We have days to make up for, and as you know, my imagination's been hard at work.'

'So's mine,' she said with a delicious little shiver. 'Show me.'

While Ella lay sprawled on the bed beside him, the midnight moonlight giving her skin a silvery glow, Adam reflected that she had been bang on with her observation about delayed gratification.

The last week in the office had been insanely tough. Never had his self-control been so tested. He lost count of the number of times he'd been forced to remind himself of his commitment to the bet and the significance of the audit for his takeover in order to stop himself from buckling beneath the overwhelming crush of desire and taking her where she sat. And he'd evidently developed masochistic tendencies, because he could have drummed up any number of meetings to spare himself the torment of having her constantly in his line of sight, but he hadn't. He could also have let her move downstairs as she'd wished, but he hadn't done that either.

So much for the assumption that arranging an affair would ease what remained of the audit, he'd thought every time he'd stepped into the shower and flipped the dial to cold. In practice, the unbearable week had crawled by so slowly it had frequently felt as though time were going backwards. The plane ride down here, during which he'd let his imagination run riot and caused himself a whole lot of pain in the process, had seemed to last years instead of hours.

And yet he'd undergo every single second of it all over again if it meant the kind of sex they'd spent the afternoon having. What they'd got up to had far surpassed anything his feeble imagination had managed to conjure up. One minute it was feverish, frantic and explosive. The next it was slow and thorough, though nonetheless earth-shattering. There was barely an inch of her he hadn't explored at length, and she'd spent a good hour tormenting him with her hands, mouth and hair while he simply lay back and surrendered. Her insatiability—and his—would be the death of him. Not even in his wildest days as a reckless teenager had he lost it so hard and so often. And best of all, they had an entire three weeks of it.

The intensity of the experience was greater than he'd been expecting. Greater than anything he'd come across before, in fact. But he had no doubt that it would soon fade. It invariably did. And most likely it was caused by a five-day run-up that had been as hot as it could be without physical contact anyway.

Nor was he overly concerned by the efforts he'd made to arrange the affair. Practically speaking, all he'd had to do was make some calls and get out his cheque-book. Annabel, who'd been intending to spend the summer at an Austrian health retreat before he'd asked her to escort him around the city, had had no problem reviving that plan. It was the work of a moment to instruct the house to be opened up and another couple of hours to purchase the plane.

Telling Ella about the bet had not been difficult either. He wasn't remotely concerned he wouldn't win it, despite what she'd said. He'd briefly checked out the *Blush* magazine website for the latest tally, and it was true that Cade and Zane had gone rather quiet on the dating front, but it was early days.

Furthermore, as he'd suspected, revealing the bare bones of his interest in Helberg had been fine too. She hadn't pushed him further on why Montague's was so important to him, which would certainly have been a trickier conversation to navigate, so on the whole, he was extremely satisfied with how everything had played out. And there was no denying that a plane for personal use would come in handy once the takeover was complete and he had more time on his hands.

The only thing he didn't much like was the fact that she believed herself to be his dirty little secret. Despite the planning he'd done, he'd failed to consider the possibility she might think that. It disturbed his already compromised principles and left the hint of a bitter taste in his mouth. But if she could get over it, then so could he.

The crucial thing was that they were singing from the same hymn sheet. They were both in this just for the sex. Why that was important to her didn't matter. All he needed to know about her was which position she fancied trying next.

CHAPTER NINE

SEVERAL DAYS LATER, although quite how many she couldn't be sure because she'd lost all sense of time and space, Ella woke late in the afternoon to an empty bed and the sound of the shower being switched off.

What a time she and Adam had been having, she thought with a languid stretch that eased the delightful ache in her muscles. There'd been so much sex. So much pleasure. He'd followed through on every one of the promises he'd made to her on the plane and she was delighted and relieved she'd suppressed her misgivings and agreed to come. She could not get enough of him. Which perhaps didn't bode all that well for getting him out of her system, but this fling of theirs was still in its infancy.

With desire once again fluttering, Ella was wondering what was taking him so long when her phone beeped to alert her to an incoming email. Lazily, she rolled over and picked up the device. She unlocked it and opened the app—and sat bolt upright when she saw that the message was from her boss.

For a moment, she didn't dare click on it, because this one message held her entire future in its hands. She thought the audit had gone well, but what if it hadn't?

What if something had gone wrong? What if somehow the conflict of interest she and Adam had both been so keen to ignore had been uncovered, the audit rendered invalid, and she was being fired?

Ella swallowed hard and pulled herself together. She took a deep breath and shook the tension from her shoulders. She was being ridiculous. Why would something have gone wrong?

Nevertheless, her stomach was tumbling and her chest was tight as she opened the email. With her heart in her mouth, she read it once, twice, a third time—and then punched the air in triumph, because she'd done it. She'd actually done it. The promotion was hers. All that hard work had paid off. She was back in from the cold with a twenty percent pay rise and assigned to a great big fat audit starting in September. Her career was back on track. Her future was secure. She could finally put the last horrible year behind her and move on. And, God, it was a *relief*, because she could now admit that she'd been more than a little nervous waiting for the verdict.

'You look happy,' said Adam, walking into the room, naked but for a towel around his waist and another around his neck.

Ella broke off the victory dance she was doing on the bed and beamed at him. 'I just got that promotion I was after.'

She thought she saw a tiny frown crease his brow, but it was there and gone so fast she realised it must have been a trick of the light. 'Congratulations.'

'Thank you,' she said, flopping back against the pillows and admiring his broad, hard chest, which was glistening alluringly with water droplets. 'I can't tell you how relieved I am. It's been long overdue.'

He pulled the towel from his neck and began to rub his hair dry. 'I remember you saying you screwed up. What happened?'

Ella stilled for a second, the bubble of happiness bouncing around inside her deflating a fraction, because, damn, that had been careless. She'd inadvertently piqued his interest, and now she was in a spot because there were only two ways in which to respond—prevarication or confession.

Since she abhorred the first—to her it seemed not only weak but also a monumental waste of time—that only left the second. Which, most likely, meant telling him everything that had happened, everything she'd been through, when the whole sorry episode was behind her and she had no intention of ever thinking of it again. Because would he be satisfied with a dismissive wave of the hand and a vague muttering about 'stuff'? She didn't think so. He was all about the minutiae. Some responses to her emails during the audit, she recalled, had run to pages.

Quite honestly, the thought of reliving the ill-judged affair with Drew brought her out in a cold sweat. She'd never shared the full story with anyone. Not even her friends knew all the details. Admitting how stupid she'd been and exposing her fallibility to a supremely confident man like Adam, a man who'd likely never put a foot wrong in his life, appealed even less.

But on the other hand, what if it *wasn't* so easy to move on? What if, despite the promotion that suggested she'd been forgiven, the memories of it continued to hound her, riddling her with doubt and colouring her every decision? How would she stand it?

Maybe she had to offload everything once and for all—the facts, the fallout, the lasting impact the affair had had on her—so she could truly let it go. Maybe it would be cathartic. And as for exposing her fallibility to this man in particular, well, he had no sway over her career any longer. He posed no threat to anything, and she certainly didn't care about his opinion of her. In two and a half weeks' time she'd never even see him again. How bad could it possibly be?

Nevertheless, bracing herself to be hit with a flurry of unpleasant memories and a surge of turbulent emotion, Ella sat up and hugged a pillow to her like some sort of shield. 'Drew Taylor,' she said on a sigh. 'He's what happened.'

'Who's Drew Taylor?'

'A year ago, he was my then boss's then boss. He's also the biggest mistake of my life.'

Adam stilled mid-rub, and while she appreciated the pose that displayed his muscles to their finest advantage, she was more intrigued by the unexpected flare of emotion she saw in his glare when her gaze met his. 'What did he do?'

'Plenty,' she said with a wince and a shudder as she fought to keep the details from flooding her head. 'But then, so did I. I had an affair with him. I knew it was against company policy, but I went ahead with it anyway. For a whole six weeks.'

His eyebrows shot up. 'You did *what*?'

'There's no need for you to be so judgemental about it,'

she said, bristling a little even though his incredulity was perfectly understandable and not nearly as great as her own. 'Believe me, I have berated myself repeatedly for it. Barely a day goes by that I don't regret my stupidity.'

Adam abandoned the towel with which he'd been rubbing his head and sat at the end of the bed, facing her. 'I'm not being judgemental,' he said, his expression softening a fraction. 'I'm just staggered that you'd risk your career like that when it obviously matters a great deal to you.'

Yes, well, quite. How very perceptive of him. 'It was an extremely stressful time,' she said, not entirely sure who she was trying to convince most. 'I'd been working long hours and was running on fumes. We were out celebrating the end of a successful financial year, and one thing led to another.' She sighed again. 'To be honest, I'm not sure what I was thinking at the time. I must have been out of my mind. I don't even do relationships. But somehow I got tangled up in it. He was very dynamic. Very persuasive. But I still should have resisted.'

The frown returned. 'Did he take advantage of you?'

'No.'

'It sounds as though he did.'

'I was a very willing participant. Too willing, as it turned out.'

'What do you mean?'

Even though she was beginning to die a little on the inside at the thought of revealing things that were so personal, so ridiculously sentimental, Ella soldiered on because there was no going back now. 'I thought I was in love, which I wasn't, but still. There was definitely some infatuation going on. For him, though, it could not have been more casual. We could not have been more at odds in terms of expectations. And so when we were found out, he threw me under the bus.'

'How?'

'He claimed I'd seduced him and that I wouldn't take no for an answer.'

For a moment there was utter silence. While she'd been speaking, Adam's expression had grown increasingly stony, and by the time she finished, his scowl could have vaporised rock. 'He deserves to be ruined.'

'He does,' she agreed, something deep in her chest twanging in response to his support, which she didn't need but for some reason felt nice to have nonetheless. 'Instead, he got promoted, I got blacklisted. The night you and I met in that bar, I'd just found out he'd been nominated for an award, while I was still battling to repair my reputation. It felt grossly unfair.'

'It's more than grossly unfair,' he said, his jaw now so tight it looked as if it were about to shatter. 'It's immoral, if not downright illegal.'

'I know.'

'I should fire them.'

Her eyes widened with alarm. 'Please do not do that. They might blame it on me and take my promotion away.'

'All right,' he conceded grudgingly. 'But the minute our contract comes up for renewal, the gloves are off.'

'There's really no need. I can fight my own battles.'

'I wouldn't be doing it for you. I'd be doing it for me. There's no place for misogyny and harassment in any of the Courtney Collection's dealings. There was enough of that going on under my father's tenure.'

'So I've read,' she said, stifling a shudder at the thought of Edward Courtney, who sounded as though he'd been an utterly abhorrent individual.

'So, because of the affair, your career stalled,' he said, bringing the conversation back to the point. 'What other impact did it have?'

'You mean apart from the realisation that I'd recklessly jettisoned the rules I'd lived by for a decade and put my whole career on the line? The humiliation and the shame and the sickening knowledge that I'd badly let myself down? The battering of my self-esteem and my confidence and losing the trust and respect of my colleagues? Nope. I think that's about it.'

Some undefinable emotion flitted across his face. 'Why didn't you leave?'

'Imagine the reference.'

'Did you think about taking the company to court?'

'Only briefly. I couldn't prove anything. And I doubt it would have done my reputation any good, even if I could. Instead, I kept my head down and bided my time until I was given the chance to prove myself. Your audit was it, which was why I was so determined to see it through. Why I repeatedly compromised my principles to make that happen, which didn't feel right when I've always done everything by the book. But I wanted redemption more. I wanted what I deserved.'

'And you got it.'

'I did. Despite my own attempts to sabotage things. I mean, I'd sworn not to mix business with pleasure ever again, and I was determined not to let the attraction I felt for you get the better of me, but I still threw myself at you the evening I confronted you at your apartment. Lately, I really seem to have been my own worst enemy.'

'I provoked you into it.'

'Perhaps,' she agreed, recalling the havoc he'd unleashed in her with his admission that he was as at the mercy of the chemistry that sizzled between them as she was. 'But I'm okay with owning my mistakes. I've always thought it important to learn from them so as not make the same ones again. Obviously, that's something I still need to work on.'

Adam appeared to have no further response to that. He seemed to be waging some sort of war with himself. His fists were clenched, and he looked as though he were ready to rip things apart with his bare hands.

But however soft and warm it made her feel, she really didn't need his outrage. Nor did she want it. In fact, the conversation had turned somewhat darker and heavier than she'd intended, and she was filled with the sudden urge to lighten it.

'Anyway,' she said with a deliberately bright smile, now focused on putting an end to the conversation before it got any more complicated. 'All's well that ends well, and you're now sleeping with a director. So what do you think of that?'

Adam thought so many things about what Ella had just told him he didn't know where to start. When he'd walked into the bedroom and seen her jumping around on the bed and beaming from ear to ear, for a split second he'd thought it was because she was pleased to see him. But that had not been the case. Which was a relief, naturally, because the last thing he wanted was to be responsible for her happiness. The quick tightening of his chest had been caused by indigestion, he was sure.

Her delight at her success had been infectious, and he'd experienced a moment of what might or might not have been pride because he knew how bloody hard she'd worked for it. He'd witnessed it. However, when she'd explained the circumstances surrounding it, those positives had swiftly morphed into a more volatile combination of emotions. Astonishment. Disbelief. And then fury, directed first at the jerk who'd messed her around and then at the company that had treated her so unfairly.

For the first time in his life, he wanted to punch something. Ella's dynamic and persuasive ex specifically, the mere thought of whom made him feel as though he'd swallowed a bucket of battery acid. This Drew Taylor should never have abused his seniority by starting something with her, even if she had been a willing participant. And then to wash his hands of her? What sort of a cowardly bastard did that?

At the very least, the guy deserved to be fired. A couple of phone calls was all it would take, and his career would be history. And once that was done, Adam would then set about taking apart the company she worked for piece by piece. The world did not need businesses with values like that. What she'd been through brought back unpleasant memories of the accusations of sexual harassment made against his father. Of the one member of staff who'd dared to sue and been so thoroughly destroyed by the process she'd never worked again. She'd been living in a hostel, broke and broken, when Adam finally tracked her down in order to reverse the miscarriage of justice at least a little. So unfortunately Ella had probably been right to question the wisdom of such a course of action.

No wonder she'd gone to such lengths to keep the audit on track and trouble-free. She was righting a wrong. Just as he was. But he had to cool it before he burst a blood vessel. He wasn't her avenger and she'd made it clear that she didn't need one. He had enough on his plate with the Helberg takeover. He didn't need to fight for justice on any other playing field. That wasn't what this was about anyway. And if she wanted to carry on working for a company that treated her so badly, that was her business.

So, deploying steely determination, Adam pushed the emotions back into the cage where they belonged and fought the clamouring urge to tell her about the challenges *he'd* faced at work, particularly when he'd taken over as CEO. About how he didn't do relationships either. About Montague's and the reason why he'd let the conflicts of interest they'd had slide.

If she wanted to share details of her past with him, that was up to her. He was under no obligation to reciprocate. And he mustn't. Because losing control physically was one thing. Losing control of his defence mechanisms that kept everyone at arm's length was quite another.

'I'll get the champagne.'

Although it pained her to admit it, a week into their affair, the frustration that Ella had experienced during the first half of the audit returned, and for a very similar reason, namely avoidance. Not when it came to sex. That was more torrid than ever. The afternoon she'd received her promotion, which they'd celebrated not just with champagne but also sex so wild and free she'd given him an orgasm that for one tiny nanosecond had actually made him lose consciousness. Ever since then, he'd been trying to do the same to her, and although he hadn't yet succeeded, his diligence had been thrilling. So no. She had no cause for complaint there. The area that was giving her grief was conversation. Or rather, the lack of it.

By definition, that was a two-way street, but currently most of the traffic was on her side of the road. While she wasn't expecting—and did not particularly want—an in-depth discussion about hope and dreams, she was interested in *slightly* more than just the basic facts about the man she was sleeping with. It was unnerving to know every inch of his body but so little of his mind, other than he had a thing about justice. It didn't feel quite right. But every time she asked him a question that ventured into the vaguely personal, he batted it away or turned the conversation back to her. When that didn't work and she persisted, he distracted her with sex.

'Our trailer park was located in California only a few miles from a swanky golf course and polo field,' she told him one morning in bed in response to his enquiry into how hard she'd had to fight for what she'd achieved. 'It was illegal. And feral. The dogs. The kids. The adults. People who weren't drinking themselves into oblivion were shooting up. We had no air-conditioning and undrinkable water. The plumbing would go down for weeks at a time, and toxic smoke from the nearby dump regularly drifted in through the broken windows.'

'How did you escape?' he asked, propping himself up on his elbow and lazily trailing his fingers over the contours of her body as if mapping her.

'It was tough. My parents dealt drugs to make ends meet. Hard ones, although they were never prosecuted because the cops tended to steer clear of the whole place. I could have easily gone down the same route. Most kids did. But even at an early age, I got the feeling that there had to be something better out there. I don't know why. Maybe I saw something on TV. Anyway, I got myself to high school, where I discovered I had an affinity for numbers and decided that accounting would become my route out. The one good teacher I had told me about charities that would help, and they did. I worked hard to catch up and got the grades. I went for days on end on only three hours' sleep a night, but it was definitely worth the pain. I graduated first in my class at college. Not that that was the end of it, of course. I had to lose the accent. I also had to learn how to read a room and network and educate myself on which fork to use, which actually was quite interesting. Did you know there was a separate plate for salad?'

'Yes.'

'And that it's generally acceptable to eat asparagus with your fingers?'

'I've never eaten it any other way.'

'No, well, you and I couldn't be more different, could we?'

He stilled for a moment, shifted minutely as if to

make himself more comfortable and then resumed his idle exploration of her. 'Do you still see your parents?'

'Not for a decade.'

'Do you mind about that?'

'God, no,' she said with a shudder. 'I can barely believe we're related and I'm very happy relying on myself. I've been doing it for years. I can't ever imagine not. They could be dead, for all I know. I really don't care.'

'You're very tough.'

He sounded impressed and a warm tingly feeling that had nothing to do with desire beginning to wind through her. 'I've had no choice,' she said, ruthlessly stamping it out. 'Once I decided to reject the life that could have been mine, it was the only option. It's been quite a journey and not an easy one, but I don't regret a moment of it. Apart from my one reckless affair, obviously. That was a bad career move. So, what about you? Where did you grow up? What was your home environment like? I've read about your father. It couldn't have been easy.'

But she didn't get an answer. His gaze that was on hers darkened and intensified and her pulse began to pound. 'I think that's best saved for another time,' he murmured suggestively, and before she could protest, he rolled on top of her and silenced her with his mouth.

He kissed her until her head emptied of everything but him. He caressed her breasts, with which he'd developed something of an obsession, and she lost what little was left of her mind. Then, when he finally stopped ignoring her desperate pleas for release and thrust hard into her, there was nothing but fierce heat, ragged breathing and the slickness of their bodies moving together. He was in no hurry. In fact, he seemed to be intent on tormenting her. He drove her to the brink and then pulled her back so often it felt like punishment. When he eventually allowed her to fall apart in his arms, she saw stars for a full five minutes.

This happened again when she tried to find out more about his sister and their relationship. And again when she recalled him telling her that the magazine article was inaccurate because that depiction of him wasn't who he was any more.

It was more than a coincidence, she felt. Just like during the first week of the audit, she suspected he was doing whatever he could to avoid her more challenging questions, and in spite of the pleasure he gave her on these occasions, the imbalance of the situation was becoming a problem. At least for her. It felt like an insult. It felt transactional, and it reminded her too much of her relationship with Drew, who, because he'd been less invested in her than she had in him, had held all the cards.

This was meant to be a meeting of equals, body and mind, and it wasn't. Knowledge was power and Adam had all of it, and it had now reached the point that this state of affairs had to be addressed.

'Do you realise that it's been a week since we got here, and you haven't told me one single significant thing about yourself?' she said over a supper of grilled spiced fish and a mango and avocado salad that had been prepared by the housekeeper who lived on the island but she'd yet to meet. 'Whenever I try to engage you in a conversation about you or anything even in the slightest bit personal, you distract me with sex.'

Adam glanced up from his plate. The flickering candlelight cast dancing shadows over the sharp planes of his face. His expression was unreadable, but his eyes twitched and a muscle jumped in his jaw. 'How is that a problem? Are you bored?'

'Of the sex? No,' she said, while thinking, *As if.* He was keeping her extremely well occupied with sex that was varied and inventive. But that was partly the trouble. 'It's just that it makes me feel as though I'm nothing more than an object of pleasure.'

He frowned and put down his fork. 'I understood you were on board with this being purely physical.'

'I am. To a degree. But I would like to know a bit more about the man I'm sleeping with. I would like some respect. I've told you a lot about myself these last few days yet have had zero in return. It makes me uneasy. I can't help wondering what you have to hide.'

'I don't have anything to hide,' he said smoothly, although tension was beginning to radiate off him in waves. 'Perhaps it's simply that I value my privacy. Perhaps I don't like talking about myself. I never asked you to tell me anything, Ella. I'm under no obligation to reciprocate. This is nothing more than a three-week fling. Don't make it something it isn't.'

At that, Ella's eyes narrowed and her hackles went up. What was he suggesting? That she'd weakened and was now after some sort of relationship with him? Heaven forbid. She was perfectly happy with no strings and no pressure. She always had been. Emotional intimacy was not, and never would be, required.

Yet it struck her suddenly that that was precisely what

would happen if she pursued her avid interest in him. She'd be creating a connection that went way beyond the physical. She might start feeling things for him she didn't not want to feel. What if warm and tingly became the norm? What if she developed the urge to rush to *his* defence? She might find herself wanting to extend this affair. Getting involved. Losing her focus. And she needed none of that.

Despite the heat of the evening, an ice-cold shiver race down her spine. Her head swam for a moment and her lungs squeezed. Thank God he'd alerted her to what was going on before she travelled too far down that dangerous path, she thought, drawing in a slow steady breath to ease the quick flare of panic. She hadn't recognised what was going on because it had never happened before, but she did now.

So going forward, she would back right off. She would respect his wishes and protect her own. She would not succumb to such weakness again. She would not allow him to damage her self-esteem when she'd only just recovered it. She would focus on getting him out of her system and nothing else.

'You know what?' she said, not wanting to even think about how close she'd come to forgetting her number one goal when it came to men—to keep it casual. 'You're absolutely right.'

CHAPTER TEN

ADAM KNEW HE was right. What was going on here was just sex, nothing more, and he'd made that perfectly clear. So when Ella finally stopped trying to get him to talk, he ought to have been delighted. It was exactly what he wanted. It was alarming enough that the desire he had for her remained so strong. But the thought of developing some sort of rapport with her that might lead to emotion of the unpredictable kind brought him out in hives, and he'd been in danger of becoming far too interested in her anyway.

At what point precisely had he stopped trying to maintain his indifference? he wondered as he sat on the terrace with a bottle of beer two evenings later and stared out to sea while she slept inside. When she'd told him about her upbringing? That had certainly shaken him up. He couldn't imagine the poverty and despair of it. Materially, he'd grown up with every privilege going—two roofs over his head, more money in the bank than he could count, a first-class education that had swept him from the country's top boarding schools to Cambridge. She'd had nothing. Less than nothing. Yet she'd pulled herself up through sheer grit and determination, and he couldn't deny he was in awe of her for it. The night they'd met and she'd dispatched her lecherous fan with a knee to the groin, he'd thought her magnificent and beautiful and fierce, and he still did. He was even impressed by the tenacity that had caused him so much trouble while they'd been working together.

But he didn't need to admire her. He didn't need to think anything about her. Or identify with her ambition and her burning drive to succeed. Wondering what else they might share apart from a non-existent family support network was not required. The fact that they weren't as different as she believed was irrelevant. So in theory, the fact that she'd backed off was a win.

However, bizarrely, he wasn't at all pleased by the withdrawal of her attention. Because she didn't just stop trying to poke around in his psyche. She pretty much stopped talking altogether, and only when it was denied him did he realise that somehow he'd got used to her telling him all about herself. He'd found himself looking forward to their conversations, wondering what she might reveal next, on tenterhooks for any titbit she gave him.

Her sudden disengagement therefore left him feeling slightly flat. The sex, while still as frequent as ever, had become a little—how could he put it?—*soulless*. There was a ripple of tension between them, and the whole point of having an affair in the first place was to clear the air of that.

He couldn't shake her accusation of disrespect. Or the recollection that by her own admission, her previous affair had knocked her self-esteem. Her comment about feeling like an object of pleasure troubled him deeply, even though no-strings sex had always been the deal. He'd found himself dwelling on it and analysing his previous interactions with women, which rarely went beyond one or two nights and never more than a week. Had he distracted them with sex too? Very probably, although it had never given him cause for concern. But somehow this was different. With Ella, such a strategy made him feel queasy. He wasn't entirely sure why.

All he knew was that they didn't seem to be on the same page any more, and that was disturbing. So rectifying the problem became his number one priority. He needed to re-establish control. He needed to put the passion back into the sex and show that he did respect her.

After drumming up and discarding a number of ideas, he eventually, reluctantly, had to accept that just one would work. However much he might loathe the thought of it, he had to give her what she wanted. At least, in part. Only then, he felt, would the equilibrium be restored and the affair back on track.

Surely there were *some* things about him that wouldn't be dangerous to share? Would the sky fall in if he revealed where he'd grown up and a few basic facts about his family? He needn't go deep. And he needn't worry about any consequences. Once this fling was over and she was out of his life for good, he could forget he'd ever said anything. Nothing he told her would go any further. He didn't know whether he could trust her to keep his confidences, but before the audit had started she'd signed an NDA. Did that still apply?

Nevertheless, if he was going to do this—even just a little bit—a change of scenery might be sensible. So far they hadn't left the confines of the villa. The furthest they'd ventured was the beach. Talking to her while enveloped in the intimacy of a bedroom felt unwise. Emotional nudity combined with physical nudity could lead to complications he really didn't need. Therefore, preventative action was required.

Somehow managing to ignore how invitingly tousled Ella looked roused from sleep, the next morning, Adam got her up and out of bed and into his open top jeep for a tour of the island.

He reminded himself to keep his attention on the wide sandy track that followed the 150-acre island's coastline and not on her in her tiny denim hotpants and vest top beneath which she didn't appear to be wearing a bra, and off they set in a cloud of sand and dust.

'You'll note that this is an incredibly beautiful dot on the map,' he said in an opening gambit as he steered the jeep round a bend in the track that took them deeper into the vegetation and obscured more of the cloudless blue sky. 'That's why I bought it. As a place to escape the city and relax. I've had it for a couple of years now. But unfortunately, I don't get here as often as I'd like.'

'No, well, I imagine you're busy,' was all she murmured in response, giving him a cool smile before turning to look at the flora.

He tried again. 'Is this your first time to the Caribbean?'

'Yes.'

'Where do you usually vacation?'

'Europe.'

'Have you ever been to London?'

'Once.'

'That's where I grew up.' He paused to navigate some gnarly tree roots while she bounced around beside him. 'Well, between there and Northumberland on the north-east coast of the country. The family has a castle that sits in the middle of a three-thousand-acre estate, complete with turrets, arrow-slit windows and flying buttresses. Parts of it date back to the twelfth century. All of it is damp and draughty.'

'I can imagine.'

'The Holland Park mansion, on the other hand, has four storeys and looks like a wedding cake.'

'How delightful,' she murmured, grabbing top of the door while he swerved to avoid a rock.

'My family can trace its history to William the Conqueror,' he continued doggedly. 'One of my ancestors was at the signing of the Magna Carta. Another was a courtier to Henry the Eighth. He managed to keep his head. I've no idea how.'

'Well, we all lose our heads sometimes.'

As the greenery thinned and the track curved to once again hug the shore, Adam wiped a bead of sweat from his brow that had nothing to do with the heat and thought that he was certainly losing his. This wasn't working out quite as he'd planned. Her ultra-brief responses to his revelations about where he'd been brought up weren't encouraging. But now that he thought about it, mansions and castles were a pretty insensitive topic of conversation when she'd been raised in poverty in a trailer park. And as for all the talk of his ancestry, who'd be interested in that?

'What do you do in your spare time?' he asked, trying a different tack as they drove past the boathouse that stored wind surfs, a couple of single sculls and other water sports paraphernalia.

'I don't have any spare time.'

A moment later, he pointed to a low white building that had magenta bougainvillea clambering all over it. 'In that cottage,' he said, 'live the caretaking couple who keep the house stocked when I'm here and an eye on the place in my absence.'

'It's charming.'

Disappointingly, she showed as much interest in the rest of the island's sights as she did in his conversation, but Adam remained undeterred. He'd caused this breakdown in communication. It was therefore up to him to repair it. So the following day, he took her up in his seaplane in the hope that the stunning scenery would aid his cause.

Who could fail to marvel at the beautiful sparkling jade waters, dotted with yachts and water sports aficionados? The islands, some of which were tiny but mountainous, some of which barely rose above sea level but spread out for miles? Who could remain unimpressed by the star-studded resorts, the virgin beaches or even the Caribbean's largest shipwreck, which rested nearby in a mere sixty feet of water?

Ella.

That was who.

Just as when he'd taken her on a tour of his property, her enthusiasm for everything was muted. She expressed polite interest in what he had to show her, but at the same time, she remained aloof. She wasn't even moved by the pod of dolphins frolicking around a catamaran.

It was as if she'd sort of switched off. The more he tried to get her to engage, the more she withdrew.

'Why are you going to so much effort to show me around?' she asked at one point as they floated on the surface of a giant blue hole. 'I thought you valued your privacy.' The glance she slid him was cool, and her voice, when she turned his own words back on him, was dry. 'I hope you're not making this something it isn't.'

The constant brush-offs were frustrating. He was getting nowhere. The prospect of injecting the passion back into the bedroom was retreating with every passing hour, and that was alarming. He wasn't used to failure, yet to his consternation, that was precisely what seemed to be happening.

However, defeat was not an option. It never had been, never would be. Not when it came to turning his life around after his mother's death. Not when it came to restoring the fortunes of his company after his father's. And definitely not when it came to acquiring Helberg Holdings, reclaiming Montague's and finding redemption.

Unbending Ella so that their last week together was as good as the first would not be the project to beat him, he vowed. He was in control here, not her. He would break through her defences. He would close the distance between them and put the heat back into the sex. Even if it meant having to tell her more. Even if it meant having to tell her everything.

CHAPTER ELEVEN

ELLA HAD BEEN finding it almost impossible to remain cool and detached when the snippets of information Adam had shared with her were so fascinating and everything he'd shown her was so stunning.

Really, she should have resisted the tour of his island. But he'd taken her by surprise. Up until then, they'd stuck to the villa, so why the sudden change in routine? For a moment she'd wondered whether *he* could be getting bored of *her*. Perhaps she needed to up her game sexwise, she'd thought with a flicker of concern. Unlike him, she didn't have many skills in her repertoire. She was more about numbers than tricks. How might one go about sourcing a pair of handcuffs while languishing incognito on an island that was a fifteen-minute seaplane ride from the nearest shop?

But whatever the reason for the volte-face, she'd figured her body could do with a break. Besides, it wasn't as if she would be making make the mistake of fixating on him again or expressing any great fascination for anything. She'd learned her lesson on that front. She was like a fortress. Rock solid and unassailable.

She'd just about held it together outwardly, but pretty

much the minute they'd set off in his jeep for the tour, she'd been captivated by the landscape—the verdancy, the crimson hibiscus that flourished everywhere, the cacti, the palm trees and the sand, so much sand. Her senses had been overwhelmed. The colours were so intense. The sounds so exotic. The scents so deliciously tropical.

When he'd begun to talk, it hadn't taken long for her curiosity to break free of its confines and batter her with the desire to know more. About life in the castle, the wedding-cake mansion and his ancestry. About the staff who worked for him, the rowing boats and how he relaxed. All of it was wildly different to anything she'd ever known. His life experiences had clearly been the polar opposite of hers, which made them all the more gripping.

Then he'd taken her up in the seaplane and dazzled her with sights so stunning she'd wanted to weep. Nature had never looked so majestic. The fact that she'd always overlooked this part of the world seemed unfathomable. What made a blue hole? she couldn't help but wonder. What was the story behind the shipwreck? Did any of the super glamorous resorts belong to him?

However, she'd pushed away these clamouring questions and reined in her curiosity. She'd repeatedly reminded herself of the need to steer clear of any sort of emotional connection with him, to resist getting caught up in the fantastical luxury of it all, and told herself that there was always the internet for the facts.

It was a challenge. The tension generated by such

self-restraint was excruciating. But she stayed strong and held off.

Until the night he insisted on joining her for a walk along the beach that she'd planned to take alone to clear her head and strengthen her defences, after a dinner during which he'd seemed distant and preoccupied.

Something was on his mind, she thought, too on edge with awareness and anxiety to fully appreciate the beauty of the dark sea sparkling in the moonlight and the tiny waves lapping gently on the shore. The sand was warm between her toes. The evening breeze caressed the bare skin of her arms and legs.

Peace and tranquillity abounded, but nevertheless her stomach churned and her throat was tight. These past couple of days she'd sensed that he didn't appreciate her lack of engagement, even though he ought to. That was exactly what he'd wanted, wasn't it? So had he had enough? Was she out of his system and was he planning to end the affair? How would she feel if he did? Short-changed? Relieved? She didn't know.

'Let's sit,' he said quietly, cutting through her jittery thoughts and making her jump.

She swallowed hard and fought back the panic which revealed that she *didn't* want this to be over just yet. 'I'd rather be heading back.'

'Please.'

Something about the tone of his voice prickled her skin and switched her senses to high alert. Her heart began to thud. He looked oddly nervous, which was bizarre when she'd never seen him anything other than supremely confident. But at least that ruled out ending things. If that was his intention, he'd come right out and say it. He wouldn't need a dinner to think it through and a walk on the beach. And anyway, this felt weightier than that. If she'd been the dramatic sort, she'd have described the atmosphere between them as momentous even. 'All right.'

He led her to a wide, spacious hammock that hung between two palm trees. She arranged herself at one end, he at the other. He rubbed his hands over his face and then gave himself a shake. 'Do you remember once asking me about my home life?' he said, his expression as serious as she'd ever seen it.

Ella's breath caught in her lungs. The question was wholly unexpected. What was going on? Was he actually going to talk to her? Now? Why? She didn't want that. Except, she did. God, she *did*. She wanted to know what made him tick. She craved information. So much so that she couldn't turn down this opportunity to get it. And so what if it did create some sort of a connection? It was hardly likely to be a deep one. They were already two-thirds of the way into their affair. In approximately a week's time, it would be over and all contact would be instantly severed, exactly as planned.

So she took a deep breath and said, 'How could I forget when you punished me so exquisitely for it?'

He gave her a fleeting smile that tugged briefly on her heart strings and was gone all too soon. 'My upbringing wasn't very pleasant,' he said gruffly. 'Not quite as tough as yours, but nevertheless, not very pleasant. You said you'd read about my father.'

She nodded, thinking with an inward grimace of the photos, the scandals and the lawsuits that had hit the tabloids over the years.

'He was selfish and volatile. On occasion he could be cruel. When he was around we walked on eggshells. When he wasn't, well, the press let us know where he was and what he was doing. I can't remember a time when he wasn't having an affair. Sometimes he brought the women he slept with home, which, even at the age of six, I knew wasn't quite right.'

A wave of nausea rose up her throat and she swallowed it back down. 'How quickly you must have had to grow up.'

'No quicker than you.'

Well, yes, that was true, but this wasn't about her. 'How did you all cope?'

'My mother dealt with it by moving to Northumberland shortly after Charley was born and hardly ever left. When I was seven I went off to boarding school, and once there, it was easy not to think about home too much. As I got older, I stayed away as much as I could. It wasn't hard. Whenever possible, I spent the holidays with friends. When I wasn't doing that, I was out. I partied hard. I screwed around. A lot. In fact, some of my behaviour wasn't that dissimilar to my father's. He once called me a chip off the old block, and he was right. I didn't give a toss about anyone but myself, and I didn't care who I hurt in the process.'

Because it was too hard to think of the boy and teenager he'd been, adrift without support, having to rely totally on himself just as she had, Ella forced the image from her head. And because she didn't want to be feeling anything for him at all, she thought instead of the *Blush* magazine article she'd read and recalled how annoyed he'd seemed about it. 'You said that wasn't who you were any more.'

'That's right.'

'So, what changed?'

'My mother died. She took a fatal overdose fourteen years ago when I was eighteen and my sister was eight.'

When that information sank in, it immediately demolished her indifference. How terribly, terribly sad, she thought, her chest aching and her eyes pricking. How devastating that must have been. For all his material privilege, his environment had been just as traumatic as hers, although for very different reasons. 'I'm so sorry.'

'She was thoroughly miserable and by that point very fragile,' he said bleakly. 'But even so, it was my fault. She rang me that night. I didn't answer the call. If I had, I might have been able to save her.'

At the guilt in his voice and the torment on his face, the ache in her chest intensified. 'It wasn't your fault. It couldn't have been.'

'It was. I was out having too much fun. I was in a nightclub at the time, with a girl, and I just didn't want to be bothered.'

'That must have been so difficult to bear,' she said, because who was she to try and convince him otherwise?

'It still is,' he said. 'But I'm trying to do something about it. You once asked me what was so important about Montague's.'

'You claimed it was all about the bottom line.'

'It's not about that. I want it back for her. While she was in Northumberland, she had an affair of her own. Just the one—with a neighbour. But my father found out. Ever the hypocrite, he took objection and retaliated. He knew Montague's meant a lot to her. Not because it was where they'd met—she as a trainee jewellery designer, he on tour of the company's North American assets—but because she'd been there since leaving school and had dreams of one day running the place. He sold it to Helberg out of spite, for a dollar.'

For a moment Ella didn't know what to say. Just when she thought Edward Courtney couldn't sink any lower in her estimation, he plumbed new depths. 'No wonder you want justice.'

Adam gave a nod and blew out a breath. 'Anyway, her death and my role in it was the wake-up call I needed. It made me reassess the way I was living. I gave up the hedonism and knuckled down. I finished university and then started working at the company back home. It was at that point that I realised how bad things were there. My father was CEO for nearly thirty years. In that time, he almost destroyed the business. When he died and I took over, I was determined to do things differently. I refuse to let his genes dominate me.'

'They don't and you have. You stopped the company from nosediving into oblivion, according to one press report I found. You turned it around in a year. That must have taken some doing.'

'It's taken sixteen-hour days, more often than not, seven days a week and a number of challenging personnel situations. But I wasn't having a company that was started by my great-great-great-grandfather vanish off the face of the earth while I was around to do something about it.'

Ella recognised his determination and ambition, and it occurred to her yet again that maybe they weren't that dissimilar after all. But that wasn't a particularly constructive thought, so she redirected her focus to his sister. 'How did Charley handle things?'

He frowned. Studied the sea beyond her right shoulder for a moment, then returned his gaze to hers. 'I don't know,' he admitted. 'I never asked. But she went through a wild patch as a teenager, so that could have been how.'

'I read up on Trouble Maker,' she said in case it helped. 'It seems to be doing well. Judging by the recent press it's had, it's heading straight for success.'

'So I've been told.'

'You sound as if you disapprove.'

'I don't. It's just...complicated.'

'In what way?'

'I don't really have a relationship with her, but I've found it hard to trust her nevertheless,' he said. 'She's made some bad decisions in the past. She quit school early and took up modelling. She got caught up in that world and went off the rails, and I'm pretty sure I don't know the half of what she got up to. That's why I made the trip to London that you questioned me about. She'd bought a flat. I was concerned it might be another bad decision. I didn't consider the implications of using the company jet at the time. I just wanted to get there as soon as possible. But when I did, she made it very clear that my concern was misplaced. And it was. The flat was fine. She had every right to be annoyed.'

In response to the flicker of discomfort that sped across his face, Ella felt her eyes narrow and her feathers ruffle. 'And was she?'

'Oh, yes.'

'Well, that's not fair,' she said, feeling quite outraged on his behalf. 'Presumably you have her best interests at heart.'

'I haven't always. I've let her down repeatedly. She once rang me, begging to come back home from the school our father had sent her to. I brushed her off. I wasn't there when she dropped out or when she got into trouble. I haven't taken the time to get to know her.'

'You weren't around. You were busy trying to sort out your father's mess.'

'It's no excuse.'

'Well, I think it is,' she said, bristling madly before thinking that she had to calm down. She really did.

She shouldn't be leaping to his defence. She shouldn't be feeling compassion and sympathy for him or dwelling on the lost boy and troubled teen he must have been. Even though she now understood that the reason he'd been so reluctant to answer her questions about Helberg and the flight to London back in the office was because both triggered deeply personal and evidently painful memories, it wasn't her responsibility to absolve him of the guilt he felt over his mother's suicide or his sister's troubled adolescence.

She must not get carried away. She must not read anything into what he'd told her at all. And why was he suddenly looking so intently at her? As if he wanted to devour her? Was the time for talking once again over? God, she hoped so, because she badly needed reminding that this was just sex. 'Why are you looking at me like that?'

'If I kissed you right now, would you assume I was trying to distract you?'

'Are you?'

'No.'

'Then what are you waiting for?'

Adam had never revealed to anyone what he'd just told Ella. In direct contrast to his father, he kept his private life private. He believed that enough of his family's dirty laundry had been washed in public and had always avoided personal interviews, partly because he feared giving up control of his narrative, partly because certainly in the early days of his stewardship of the company, he'd felt it would severely weaken his position. He'd certainly never been tempted to spill his guts to any of the women he dated, who'd never meant anything to him anyway.

So he hadn't known what to expect when he'd taken a seat in the hammock and begun to talk to Ella. Fire and brimstone? A crash of thunder or lightning strike? At the very least, he might have anticipated severe discomfort. Judgement and disapproval had not been off the cards either.

However, there'd been none of that. No rent heavens or plagues of locusts. She'd just listened, without prejudice. And the only moment of unease he'd experienced was when her eyes had filled with sympathy at his mother's suicide, which he did not deserve despite what she might claim.

Voicing it had been no worse than thinking it. In fact, he was more preoccupied with the outrage she'd displayed when they'd been talking about his visit to Charley. No one had ever come to his defence before. He'd always fought his battles on his own. He'd never had anyone in his corner. Yet in it she'd been.

His chest felt tight, his heart beating too fast. His head was spinning, even though he was half lying back. Above them, a vast canopy of stars twinkled in the inky blue night sky. Beyond the beach stretched the huge sea dotted with the odd light of a moored yacht. But all he was interested in was this hammock, which contained this woman. His gaze locked with hers. Her eyes were shining with invitation. A faint smile curved her mouth.

His pulse was thundering even before she removed her T-shirt, unclipped her bra and dropped both onto the sand. She shimmied out of her skirt and underwear until she was naked in the moonlight, and he thought he'd never seen such a beautiful sight.

'You're overdressed,' she said, her gaze slowly roaming over him and setting fire to his blood. 'I would help, but I wouldn't want to tip us onto the sand.'

It was a matter of moments to get out of the hammock, remove his clothes and apply protection, even though his hands seemed to be trembling. Then he climbed back in carefully and arranged himself on top of her, lowering his head to hers and kissing her until she was panting and moaning and the world around them disappeared.

Her hands were in his hair, on his shoulders, holding him to her as if not wanting to let him go. Carefully, smoothly, he manoeuvred her onto her side and wrapped himself around her, her back tight against his chest, their legs entwined. She twisted her head round and he kissed her again, one hand tangled in her hair, the other on her breast.

Desire poured through him. His heart was pounding so hard she had to be able to feel it. When he slid his hand down her body, she shivered and pressed herself against his erection, which ached and throbbed. His fingers parted her and she raised her leg to grant him better access. He found her warm and wet, and when she reached behind her to take him in her hand, he couldn't wait any longer. He held her hip, allowing her to guide him to her entrance, and when he was there, he surged into her slick velvety heat.

Ella gasped. His entire body shook. And then, cocooned in the hammock, so closely connected that not even the night's breeze could find its way between them, they began to rock together. Slowly, steadily, yet with an intensity that built and built and built, until she cried out softly and shattered, trembling against him as her fingers dug into his hip.

The powerful convulsions went on and on, clamping around him so relentlessly, so exquisitely, that they tipped him over the edge. With a hoarse groan, he pulled her against him and climaxed in a white-hot rush of ecstasy, pulsating into her harder and for longer than he ever had before, until he was limp, blitzed, completely hollowed out.

And just like that, he thought dazedly as they lay there, catching their breath, the sweat cooling on their bodies, the soul in the sex was back.

CHAPTER TWELVE

THE NIGHT ON the beach was something of a turning point as far as Ella was concerned. She had no idea why Adam had chosen to suddenly lower his guard after days of keeping it firmly in place, but she didn't much care. All that mattered was that this affair of theirs was now about as different to her last relationship as it was possible to get. There was balance. There was mutual respect and developing trust. There was also fun, because quite apart from the physical pleasure Adam continued to give her, he was also proving a most excellent host.

One afternoon he took her back up in the plane and patiently answered her *many* questions about the shipwreck, the islands, the resorts and the structure of a blue hole.

Another they went snorkelling, which was something she'd never tried before, European city breaks not really lending themselves to the activity. As impressive as the Caribbean was from the air, from beneath it was breathtaking. Just when she thought she saw the most beautiful creature on earth, along came another. Shoal after shoal of brightly coloured fish darted through coral the colour of amethyst, emerald, amber. A ray glided gracefully by not six feet away from her. One turtle that hung around for a while was half her size.

The following morning, Adam put her into one of the single sculls he kept in the boathouse, fitted himself into the other, and tried to teach her to row. Scything through the crystal-clear water, his upper body muscles rippling with every stroke he took, he made it look effortless.

It wasn't.

'Do you do this a lot?' she said, frustratingly unable to find any sort of co-ordination.

He rested his arms on his up-bent knees and watched as she went round and round in circles. 'I used to back in the UK. Now I have a machine in my apartment.'

'Handy.'

'In more ways than one.'

'What do you mean?'

'Lately, it's borne the brunt of my extreme sexual frustration. I must have rowed the length of the Mississippi since I met you. The morning after we first kissed, I completed ten thousand metres in thirty-nine minutes and twenty-four seconds. It was a personal best.'

Thirty-nine minutes and twenty-four seconds of bunching muscles and bronzed glistening skin? she thought, gritting her teeth as she accidentally loosened her grip on the oar and down went the blade. That, she'd liked to have seen.

'You just caught a crab. You won't make any progress if you don't concentrate.'

'Then you should put on a shirt.'

He just grinned, dazzlingly, at which point she promptly fell in. While she dashed water from her eyes, he paddled over. In revenge, she wobbled his scull until he toppled in too, a move she paid for with a long, hot kiss that had them dragging the boats up onto the sand, then rushing into the boathouse and tumbling onto a pile of tarpaulin.

Happily, conversation was no longer a one-way street, in either direction. There seemed to be nothing he didn't want to share with her. It was as if he'd kept everything bottled up for years, and now that he'd popped the cork he had no intention of sticking it back in. He told her more about his ancestry and his sister, with whom he was hoping for a better relationship. He detailed all the challenges he'd faced after taking over from his father, which sounded as though they'd been equally as tough careerwise as anything she'd undergone.

Because it was clearly a difficult subject for him, she didn't press him on his mother's death and the role he perceived he had in it, at least not initially. However, she became increasingly troubled not only by the thought that he blamed himself but also by the fact that he believed reacquiring Montague's would absolve him of his guilt.

She wasn't quite sure why she felt this way. She realised it wasn't up to her to persuade him to see the situation in any way other than his, yet she was filled with the urge to try, because for some reason it just didn't feel right. But how could she broach the subject? It wasn't something she could just drop into conversation, and it was the one topic he hadn't brought it up again.

The opportunity to do so arose the evening after the morning they'd spent rowing, when Adam took her by motorboat to a long curving beach on the northwest side of the island.

The sun had recently set and the darkening sky was streaked with orange, pink and red. As he switched off the engine and they glided through the shallows and onto the sand, she could see that a table had been set up beneath the spreading branches of what he had informed her as he'd driven her around the island a couple of days ago was a fofoti tree. It was draped with a white cloth, and on it were laid two places facing out to sea, complete with what she later discovered to be bone china crockery, polished silver cutlery and sparkling crystal glassware.

All around flickered dozens of candles and fairy lights wound through the branches above. To one side was a firepit in which bright flames danced. Two rows of tiki torches lined a path from the landing point to the table, and as he alighted to pull the boat farther up the shore, she thought that she'd never seen anything like it before. It was the sort of scene that sold holidays. It was the definition of paradise.

It was also extremely romantic, which meant she ought to be clambering back onboard and demanding he speed her back to the villa as fast as he possibly could, because what exactly was going on here? She wasn't remotely interested in romance. She'd always avoided it like the plague because raised hopes and false expectations would do no one any good.

But instead, her heart was racing, her throat was tight and she was thinking that, whatever the reason for this intimate dinner à deux, would it really be such a bad idea to enjoy it? She'd never been wined and dined by a gorgeous man who repeatedly rocked her world. She'd never been wined and dined at all. And how many hopes and false expectations could be raised in a paltry couple of hours when neither of them wanted anything more? None. So when Adam raised his arms to lift her off the boat, she willingly went into them.

'This must have taken a lot of effort to organise,' she said, her heart beating a little faster than normal once they'd walked between the torches and sat down at the table.

He reached into a cool box and extracted the ingredients for two piña coladas. 'Not particularly,' he said, mixing the drinks with impressive skill. 'We've exhausted the sights here, and I thought that since I couldn't take you to Aruba for fear of discovery, I'd transport Aruba to you.'

Determined to keep a lid on the wild tangle of emotions swirling through her, Ella swallowed hard and sought to keep things light. 'Is this how you seduce all the women you bring here? Because you needn't have bothered, you know. That horse has bolted.'

'I've never brought anyone here.'

She shot him a smile. 'Not even one of your many, *many* dates?'

He raised one dark eyebrow in her direction and handed her a glass. 'You read the article.'

'Along with half the female population of the country, it would seem.' She took a sip of her drink through the straw, the delicious flavours of rum, pineapple and coconut exploding on her tongue. 'I can see why you were concerned about the effect of all that gossip on your reputation and why you were so keen to stop it.'

'I couldn't take the risk of it upsetting the holders of the Helberg shares that I'll still need to acquire after taking Zane's and Cade's on Labor Day.'

This was the opening she'd been waiting for, she realised with a skip of her pulse. The chance to offer him a different version of events, perhaps. 'I know you're convinced that you'll win it,' she said, 'but what if reclaiming Montague's doesn't give you the absolution you're after?'

'It will,' he said, without even a second's hesitation. 'It has to. I've lived with the guilt of being responsible for my mother's suicide for fourteen years. It's crushing. It's stopping me from pursuing a relationship with Charley. This is my one shot at redemption. I'll never get another.'

'I'm not sure you even need it.'

Momentarily stunned into speechlessness, Adam set down his drink and stared at her as if she'd sprouted horns. 'Of course I need it. You even know why.'

'I think you're wrong,' she said, more certain of it than ever. 'I don't think you're responsible for anything at all. Obviously, no one knows the workings of your mother's mind at the time, but you said yourself that she was fragile. If she went to Northumberland straight after having Charley and left her behind in London, it's possible she may even have had postnatal depression.'

He sat back, his expression unreadable. 'What makes you the expert?'

Ella ignored the note of warning that tinged his voice

because she was on a roll. 'Clearly, I'm not,' she said, wishing he'd give her a chance at least. 'Especially when it comes to maternal instincts. But that doesn't sound like normal behaviour. It sounds as though her marriage made her miserable right from the start. Do you know if she'd tried it before?'

'No.'

'So she might have done. She might also have called a dozen people before you who didn't pick up either. And even if you had saved her that time, she might have succeeded another. If what happened to her is anyone's fault, it's your father's. I really don't believe it's yours.'

'Well, I do.'

'I think it would help if you tried to let the guilt go.'

'I think we should agree to disagree and talk about something else.'

Adam got up to prod the fire, and the conversation did indeed turn to something else, because even she could see that she was banging her head against a brick wall. But it stayed with her nevertheless. Even though she thought him deluded, he was clearly tormented by what he believed to be the truth, and her heart continued to break for him. Whenever she remembered all he was doing to assuage his conscience, she couldn't help but worry. If only he'd take on board her points. But this was evidently a red line for him, and there was nothing more she could do.

It hadn't escaped her notice that since the night he'd decided to open up to her, she too had been experiencing a new dimension to their affair. Whenever she had a moment to herself, she kept replaying the intimacy of what had happened in the hammock after he'd finished talking. The minute she'd turned on her side and he'd wrapped himself around her, she hadn't just felt wanted. She'd also felt safe and protected, which was unexpected, because she was used to providing her own safety and protection. Even more bizarrely, she hadn't wanted to shake him and the feelings off. She'd wanted to pull him and them closer. Then, as they'd rocked together, slowly, steadily, her heart had swelled until it seemed too big for her chest.

But this didn't unduly trouble her. Nor did her growing fascination with him or the connection that was developing. However great this affair was turning out to be, she wasn't remotely concerned that she wouldn't be able to walk away from at the end of it. Her promotion still flashed as bright and shiny as ever. Her career was still her number one priority. This was still just a celebration of her promotion and a bit of fun until real life called. And that was the way it would stay.

To Adam's gratification, opening up to Ella had been a truly excellent idea. She was no longer holding anything back. The tension had gone. The sex was even better than before. Their goals were once more realigned, the equilibrium restored, and it was all deeply satisfying.

They shared the values of hard work, determination and integrity. Right from the start, she'd kept him on his toes. And she seemed to get him—their difference of opinion about his role in his mother's death notwithstanding, because he would never agree that he wasn't at fault for that. His mother might have been suffering from depression. She might have called someone else that night who hadn't picked up either. She might have tried it before and maybe she would have tried again, even if he had saved her. He'd never know. All he had to go on were the facts, so he could never just 'let the guilt go' as Ella had suggested.

They even had the same approach to relationships, as he discovered over a platter of lobster at lunch one day.

Having once done a course on dining etiquette which had covered crustacea in week three, Ella picked up a claw and carefully bent back the thumb to pull out the cartilage before cracking the shell and neatly extracting the flesh. He, on the other hand, simply twisted the body from the head and then bashed it with a hammer.

'That's what I'd quite like to do to my ex,' she mused as the shell shattered and he pulled it apart.

'So would I.'

'But then I only have myself to blame.'

'How?'

'It was my fault for reading more into the relationship than there was there. I completely forgot my rule to keep things casual.'

'Are you not a fan of commitment?' he asked, now applying the hammer to the claw in a move that would no doubt appal her course instructor.

'I've fought too hard for my independence to let myself rely on someone else, and I've worked way too hard to sacrifice everything I've achieved for the demands of a husband and kids. I have a plan to reach the top, and I won't let anything get in the way of that ever again. Not even myself.'

'That makes sense.'

'What's your excuse?'

Adam swapped the hammer for a fork and thought he couldn't even begin to answer a question like that. How could he tell her that he was a control freak with a fear of his world disintegrating if he relaxed his iron grip on it? How could he explain that rampant desire and volatile emotions threatened that control, so it was easier and safer to steer well clear? He'd have to explain why he'd made an exception for her, and he definitely couldn't answer that, because he didn't know why.

'I just don't have the time,' he said instead with a nonchalant shrug. 'I have too many responsibilities as it is. There aren't enough hours in the day to maintain a relationship as well.'

That seemed to satisfy her, judging by the thoughtful tilt of her head and then the nod. 'Well, it's good to know that our expectations are the same.'

'It certainly is.'

The more time he spent in her company, the more he came to realise that he didn't just enjoy the sizzling chemistry that showed no sign of burning out—he liked her. A lot. He admired her willingness to give everything a go and then put one hundred percent effort into it. He could listen to her talk about herself for hours. He'd never thought of auditing as a particularly exciting field, but she did. Her face lit up when she expanded on the subject, and so suddenly and unexpectedly, he found it fascinating too. When she told him more about the trailer park, he wondered what his company did to help the disadvantaged in life and whether it could do more.

Their affair was soon coming to an end, and that had

always been the plan. But now he couldn't quite recall why. It felt wrong. He wasn't nearly done with her. She wasn't out of his system at all. His desire for her had not waned, and although their conversations had sometimes lasted long into the night, he was certain there was still much left to learn.

So, why couldn't they continue this back in New York? Not forever, of course, but perhaps until it petered out of its own accord. Night after night, he lost control with her and the world hadn't imploded. Indulging the still raging desire he had for her had led to no recklessness here, and he saw no reason why it should anywhere else. He didn't know what he'd been so afraid of. They had a good thing going, and it felt wrong to bring it to an unnatural close.

As he stood in the kitchen and fried up some plantain for breakfast, Adam wondered what Ella would think of that plan. If he'd read the situation correctly, he suspected her expectations might have moved in that direction too. Every now and then, he'd caught her looking at him in a way that suggested that she wasn't done with him either. He would ask her and find out. Once he'd answered this call.

In the back pocket of his shorts, his phone rang and vibrated. He turned off the gas and pulled it out. It was Maggie, his secretary, on the other end of the line, who he hadn't heard from since he'd left the city, other than receiving an email about some upcoming travel plans that he'd yet to open. Strange how all that seemed very far away.

'Good morning,' he said, and thinking that if Ella

agreed to extend this affair of theirs, it could turn out to be a very good morning indeed.

'I apologise for disturbing you while you're on vacation,' said Maggie, sounding not quite as thrilled with the day as he was. 'And I hope you're having a lovely time. But I thought you'd like to know that I've been sent a photo by one of my contacts at *Blush* magazine. Of you and a woman who is not Annabel St James disembarking the plane in Aruba. It's due to go live on the website in an hour.'

Because his thoughts had been so wrapped up in other things, it took Adam a moment to process the information. Once he had, he went very still. His pulse spiked and his blood ran cold. White noise rushed through his head and his stomach heaved.

'Send it to me,' he said, his voice sounding to him as though it came from deep under water.

'I just have.'

Numbly he switched apps and opened up the picture. He and Ella were walking down the steps of the plane. They weren't touching. They weren't even looking at each other. But something about it nevertheless suggested intimacy. They were far too close to each other for him to ever be able to pass it off as anything professional. And there was no mistaking it was them. The focus was that sharp.

As the implications of what he was looking at sank in, an icy sweat coated his skin. His breath stuck in his lungs. He felt sick. Dizzy. As though he were about to pass out. With superhuman effort, he forced himself to exhale and get a grip. 'Put a stop to it.'

'It'll be pricey.'

'Whatever it takes.'

'Consider it done.'

He cut the call and put the phone down, and it was then that the numbness vanished and all hell let loose. His vision blurred and his heart crashed wildly against his ribs. The strength drained from his limbs, and he had to sit down before he collapsed. All he could think was that if this photo had appeared in the public domain and caught the eye of Cade and Zane he'd have lost Helberg in an instant. Montague's would have been gone. Redemption would have been history. Everything he'd been working so hard for recently, over.

How the hell could he have let it happen?

How could he have lost control of the situation so badly?

Because he'd been overwhelmed by chemistry so powerful he hadn't been able to resist its allure, that was how. Because he'd been arrogant and reckless in assuming he could have both Helberg and Ella. Because somehow he'd managed to forget that from the moment they'd met, the second their eyes had met in that bar, she'd repeatedly had him throwing caution to the wind.

At what point had he completely lost his mind?

What the hell had he been *thinking*?

This affair should *never* have happened, he thought, his breathing harsh and choppy. He should never have succumbed to temptation. Fourteen years ago, in the aftermath of his mother's death, he'd sworn to avoid the kind of desire that wreaked destruction and ruined lives, and he'd stuck by it. But he'd broken those rules, and bent many more for the sake of a fling with a woman who he'd even recognised was dangerous.

And as for extending it, was he mad? How would that even have worked? How had he thought they'd be able to continue seeing each other under the radar in a city of twenty million? Labor Day was still three weeks away. They'd have eventually been caught by *someone*. *Blush* magazine would have had a field day. To the world at large, he'd have cheated on Annabel and his reputation would have taken a huge hit, which would have displeased both his board members and the Helberg shareholders. And it wasn't as if he could have simply fixed up a three-way meeting between Annabel, Cade and Zane to clarify the situation. They'd never have let him get away with it, even if they had believed him.

The truth was, since he and Ella had arrived on this island, he'd barely given the bet a second thought. He'd barely given *anything* a second thought. His laptop had been gathering dust. He'd let numerous calls go to voicemail. For the first time ever, he'd put the executive team he'd created in charge, and he hadn't even wondered whether they were doing a good job of running the company in his absence. He'd been wholly wrapped up in Ella, in some sort of a make-believe bubble with her, so far from reality that they might as well be on another planet.

Well, that bubble had burst. Reality had stormed in like a horseman of the apocalypse, and here was the chaos he'd feared. He'd put a stop to this particular photo, but he couldn't risk another. He'd had a very close shave, and he wouldn't put in jeopardy everything he was trying to achieve again.

When he thought of Montague's in the hands of Zane or Cade, his heart practically stopped. If that happened, he'd never get justice. He'd be carrying the guilt he felt over his mother's death for the rest of his life. His sister would remain at a distance forever, and he simply couldn't allow it.

So forget how much he liked Ella. Forget the incredible sex and the appreciation he had for their conversations. She turned him into the man he'd fought hard to erase, the man he didn't wish—and could not—afford to be. She had to go, and she had to go for good.

CHAPTER THIRTEEN

ELLA WAS CLIMBING out of the pool when she saw Adam bearing down on her like a thunderstorm. What could possibly be wrong? she wondered with a frown as she picked up a towel and wrapped it round herself. She'd left him in bed, limp, sated, with a huge smile on his face, but that was nowhere to be seen now.

He came to an abrupt stop in front of her, the tension radiating off him in waves that were so huge she felt buffeted. His jaw was set and his face was as dark as night, and great big fat alarm bells started ringing in her head because, whatever it was, it had to be serious.

'I've just been sent a photo of us getting off the plane in Aruba,' he said grimly and without preamble. 'It was scheduled to appear in *Blush* magazine online. I don't know who took it, but there's enough detail to suggest that we're more than just colleagues. Take a look.'

He thrust the phone in her direction. Stunned, unable to quite comprehend what he was telling her, Ella took the device from him and glanced down, her mind instantly spooling back to nearly three weeks ago. She recalled the moment only too well. The two of them had just stepped out of the plane and onto the steps. A second earlier he'd reminded her of what he was planning to do to her when they got to the house, and she was wearing a secretive sort of a smile that somehow managed to imply that she couldn't wait to get her hands on him.

'How did this happen?' she said, her mouth dry, her heart thudding while she struggled to absorb its implications.

'I don't know, but I intend to find out,' he said with such icy steel that for a second, she felt sorry for the perpetrator. 'I've stopped it going public. However, it was an extremely close call. We got lucky this time, but I can't risk it happening again and putting into jeopardy everything I've worked for. You know what that means to me.'

'I do.'

'This island is not as safe as I assumed. We could be discovered any moment now.'

As that observation hit her brain, Ella's blood drained to her feet. No. God. That couldn't happen. What if her colleagues found out what she'd been doing? The gossip would be unbearable. They'd never trust her again. And if the picture reached her boss? She'd be fired in an instant, because an auditor and a client in cahoots on a Caribbean island the day after winding up a job was about as big a conflict of interest as there could be. The audit would have to be redone. Her reputation would be trashed. She really would never work again.

Despite the heat of the morning, a rash of goose bumps broke out all over her skin and she found she was trembling. All right, so Adam had blocked the photo's publication, but that wasn't the point. The point was that she too had jeopardised everything she'd worked for—not to mention the promotion she'd literally just received—and for what? Sex. A man. Again.

So, what the hell had she been thinking? How could she have let desire once more hurl her off her path? Hadn't she done enough damage to her career already? Had she learned *nothing*?

Ella had never regretted agreeing to this affair, but she did now. She regretted it with every fibre of her being. It had been a mistake from the start. She shouldn't have allowed Adam to persuade her into it. She should have been resolute. She couldn't *believe* she'd let history repeat itself, despite telling herself over and over again that it mustn't.

'You need to leave,' he said curtly, his voice slicing through the tumbling chaos in her head. 'Now.'

He was right. She did. She needed to find her things, pack up and get out of here as fast as she could. Back to the city, back to the plan, with her fingers crossed that this one photo was it. Once there, she would revert to eating, sleeping and breathing work. She wouldn't so much as *talk* to a man, let alone touch him, kiss him or lose her mind over him.

Yet, for some reason, she couldn't move. Her feet seemed to be rooted to the spot. She couldn't tear her gaze from his, and suddenly she was finding it almost impossible to breathe.

What was going on?

Why wasn't she moving?

Why was her chest so tight?

More pressingly, why was the realisation that leaving here would mean never seeing him again now the only thought in her head?

Surely that shouldn't matter. She'd been due to go home the day after tomorrow anyway, and she'd never had a problem with that. In fact, she'd relied on the time frame to keep her on the straight and narrow.

But it seemed it was a problem now because she didn't want to go. She wanted to stay here. With him. And not because she still had to get him out of her system but because she simply couldn't contemplate *not* staying.

Which meant what? she wondered, her head spinning and her stomach churning with confusion. That, despite her best efforts, she'd become emotionally involved with him? Well, she had. She'd known that days ago and had accepted it. Only she'd badly underestimated the effect it would have on her. She'd thought she'd be able to stay in control. But at some point she'd clearly lost it completely, and now she was in so deep she couldn't get out. Worst of all, she didn't *want* to get out.

The idea of leaving him cleaved her in two. It made every cell of her body rise up with denial. Was she truly never going to be able to touch him again? To kiss him? To close her eyes and inhale him? It didn't seem fair. It made her heart physically hurt.

If she was being honest, these last few days, whenever she'd thought about returning home to the city she loved, alone, without him, her spirits had dipped. How would she fit back into her little life after this whirlwind of an experience? It was going to be like switching from Technicolor to black and white. Who would she talk to? Who would she laugh with?

And surely he couldn't *want* her to go. He seemed

as invested in this as she was. Look at the steps he'd taken to get her here. The control he lost in her arms. He'd opened up to her. He'd given her Aruba. This was no more purely physical for him than it was for her, she was certain of it.

So maybe they didn't have to go nuclear.

Maybe there could be an alternative solution.

Straightening her spine and fighting the fog clouding her thoughts, Ella swallowed hard. She took a deep breath, summoned up every drop of courage she possessed and said, 'I agree that we've had a lucky escape. And I understand the need to leave. But what if this doesn't have to be the end?'

Adam went very still, not an inch of him moving, apart from the muscle that flickered in his cheek. 'It does,' he said flatly. 'You know why it does.'

'We could put this affair of ours on hold until Labor Day. You win the bet. I focus on my job and put some clear blue water between the audit and us. And then we start up again in September.'

He gave his head a sharp shake. 'It's out of the question.'

She frowned at the bluntness of his tone. Wasn't he overreacting? 'Why?'

'That was never the deal. We said three weeks.'

'I know. But am I out of your system? Because you're not out of mine.'

'You absolutely are. And there is no "us."'

Ella inwardly flinched, as if she'd received a thump to the gut. But she wasn't going to let this go when she believed him to be so wrong, when they didn't have to destroy something this good. 'Then, what have the last few days been about?'

'Sex.'

'Nothing more?'

'No. Why? What have they been about for you?'

Falling in love.

She stilled at the thought that darted through her head, and her whole body froze. No. That couldn't be right. She didn't want to be in love, ever. Look at what had happened the last time she'd tried it. Not that that had been love, she'd realised when she'd fallen out of it so swiftly. But the real thing would be even more unacceptably distracting. It would mean having to consider someone else's feelings and wishes. It would mean compromise, sacrifice and distraction. She'd never get to the top of her profession, ideally running one of the big four firms, without total single-mindedness. She couldn't think of anything worse than constantly battling for control of her career as her private life got increasingly complicated.

Yet, was love the extra dimension to the affair that she'd noticed following the night the hammock? The warm fuzzy feeling she'd developed? It could be. And when she thought about it, the rest of the evidence was pretty damning too. She adored sleeping with him. She couldn't get enough of his company and she was riveted by his conversation. The minute she was in his vicinity, every sense she possessed sharpened. He blew her away with his strength, his resolve and his determination to do the right thing. He made her feel safe and protected. He was steadfast and reliable. If she allowed him to, she had no doubt he would take on her ex and her firm, just as he'd been prepared to confront the lech in the bar who'd chatted her up the evening they'd met.

She'd always believed that she had to depend on herself and herself alone. She'd been let down so many times—by her parents, her employers, Drew—and had learned from an early age that she was her best and only champion. But she'd be able to depend on Adam. He would never let her down. He fought for the things he cared about, whether it was justice, his company or his sister. Would it really be such a bad thing to have him fight for her too? She'd been marching through life on her own for as long as she could remember, and it was exhausting. And lonely. So very, very lonely.

Perhaps she'd been ever so slightly overdramatic with the whole must-stay-single thing. Perhaps the key lay in choosing a partner who had similar values and an identical work ethic to her own. Similar drive and ambition. Someone who would totally understand when she had to stay late or work weekends because they did that too.

Adam was that man. He wouldn't demand she make sacrifices to accommodate him. He wouldn't feel threatened by her need for independence. He operated entirely on his own too and he wasn't threatened by anything.

Okay, so he'd said he didn't have time for a relationship, but everyone made time for the things they wanted to do and people they wanted to be with. She just had to show him she was one such person. They could figure out the details later. They could be great together, a power couple taking the city by storm. She could have everything she hadn't even known she wanted.

'I've been falling in love with you,' she confessed giddily, her heart feeling too big for her chest, the wild jumble of emotions too great to contain.

Adam tensed and paled, which wasn't very encouraging. But he had a habit of backing off when she got too close for comfort and, as he'd discovered repeatedly over the last few weeks, she was extremely tenacious, so there was no way she wasn't going to add, 'And I think you've been falling in love with me.'

He flinched as though winded and took a step back. He gave his head another sharp shake, his denial unequivocal. 'You're mistaken.'

'Am I?' she said, the image of the future they could have together so dazzlingly brilliant that she could see nothing else. 'Do you talk about your mother with everyone? Do you resort to subterfuge and buy a private jet for all the women you sleep with? And what about the romantic dinner you arranged the night you brought Aruba to me? Is that standard practice?'

His body was now rigid with tension. His expression turned even stonier. 'I warned you not to read more into this than there actually is, Ella.'

'I don't think I am.'

'It wouldn't be the first time you've made the mistake of thinking yourself in love, would it?'

At that, the dazzling future vanished. Ella stifled a gasp and reeled, his callow observation shredding her heart to ribbons. She couldn't believe he'd said that. How dare he turn her confession on her like that? Who was this man? Where had the Adam of the past few days gone? How could she have forgotten how ruthless he could be?

'That's a low blow,' she said hoarsely, her throat oddly tight. 'And this is quite different.'

'How?'

Well, quite. How? Her heart hammering, she mentally sifted through the last three weeks, her temperature steadily rising when she realised that it *wasn't* different. He'd never promised her anything. She'd just assumed. She'd done what she'd sworn not to do. She hadn't kept it casual. She'd allowed her starry-eyed self to be swept off her feet and ended up far more invested in their affair than him. Just as she had before.

'Are you honestly saying you feel nothing for me?' she said, her head spinning with confusion and despair.

'That's exactly what I'm saying.'

For a moment, she couldn't breathe. The ground seemed to be shaking. She felt as though he'd reached in, pulled out her heart and then trampled all over it while she lay beside it, bleeding, dying.

But what could she do? She couldn't force him to feel the same way about her as she did about him. No amount of tenacity would make him love her. She wasn't wanted. And that meant she couldn't be here any more. There was only so much humiliation she could take. Only so long before her strength drained away and she collapsed into a soggy heap on the tiles.

So she lifted her chin and pulled her shoulders back, and before she lost what was left of her dignity, she said, 'I'll get packing right away.'

CHAPTER FOURTEEN

EMBARKING ON THE travel plans Maggie had discussed with him back in the office nearly six weeks ago and then followed up with an email he'd eventually opened once Ella had gone, Adam touched down in Rome first thing on Tuesday morning, certain he'd done the right thing in cutting off all prospects of a relationship with her and denying any feelings for her that he may or may not have had.

That photo had been far too close a call, he thought darkly as he listened to the plans for refurbishment outlined by the general manager of the seven-star hotel the Courtney Collection owned there. She was safe. As was he. They'd both had an incredibly lucky escape—for him that had been personal as well as professional—so he booted both her and their conversation firmly from his head with no regrets about any of it. He didn't miss her or wonder how her promotion was going. He didn't think of her and their three weeks together at all.

A week later, however, as he toured the factory in Hanoi, which manufactured leather goods for one of the businesses in the Collection, he had to admit he was struggling. Ella filtered into his head annoyingly often, and that scene by the pool kept nagging at his thoughts.

But he still held firm the belief that sending her home had been the best thing to do. He couldn't have agreed to a continuation of the affair from Labor Day onwards, even though he'd had to bite back the *Hell yes* that had been on the tip of his tongue. She'd still strip him of control and civility and tempt him into recklessness, and from there it would be a quick descent into chaos and destruction.

It was only natural to miss her, he reflected in between meetings that felt interminable. They'd packed a lot into three weeks. The memories would soon fade. And he'd eventually shake the image of her stricken face when he'd accused her of making a mistake about her feelings for him. He had not been proud of himself for that, but he'd had to get her away before he'd caved in and agreed to—and with—everything she'd said.

But by the time he arrived in the Blue Mountains wine region of New South Wales at the end of August, he was wondering what the hell he'd done. Every moment they'd spent together and every conversation they'd ever had were etched into his head. And now, as he sat in a presentation about the projections for next year's Shiraz sales, all he could think was, had he completely lost his mind? How could he ever have believed himself not in love with her? He was wild about her. He probably had been since the moment she'd dealt the jerk in the bar a knee in the groin and a martini down his shirt the night they'd met.

She was the only person who knew everything about him. She was the only person for whom he'd bought a private jet, resorted to subterfuge and arranged a romantic dinner. He thought she hung the moon and the stars. He worshipped the ground she walked on. She was magnificent.

She was also totally right about the hold that the past had on him.

En route from Hanoi, he'd happened upon an article in a magazine entirely dedicated to the green credentials of the Courtney Collection. The article was great—and so it should be when, where possible, he'd invested heavily in sustainable, ethical manufacturing and clean energy—but that wasn't the point. The point was that two months ago, not that he'd have known exactly who was writing the article, when it was to be published and in which publication, but he would also have demanded to see a copy before it went to print. This one, however, he hadn't even been aware of.

It had hit him, then, like a blow to the head, that he'd almost entirely stepped away from the company in order to focus on Ella and their affair. He'd ceded control and disaster hadn't struck. His recklessness had not led to chaos and devastation. Everything he'd worked for was still standing. He'd built something strong and lasting. Which proved he *wasn't* like his father in that respect, and perhaps not in any others either.

For years, he had feared that if he didn't keep a tight control on everything and everyone, the genes he shared with his father would overrun him, but although he looked like the man, he *wasn't* a chip off the old block. Yes, he'd once been selfish, thoughtless and irresponsible, but he'd been a teenager in a mess. Fourteen years had passed since then—years he'd spent knuckling down and forging his own path—and they counted.

The three weeks he'd spent away from the helm suggested that he didn't have to keep quite such an iron grip on everything as he'd always believed. He could afford to take his foot off the pedal from time to time. He could afford to let go.

And not just of his issues with his father. But of those with his mother too. Because he wasn't responsible for her death. Or maybe he was. Either way he'd never know.

Acquiring Montague's certainly wasn't going to give him any answers, he'd come to realise when he revisited the conversation he and Ella had had over piña coladas, awake and alone in the early hours in one hotel room or another. And it wasn't going to bring his mother back. How could it? And what if it didn't give him the absolution he craved? What if nothing would?

Did he really want to spend the rest of his life trapped in the past, hounded by his fears? Shouldn't he try and take a leaf out of Ella's book by accepting what had happened and moving on? If he just let it all go—as she'd suggested—he wouldn't need redemption. He'd be free. Free to explore a relationship with his sister. Free to look to ahead instead of behind. Free to have Ella in his life with all the challenge, excitement and love she would bring to it.

So the only question that remained was, would she feel the same way?

It didn't seem likely. When he thought of the manner in which he'd spoken to her, he felt physically sick. Driven by a ridiculous need to protect himself, he'd lashed out and hurt her. Devastatingly. He didn't think he'd ever forget the bewilderment and pain in her eyes when he'd dismissed her feelings for him and denied his for her. The memory of it tore him apart and brought him to his knees.

He had to fix the mess he'd made of things, he thought grimly and repeatedly on the twenty-hour flight back to New York. He missed her more than he'd ever imagined possible. She was the most incredible woman he'd ever met and he couldn't contemplate a future without her in it. He wanted her in his corner, in his bed, in his heart. He wanted everything she had to offer and give her everything he had in return. He would do whatever it took to get her back, he vowed above the Pacific, the southern states and then as they came into land. He just hoped he hadn't left it too late.

For the first few days that followed her return to the city, Ella kept herself so busy she barely had time to breathe. Focusing purely on the practicalities, she filled the fridge and did the laundry. She watered the plants, sorted her post and then started prepping to go back to work and take up her promotion.

She had no intention whatsoever of wasting any more time on Adam, she reminded herself firmly whenever she was unexpectedly hit by a memory of something they'd done together or a conversation they'd had. She had never shed tears over anyone, let alone a man, and she wasn't starting now. It was the super strong air conditioning that had stung her eyes on the long flight home, nothing else.

She wasn't some wilting Regency heroine, pining over

an unrequited love. She wasn't a romantic any more than he was. She was a realist, a pragmatist, even if for those three crazy weeks, she'd temporarily forgotten that.

Every time she revisited that scene by the pool, which was far too often for comfort, she cringed. The things she'd said to him… The mortifying assumptions she'd made… The foolish feelings she'd thought she'd developed…

What on earth had she been *thinking*? she repeatedly wondered with incredulous despair. Where had that soppy, sentimental wreck of a woman come from? That wasn't her. That had *never* been her. Going all gooey at a few fairy lights and candles on the beach? Please. Fancying they shared some sort of an emotional connection? Honestly.

She simply couldn't fathom how she'd actually believed herself to be in love with the man when she'd known right from the start that it was nothing more than a fling and he'd made her no promises. And as for putting him on some sort of a pedestal, as if he were a paragon of strength and protection to be worshipped, well, who knew what that had been about? She must have entered a parallel universe for a while.

But she was back in the real world now, back on track, and she needed no further distraction. So with more effort than she'd have liked, she shoved Adam from her head and forced herself to look forward. Which worked. Mostly. Enough, at least, to mean that come Monday morning, she was cool, calm and raring to go.

This was the start of the rest of her life, she told herself as she leapt out of bed and into the shower and resolutely did not think about the many showers she'd shared with the man who'd turned out instead to be a paragon of disappointment. It was what the whole of the last twelve months had been about—the chance to put everything behind her and move on with rising to the top of the auditing world.

However, the minute she stepped across the threshold of the company that had been her spiritual home for the last three years, something felt wrong. She ascended the lift to her floor and headed to the new office she'd been given, but with oddly little enthusiasm.

Nothing about the building had changed. Her colleagues were perfectly pleasant, even congratulatory, which should have delighted her way more than it did. It was just that she had the bizarre feeling she wasn't the same woman who'd walked out the door six weeks ago.

Although supremely confident she could do the job, she felt off balance. For some reason, she was on edge. She couldn't seem to shake the conversation she'd had with Adam about the circumstances of her promotion. She was hounded by the voice in her head, which sounded annoyingly like his, demanding to know whether she was really okay working at a place that was prepared to treat her so badly.

Despite her best efforts to banish it, it stayed there, relentlessly hammering away at her and dredging up memories of horrible conversations with management, the same management who'd so recently authorised the promotion that should have been hers all along.

It took the shine off her new role. It made her question her judgement and kept her up at night, tearing her apart in the early hours because she'd fought so hard for it and wanted it for so long, yet now…she didn't. In fact, it gave her self-respect so much grief that in the end she had to resign, so yet again her career was disrupted because of a man she'd become involved with.

But even though it had been a tough call to make, the subsequent absence of angst absolutely confirmed that resigning had been the right thing to do. The company's values did not match her own, and hers mattered a lot. And at least this time, *she* was in control of the professional decision she'd taken. It was now five days since she'd quit—Labor Day, in fact, not that the date held any significance for her at all—and she already had half a dozen interviews lined up. She had no doubt she'd have her pick of offers. So it was all good. It was all very good indeed.

Of course, resigning and leaving the office immediately to work out her notice at home had meant that she now had a lot of time on her hands with nothing much to occupy her brain. Endless trips to the gym might exhaust her body, but her mind seemed to be on overdrive.

But if she caught herself increasingly dwelling on her secret Caribbean affair, well, why wouldn't she? It had been intense. She and Adam had packed a lot in. It was only natural that she experienced the odd moment of regret that he hadn't wanted to continue their relationship, because she did miss the sex. Who wouldn't?

She didn't miss him, though. Oh, no. These days, she barely ever thought of the conversations they'd had and the things they'd done. She was over him. They were done. She wasn't remotely interested in whether he'd won Helberg today and found the peace he sought.

And, yes, she might very occasionally have expended some energy reviewing how it had all ended, trying to figure out what had gone wrong, whether she could have done anything differently, but that was the analyst in her.

It would soon stop, she assured herself as she arrived back home after an hour on the treadmill. She was sure of it. At least she hoped it would. Because what choice did she have but to forget about him and forge ahead? It wasn't as if he was suddenly going to appear right in front of her and declare his undying love for her. Heaven forbid.

Keys in hand, determined to fill the rest of the holiday with something productive, whatever that might be, Ella stepped out of the lift onto the fourth floor of her building—and froze. Adam was pushing himself off the window sill outside her condo as if he'd been waiting for her, as if she'd conjured him up just by thinking about him.

Her heart stopped. Her breath caught in her throat. Her vision blurred and her head swam, and for a second, all those defences she'd built to protect herself trembled because it had been so damn long and she felt like someone dying of thirst coming face to face with a glass of water. But she kept them in place. She steeled herself to stay calm and held at bay the emotions she could feel trying to muscle their way in. She'd been vulnerable before him once and he'd crushed her. She would not allow that to happen again.

'What are you doing here?' she said coolly, noting that he looked tired and drawn but stamping out the urge to take him in her arms and smooth away the lines, because how he looked was none of her concern, and he didn't deserve her care anyway.

'I've been travelling,' he said gruffly. 'I came straight from the airport. Can we go inside?'

Absolutely not. She couldn't have him in her apartment. Even if she physically got him out, the memory of him in her space, space which she'd worked so hard for, would be unbearable. 'No.'

He frowned. Rubbed a hand across the back of his neck, then gave a short nod and cleared his throat. 'Right,' he said, shoving his hands into the pockets of his jeans and locking his gaze on hers. 'Then I'll just have to do this out here.'

She ignored the slow burn of heat that looking into his eyes always generated and lifted her chin. 'Do what?'

'How have you been?'

Was that why he'd come? To enquire into her wellbeing? Surely a phone call would have sufficed. Not that she'd have answered it. 'I could not have been better.'

'Promotion going well?'

'I resigned.'

He went very still. 'What did they do?'

'*They* did nothing. I just kept thinking about how they treated me and decided that it wasn't good enough. It was less than I deserve.'

'That was brave,' he said, a glimmer of what could have been admiration lighting the depths of his mesmerising blue eyes, although what did she care? It mattered not one little bit what he thought of her decision. 'I have contacts if you need them.'

'I have plenty of my own.'

'Of course you do.'

For a moment, he just looked at her intently, as if trying to get a glimpse into her soul. Her heart thudded heavily, and a flurry of jitters flitted around her stomach, which was not how she wanted to feel, so she blinked to break the connection and pulled her shoulders back. 'What do you want, Adam?'

He hauled one hand out of his pocket and shoved it through his hair. Then he took a deep breath and let it out slowly, and she might have thought he was nervous if how he was feeling was of any consequence, which it wasn't. 'First of all,' he said with another quick clear of his throat. 'I need to apologise for what I said to you by the pool just before you left the Caribbean. It was unacceptable and cruel. I was thrown off balance by the photo. It triggered a reaction I'm not proud of. I'm sorry.'

Ella's heart skipped a beat, but her guard remained up because an apology was the least he could give her. 'Don't worry about it,' she replied with a shrug that didn't feel quite as casual as it should. 'I was thrown off balance, too. We both said things we regret. Forget it. I have.'

He stilled. Frowned. A muscle jumped in his cheek. 'Have you?'

She gave a short nod. 'Oh, yes,' she said firmly. 'Totally. I really don't know what I was thinking. Perhaps I was suffering from sunstroke. Anyway, it's all water under the bridge, right?'

'No,' he said, taking a step towards her, a move that enveloped her in his scent and would have made her swoon if she'd let it. 'It's not all water under the bridge. And it's not right at all. Although you were. You were bang on. About everything. I *don't* buy private jets or arrange romantic dinners on the beach for anyone. I've *never* compromised my principles for an affair. I've only ever done those things for you. I am in love with you. I think I have been since the moment we met. You are the strongest, most incredible woman I've ever met. You frustrate me, you challenge me, you thrill me, and I want you in my life forever.'

Ella's heart crashed against her ribs and then began to gallop. But she must not weaken. She must not give rein to the emotions battering at her defences. She must not let him crush her again. 'Yet you hurt me,' she said, her voice nevertheless cracking. 'Badly. I told you I loved you and you denied it. You took something I told you, something personal, and turned it back on me.'

A flash of anguish sped across his face. 'I know,' he said, as earnest as she'd ever seen him. 'And I'm sorry. I was spooked and lashed out, and I deeply regret it. The thing is, Ella, ever since my mother died, I've feared losing control. I've always believed that without it, I'd cause the sort of chaos my father did. That night in the bar, you stripped me of it. I immediately reverted to type, acting without a thought for the consequences. You continued to remind me of the recklessness I am capable of, and I resisted that. The photo did too, and I reacted in the worst way possible.'

'So you got scared.'

He nodded. 'Yes.'

'That's no excuse.'

'I know,' he said, his tone filled with remorse. 'I have no excuse for any of it. But your take on my feelings for you wasn't the only thing you were right about. I've been doing a lot of thinking recently. And I've realised that I *do* need to let go of the control and the guilt that have kept me trapped in the past. I am not my father's son. I build things, not destroy them. And whatever my role in my mother's death, I'll never know for sure.'

His steady gaze continued to hold hers. 'I don't want to carry on living like this. I want to be free of it all. So this morning, I withdrew from the bet. I don't need Montague's. I don't need redemption any more. I don't need anything but you. If you'll have me. If I haven't screwed this up for good.' He stopped, his breathing a little shallow, a faint flush tingeing his cheekbones. 'Have I done that, Ella? Do you still love me? Or have I killed any feelings you had for me stone dead?'

Ella didn't know where to start with answering Adam's questions. She couldn't think straight. She was reeling. Struggling to process everything he'd just told her. He loved her? He'd listened to her? He was ready to move on and had given up Montague's?

As she stood there staring at him, her heart pounding so hard she felt as though it were trying to escape, one by one, her defences shattered. Every single lie she'd told herself vanished. And into the vacuum, every emotion she'd been battling to keep at bay flooded with the force of a tsunami.

God, she'd missed him, she thought, her chest aching, her throat tight. So very, very much. Despite her every effort, she hadn't been able to stop thinking about him. She'd been utterly miserable since she'd been back. And not because of the job, but because of him. Because he hadn't shared her hopes and dreams. Because she'd taken a risk and lost.

Returning to the city *had* been like switching from Technicolor to black and white. Everything had felt so flat. She missed feeling alive. Being kept on her toes. When she'd been struggling to work out what to do about her promotion, even though she was perfectly capable of making her own decisions, she'd wanted his advice and support. She'd had a glimpse of what a proper relationship could be like and to have it snatched away had been excruciating.

But now he was here, putting everything on the line, and perhaps she ought to make him pay for the agony he'd put her through, but it hadn't been deliberate. They'd both made mistakes. Neither of them was flawless.

'You haven't killed off anything,' she said, wondering if the floor beneath her feet was actually shaking or whether it was simply the force of the emotions swirling around inside her. 'I do still love you. But I'm not entirely happy about it. You crushed me. You sent me away. You've caused me nearly a month of misery.'

He closed the distance between them and took her hands in his. 'If you'll let me,' he said, tightening his hold on her as if he wanted to never let her go, 'I'll spend the rest of my life making it up to you. You're not the only one who's tenacious, Ella. I will do everything in my power to prove how sorry I am and how much I love you. I will fight for you and I will not fail. I will date you. I will woo you. I will bombard you with texts filled with heart emojis and emails laden with innuendo. You'll have to give in eventually, if only to get some peace.'

Her heart pounding, Ella gazed up into his eyes, which were filled with sincerity, determination and the steadfastness that she loved so much, and the last of her resistance melted clean away. Who knew what the future would hold? she thought a little giddily as happiness began to spread through her, warming every inch of her as it went. There'd be much to discuss. Much to sort out. But they'd both taken giant steps into the unknown recently—him relinquishing Montague's, her quitting her job—and so maybe now was the time to take another one. Because she loved him and he loved her, and the one thing she did know was that life with him would never be boring.

'Well then,' she said, her smile wide and bright and filled with everything she was feeling as she drew him with her towards her front door, 'you'd better come in.'

EPILOGUE

Fourteen months later

STANDING IN THE centre of the ground floor of the newly refurbished Montague's, listening to the hubbub going on around her, Ella couldn't remember the last time she'd felt so nervous.

Three hundred guests were in attendance at this launch party, and she'd spoken with many of them, but she could not recall a word of their conversations. She felt as though she'd drunk a dozen glasses of champagne instead of just the one. Her stomach seemed to be on a spin cycle.

She glanced around for the man of the hour and spotted him by the jewellery case that contained a million-dollar diamond necklace and matching earrings. At the sight of him, in a black dinner suit that emphasised his dark good looks, her heart turned over as it always did.

They'd come a long way since the Labor Day Adam had stepped into her condo and started the rest of their lives together with a kiss that she could still recall. With his support and advice, she'd decided not to take up any of the many job offers she'd received and to set up her own business instead. Now she employed two other auditors, and in time she hoped to expand her workforce and maybe, just maybe, even add a crèche.

True to his word, Adam had dated her and wooed her, even though she'd repeatedly told him that he didn't need to, because she'd actually forgiven him the moment he'd explained why he'd fought his feelings. He'd loosened his grip on the company and it was flourishing. He'd also let go of the guilt, and, free of the cage the past had trapped him in for so long, he'd pursued a relationship with his sister, which had gone from strength to strength.

When Montague's had become available, Ella had encouraged him to take it. He'd said he didn't need it, but because she'd thought he might nevertheless regret it later, she'd prevailed, and it had not escaped her notice that he'd taken more than a casual interest in the relaunch.

Once in his possession, he'd begun to raid it for gifts. A tennis bracelet here, a pair of diamond stud earrings there. Not an engagement ring, however. He'd broached the subject of formalising their relationship a mere three months into it, but she'd been a little more circumspect. It had felt too soon. He'd never given her any reason to doubt his commitment, and she knew he loved her, but she'd spent over a decade fretting about compromise and sacrifice and her independence, and old habits died hard.

However, a lot had happened since then. Six months ago, he'd persuaded her to move in with him, which had been a major step for her. But as it had turned out, compromise and sacrifice weren't a problem at all when the person you were accommodating was doing the same for you. Independence didn't disappear just because someone else's wishes became as important as your own.

And so now she was going to take an even bigger one.

'I need you for a moment,' she murmured when he reached her side, drawing him behind a pillar and away from the throng, her heart practically in her throat.

'That's something I'll never tire of hearing,' he said warmly, gazing into her eyes and smiling.

'I love you.'

'I love you too. More and more each day. Body, heart and soul.'

'That's how I feel,' she said, her voice a little shaky. 'I love how I can depend on you. I love how you lean on me. You make me feel protected and secure and at the same time, as if I can take on the world. I never thought I could ever have this. I thought I was destined to be alone for the rest of my life. You've made me happier than I ever believed possible.'

'Right back at you.'

'So I have a question.'

'What is it?'

She took a deep breath. Then she got down on one knee and held up a band of platinum. 'Will you marry me?'

* * * * *

FIANCÉE FOR THE CAMERAS

TARA PAMMI

MILLS & BOON

For Soraya, my fabulous new editor, for giving me new energy for so many more delicious Presents.

I can't believe we're already at three books! Here's to many more together.

CHAPTER ONE

HER BRIDEGROOM WASN'T COMING.

Monica D'Souza realized the awful dawning truth even as she dialed Francesco's number one more time. It continued to ring, as it had done over the past hour, and with each unanswered call, she was beginning to feel like something a careless tourist had chewed up and spat over the steps of the piazza.

Or worse, something forgotten or abandoned. Or both. Which she'd already experienced far too many times in her life.

Had Francesco been in an accident? He drove that moped pretty recklessly, and Monica could just imagine him bleeding out on some tiled floor a few streets away. Why else would he not only be late but also not even call her? He *had to* be indisposed in some way. He had to.

Standing outside the marvelous Sala Degli Specchi hall in Palazzo Reale for the past two hours—because of course she had to arrive at least an hour early—in the elaborate puffy white dress that she had bought online, she was beginning to draw attention of the worst kind.

The dress was nothing like the website posting had said, with a cheap, plasticky feel to the fabric and worse, a weirdly pungent chemical smell that was beginning to make her feel faint.

Breaking all her rules, she'd stolen a sachet of lavender from her boss's private bathroom at work and pressed it between the folds. But the smell of the dress was as tenacious as she was and now it clung to her skin, creating her very own scent of desperation.

Granted, she hadn't paid a lot for the dress—not after putting the little nest of her savings from the past three and a half years into the tiny studio flat she and Francesco wanted to move into later this week.

A new home, though it was tiny, a new life, with someone who wanted to be with her… It was all she'd ever dreamed of.

With a frustrated exhale, Monica pushed away the ridiculous veil that had come with the dress out of her eyes, blinking back prickly tears. The June sun beat down mercilessly, probably melting her sunscreen and makeup. All she needed now was mascara tracks running down her cheeks to complete the picture of the ghastly, pathetic bride.

No, she refused to believe that Francesco would do this to her. She'd seen him only last night and while there had been a desperation to his kisses and more than usual urgency to his demands about making love to her, he'd said he couldn't wait to begin their life together.

She had only known him two months but discovered they had so much in common. They were both orphans and had grown up in care homes all over the country—she in the US and he in Italy—and they both wanted desperately to build a family, both eager for belonging. Like her, Francesco loved art and history and languages, and on their first meeting they had chatted for hours and at the end of it, she'd been absolutely head over heels in love. And he had expressed with that European flair that he felt the same toward her.

Over the next few weeks, she'd seen him at least three times a week, the only impediment to their relationship being her very demanding boss and the rigorous work schedule he imposed on her as his assistant.

Monica had been floating on cloud nine, so much that even *he*—of the brooding glower, grumpy manners and workaholic energy—had noticed and questioned her.

Then, a week ago, Francesco had proposed to her right in this very spot, his grin that charming, naughty one that had tempted her more than once into almost breaking her rule that she'd only have sex when she was fully ready.

She'd always been a little dull, averse to risk. Dependable, definitely. She would have liked to spend, and would have spent, her entire life under the radar if not for the fact that whoever had abandoned her to an orphanage when she'd been a baby had passed on genes that made her "stunning" and "beautiful."

While she could appreciate the symmetry of her angular features, her golden-brown complexion and the uniqueness of her yellow, catlike eyes, her face and body had always drawn attention of the worst kind, first from boys in all the foster homes she'd bounced through and then men—even the ones who were supposed to protect a homeless teen.

But her face had drawn Francesco to her. Francesco, who was fun and charming and sexy. She took everything too seriously and he took it very easy, breezing through life, making bets upon bets. No wonder he was late now. She wouldn't be surprised if he'd gotten caught up in arranging a fun surprise for her or some other daring activity for their honeymoon.

He's only late, she kept telling herself.

Not dumping her here. Not leaving her like everyone eventually did. Not deciding that something else was more important than her.

More than one woman had given her a piteous look and

more than one man had whistled, laughed and asked if she wanted to celebrate a wedding night without getting married. After studying Italian for two years at a community college in New York and living in Milan for four years now, she had a good grasp of the language.

She wiped at the beads of sweat over her upper lip and licked her parched lips. Opening her small backpack, she was pulling out her water bottle when her cell phone chirped.

"Francesco? You're late," she said, unable to keep a sliver of frustrated anger out of her tone. "Our appointment was for an hour ago but I've sorted it out with them. If you can—"

"I'm sorry, *mia cara.* A golden opportunity came up for my business and you know how hard I've been working to get cash infusion, *sì*?"

"I do," Monica said, blinking a mixture of tears and makeup out of her eyes. "And I fully support you," she added softly, as compensation for her miserable tone. "But I'm waiting for you. At the Palazzo Reale. To get married."

"Ahh...*bella.* Unfortunately, this opportunity means I have to postpone the wedding. At least for a year."

Unfortunately...

Misery and pain swamped Monica, bringing her back to that time the public school she'd attended had gone on a trip to swamplands in sixth grade. The whole trip to Florida, she'd been reminded by most of her classmates that she was the charity case their parents had chipped in extra for. She hadn't cared—it was the first time she was seeing something other than the orphanage and foster homes and her school—but then Olivia Kent had pushed her head down into the water because Timothy Evans had smiled at Monica and not her.

This felt exactly like that. Like she couldn't breathe.

"I don't understand. What does your business opportunity have to do with our getting married? You know how much I support all your dreams. If you want, I'll even ask my boss for a loan if you really—"

"No need. You didn't want to ask before, *si*? Now I don't need that big shot Valentini's help. This whole marriage thing was your idea."

"What? That's not true. You proposed to me. You wanted us to get that flat to live together. You made me shell out—"

"*Basta!* I will return your puny money. I'm not a man who depends on a woman. Especially one so clingy and needy. All the time, you are cooking and doing my laundry and offering your services up. A man can get confused when a woman throws herself at him like that. I only thought you were a good goose after—"

Monica felt like she was getting whiplash, and it wasn't her dress or the sun beating down on her. Francesco thought she was…*clingy and needy*. He thought she had thrown herself at him. He thought…

Of course, Francesco didn't love her. Or at least not more than himself and his business ventures. Not when loving her meant giving up bigger, better opportunities. Not when it was inconvenient. Maybe what he felt for her wasn't love at all.

"You are a beautiful woman with a sexy body. You always smile and maintain good cheer. I thought hey, she is a hot American woman with good connections in Milan. But it was convenience, Monica. Especially since you don't even give out sex. If you still want to celebrate our wedding night without—"

Hands shaking, Monica hung up and fought the maddening urge to throw her cell phone across the steps into the cheerful fountain.

No. She couldn't. It was her work phone and there was no point in taking her misery out on it when she'd have to fish it out of the fountain, then get a replacement, then explain to the IT department how it had fallen into the water in the first place. And God forbid if the phone got clogged up with water and she missed a call from her very demanding, very important, boss.

Especially today of all days, when Mr. Valentini might well announce his engagement to his ex, Mrs. Chiara Rossi. She'd been expecting it for more than six weeks now, given the impending merger between Valentini Luxury Goods and Chiara's father's company, Brunetti Leathers. Especially ever since she'd run into Mrs. Rossi at a dinner party and had been warned off setting her sights on her boss.

Hurriedly, she made sure the ringer was turned up all the way.

This was her, she thought, tears falling down her cheeks, with an edge of hysteric laughter setting into the sound. This woman, who minutes after being dumped at the altar—though technically it was city hall—balked at the idea of even throwing her phone because it might give rise to unnecessary questions and inconvenience for someone else. Especially the man to whom she owed so much.

But even the usual nerve-racking urgency she felt around Mr. Valentini wasn't enough to cut through the weight of her misery, which sank through her belly as if she'd swallowed one of Francesco's enormous dumbbells.

This was her—Monica D'Souza—once again alone in the world, with no place to go, once again abandoned and unwanted.

Andrea Valentini, CEO of Valentini Luxury Goods, did not usually involve himself in the personal lives of his employees. He could barely remember their full names and personal situations. All he did remember was their abilities and efficiencies and how loyal they were to his company. He didn't need to know more than that. And he didn't have the bandwidth to know more than that. Which was why he, nearly two years ago, when another assistant had quit on him, had jumped on the opportunity to promote his mother's rescuer, the walking, talking human resource machine that was Monica D'Souza.

He prided himself on seeing people for who they were and once again, he'd been right. During her convalescence at the hospital after she'd saved his mother from a dangerous mugger, Andrea had seen the magic Ms. D'Souza could weave with numbers and interpersonal affairs.

Offering her a job as one of his junior assistants in exchange for saving his mother's life had been a small price to pay. As he'd expected, her sharp mind and her extraordinary talent in dealing with people who always needed something from him, which meant he could actually focus on the business, had had her climbing the corporate ladder super-fast. Until he'd had no choice but to steal her for himself exclusively.

Now Ms. D'Souza pretty much ran his professional life, and his personal life, too, though he didn't really have one. She made him an approachable package for the media, for his shareholders and even for his own family.

He'd never really had any complaints about her, until a few weeks ago when she'd met Francesco Ricci—a charming conman Andrea could scent a kilometer away. How Ms. D'Souza didn't see his true character was a mystery to him.

While it had irritated the hell out of him to see her throw her breathtaking smiles and her generous compliments at such a rascal, Andrea had set her little flirtation out of his mind. She was not only naive but also young at just twenty-three. She deserved to have fun, even if it was with a rogue who didn't deserve to kiss her little toe.

Except his mother had called his attention to the fact that Francesco had not only proposed to Ms. D'Souza but he had also talked her into giving up her savings to finance some ridiculous hovel he wanted to rent, a week ago.

On impulse, Andrea had had his chauffeur drive him to that dingy, unsafe neighborhood, only to realize that Francesco had fleeced Ms. D'Souza. If it was just that, Andrea could have called in his connections and had him hauled to prison.

But no, Francesco had found his golden goose in Ms. D'Souza and meant to fleece her for the rest of his life. Especially with her close connection to his own family. That, Andrea could not allow.

So here he was, after having one of his associates pay off the thug to dump Ms. D'Souza. And while it was cruel, Andrea hoped this would cure Ms. D'Souza of her naive faith in every scoundrel she came across. The woman needed a crash course in the reality of people.

But of course, it wasn't enough that Andrea had taken care of the mess she'd gotten herself into. Mama wanted him to make sure Ms. D'Souza was okay in the aftermath, when the last thing he needed was a distraught woman on his hands.

As if his ex's machinations to force him into accepting her as his wife as a bonus prize along with the merger with her father's company wasn't bad enough.

Once, Andrea would have done anything—*had* done anything—to win Chiara's hand and heart. But she had chosen a different man, a man more suited to give her the lifestyle she was used to and the kind of commitment she'd wanted. Her gamble hadn't paid off quite the way she'd foreseen, for her husband had failed at a few business ventures before dying in an accident.

And now his mother, and Chiara's father and Chiara herself apparently expected him to pick up where they had left off ten years ago and enter wedded bliss with her. Or the merger wouldn't go through, her father had the gall to say, when Andrea hadn't immediately jumped on the condition.

The very thought made his temper boil over. The fact that Brunetti now tied the fate of this merger—a merger Andrea had sunk everything into—to his marrying Chiara...

As of now, Andrea had no solution to a problem that was suddenly a big headache. He wanted to say no without saying no, without upsetting the delicate balance that was his business negotiations with Chiara's father.

He leaned back in the car, gritting his teeth, and found his mind drifting to Ms. D'Souza. Suddenly, it didn't feel like such a chore to rescue her from the clutches of the rogue. At least with her, Andrea knew there was no honeyed trap, no sweet nudges toward the altar. Nothing but painfully naive honesty packaged in a goddess's body.

Monica flipped through the few contacts on her phone, holding up the train of her dress high off the ground, even as she felt a slow, relentless burning across the skin of her upper back.

After calling Francesco a few more times and finding it going straight to voice mail, she'd just been standing there feeling lost. Unraveled. Facing the very real truth of her situation—she had nowhere to go.

After plucking her water bottle out of her bag, she took the last sip and pressed the cool metal to her cheek. She wanted to rip the dress off her skin and jump into the fountain herself. Drench herself from head to foot in the cool water. Wash off this nasty day. Would anyone stop her? Was the last event on this crazy day to be arrested for public indecency in Milan of all places?

Letting the hem fall to the ground, she peeked over her shoulder to see why the skin on her back felt like someone had lit up a matchstick and pressed it unrelentingly against it.

She couldn't see much. Blinking, feeling a strange nausea well up at the back of her throat, she frowned. It was summer in Milan, so yes, it was hot. But she'd never felt this…scorching sensation on her skin before, nor this lightheadedness. Something was wrong.

There was only one person she could call, only one person who had been unflinchingly kind to her for close to four years now. Mrs. Valentini would welcome her with open arms, and yet, Monica felt the strangest reluctance. Everything Flora knew, her older son would be made aware of. The thought of Andrea Valentini finding out what a pathetic mess she was made the scorching burn on her back feel like a cool glaze.

Suddenly, a very familiar Bugatti with tinted windows came into view at the end of the street and Monica stiffened. Any doubt she might have had turned into dust when the chauffeur parked the car right in front of the huge steps leading to the Palazzo Reale, uncaring of whom he was blocking.

As if his boss belonged there.

Because he did.

And Monica knew that her nightmare had one last cringeworthy humiliation to deliver. Her day wasn't over yet.

CHAPTER TWO

SHE SHOULD HAVE looked pathetic.

If Andrea was honest with himself, she did, a little. But standing on those steps, with people watching her and mocking her, in that ghastly overpuffed, overlaced, frothy concoction that someone like Chiara wouldn't let a staff member wear in her household, Ms. D'Souza also looked brave. As if she'd entered a battle and lost it spectacularly, and yet somehow remained full of that fierce little heart he had never seen in anyone else.

He should have sent his chauffeur, Pascale, to pick her up, throw her over his shoulder if she offered her useless, prideful resistance and dump her inside the car and speed off, so that he could leave her piteous…situation in Mama's capable, caring hands.

But a little something went off track—a little blip in the fold of the universe, as his brother was fond of saying—and Andrea decided to get out of the car and pick up the wretched baggage himself.

That little lift of her chin as Monica's catlike golden eyes met his when he lowered the tinted window—even as her hands trembled at her sides, even as her face looked like it was made of myriad shades of red and brown and gold with a little green around her mouth thrown in for good measure, even as she looked like a jilted bride who had crawled out of some haunted mansion in a cheap gothic novel—was the thing that provoked some base instinct that Andrea had never known existed in him.

He raised a hand to his chauffeur to turn the car around on the busy junction, aware that they were already attracting attention. Usually, he hated spectacles like this. He was a well-known figure in Milan and his face was the one that had turned a small leather goods company into his current billion-dollar machine that had resuscitated a sinking economy on its last breath. Flexing his power and prestige and connections in this way had never been his style.

But something egged him on and he didn't even calculate the risk like he usually did when he encountered such a situation.

He finally reached his assistant and felt a sharp spike of awareness as she looked down at him from a few steps above. Whatever hairstyle she'd started the day with had unraveled, leaving her silky brown waterfall of hair falling to her waist. Her skin was flushed and blotched at the same time, as if she'd been trekking in the sun without water for too long. Her lips were chapped and she kept licking them.

Even with the overdone lace puffs at her shoulders and too much lace fluttering at her neckline, the bodice paid homage to her high breasts and then nipped tightly at her tiny waist. How she had managed to find a dress that fell too far to the ground when she was so tall, Andrea would never know. His leisurely traversing revealed a tear at the hem and one at the waistline, as if she had pulled and torn at the dress to get it away from her body.

But what alarmed Andrea when he would have otherwise found the whole thing comically tragic was the reddish flush to her cheeks, her neck and the skin beneath. And the way she couldn't seem to stop trembling.

She looked like she was unraveling, providing a spectacle for bored tourists and Milanese alike.

The stubborn tilt of her chin was gone. Had he imagined it, the little flicker of bravery? Was she that same lost little lamb who gave foolishly and generously of herself to one and all?

"Come, let's go," he said when he reached her, employing his usual brisk tone, hoping to devolve whatever emotional outburst was building inside the woman like a damn geyser. The last thing he wanted was to be near her when it erupted.

Have a little care, Andrea. She's twenty-three years old, years younger than you in age and experience and she just got dumped.

Suitably chastened, as if Papa were standing next to him and speaking those words, Andrea extended a hand toward her. "There is no point in lingering here, Ms. D'Souza."

"I can't, Mr. Valentini," she said, her usually husky voice paper-thin. "At least not until I get this thing off me."

Andrea frowned. He tried, *tried his best*, to modulate his tone but he was now regretting the impulse of getting out of his car at all. This had disaster written all over it, for her and him. "You're very well aware of how much I loathe public scenes, Ms. D'Souza. It is bad enough that Mama wouldn't leave me alone until I picked you up here and delivered you to her care. Bad enough that I had to come here all the way from Mr. Brunetti's estate at the outskirts of the city. You're also well aware how busy this week has been at work and how much your leave today has inconvenienced me already. Enough with your—"

"All I need is that Swiss blade you keep on yourself all the time," she said, eyes not only watering but also shedding tears, which were running tracks down her cheeks and into the grooves of her delicate clavicle.

Cristo, the woman was stunning and sensuous even when she was a hot garbage mess, as one of his younger cousins was fond of saying. Now Ms. D'Souza was swaying where she stood and Andrea thought she might disappear in a whiff of smoke if he so much as breathed wrong.

"Then you can turn around, forget this little scene ever happened and return to your air-conditioned suite and that Brunetti contract. If you do me this favor, I'll even put in a few hours of work tonight. And I'll return the blade back to you. I know it is a cherished gift from Mrs. Rossi."

Andrea stilled, shocked at her request. Shocked at how much of his personal life she was privy to. That he held on to the blade that Chiara had gifted him almost a decade ago, not even his mother knew. It had been foolish sentimentality at the beginning. And now he was simply attached to the master craftsmanship of the blade. Not that he had to explain his uncharacteristic fondness of the blade to this woman.

"Do not be ridiculous, Ms. D'Souza. I'm not so much of a monster that I would make you come in to work when you're in such a…pathetic state." It was a bad choice of word, yet again. Andrea regretted it the moment it found shape, even before it landed and she flinched.

Dio mio, what was wrong with him? He was called ruthless, arrogant, but casual cruelty had never been his weapon of choice.

She did draw her chin up then and he knew he hadn't imagined the same earlier. "If you're not going to help me, leave me in peace."

"What good will a Swiss blade do you now? You should have taken better care with your money and your heart before you trusted such a scoundrel. All these dramatics are of no use. Walking naked through these streets is not going to bring him back."

"That's not what I mean to do at all," she said, mouth falling open at his suggestion. "Wait, how do you know that he…" Closing her eyes, she took a bracing breath.

Once again, Andrea was struck by her quiet dignity.

She rubbed a hand over her cheek and neck and opened her eyes. There was a flatness to her gaze that he disliked intensely. "You know what? Like you said, it doesn't matter. Francesco dumping me here has no more or no less significance just because you found out and use it to talk down to me. If you'll excuse me, I have other things to take care of. I'm sorry that Flora inconvenienced you and I will see you tomorrow morning at work."

He should have let her go, let *it* go. In fact, he was glad to see she had some backbone. But he didn't. Apparently, today was full of surprises.

When she sidestepped him to take the stairs down past him, he grabbed her wrist. "I'm not talking down to you," he said, stubbornly wanting the last word. "And you are…"

His words stilled. She was burning to his touch.

Andrea dropped her wrist and touched the back of his hand to her forehead and then her neck, like he had seen Mama do countless times.

"Are you dehydrated?" he demanded, pushing into her space, touching her compulsively in a few more spots. "You're flushed and sweating and…you need a doctor. You're a stubborn creature to stand here and argue with me when you—"

"I need your blade," she said, shoving away from him. "If you have even a tiny bit of respect for me, you'll listen to me when I say I know what I need. Now, Andrea."

It was how she said his name that convinced him. With

an easy familiarity, as if she had said it many times. When in reality, he had always been Mr. Valentini—his last name almost a shield. Now, in that low-pitched husky voice, it sounded intimate and strangely like something he had imagined before.

"I will not let you do anything foolish, Monica." Her own name fell easily, effortlessly, from his lips. As if some hitherto closed door had been unlocked, never to be shut again. *Cristo*, the heat must be getting to him, too, because that was a load of bullshit if he'd ever heard, in his own head.

She scoffed then, and he felt the loss of her innocence keenly. "I have lived through too many shitty foster homes, evaded too many incoming hits, fought too many roving hands, to now harm myself over a man who has no…loyalty."

He placed his blade into her outstretched hand. "You're an orphan, then?" How had he not known it in two years of working together so closely? Or the nearly four years that she'd been close to his mother and brother? How had he compartmentalized this woman so easily?

She didn't answer and Andrea knew that it was a choice, that he hadn't made the cut to her inner circle. Damn if it didn't irritate the hell out of him.

She palmed the blade, as if to test its weight and slant, and then turned the pointed edge toward the bodice. Andrea nearly leaped at her, his pulse jumping into his throat. Only to realize that she meant to rip the bodice off her flesh.

"Put some pressure on my hand," she said, and he clamped his fingers over hers automatically. "The zipper is stuck."

She was different now, her calm voice and the rigid resolve showing something else beneath the soft-spoken, highly efficient shadow he'd gotten used to for years.

Too close, they were too close. Any protest he had that they were creating a spectacle disappeared as he noted the slight swelling of her lips and the small reddish bubbles near her neck. Her eyes flickered for a second, meeting his, then she groaned as the fabric finally rent under their combined pressure. It fell open, revealing an ivory white lacy bra that was clearly much more expensive than the cheap dress. Her breasts were thrust up, falling and rising with her labored breaths.

"Now the back, please," she said, and turned around, presenting him with her back.

Shaking himself out of the sudden haze, Andrea cut through the fabric of the dress in the back. He'd barely gotten it down to her waist when she ripped it off her skin as if it...burned her.

He saw it then. The angry red rash all over her back, dipping all the way to the slope of her buttocks. A combination of blisters and rash that looked...intensely painful. Alarmed, Andrea pushed the dress down her shoulders and then down her waist and hips. He pulled the bra away from her skin and cut through that, too, realizing now that her skin must burn when anything touched that ghastly rash in this heat. He hated himself a little for making her wait so long before listening to her.

"That feels...better," she said, turning around and burrowing her upper body into his. The blaze of heat from her body nearly seared him. Her hands were shaking as she held the torn dress against her breasts, her mouth a rictus of pain, her eyes cloudy.

"You'll be fine now, Ms. D'Souza," he said stiffly, shrugging off his jacket, feeling a strange powerless anger thrum through him. He recognized the familiarity of it and loathed it so much that he almost pushed her away. But the wobbling of her delicate chin stopped him.

He had barely draped the jacket over her shoulders when she swayed, lost consciousness and folded into his arms like a doll.

Andrea picked her up in his arms with as much gentleness as he was capable of, his heart in his throat. Why had he not listened to her immediately? How had he not seen her pain in her eyes?

His chauffeur helped him lay her on the backseat with her head in his lap. Grabbing a bottle of water, Andrea uncapped it and sprayed a few drops onto her burning forehead, even as he barked orders at Pascale to rush them to the company-owned flat close to the financial district.

He held her head in his lap, arranging her long, bare legs to stretch out onto the seat, and softly tapped her cheek. She didn't respond. His fear grew in his throat, choking him out of air. If anything happened to her because of his arrogance… *Cristo*, he would not forgive himself!

Having drenched a napkin in ice-cold water that was now puddling at his feet, Andrea ran it over her forehead. Slowly, her eyelids fluttered open and she made a half-hearted attempt to sit up. Her hands scrabbled for purchase on his shirt, her lithe softness pressed against him.

He helped her recline against his side, making sure not to touch her back, and held a bottle to her lips.

She drank it down eagerly, coughing and sputtering water until he had to drag the bottle away from her mouth. With a soft gasp, she grabbed the bottle from his hands and poured it over her back and front, dumping cold water all over his leather seats.

"Better?" he asked, as he fished his cell phone out of the jacket that was draped over her shoulders.

"Much, thank you," she said, bare shoulders trembling, whether with the fever he could clearly see in her eyes or with cold, he didn't know. "If you can have Pascale drop me off at—"

"You're not going anywhere alone. You need to be looked after."

"That's not your decision." She licked her chapped lips and softened her tone. "Please, Mr. Valentini. I would prefer—"

"What? No more *Andrea*?" he said, just as the call he'd made on his phone connected.

He wondered what her answer would have been while he barked orders on the phone.

She would not like his high-handedness come tomorrow. She would actively loathe his thoughtfulness and care and generosity tomorrow. But he didn't give a fig.

What did concern him was the couple of cell phones he'd seen focused on him and Monica when he'd been busy cutting the damned dress off her and when he'd carried her to his car. Any other time, he would never have left himself vulnerable to being recorded in a public setting. But the state of her… It was done.

And whatever the consequences, he'd have to deal with them.

Monica had barely discarded his jacket and was holding the bedsheet around her front without it touching the rash when Mr. Valentini returned from his brother Romeo's bathroom with a tube of aloe vera gel that she had told him where to find. Numerous peeks over her shoulder had been unsuccessful for her to get a good look at her back.

With each passing moment, she was aware of what a nuisance this situation was for a man who abhorred any kind of drama or mess, professional or personal. What a nuisance she herself had become for him today.

The last straw in her miserable day had been to find that he had brought her to the apartment he used in the city.

His younger brother, Romeo, had taken one look at her—holding his brother's jacket against her near-naked body—and opened his arms wide to her from his wheelchair. Monica had thrown herself into his arms shamelessly, nearly crashing them both to the floor, and sobbed her heart out while he whispered soft endearments into her ear and cursed Francesco to hell and beyond.

The kindness in her friend's eyes had broken through whatever fake armor she'd put on around his brother, making today's loss unbearably real.

Now, with Romeo busy with his physiotherapist, Monica wished she hadn't let go so…completely of her emotions. At least, not where Andrea's frosty gray eyes watched her and judged her and found her so…*pathetic.*

That was the word he had used for her. She couldn't let herself forget it. Not because the ruthless Andrea Valentini had pronounced it so, but because it was what her foolish desperation for love had reduced her to.

Now, looking up at Andrea as he prowled toward the bed, toward her, Monica tried not to be caught up in the indescribable masculine energy of the man. It had been so from the first moment she'd met him four years ago. Even then, it had been her on the hospital bed and him glaring down at her with those inscrutable gray eyes, making her skin prickle with awareness, even amidst the happy haze of painkillers. As if he blamed her for his mother's mugging incident, rather than thanking her for saving her life.

Nearly three years of close proximity hadn't dimmed his frightful appeal one bit. Proving her efficiency and efficacy to him and the company hadn't stopped her insides from tying into knots every time he stepped close. Understanding his work ethic and his care for his employees and his utter intolerance for incompetence and greed hadn't helped conquer this…ridiculous attack of nerves whenever she was near him.

He's just a man, she told herself, like she always did. Made of flesh and bones and hand-stitched designer suits. *But what a man*, the same voice whispered, the bold, brave one she never let out.

With his jacket gone, his cuffs rolled back to reveal hair-roughened corded forearms, the front of his shirt damp and wrinkled thanks to her, he looked less like the suave, sophisticated, steely-eyed businessman and more like…the big, bad boss of a nefarious enterprise. Even his hair, always slickly pushed back, looked as if he'd run his hands through it multiple times, and his mouth had the pinched look that conveyed strain he rarely let rise to the surface.

His meeting with his ex and her father...

Monica's gaze slipped to his left hand, looking for the ring she'd been expecting for weeks now.

"What are you looking for?" he said, leaning one knee onto the bed while she instantly scuttled back like a frightened cockroach.

His mouth flattened at her reaction.

Her cheeks heated, and she hoped he would just put it down to the feverish haze that still racked her body. "I wondered if I should offer congratulations," she said, feeling a boldness she'd never known before. Maybe this moment of bravery came with him having seen her at her worst already. Maybe this was the illusion of wisdom since she'd paid dearly for her naive foolishness.

"Congratulations?" he asked, frowning.

"On your engagement to Mrs. Rossi."

"How the hell did you know that her father was going to demand that as a condition to the merger?" he said, a sudden coldness to his gaze.

She shivered, his anger a freezing blast against her overheated skin. "We ran into her at dinner one evening, almost six weeks ago. Even before your mother invited her, she joined us."

"Ran into whom?"

"Chiara Rossi," Monica said and sighed. "Flora told me she's Mr. Brunetti's daughter. She was very warm toward your mother. When Flora introduced me as your assistant, gushing how invaluable you find me and couldn't do without me and that I was almost a Valentini family member—" Monica blushed as he watched her with that relentless gaze, though he didn't deny his mother's claims "—it was like a switch had flipped. She kept probing about our working relationship and..." She bit her lip. "When Flora went to the restroom, Mrs. Rossi asked really pointed questions about how well I know you and how much time I spend with you and other intrusive stuff that made me very uncomfortable."

"You could have refused to answer her."

Monica stared at him. "She's your...friend," she said, instead of "apparently the lost love of your life", "and I... didn't want to give offense." She blew out a breath at having gotten that much out.

"You're not answerable to anyone other than me, Ms. D'Souza," he said, running a hand through his hair. "What else?" he asked, his gaze taking in every nuance of hers.

"At the end, she said to make sure I had my head screwed on straight around you, to not lose myself in silly, girlish dreams. To remember that I was nothing but your employee. And then she..."

"What, Monica?"

"She muttered something in Italian, obviously assuming I wouldn't understand."

"What?"

"That she would make sure my time with you was limited, beginning right then."

"You didn't think to warn me of this?"

"Warn you?" Monica said, frustration creeping into her tone. "Of what? That a stunning, sophisticated woman, your ex, apparently a…member of your family's intimate circle, interrogated me about…us? You would have thrown me out of your office before I could get started on that story, calling it gossip. And even if you did hear me out, I didn't know if you would trust my version."

"When have I ever given you the belief that I don't trust you? *Dio mio*, give yourself some credit," he said through gritted teeth. "I could have walked into that meeting with Brunetti without being blindsided by his ultimatum."

"You've been out with her to the opera and that charity gala the last few months. Spent time with her more than I've ever known you to, with any woman, in four years. I thought it was a foregone conclusion. Flora said mergers and marriages were interchangeable in high society."

"You didn't even want to know if her threat had credibility with me? About your position?"

Monica sighed, wondering if he really didn't see. "Pit myself against a woman who knew you for years, who was about to marry you, who has power and prestige and wealth and ask you to pick her or me?"

"You continue to sell yourself short and that is a pathetic trait," he said, shoving away from the bed.

She flinched, feeling his disappointment worse than the

sudden crack in his temper. Still, she couldn't stop herself from asking, "So it is not…a done deal?"

Turning, he glared at her.

"I'm not fishing for gossip. I'm merely asking, especially since I've pulled you away from a meeting with her father. I know how much you've sunk into the merger and how many livelihoods depend on it, and how hard you've worked on this. If—"

"Your little drama today hasn't affected the merger. Now drop it. When you need to know anything more, you will."

Monica bristled at his dismissal, though she should be used to it. On one hand, he told her to value herself when it came to him and on the other…he shut her down. Not that she didn't understand his frustration.

Mr. Valentini thrived on being in control, and Carlo Brunetti's addendum must have come as a shock.

While he had shut her line of questioning down, it was clear that he wasn't dating his ex, wasn't the least bit interested in getting back with her or marrying her. Suddenly, it felt like a weight she hadn't known she was carrying had been lifted from her shoulders.

And then, in that feverish haze, it dawned on her that even Francesco abandoning her had less weight in the face of her boss's continued single state. Pressing her hand to her forehead, Monica shivered anew.

Had she been so shaken by Mrs. Rossi's threat that she'd soon cut Monica out of Andrea's life that she had thrown herself into seeking security with Francesco? For nearly three years, her boss had been the locus of her life, the sole foundation to the kind of security she'd always craved. Andrea's needs and demands and requirements of her had become her sole focus, her reason to get through the day.

Had she so feared losing what little she had of Andrea

that she had taken such a reckless, uncharacteristic move and thrown her lot in with Francesco? Had she made him into something he'd never been because she'd worried she was losing her place in Andrea's life?

How bad was her fixation with Andrea Valentini? How had she not seen it?

She was shaking over this new realization when Andrea reached her and opened his palm to reveal two painkillers. "I've spoken to Mama's doctor. He will visit you before nightfall. In the meantime, he suggested these for that fever. He will do blood tests to make sure no lasting damage was done."

"I'm sure it wasn't," she said, wanting not to discuss this with him anymore. Needing this torment to be over. "It's not late. You could just send Pascale to drop me off at the doctor's. That way—"

"And then have Mama castigate me that she didn't raise me to be such a thoughtless, uncaring brute? Save me from a lecture, an extra trip and the headache of an argument with you now, Ms. D'Souza."

CHAPTER THREE

APPARENTLY, ABUNDANCE WAS the name of the game today when it came to Mr. Valentini's choice words for her.

Monica tried to take the pills out of his hand without touching him unnecessarily, resulting in the two red pills dancing off his palm onto the bed. With a curse, he flushed them out, picked up the glass of water and said, "Open."

Feeling like a child who'd gotten in more trouble while actively trying to avoid it—the story of her life—Monica swallowed the protest at his manner and opened her mouth. The faster she could get him out of here, the better she could wallow in her misery.

But it was impossible to follow her head's warnings when his fingers gripped her chin in a firm grasp and her nostrils were full of that dark clove-and-pine scent of his, and the corded column of his throat and his angular chin and that thin slash of his mouth filled her hazy gaze. And then there was the scar that ran from his temple to the side of his mouth, somehow adding to his appeal as a grumpy beast of a man.

Monica shivered again and it had nothing to do with whatever fever the chemicals from the dress had induced in her.

He noticed that, too. "The doctor said the aloe was a good idea until he can give you a stronger steroid. He recommended we air out your skin as much as possible. So, lie down so that I can—"

"That's not necessary at all," Monica said, trembling from head to toe now at the thought of his fingers on her bare flesh.

And there was the second part of the thing she'd missed.

There was a reason she'd always avoided anything even remotely nearing forced intimacy with Mr. Valentini—not even risking a nightcap in the confines of his office after thirteen hours of constant negotiations resulting in a deal last year; not a ride in his car after a long day to the apartment she shared with four other women—and she was becoming aware of the why of it only now.

Shame burned through her chest, adding to all the other burns currently attacking her tender flesh and battered heart. Had she convinced herself that Francesco was it for her because of how out of control her life felt with her boss's alleged upcoming engagement? How long had she been attracted to him without even being aware of it?

It took Mr. Valentini's hand on her wrist to realize she'd started crawling away from him, the sheets now tangled around her legs. The frost of his gray eyes should have been enough to cool down her burning flesh in an instant. "There's no one else to tend to you here and I would rather not move you tonight. If you prefer Romeo to me, I can call him. Only then he'll insist on missing his physiotherapy session and remain here with you. Your choice."

"That's not a choice at all," Monica whispered in a small voice, knowing that she was making it worse by stretching this out. For both of them.

"Lie down," he said in that firm voice, and her body automatically began to obey him. "It's nothing I've not seen before, Ms. D'Souza. And maybe this will teach you to not act so prideful when Mama offers you a present once in a while."

Halfway through her turn, Monica straightened and glared at him. "I can't accept monetary gifts from Flora any more than I can accept them from you."

"I've not offered you any," he said, something flickering in his gaze.

Monica wondered how she wasn't going up in smoke at all the embarrassment she was causing herself. "I know that. And I wasn't hinting that you should," she said, feeling more and more flustered by the second. "I'm just saying it would be the—"

"Please, continue…enlightening me about how your mind works."

"I know what you think of Romeo's friends who come to him for his clout and his wealth. I know what you think of your cousins who are forever asking you or Flora for handouts. I know how easily people fall in your esteem and how ruthlessly you cut them out of—"

"I did not realize you held my opinion in such esteem," he said, frowning. "*Dio mio*, why would I count you as one of those leeches if you accept a frivolous dress or a handbag from Mama? What's the big risk if you accept it?" His frown morphed into a thunderous scowl. "You're afraid I will take your job away? You should trust in—"

"What? Of course not. You would never do anything so unethical. I just…" She hesitated, feeling as if she was baring herself to him on more than one level. "Please, just forget it."

She was about to turn around when he arrested her once again. This time, his fingers spanned more of her flesh, her shoulder to be specific. Her bare shoulder.

Monica could feel the ridged abrasions of each of his

fingers like a divot on her flesh. As if the mere touch was stamping her *Property of Andrea Valentini.* And the worst thing was that she didn't even mind the feverish jumps her imagination was taking. What the hell was wrong with her?

Her attempt to stop jerking away made her do a weird convulsion on the bed, pulling her closer to his hard body. She wiped at her damp lip and wondered what she'd done wrong in this life to receive such torment. "You trust me in a professional setting, then?"

"Of course, I do. In a personal setting, too. Because you operate it with the same principles."

He pulled back as if he needed a wider view of her, and his mouth—why was she looking at his mouth constantly?—lost that annoyed set. "Then what is it you fear would happen if you accepted Mama's gifts? If say, you had let her buy you a nice wedding dress instead of this chemical-soaked death trap that has caused you so much pain? If you had let her meet Francesco a few times and make sure he was right for you?"

Monica blinked back a new spurt of tears. When he put it like that, when she thought this all could have been avoided, she truly felt pathetic. "I have gotten so used to all the time I spend with Flora and Romeo. I like having them in my life. I adore meeting her for dinner every Wednesday. I adore playing chess with Romeo and practicing Italian with him and just...being around him. I have never had such wonderful people who...cared about me in my life before. I don't want to do a single thing that would jeopardize that."

"And my second question?"

"I..." Monica met his gaze and then skittered away. Clearly, he wasn't going to let go until she admitted what a fool she'd been. "Francesco was desperate to meet Flora. And Romeo. And you. Especially after I confessed how sweet it was that Flora wanted to buy me jewelry for the wedding. Then there was that one time when you picked me up in the middle of our date and demanded that I find that communication with the Japanese company… He was elated that whole day. I think because he realized how much you valued my work."

In retrospect now, Monica could see that Francesco had proposed soon after that. He'd also been unbelievably annoyed until she agreed to bring him to the Valentini estate sometime to meet them all. "Something about his eagerness didn't…sit well with me."

"And yet you chose to bury that instinct?" Mr. Valentini sounded so angry that Monica felt herself shrink under his gaze. But enough was enough. She'd already let one man treat her like garbage.

She looked up, meeting that gray gaze straight on. "He is an orphan, like me. Wanting shiny things like a new car or nice clothes or wanting to use my connection to you to establish himself in his life is not wrong, Mr. Valentini. Not all of us are born into wealth *and* a loving family."

A curse escaped his mouth, the contempt in his eyes deepening. Monica swallowed at the intense reaction, fighting the need to fix it.

"So you think he was right to use you like he did?"

"Not if he loved me a little and thought it was an advantage we could use to build our future. Not when I've worked hard to build that reputation with you. Not when life is… hard and unfair. But he didn't love me at all and he thought I was a foolish girl with outdated ideas. He's made that clear."

His rough fingers lifting her chin sent Monica's pulse skittering across her body like an unearthed wire. If she'd expected to see tenderness in his eyes, she'd have been disappointed. "Whatever you do or don't do in the future, it would be impossible to separate Mama and Romeo from you, Ms. D'Souza. Even if I wished it. Neither of them will stand for it. Trust me in that, too, *si*?"

"Si," she said, trying to not drown in the warmth that promise drenched through her.

"Once your fever goes down, you're moving to the estate while you recover." He pressed a finger to her parted lips before she could protest. "Let Mama look after you. Spend more time with Romeo. He's always complaining that I work you too hard. *Si*?"

"Si."

"Mama thinks of you as her daughter and wants to spoil you, just a little. With me and Romeo, she does not have a chance to indulge that side of her. So next time, when she begs to buy you a little something, just for her own pleasure, let her, *si*?"

Monica licked her dry lips. If he asked her in that tone, she was afraid she'd agree to anything. *"Si."*

Something hot and feral sparked in his eyes and was shut down before she could even be sure she'd seen it.

Andrea Valentini was not attracted to her, no. Not at all. Never in a million years. He was too old and experienced and sophisticated and cynical and gorgeous and way too out of her silly, safe, secure sphere to *like her* like that. God, she couldn't even say it right in her own head.

This wasn't a relationship she would ever mess up by forcing her own stupid romantic ideals on it. Never. Her fever was clearly making her hallucinate.

"Now, lie down and let me finish this."

"Si," she said automatically and plopped, facedown, onto the bed.

There were two different fevers going on in her body, she thought with a near hysterical giggle trapped in her throat.

One was caused by the rash on her back, and the other made her nipples pinch deliciously against the cool sheets, her entire body thrumming in anticipation of his touch.

His sudden laughter exploded into the space between them, running down her spine like a warm, delicious trickle that was both comforting and arousing. Just the husky, deep sound of it did things to her belly and lower, more effectively than Francesco ever could have. She burrowed her cheek into the cool pillow, grateful that he couldn't see her face right now. The last thing she needed was for her expressive face to give away her…arousal.

"You are dangerous, Ms. D'Souza. A man could get used to hearing all those yeses from such a mouth."

Monica tried to stay stiff, even as his words filled her with a delicious ache.

No, he wasn't flirting with her. Not at all.

"Surprising that you think it might go to your head, Mr. Valentini," she said, fighting the urge to catch his gray gaze, "when you're unused to hearing anything but yes from the whole world."

"You're not as malleable and lacking in spine as you think you are," he said gruffly, after a beat of silence that crackled with tension. "I definitely do not remember you blindly agreeing to anything I proposed. In fact, your meteoric rise through the company to my side has to do with how well you stand up to me, even as you act like a scurrying mouse."

Monica blinked back the surge of grateful tears and wriggled against the sheets, feeling an ache between her thighs. "Mouse, huh? That's the nicest thing you've ever said to me." Feverish or not, those words of affirmation out of Mr. Valentini's mouth made pleasure skitter through her. "Maybe what I have is a praise kink and not this crazy attraction to him," she said into the pillow, not realizing she'd spoken aloud until it was too late.

Behind her, she could feel Andrea still.

God, please, don't let him have heard.

"I'm ready," she said loudly, desperate to get this over with.

She stayed stiff and unmoving when the cool, soothing gel landed on her back.

She somehow kept her breath steady as his fingers spread the cold gel over the rash, skating nearly to her buttocks and upward, his touch incredibly gentle, as if he was an experienced skier in full control of his path.

When his fingers moved up and around to spread the gel to her side boob and to the back of her neck, and when the bed shifted and groaned under her when he leaned forward to reach her other side, and when she felt his breath on her back and his scent filled her nostrils, Monica could do nothing about the dampness that bloomed between her thighs. Or the sudden, painfully alive ache that pulsed at her core.

So much for Francesco calling her prudish and unresponsive. His touch, his kisses, just hadn't done it for her, because he wasn't the one she really wanted.

Especially when she'd spent most of her life trying to downplay her body, dressing in frumpy clothes, wary of attracting the wrong kind of men. In the end, she'd started believing that she wasn't much of a sexual creature to begin with. At twenty-three, she'd never felt the need to try sex. Even with her fiancée, she hadn't been eager.

And yet, apparently, all her boss had to do was breathe in her direction and she was ready to go up in flames. It was knowledge she could have done without.

For the first time that miserable day, she cursed Francesco for putting her in this position, even though she was beginning to understand that he wasn't really to blame. For proposing to her. For making her buy this shitty dress. For making it all gray and confusing and yet...*deliciously right.* For putting her in a situation where she knew without a doubt that Mr. Valentini's touch made her shiver, always had, because she was unbelievably attracted to him.

She was attracted to her ruthless, grumpy boss, and if she so much as betrayed the fact, it didn't bode well for her future with his company, or with his family.

Andrea had never been in this place where desire thrummed through his veins in a sluggish beat, slowing down the world itself around him. The only time that came remotely close had been when he'd tried a cannabis brownie with Romeo because his brother's pain had been unbearable and he hadn't wanted to do it alone.

Never again, Andrea had promised himself when all it had done was intensify his feelings around the loss of his father.

Not even as a twenty-year-old who'd been deep in the throes of lust with Chiara and had been determined to win her at any cost, had he felt this delicious heaviness in his limbs.

Now, as he covered his assistant's bottom with a sheet and applied the goopy gel to her back, it felt like he was charting the dips and valleys of her smooth, golden-brown skin. As if he was compiling a database of how she reacted to what kind of touch.

Her soft groans of relief shouldn't tighten his own muscles so much that he wanted to send his fingers on further exploration of her unmarred skin, of the tight cinch of her waist, of the swell of her hips...until she knew his touch everywhere. And it wasn't just the physical hunger he felt for her.

It was an inexplicable, overwhelmingly possessive urge to fix all the wrongs that had been done to Ms. D'Souza, to give her everything she'd ever dreamed of in her life.

Cristo, the woman's back was red and angry and she was literally in pain, on top of the humiliation she'd endured today. And still, some invisible spark she'd set off banged against the outer shell Andrea had covered himself in over the years.

It was her vulnerability—as raw and visceral as the rash on her back. He found it…tasteless, and yet it clung to him, making him wish he could pull something over to cover them both from his sight.

Maybe because it reminded him of how he'd once felt. How the accident had left him raw and aching with loss and fear. He never wanted to be at the mercy of such fear again.

And truly, something had been cauterized in him with his father's death. He had gone from a wild, incessant partygoer who cared about nothing but soccer and women to a responsible businessman whose duty was to his family overnight. But something more had been lost, too.

And he didn't regret that loss just as he didn't regret the loss of that wild lifestyle. Only that his father had never had a chance to see how responsible and capable Andrea could be, that he had died terrified for Romeo and for his family.

Ms. D'Souza's face when she'd revealed how important his mother and brother were to her and how she never wanted to lose them…that kind of attachment would only set her up for pain and disappointment and loss. And yet, he had made the foolish promise that she would not lose them.

He jumped off the bed, wiping his hands on the end of a sheet. He needed to get out of here and figure a way out of Chiara's father's ridiculous ultimatum. He hated being manipulated like she and her father were doing. Didn't like being pushed into a corner.

And now there was this…headache, in the form of this innocent, naive creature lying down in front of him. With whom he spent more time than he did anyone else in a given week. The last thing he needed was this attraction messing up a perfect professional relationship. If it was simply lust, he wouldn't give a damn about it. But he had a feeling it wasn't.

It was…more. Even admitting that stuck in his craw, but he wasn't a man who thrived on delusions. He'd rather face the problem and fix it than drape himself in lies.

"When you come back, we'll find you a position with a different department. Maybe you can go back to the CFO. Maria has been bitterly vocal that I stole you from her."

Her silence told him he had hurt her. But Andrea couldn't afford to care. She needed toughening up to begin with and she had failed in not communicating to him that Chiara had acted like they were already married. Her usefulness had been defeated by this…inconvenient attraction, on his part, and her awe of him.

"It will be the same designation and pay," he added, wanting to clarify that he wasn't punishing her.

After tense moments of silence, she shifted a little on the bed, clutching onto the sheet as if it were a lifejacket, and hissed out a pained breath before she faced him.

Her eyelids were swollen, and the tip of her nose was flushed pink. Sweat made silky tendrils of hair stick to her forehead and she dug her teeth into her lower lip, making it glisten a dark pink.

But it was the expression in her eyes that caught him. There was so much there, too much that he didn't want to see. She released her lip and sighed. "That's for the best.

Although—" a small smile blossomed "—you might have to tone it down a bit if you want to keep an assistant. Not everyone is as…"

"Brave as you are?" He raised a brow.

"I was going to say *efficient*."

"So you're not upset about it," he said, wanting to poke and prod a little. *Dio mio*, why was he being so contrary?

She shrugged and the sheet slipped a bit to reveal the curve of a plump breast. Andrea had to look away, though he couldn't ignore the jolt of lust tightening through him. "You've never hidden how much you loathe the personal crossing over into the professional. Flora's…fondness for me would have put us at odds sooner or later. This way, at least I haven't…" She trailed off.

"Haven't what, Monica?" he said, insulted and injured, like a young cub trying to prove himself. Apparently, working for him had less hold for her than her attachment to his mother.

"Made a fool of myself."

"What do you…" His curiosity disappeared when his gaze landed on the scar that was the length of his hand span on her waist. The scar she'd acquired when she'd saved his mother.

Andrea felt as if he was suddenly drenched in a cold bucket of water. He could have lost his mother if not for this foolish, brave woman's rash actions. *Cristo*, she hadn't even been a woman but a mere girl of nineteen, jumping to a stranger's rescue. And in return, she'd gotten a blade to her belly, nearly cleaving her waist in two.

A rush of shame swamped him. How had he not made it a point to learn how badly she had been hurt? How had he just shrugged off her injury as if it was a minor inconvenience, a small price to pay for his mother's safety? How had he thought her unwillingness to accept cash in return an irritability?

"Turn to the side," he said, unable to even modulate his tone toward a request.

"What? Is it the sheets? I will wash them and make sure—"

"Forget about the damned sheets. Turn to the side, Monica," he repeated, his strides eating up the distance to the bed.

Slowly, looking like a frightened rabbit, tugging the sheet higher between her breasts, she followed his command.

He couldn't help it, even if he tried. And he didn't try that hard to stop himself.

He rubbed a finger over the scar that inched from front to back on her right side, at the tight, tiny juncture of her waist, as wide as the span of three of his fingers together and reaching back.

The gash must have been deep to leave such a scar, despite the fact that Mama had had her transferred to the best doctors immediately. All he had cared about was that his mother was unharmed.

"I didn't realize you were hurt this badly," he said, in a thin voice that shivered with anger and fear that felt as fresh as it had when he'd first learned of the mugging incident. And yet, the source was different. The source of those thorny emotions was new.

"I don't even remember that it's there anymore," she replied in a muffled voice, and he realized the painkillers had finally kicked in. "Sometimes, though, when I leave work after dark, and you know that street behind the bus depot, I get a flash of like…fear. And you know the weirdest thing? The scar burns then. I know it sounds ridiculous because as you can see, it's all healed but—"

"Just because the burn is not real doesn't mean you don't feel it."

She sighed, her body trembling and then settling. "Francesco said I was being a scaredy-cat."

"Do me a favor, Ms. D' Souza. Stop telling me about all the foolish, idiotic things that man led you to believe."

"I think that's a fair ask," she said.

"If you would like, I'll take you to see a specialist. We can get rid of the scar," he said, running his finger again over the thick pink-white scar tissue. "It mars your beauty."

She laughed into the pillow, the sound half-muffled and half-airy, as if she couldn't get enough breath into her lungs. "My so-called beauty has never done me any favors. And honestly, I don't care about the scar. I'm only glad Flora remained unhurt that awful day."

Andrea ran his hand one last time over the scar, knowing that he was crossing a line she and he had both clearly demarcated between them. But the damned thing was that he wanted to touch the scar again. He wanted to press his mouth to it, lick it, take away whatever phantom pain it had left behind and make it mean something else for her. Make it a source of pleasure.

He wanted to lie down beside her and turn her to face him, until her breathtaking features lit upon him. Until she bared herself to him willingly, until she stretched into his touch. Until she begged him to explore this…prickly heat between them. Until she of the generous smiles and the gushing compliments and brave little heart was all his to do with as he wanted.

Oh, how he would play with her and tease her and taunt her until that shyness faded and she came to him, ready and brave, willing putty in his hands.

He jumped off the bed as though he was the one scalded, as though it was his back that was on fire.

Cristo, she was twenty-three and naive and not for him. *In any way.* Not even for a single night, he told himself, crushing the wicked whisper of desire.

"Andrea?" she whispered when he was almost at the door.

He turned to find her watching him, a sudden alertness to her drowsy gaze. *"Si?"*

"Can I ask you something?"

"Si."

"Are you angry with me?"

"Yes," he said, letting his irritation flare. "You know how much I don't like unnecessary headaches in my life. I know way too much about you that I didn't need to."

"I won't fight the transfer but you…you won't let this change—"

"*Si*, Monica. Now, sleep."

She giggled then and it made him still. When he looked back, *one more time*, her eyes were closed, the thick, long lashes casting crescents onto her cheeks in the shadows as he closed the automatic blinds. Her nostrils flared, and a small secretive little smile split her mouth. "You also said yes three times. A girl could get used to that. A girl could feel heady with the power of hearing so many yeses from *Andrea Valentini.* Any girl. Even silly, stupid, pathetic me."

Then she snored and drifted off to sleep and Andrea knew he had to stay away from her. Completely.

Before the little good sense that was left in him was consumed by raw want. Before he gave in and did something his father would have been appalled by. Before this inappropriate lust for a woman under his protection turned into something more dangerous that would only end in hurting her.

CHAPTER FOUR

IN THE FIRST two weeks that Monica was at Flora Valentini's house—their family home in a postcard-like village near Lake Como—Andrea hadn't come to see her once.

No, not to see her, but to visit with his mother, Monica modified in her head. The fact that in two weeks, Andrea hadn't visited Flora and Romeo once *was* kind of alarming.

If there was one thing she knew about him for sure, it was that he was devoted to his mother and brother.

Was it because she was here? Because after all the drama she'd inadvertently started, he couldn't stand to see her pathetic face?

Monica had resisted the idea of staying at his home—his high-handed order—for the first two days. But under Flora's gentle care and with Romeo's cheerful company, she had decided not to fight one of the few favors life had handed her. It wasn't like she caused an imposition to either of them.

Flora was exactly the kind of mother she'd have chosen in any universe, if she was given the chance. And learning that the older woman thought of her as a daughter was a gift Andrea had given her. The one gift she didn't resent, when she was already buried under obligation for all the favors he'd done her.

Monica had cried a lot the first two weeks. Some of it

had been tears of pain and relief because the doctor had told her that Andrea's immediate intervention and having seen her the very day she had collapsed had staved off infection and scarring. Some of her tears had been for this new consuming awareness of a man who was so out of her sphere. To think she'd nearly married a man she didn't even love just to escape the pain of being thrown out of his life…

But she also reminded herself that, if not for Flora, Mr. Valentini would have no interest in her personal life. He wouldn't have noticed if she had dropped dead that day at those steps. Until she was absent from his life and it fell apart without her brisk efficiency, Andrea Valentini wouldn't have taken note of her absence any more than he'd taken note of her presence over four years.

So yes, while she'd recovered and screwed her head on straight under Flora's gentle care, she wasn't going to read anything into the sudden flare of heat that had arced between them that afternoon. Any woman would feel discombobulated when seeing a man like him—gorgeous and smoldering—attend to her personally. And she had already been under such shock and in pain, had been vulnerable and desperate for a small kindness.

The little hope she'd nurtured the beginning of the third week that she could slowly transition out of his life and into her new role with the CFO was blown to bits when Romeo shared the little clip of her and Andrea that had gone viral. Of him cutting through the dress and then carrying her to his car, while she was half-naked and delirious and the accompanying narrative the press had spun around it. If he'd thought her a nuisance before, he probably actively hated her now. When she'd called Mr. Valentini yesterday, she'd been unable to reach him.

Then he arrived suddenly the next evening, like the storm

clouds that had suddenly gathered, threatening a downpour. Romeo and she had just finished an invigorating chess game that she had lost, yet again, sitting in the small garden that separated the manicured lawns from the thick orange groves and dense woods beyond.

A prickling at her nape was the thing that intimated Monica of her boss's arrival, as if there was now a chip sewn under her skin, programmed to detect his proximity. She looked up to find him standing on a wide balcony off the second floor, kissing Flora's cheek while the older woman animatedly greeted him. His gray gaze was, however, intensely focused on Monica.

Even across the field separating them, she could see the pinch of his eyebrows because he didn't want his mother to know of his thunderous mood. Unable to hold his gaze any longer, Monica swallowed and looked away. Butterflies took flight in her belly, making it impossible to sit still. Her muscles called for action, either to run toward him or far away, into the woods maybe.

"What was that?" Romeo asked from across the small table, his gaze switching between her and his brother.

"What was what?" Monica asked, trying a fake casualness with all her might.

"That look in your eyes. Monica, are you scared of my brother?" he asked, reaching for her hand across the table.

"What? No," she said, warmth cresting her cheeks. At Romeo's unconvinced expression, she sighed. "Maybe a little, yes. Especially after this…episode I've caused."

She pulled his hand forward and draped it across her cheek. All her life, she'd been starved for touch. And Romeo was one of those very few men on the planet, in her limited experience of them, who seemed to need it as much as she did, without thinking it somehow decreased his masculinity. When he cupped her cheek, she pressed herself into it. "I'm a coward."

He *tsked* and she looked up. His gray eyes—so much like Andrea's, except tempered with natural kindness and constant pain—gleamed with warmth. "You're the bravest person I know."

She scoffed. "Is it open season on me, then?"

"Or maybe the wisest?" He scrunched his nose. "Very few people on this planet understand my brother's moods."

"Yes, that," she said, jumping on the lifeline he offered. "I know An— *Mr. Valentini's* moods better than anyone. Right now, you might imagine he's simply listening to your mother talk a mile a minute at him, but he's in a foul mood. And obviously, it's to do with me."

Romeo looked at his brother and then back at her. "Perhaps, but not in the way you imagine, *cara.*"

"You're just having fun at my expense, you scoundrel."

He picked up her hand and kissed the back of it, a sudden unholy glint to his gaze. "You never told me what happened that day, after he brought you home. The fact that my sainted brother hasn't visited in three weeks to check on Mama and me is…shocking. Something must have happened to keep him away so thoroughly."

Monica shrugged, her mouth suddenly dry, her heart palpitating at a dangerous rate. By the time he'd left, she'd been out of it. Had he made the decision to transfer her because she had said something she shouldn't have? Had she betrayed her stupid attraction? "He took care of my back, told me what a nuisance he considered me, declared he was transferring me to another department and left."

"And yet, you have been helping smooth over things these last two weeks, *si*?"

"Just some knowledge transfer," she said dismissively.

But at least, in this, she could feel pride in a job done well. While she had left behind systems to deal with everything he worked on, no other person could come close to understanding him.

"Oh, come, don't downplay your virtues, *bella*. I bet Andrea can't do without you. And that dark scowl he's wearing is because he has realized that, too. If there's one thing I know about my brother, it's that he hates needing anyone."

Her gaze finding Andrea unerringly, Monica mulled over Romeo's insight into her boss. "What about Mrs. Rossi, then?" she asked, before she could curb her tongue. The question had been burning a hole through her for three weeks. Every morning, noon and evening, she expected to see the sophisticated woman walk in and declare that she was Andrea's fiancée and throw her out. Or at least express her satisfaction that he had already moved Monica to a different department. Even though he'd told her the engagement wasn't happening.

She had literally stood in front of a mirror every night and practiced the facial expression she'd put on when she congratulated the happy couple. She was determined not to betray her own tangled thoughts on the matter, nor the belated feelings of righteous resentment that Chiara Rossi had no right to talk to her like she had.

"*Even you* can't believe that Andrea marrying Chiara would have anything to do with needing her. My brother is incapable of the particular emotion you walk around looking for."

"Now you're beginning to sound like him," Monica said, hearing the unspoken ache in Romeo's voice.

She reached for his hand again, her heart aching for this man who had become such a good friend to her in the past four years while his brother had remained a fascinating mystery. And he needed to remain one. While the transfer had hurt, Monica realized now that it was a blessing in disguise. She needed to stay away from Mr. Valentini, far away.

Turning, she focused on her friend. "Now, how about we leave Mr. Valentini to his brooding and you tell me about that waitress who begged for your number at that restaurant last week?"

"What will you do? Andrea?"

Andrea had to tear his gaze away from the scene being enacted out in the garden, no doubt on purpose, by Romeo. A part of him was delighted that in Monica's company, Romeo was rediscovering the fun-loving, outgoing, stunt-per-day rascal that he had been as a teen before the accident had bound him to the wheelchair. Papa had been driving in a dangerous snowstorm, while Andrea had been screaming at him like a thwarted toddler, leading to the accident that had stolen him from them.

Another part of him, the part that he'd unsuccessfully been trying to beat into submission, roared like some low-cognitive-capacity Neanderthal watching his woman being chummy with another man.

His woman... Madre de Dio, where was this uncivilized possessive streak coming from?

Maybe because he hadn't spent a single day since the accident doing one thing for himself, he told himself now, searching for some rational explanation. Those first few years, he'd simply functioned on autopilot, running himself ragged between stopping a hostile takeover and getting Romeo everything he needed, and relieving Mama whenever he could at his brother's side so she could rest and grieve losing the man she had loved.

After that, after they'd learned to live with the gaping hole his father had left behind, after Romeo had made peace with the fact that he might never walk again, Andrea had still continued in the same way.

Even now, as he watched, Romeo pulled Monica into his lap and hummed some melody that Andrea could just barely hear. With one arm thrown around his neck, one clasped in Romeo's, Monica was laughing.

He could hear that inelegant snort that came at the end of her laugh, see the way her whole body shook, and he could just imagine how she would smell of sun and vanilla, a strange, erotic scent he associated with her now.

With his other hand, Romeo was wheeling the chair forward and backward, moving their clasped hands. When Monica bent down to kiss his cheek, her long dark hair fell forward like a curtain, covering them both in whisper-thin darkness. As if to taunt him.

"Andrea? What will you do about—"

"Is he more than fond of her? Romeo?" he asked, suddenly remembering the frantic call Romeo had made, right after Mama had, demanding that Andrea do something about Francesco and the sudden wedding.

Andrea had known they were both fond of her, but this possibility… A sick feeling twisted in his stomach. If his brother really *liked* Monica, when Andrea had just discovered such deep… It didn't bear thinking. Out of the miasma of confusion, a selfish, primal, competitive want roared.

"Of Monica?" Mama said, an instant smile teasing her mouth. "Wouldn't it be wonderful if he were? She is such a lovely girl, Andrea, and she does make him laugh like before…the accident and that business with that girl." His mother pursed her mouth and sighed. "I know Monica might be open to trying something but I also know it is not fair to her. His heart and mind are not yet in a good place."

Andrea grunted. Everyone she came across, at work or in personal life, whether it lasted a day or a week or a moment, Monica seemed to win them over. He found it both infuriating and fascinating. "She just got dumped at city hall at the last minute, Mama. How are you so confident that she would welcome Romeo's advances—" he had to inhale with a conscious effort "—whatever they might be?"

"All Monica wants is family and security and to belong somewhere, and she fits so well already into our family and we all like her, even you, and..."

Whatever she saw in his face, her words trailed off.

Andrea turned just in time to see her gaze widen, her mouth fall open with a soft gasp. As if she'd just seen a tiger setting its target on a doe.

Cristo, he was a thirty-four-year-old man. The last thing he needed was his mother to know he lusted after his very capable, very young, assistant and that it had him thrashing around like a randy teenager. Or that he wanted to act on it, forgetting all his own personal ethics. "Mama, do not—"

"She's too...young, Andrea. And so pure at heart," she finally said, a thread of outrage in her tone.

He laughed and pulled her close, loving her a little more for being so protective of the stranger in their midst. Though he wasn't at all surprised. The Valentini name had always stood for ethics and sound business morals, and his father had made loyalty the highest badge of honor. His mother's warning only reminded him of his father and all the values he had tried to instill in him and Romeo, beginning with the fact that power and privilege shackled a man as much as they liberated him.

"And now this...media scandal about that video..." his

mother said, bringing him back to the present. "I demand to know what your plan is."

"I have no plan, Mama. This has already blown up beyond my control."

"So marry Chiara, bring Monica back to work for you and all this…speculation is over. You wanted a future with her once, Andrea." She turned completely and studied him. Her voice softened as she cradled his cheek. Andrea marveled at how little she did that with him these days. All her softness and her maternal instincts were limited to Romeo. *And Monica*, he thought, without an ounce of rancor. "Chiara is sophisticated and smart and she will make you a good wife."

"I am not the same man I was ten years ago."

"Then it is good that she has matured, too, no?"

"It doesn't look like that, given she's letting her father trot her out like some show horse, attached to this merger. If there's one thing I know, it is that Chiara wants power and prestige more than anything. I have nothing against her wishes for her life. But I will not play her games."

His mother looked alarmed, as if she couldn't imagine so much scheming. The simple soul she was, he wasn't surprised. Still, she persisted, taking his hand in hers. "Is it simply wounded pride that she picked a different man over you a decade ago that drives you to say no now?"

"Pride has nothing to do with it. And believe me, I'm grateful that she didn't accept my proposal then. Because now, I'm not that young, prideful buck who needed to prove himself by gaining the biggest prize around. Now, she or marriage…have very little appeal to me."

It was both relieving and sad that his mother did not push him harder toward matrimony or hold the Valentini legacy over his head like some hanging sword. Maybe because she knew where his opposition came from. She had once known the real thing and the loss of it had nearly shattered them all. Once you were witness to something as holy and real as his parents' marriage had been, it felt like blasphemy to enter one that was nothing but a mocking illusion of it. Neither did he think he was made for the real thing, even if it was available to him.

He had lived through enough pain such love wrought on one.

"She and her father are playing a dirty game, threatening to pull back from the merger at this critical point when so many livelihoods depend on its success. They need to learn that I will not bow."

"So you will use Monica?"

"Use her? She's not a doll, Mama, to arrange wherever you or I please. This situation was not of my making and if I twist it to my own advantage, it will be because there is no other choice left. I have my reputation and Valentini's to protect."

Before his mother could further lecture him, Andrea turned around toward the stairs. He had tried to stay away. He'd already had her moved to a different department, though that had only seemed to blow up in his face because Monica was the linchpin for so many matters that came through to him.

But the video circulating on the internet and the story that the media had already woven around it besmirched the Valentini name. The very name his father had given a new meaning to. Andrea could not let it continue. So he would take care of two birds with one shot.

CHAPTER FIVE

One look. One exchange between him and Romeo in which Andrea tried to keep his expression vacant—not completely successfully—was enough to know his brother's heart. Conversely, Andrea had no doubt that Romeo now knew what was in his heart, too. Or to be precise, what was swimming like lazy wine in his blood a lot farther south of his heart.

"I was just asking Monica if she is the reason you have neglected us for three weeks," Romeo said, grinning. "Quite the precedent you're setting, Andrea."

Standing by his brother, her gaze landing on and quickly skidding away from Andrea's face, Monica looked like she wanted to run.

"I could be a gentleman like you," Andrea said, unable to stop himself from ruffling Romeo's hair, "and lie, but I'm not. Monica is indeed the reason I couldn't visit. There's a media scandal in the making with her in the middle of it and I have been trying my best to thwart it before it muddies the Valentini name beyond repair."

Monica stiffened and finally, finally, met his gaze. "I called you several times since I found out two days ago, Mr. Valentini. You didn't pick up."

Andrea felt that same lazy thrum again. His gaze traversed her length, greedy, and all-consuming.

In four years, he had never seen her dressed so casually. In denim shorts that showed off her legs that went on forever and a tiny, tight V-neck crop top that bared her shoulders and a strip of her midriff, she looked like the gelato he used to be eager for on a hot summer day. Her hair was tied in a high ponytail, highlighting the angular gauntness of her features.

"I know it looks bad but—"

He finally responded to her. "It's not just that someone recorded the entirety of me undressing you and carrying you to my car or that the short clip has been edited with salacious commentary. Today, some investigative reporter decided to inquire after your well-being at Valentini headquarters and she was told that you'd not only been sent off somewhere no one knew by me, but she's now also saying that I abused my power and then when I got bored, fired you."

Monica pressed her fingers to her mouth. "That's… awful."

"The best version is where they speculate that we've been sleeping with each other for a while and that day, I came to sweep you off your feet at the city hall and that you're now a very satisfied but secretive bride. There are memes being made about me."

"This is my fault," Monica said, rubbing her temple.

"I'm not arguing that point," Andrea said dryly, more than irritated by how she leaned automatically toward Romeo, when he was the one who had actually come to her rescue.

"Andrea!" Romeo said, a quick flash of anger in his eyes. "You can't blame Monica for this. She was unwell. Where was *your* head?"

"No, Romeo. He's right." She moved toward Andrea like

a doe walking into the lion's den, shoulders painfully rigid. "I'll do whatever you need to fix it."

Andrea extended his arm, and she licked her lips, considering it as if it were a snake. "Come. I have a plan in mind."

"Why can't we discuss it here?"

"There is the very real danger of my own family coming after me with pitchforks, if I put one step wrong with you, Ms. D'Souza. I did not think you so much of a coward that you would hide behind them."

"I'm not hiding behind anyone," she said, rushing around Romeo, cheeks red, ponytail flying around, gloriously indignant. "You ordered that I stay here, transferred me to a different department and…don't even answer my calls. You decided I was a headache, a pathetic loser, and shuffled me off."

Andrea stilled, watching the finger she poked into his chest. Hurt and something more flashed in her beautiful eyes. "And if I admit that I had more reasons than your so-called flaws—all your words, by the way—to have you transferred?"

"Did you?"

"Si."

"Oh," she said, color rising to her cheeks. "But you think I can help fix this…mess?"

"Si."

"Fine. Tell me what I need to do."

A surge of desire wrapped its fingers around Andrea's muscles. "Go wait for me in my suite. I need a moment with my brother."

She nodded, squeezed Romeo's hand one more time and then left.

"Do you know that Mama wishes you were together?" he said to his brother, once Monica was out of earshot.

Romeo's face tightened. "Mama has many wishes, Andrea. Pity we can't make them all true, *sì*?"

Feeling as powerless as he did years ago, Andrea shook his head. "Romeo—"

"You're not stealing my chance with her."

"She makes you laugh, like before," Andrea said, repeating his mother's words, knowing the precious truth of them.

"She does. She has reminded me of all the things I'm still capable of. She's been a wonderful friend to have in my life. But neither of us is drawn to the other in that way. In the way you're drawn to her."

"That's not what I want to discuss."

"And yet you interfere in *my* life? Keep track of all the waitresses I hook up with? I'm not some fragile princess whose virginity you've been tasked to protect, Andrea."

Andrea's cheeks crested with guilty heat while his heart jumped with joy that his brother had...*scored*, as tasteless as that sounded. It meant Romeo's heart was also healing.

"While I appreciate the grand sacrifice you were about to make on my behalf," Romeo said dryly, "it is unnecessary."

"Don't be so sure that I would *make the sacrifice*," Andrea said, still feeling the pinch of acute selfishness. "I simply would have said may the best man win."

A flicker of shock passed through his brother's eyes before he scoffed. "Just what Monica would like, no? You and me fighting over her like she was a bone." Then his gaze searched Andrea's, as if it had only now dawned on him what his brother had unwittingly betrayed. "You're thinking at less than your usual capacity if you think Monica will be easy to bend to your...strategies. Mama, like the world, only sees part of her."

"*Cristo*, my own family thinks I'm some kind of...twisted monster, getting ready to prey on the innocent lamb."

Romeo laughed, grooves forming around his mouth. "I understand the bind you're in, even if Mama doesn't. I know you need to take aggressive action. Against the scandal and against Brunetti."

"And?"

"I know the tack you're going to take. Probably the only one available to you. And I know where it will lead."

"Romeo—"

"I have seen the way you looked at her just now, Andrea, when she was laughing in my lap. I will even admit that I once felt what you feel—the selfish want that takes you out at your knees, when you as a Valentini man should be the one in control. The one to whom everything should bend and bow."

"And you're going to warn me off?"

"*Cristo*, no. Mama does you a grave injustice by behaving as if I was the only one who lost something in that accident. Why would I warn my brother against something he desperately wants, something that makes him look like he's gloriously alive for the first time in a decade?"

Andrea thrust a hand through his hair, shaken by his brother's depth of perception. Shaken by how his deepest desire sounded so…stark and all-consuming when put into simple words.

"What of your little friend?"

"My *little friend* has more courage in her pinky finger than the rest of the world. You know the biggest gift she's given me in the last four years, Andrea? She showed me what a glorious, wild, wonderful world is out there and how much I still crave to experience it. She just needs to come to that realization, too. And if something does happen to her once she sets her tremendous will to it—" Romeo's gaze, so much like their father's, pinned Andrea to the spot "—

then she has me on her side. But I cannot bubble wrap her, just like you can't do to me."

Andrea bent and kissed his brother's rough cheek, feeling a wellspring of gratitude for the woman who had shown his brother who he could be with the simple, expansive, unconditional gift of her friendship.

"You got all the wisdom from Papa. All I got were his good looks," he said, blinking away the tears that rose to his eyes.

Romeo thumped him on his shoulder, his serrated laughter music to Andrea's ears, and wheeled himself along the path back to the house by Andrea's side. "You're not alone in this either, Andrea. If this merger falls through, I mean."

Andrea nodded, feeling like his world might finally be settling into a new place after being shattered a decade ago. It would never be the same without Papa, but it wasn't as horrible as he had let it get over the past few years.

It was like entering a treasure vault, if the treasure was the inside of Andrea Valentini's intensely private mind and life. With each step she'd taken up the stairs, Monica felt as if she was embarking on some momentous journey that she could not turn back from.

The odd day or two she'd stayed here in the past, and even the past three weeks, she'd always stayed in the guest suite, close to Flora's own. She'd never even been up here.

His suite on the first floor was a paradise made for solitude, different from his steel-and-chrome office. Here it was all glass and wood, with minimum decor, while sunlight poured in, bathing everything in a warm, golden glow. And yet, the space was also innately masculine, sober and serious like the man himself.

One entire wall was taken up with bookshelves, which

on further scrutiny revealed to be on racing cars and other extreme sports as well as some business tomes. There were even a few glittering trophies, but Monica's attention was quickly commandeered by the other wall.

By a large portrait of Andrea and Romeo and their father, Giovanni. His arms around his sons' shoulders, Giovanni was clearly full of pride and joy. Tall and distinguished, he had been a handsome man, like his sons, but the thing that radiated from him was an easy kindness that Monica had found in few people in her life. Even with him gone for so many years—in the same accident that had hurt Romeo's legs, Flora had told her—she could sense the older man's legacy in his sons and in the company ethics Andrea so staunchly upheld. To have known such love as they did... That sweet ache for something she'd never known came back to her chest.

Monica lingered in the cool foyer until Andrea swept past her to the massive desk in the adjoining study. For a moment, she wondered if he'd forgotten that he'd invited her up here. Then, his gaze was potent on her back, like a physical caress.

"You were supposed to recover here. Not lose weight."

The chastisement was the last thing she'd expected. She wrapped her arms around her belly self-consciously, her skin feeling far too tight to hold the sensations quivering through her. If she'd known he would be visiting, she'd have covered herself up from head to toe. "I'm sorry my body doesn't perform automatically to your wishes and desires," she said, shocked at her own daring.

His laughter at her back felt like a reward. "Your spirit seems to have more than recovered." The tiny hairs at the nape of her neck prickled with awareness as his gaze moved over her back, mostly left bare by threads of fabric holding the crop top together. Going without a bra suddenly seemed liked the worst idea she'd ever had.

"No pain anymore?"

"None at all."

"I'm glad."

He was not a man to make pageantry of anything, and yet this felt like that. As if something big was looming on the horizon, something she hadn't foreseen in her wildest dreams. Or nightmares.

She needed to take control of this conversation as much as she needed to take control of her life. Turning around, she blurted the first thing that came to her lips. "If you're going to fire me to do damage control, Mr. Valentini, I'd rather—"

"Mr. Valentini? And, *Cristo*, I'm not firing you. Where is that faith of yours?" His gray gaze flashed with a thread of...hurt?

No, she was seeing things again, apparently a condition she suffered when it came to only him. "Of course, I have faith in you. But I realize how bad this is."

"So the solution is to get rid of the one person who's innocent and powerless in all this?"

She jerked her chin up, a defense mechanism, hating that that was how he saw her. Though it wasn't far from the hard truth, like the dog with the broken leg Romeo had nursed to health a year ago. "No, it isn't. But I also know that you wouldn't just cast me out on the streets or hide me away like some taint upon your name. I was just thinking of the company and your reputation. I...misspoke out of fear and urgency."

"Monica... Whatever else the future holds...with the company, with this scandal, with us, I need you to understand that I would never abuse my power in any way."

"I know that, Andrea," she said, letting him hear the conviction she held deep in her bones. His name on her lips, this time when she wasn't delirious with pain, landed between them like an invocation. To what, she had no idea. But she didn't scuttle her gaze away from his.

It was the one truth she'd always known, even if she hadn't understood anything else about her reaction to him. But uncertainty about the current problem was another beast. She addressed the thing that was bothering her, trying her best not to look like a startled hare. "Why are we having this discussion in your suite?"

He sighed. "It's the only place Mama won't try to send some staff member to spy on us. And I need a shower before I can deal with the—"

"—mess I created," she automatically finished for him, wondering why Flora would involve herself in this when she usually stayed outside of Valentini company concerns.

"That was unfortunate phrasing on my part," he said, rubbing a hand over his temple. Was that regret that laced his words? That would have been strange enough to capture her focus, but something else stole and held her attention.

He leaned against the massive desk, stretching his long legs out in front of him. Custom-stitched Italian trousers pulled tight, displaying the hard lengths of his thighs. With that economy that imbued his every action, he undid the cuffs of his white dress shirt and slowly rolled each one back. The sight of his corded forearms, liberally sprinkled with hair, made Monica compulsively run her fingers over her own smooth forearms. Then his fingers went to his shirt and he unbuttoned a couple. Her pulse sped up, in direct proportion to each strip of olive-toned flesh that came into view.

His gaze snapped to hers and something else snapped

into place between them. "It's not like you forced me to strip you in the middle of the piazza," he said, easily cutting through the growing tension. "Or made me carry you or begged to be transferred to a different department. I didn't handle that whole day well."

"Can I ask why?"

"Why what?"

"Why are you so…angry with me?"

"I'm not angry with you."

"You seem it. It's fair in a way, because I've brought your professional reputation into question. But it feels somehow…personal."

One hand thrusting through his hair, he stilled at her question. And while he only continued to stare at her thoughtfully, Monica realized his silence was assent.

It *was* personal. And then it came to her. "Is Mrs. Rossi upset by all this talk about our supposed affair?" How could she doubt a man like Andrea? "I'll talk to her and explain it all. Make it clear that there was never anything other than work between us. That all you've done is show me kindness, that you pitied me, that Flora forced you to—"

"Basta!" he said, looking even more disgruntled than before. "You're not some charity case. As to why I reacted badly, that's neither here nor there. Believe me, if Chiara was to be my fiancée, she would not doubt me."

"So she's not going to be your fiancée?"

"I have no interest in her, or in her father's deal when it comes with such strings. Especially when it's nothing but manipulation."

"You were never interested in marrying her?"

A soft, swift smile broke his serious expression, stealing Monica's breath. She flushed, reacting to that knowing glint in his eyes. Though she had no idea what the knowing was of. And then the other, bigger truth slammed into her.

"So all the hard work we put in for the merger is going to waste? All those jobs, that new manufacturing plant in Vienna..."

"Brunetti has always put his business before personal life and family. It was the reason Papa never liked him. But that could be to our advantage right now. Chiara has always been a spoiled child and if she had told him that she and I were a sure thing, he would have attached her as an addendum clause, happy about the extra level of connection it would bring us. He would think nothing of abandoning her now, when he realizes I have no interest or intention of taking her on. Except it's become a..."

"A matter of pride that you have said no to his daughter. He wants the merger to go through but wants to save face as well," Monica finished his thought process.

"Exactly!"

She frowned. "I don't understand Mrs. Rossi's thinking. Why risk losing you by playing all these games? Why not be straightforward with you about her affections?"

He chuckled, though not quite to mock her. "You and Mama are peas in a pod."

Monica had no idea what he meant but she knew what she had to do. "I'll make a statement to the press immediately that the whole incident has been twisted and that I've been simply recovering at your mother's—"

"I thought you were terrified of talking to the press?"

"I am, but your reputation is not something I take lightly. I..."

"I have a different solution. One that would address *both* problems."

And here was the thing he'd clearly been reluctant to

bring up, even as he'd made up his mind. Monica braced herself for anything, even though her heart ached at the thought of being sent away from Flora or Romeo or even… him.

Three weeks ago, as distressing as it had been, her transfer to a different department had felt necessary. To keep at bay all the feelings she'd discovered in her near delirious state.

But now, hearing this confirmation that Andrea had no interest in Mrs. Rossi, knowing that he cared about *her*, albeit in his own autocratic way, she didn't want to go away. She didn't want to stop working for him, or being near him. Which was really the pinnacle of the kind of foolish, clingy attachment she couldn't afford in a million years.

It wasn't as if anything could happen between them. So what was she doing feeling like this? Was she simply attaching herself to him because he was the most stable, genuine man she'd known in a long while? Why didn't she feel like this with Romeo, who was not only more handsome but also warm and open and approachable?

Something about him consumed her, as if finally, she had tuned in to the right frequency of her own heart and body. "What's the solution?"

"We will pretend that the story the tabloid press made up is true. That we've been in a relationship for months and that day, we had planned to elope to city hall but realized that Mama would be heartbroken at not being able to throw us a wedding. At the last minute, it became necessary to cancel it anyway because you were sick and had to be hospitalized. In two days, we'll arrive at a charity gala together. That will be enough of an announcement that we are together."

Try as she might, Monica couldn't muster up a response.

Shock enveloped her so fully that all she could do was freeze and stare and…

Pretend they were together, that they'd been in a relationship for months. Go to a party with him. Pretend like she had the right to touch him, and kiss him, and want him...

Suddenly, she felt feverish all over again.

CHAPTER SIX

ANDREA'S HANDS CAME over her shoulders when she swayed. He smelled like pine and cloves and the deepest, darkest want she hadn't admitted to herself. His fingers on her flesh reminded her of the ache between her thighs when he'd touched her scar. Two more steps and her nipples would brush against his chest, and it was such an overload of sensory pleasure that she felt dizzy. The back of his hand came against her forehead. "Do you feel faint again?"

The pang of concern in his tone dissipated the shivers. God, she was acting like some Victorian virgin given to swoons at the slightest touch of a man. She needed distance, needed to fight the haze of desire he enveloped her in with his mere presence. Slowly, she edged back from his touch. "No, I'm fine. I just…"

"Ah…is the very idea of being affianced to me that frightening?"

"Of course not," she said, raising her gaze to him. "Are you sure you want to do this?"

"As sure as I can be."

"And it has to be an engagement? Not just…a fling." Just saying it made a lick of heat flash through her.

"If it's a fling, that just proves the media's point, no? That I used you when you were under my power and then discarded you? An engagement also gives me armor against

Chiara's mind games. Her father can come back to the table to discuss the merger without thinking that I rejected his daughter."

"Because you were already serious about me! And everything Flora said that day at the dinner to Mrs. Rossi adds up to it," she said, nodding. Then she blew out a breath that seemed to settle right between her throat and chest. "But what about Francesco?" Just saying his name made shame sit on her chest like a boulder. "He won't keep quiet when he hears this version. While he's not evil or anything, he'll try to twist this into some kind of gain for him and—"

"I will deal with him."

She raised a surprised gaze to him. "You will?"

"I'm Andrea Valentini. I have *some* resources available to me."

"As if anyone can forget who you are," she said, warmed by his attempt at humor.

Silence grew between them, gathering every twitch of her hands, every hitch of her breath, saying more than she wanted to say, betraying her.

"I know it puts you in an awkward position and I will understand if you refuse," he said, turning back toward his desk. When she didn't say anything, he gave a hard nod. "We will begin with the statement you can make to the press tomorrow and—"

"No, I…want to help sort this out. I want to pay you back in some small way for all the kindness you have shown me for four years."

He whirled around, every lean, hard inch of him radiating anger. "You will make a monster of me, just as the media says?"

"What? No. Why is it wrong to want to return—"

"Because if it was a kindness, then you insult Mama

and Romeo and me by constantly talking about wanting to pay it back and—"

"No, that's now how I meant it. I had nothing and no one when I arrived here that summer on a whim. Now I have so much and I just want to contribute—"

"If that's why you want to do it, then let's stop now. If I had taken your overinflated sense of obligation into account, I'd have never considered it. Do you count us obligated to you since you nearly died to save Mama? What is the price for that?"

Frustration made Monica groan. Why was she botching this so badly, alienating him with her words? "I'm sorry for how I said it. I meant that if there's anything I can do to…help you out of this tricky situation, part of which I'm responsible for, I'm more than willing. I just can't help but wonder if you've thought this through."

"Three weeks with Romeo has shown you your claws, huh, *bella*?" His gray gaze swept over her face, as if he was seeing her anew. And yet, instead of irritation, admiration glinted there. "You never would have asked me that before."

"Yes, well. Humiliating life experiences have one upside to them. You're forced to think what's the worst that can happen and then come up with *Been there, went through that.*"

"This new boldness suits you," he said, and a thrill shot through her. "Now, tell me your reservations."

"I'm not…used to the high society you move in. Just speaking to Mrs. Rossi—who was so sophisticated and poised—gave me the biggest fright. Luckily for us now, I couldn't mumble a word in my defense when she kept warning me to stay away from you. But I worry that I might cause your reputation more harm than good. I might be found out as an impostor of the worst kind. I know nothing of arts or fashion except for reading about them."

"All of those can be learned. You know enough about me, and that's more than most women, even Chiara, can say. Don't let anyone tell you you're less than who you want to be. Even me."

"Believe me, I'm trying," Monica said, liking this new, charming side of him as much as she liked the serious, ruthless side.

"*Bene.* What else?"

"This one's a big one." To avoid losing herself in those eyes, she started walking around the room, her pulse skyrocketing with every step she took. But she had to tell him. She had to make sure he understood before they got deep into this. "You might even decide that it's a deal breaker. But I…don't want to play games with you and I don't think I could, even if I tried. And I'm afraid it might just be—"

"Monica, what is it?"

His impatience made the words burst out of her. "I'm attracted to you!"

Dio mio, it was the last thing he'd expected her to own up to. And with such open, artless naiveté.

The primal attraction he'd felt toward her that day… It had taken him by shock, too. Still, he was experienced enough—Cristo, he'd thought his manly prowess was in winning as many women as he could as a cocky twenty-year-old race-car driver—to know that it wasn't one-sided. In the three weeks since he'd left her in his mother's care, he had wondered, multiple times, if she simply hadn't seen it. Or if she'd lied to herself that it didn't exist, since she also clearly believed that she was in love with that rogue. People clung to intrinsic beliefs like lifelines, even when the evidence to the opposite was in front of their eyes.

And here it was. The answer he'd desperately wanted to hear, delivered in such easy but complicated words.

Her arms were wound around her belly in a gesture of defensiveness that tugged at a part of him he hadn't known existed. *Dio mio*, did she think this attraction was wrong? As if everything around them and about them wasn't complicated already.

"Look at me, Monica."

It was the first time she defied his command, refusing to meet his gaze, continuing to walk around the study. "It feels…awful to feel all these things about you. And I don't even fully understand it. I've never felt like this before. Even with Francesco, it was never—"

"You don't need to draw a comparison chart, *bella*!"

She shook her head. "It could be that I'm just attaching to you because you were so good to me that day and I was half out of it. I had hoped these three weeks would be enough to wake me out of the trance but no, it's still there." She rubbed a hand over her neck and when his gaze went to the smooth column and the rising swell of her breasts, she pulled away from her own body, as if scalded. "It's still there and I am afraid that you…"

"Will take advantage of this…thing that you're not even sure about?" he bit out, his mind stuck on the word *awful*. She thought her attraction to him was awful? He hadn't required his masculinity or his ego to be validated on any basis in a long while, but *Dio mio*, if her assessment didn't rankle like a thorn stuck under his skin.

"What? No?" Alarm widened her big eyes. "I'm afraid that you might be…disgusted by me and my reactions and my little twitches every time you come near me when we put up this pretense of an affianced couple. I'm not sophisticated enough to play it all cool. Not that I would make a move on you. And I'm not even sure if this is some kind of reaction to Francesco and you're like this giant rebound blanket—"

"I would prefer it if you didn't bring that bastard up in our conversations."

She tilted her chin up, and then everything about her stilled. "You're angry with me again."

"It seems you're better at gauging my moods and my reactions than understanding your own feelings."

Now, when she should back off at his grumbly tone, she stayed put. "Why are you angry, Andrea?"

He sighed. "Let's just say my fragile ego got dented."

She smiled then, and it lit up her entire face. Those unique amber eyes of hers glowed with pleasure and he wondered how they would look full of desire. "That's not possible, is it? Will you not tell me? Please? If there's one constant, one anchor around me, it's you and where I stand with you. I'd like to—"

Andrea had to stifle his groan. If she used that pleading tone with him, he ran the risk of granting her whatever she wanted. "I'm not angry with you."

"More like frustrated?"

He shrugged. Then he asked the question he shouldn't. "Do you want to act on it?"

She looked as if he'd asked her to jump from a running train. Also something he'd attempted once to show off. She licked the curve of her thick, shapely lower lip, her pulse fluttering like a butterfly's wings at her neck. He wanted to press his mouth to that delicate spot, lick up the susurration and bite down on the sensitive skin, leaving a mark.

Usually, he preferred experienced partners, women who

liked and demanded pleasure as much as he demanded his own. And here was this creature, looking like she might be blown off her feet by a strong kiss. So where was this coming from?

She was beautiful, yes, but simple beauty had never done it for him. Not since he'd finally grown up.

"What?" she whispered, her entire body trembling from head to foot now.

"Do you want to act on the attraction?"

"Why would you… What does that mean?"

"It means that this—" he motioned a hand between them, wondering at how convoluted this was "—is not one-sided."

"Oh! You mean you're attracted to me, too? You want…" Her mouth fell open on a soft gasp, her gaze finally, finally, landing on his mouth and staying there. "You want…"

"You. I want you."

She swallowed audibly.

He scoffed. "In case you haven't looked at a mirror recently, you're hot, *bella*."

"I'm a selection of symmetrical features and in-trend arbitrary body constructs that we've been programmed to like, but *you* are…" Her gaze moved over him—from his hair to his mouth to his neck to his chest—with a sweeping, overwhelming thoroughness, before she jerked it back up to his eyes.

"What? A slab of unfeeling rock?" he taunted, feeling as unbalanced and on edge as she seemed to be. Which made him wonder at how new this felt. "I would take you to my bed right now and give you what you want and demand you give me what I want, if you said yes. That's what I mean when I say acting on it. My only hesitation would be that I can't be a hundred percent sure Mama won't come banging on the door to protect her innocent lamb from me."

The reddish streak warming her cheekbones intensified as she pressed a hand to her mouth. "Flora knows."

"I think the entire goddamned world knows by now. Except you."

She walked toward him then, surprising him yet again. He could feel the pull between them as easily as if there were opposing poles embedded deep in their bodies. Her gaze, usually so meek, met his, pupils blown wide already. A breathless gasp left her as she seemed to find whatever confirmation she sought. Her hands fisted at her sides, and Andrea understood the need for that, too.

"This is a lot," she said, after what felt like an eternity stitched of hot, hungry moments.

"It is," he said, trying hard not to let his disappointment seep into his tone. "But chemistry is nothing but nature and instincts. It doesn't mean we have to give in to it."

"But you want to?"

He touched her then, just the pad of his thumb skimming over the soft, silky swath of skin on the inside of her wrist. Her pulse went haywire under his thumb, and her shallow breath was a symphony in his ears. "Yes. But it would be an affair, *a fling*, in your words. A…finite thing. I won't make false promises. I won't dress it up and call it dating. I won't lie and tell you that I'm interested in a girlfriend or a partner or a future wife. Because I'm not. I have no interest or any inclination toward love."

"How long would it last?"

He laughed then, and when she made a moue of her lovely mouth and made to pull away, he stopped her, all the while gentling his grip on her arm. She was so fragile in his hands. And more than just her wrist.

"Such anger, *bella*? I wonder that I know you at all, mouse."

Her catlike eyes flashed at him. "You're mocking me."

"I've…never been asked to fill out a questionnaire before I embarked on an affair."

Her eyes searched between his and then zoomed down to his mouth with a helpless eagerness that made him want to groan out loud. "And I've never just jumped into an affair with a man like…you."

"A man like me?"

"So out of my league. Who radiates confidence and sexuality and…"

Her open admission sent lust spiraling through him. *She was new to this and that meant it could go wrong in so many ways*, that rational voice he lived by whispered. "I wish I could put a shelf life on it. But I have no idea how long it would last. You might grow bored long before I do."

"Maybe in an alternate universe," she said, her own fingers coming to grasp the base of his palm in a tentative touch. He felt the contact shiver down his spine, wondering if he was so deprived of all touch or if it was just hers that had him reacting like this. Wondering if there would come a day when she realized the hold she could have over him.

"I guess the timing is convenient," she said, her voice gone husky.

"How?"

"The fake engagement, the forced proximity is a good cover to get it out of our systems." When he stared at her, she blushed. "That's the technical term."

He had never in his life discussed the terms of a maybe affair and the naiveté, the sheer lack of worldliness with which she asked the questions, told Andrea why his mother had been so outraged. Releasing her wrist, he moved away from her. "I tend to take people at face value. And yet, I cannot forget that you've just been through a painful, life-changing experience. And, by your own admission, you're not even sure what this is. What did you call me earlier? A giant blanket?"

"As much as I can cuddle a grumbly, grouchy bear," she said, coming up to the other side of the desk, her eyes wide in her face. When she gripped the edges of his desk and leaned over it, want made every inch of him curl tight.

He watched her, feeling a slow hum of pleasure through his veins at her aching beauty. Emotions flickered through her eyes. When the silence lengthened and he still didn't say anything, her mouth pinched down at the middle. "You're changing your mind about this. About wanting me."

He rubbed a hand over his face, feeling all of his thirty-four years in his bones. "No, I know I want you, Monica. And I know all the ways I want you. I cannot stop thinking of how many of my own rules I'm breaking by even admitting how much I want you."

"And if I said I was sure, Andrea? If I want to do this with you no matter what?"

"It *is* a lot. I should've never told you—"

"Then why did you?" she demanded, pushing her upper body over the desk like a bow bending toward him.

"Because I lost control. Your sweet admission made me forget how complicated all of this already is. When I invited you in here, all I meant to do was suggest the fake relationship. Not propose an affair."

"I know that. I started this. I was the one who said it first."

He stared at her, willing her to leave it, willing her to go.

"Do I need to sign a contract that says I won't ask for more than you give, or cling to you when it's done or that I'm old enough, wise enough and savvy enough to have sex with Andrea Valentini for pleasure without making it too much in my puny head?"

He let out a pithy curse.

She nodded, as if he had given her answers to all her questions. Then she wrapped her arms around herself again, as if she was pulling her dignity around her, and turned to leave. She was almost at the double doors when she turned back and said, "What time do we have to leave for the gala?"

"Monica—"

"We're not losing that contract. I'm not going to stop working for you because of something that didn't even happen, because of what that jackass did to me. And we're not going to let your reputation get tarnished." There was steel hidden in her quivering voice and it made him want her a little more.

She rubbed a palm over her flat belly and then glanced down at herself with a frown. "I need better clothes and shoes and maybe a little help with makeup."

"You're the most gorgeous woman I've ever met. And believe me, I have met some."

"Ri-i-i-ght," she said, stretching the word out. "I keep forgetting you had a playboy phase." Then as quickly as it came, the teasing left her eyes. "I don't want to let you down, Andrea."

"You won't."

"I don't want to let myself down, either. After everything with Francesco… I need a little boost of confidence. As the fake fiancée of the CEO of Valentini Luxury Goods, I'm allowed a little trip to the designer freebies showroom, aren't I? I've heard so many stories about it and I've been dying to go."

"Why didn't you just ask?" he said, then scoffed. "Right, the list of obligations and all that."

She nearly danced on the balls of her feet. "Can I, please?"

"Si."

"And just for the gala, can I have a stylist, and a makeup artist to help me get ready?"

"*Si.* Mama will arrange it for you."

"And who do I see for a little insight into how to seduce the man who's brilliant and ruthless and so gorgeous that he makes my knees quake even when he glares at me and calls me a damned headache?"

His mouth twitched and Andrea had to fight the insane urge to jump over the desk and tackle her to the floor. He would rip that ridiculous thing she called a top off her and bury his lips against her golden-brown flesh, dig his teeth into the curve of her breast, flick his mouth against the bold nipple that poked against the fabric even now, until she arched into him completely. Until she was begging for his mouth somewhere else.

The urge was overwhelming in its intensity.

Instead, he simply took in the breathtaking beauty of her, savored the thundering of his own pulse thrumming with a rich awareness he hadn't known in years.

He wanted to say yes to this, too. He wanted to say yes to anything she'd ask of him, if she asked him in that tone.

The little mouse was getting so bold. And it sent a thrill through him. Maybe he would never take her to bed, but *Cristo*, he felt like a new man when she flirted with him, when she crossed that edge of caution just for him, when she glared at him.

"You're growing bold."

She waved her fingers in the air, her eyes dancing with a wicked pleasure he'd never seen in her. Energy seemed to radiate from her, and he wondered if he was shortchanging her. If he was projecting the vague unease he felt at the back of his mind onto her. “Just flexing my newfound claws.”

And then she was out the door.

For a long while Andrea stayed in his chair, wondering what he’d unleashed between them. And yet, there was not even a hint of regret to be found anywhere within him.

CHAPTER SEVEN

TWO EVENINGS LATER, Andrea stood waiting in the lounge of his family home, impatience and anticipation swirling through him in equal measure. He hadn't been this…invested in even the damned merger. But then, he knew the rules of that game. He'd written most of them.

With his assistant turned temptress…all bets were off. He felt as immature and unsure of himself as he'd felt with Chiara all those years ago. But for entirely different reasons.

For one thing, she was late.

Which was uncharacteristic enough of Monica that he couldn't help wondering if she'd changed her mind in the two days since they'd seen each other, since she'd declared with a steely resolve that she was going to be a part of the solution for the mess they had both had a hand in creating.

He wouldn't blame her if she did back out, though. He would even try to see it as the better outcome—notwithstanding the problem of Brunetti and the merger—because then he wouldn't have to spend God only knew how many months trying to avoid giving in to temptation.

How do I seduce a man who makes my knees quake?

Dio mio, that innocent and yet infinitely provocative question of hers had haunted him for two days and nights. An echo of her sunflowers-and-vanilla scent had lingered in the air long after she had left his bedroom. He'd woken up close to dawn, hard as nails, the sheets tangled around his lower body feeling like those fingers that had tingled against the base of his palm. *That* was all the contact they'd had and yet it felt like she had left the echoes of her tentative touch all over his body.

For the first time in years, he'd thrown off the sheets, sunk back into the bed and taken his erection in hand. Eyes closed, he'd spent long minutes running through the images of her in his head, like a slow reel he'd been saving up for his leisure.

The upswell of her breasts when she'd leaned over the desk, all anger and outrage that he was changing his mind. The lean, muscled lengths of her thighs as he'd carried her to the car. The relentless flutter of the pulse at her neck when he was close. The soft gasp that fell from her sensuous mouth when he touched her.

He flicked through every image while he pumped himself in his hand, reveling in the pinpricks of pleasure sparking all over his body and corralling down his spine, coalescing into a storm that made him thrust his hips up off the bed. The moment he reached the image of her gaze lingering on his mouth…he spilled all over his sheets, his climax a sudden, riotous explosion that had left him shaking.

For long seconds after, he'd lain against the sheets, his skin damp, his breaths bellowing through his lungs, lingering aftershocks making his muscles shake. It was a luxury of time, of experience, of mind and body, he never allowed himself anymore. Had not for more than a decade.

And as he'd gathered the sheets and thrown them into the laundry hamper, as he'd checked his phone like some gauche emo teenager after a first date to see if she'd texted him, as he'd padded naked into his shower and turned the water to an icy blast to cool down his overheated skin and suddenly rampaging libido, he wondered if that was why he was so attracted to Monica. Not just attracted, but attuned…in a way he had never been to another woman. If he'd deprived himself of even the smallest pleasures, like lying in bed thinking of a beautiful woman, of feeling the silk sheets against his skin, of the blood-tingling chase of wanting a woman, of letting his mind and body linger and revel in all that he'd built through sweat and tears.

He decided that was it, as a man who needed things to sit in clear, defined boxes. He'd been driving himself at a relentless speed, working eighty-hour weeks, pushing himself and the company and his staff to put out more products, more innovative designs, more investments, for thirteen long years…until Brunetti himself had reached out to him with interest in a merger. Driving himself toward another milestone, another million, another meteoric development, until his father's dream became true. Until he built enough wealth and power that Romeo and his mother would never need anything. Until Valentini Luxury Goods had become synonymous indeed with luxury and design and innovation. All the while, he… He had never learned to rest on his laurels, to celebrate his achievements, to simply enjoy the hard-won pleasures.

No wonder Brunetti's ridiculous condition had driven him to the brink so easily. No wonder he felt so…burned out. No wonder a delicate, inexperienced, almost fragile woman like Monica was catching him unawares, knocking him to his knees without even trying. God help him the day she decided she wanted to flex her sensuality, though.

"Andrea! What has come over you? That is the third glass of wine you have drunk in twenty minutes."

His mother's probing pulled Andrea out of the reverie. He turned to her and for the first time that evening noted the bright red lipstick, the complicated chignon, the navy blue designer dress and the simple diamond choker at her neck that had been a present from his father.

She was dressed up to the hilt, not something he'd seen in years. Her skin glowed with health and there was a simple joy to her gaze that made his heart swell in his chest. "What a beast I am, Mama, for not telling you how pretty you look this evening. Papa loved you in that color, I remember."

His mother blushed, scoffed and then slapped his arm, making sure he knew that she knew what he was doing. Romeo chuckled on her other side.

"*Grazie mile*, Andrea. But what is making you so restless that you drink so much?" At whatever she saw in his face, her words drifted away. "You are impatient to see her. You...like her. More than for—"

Andrea groaned. "Have we traveled in time back to my eighth grade, Mama?"

Turning so that she could see him fully, his mother clasped his cheek. He chafed under her scrutiny, not because he was thirty-four damned years old and she was trying to fix his hair, but because he couldn't bear to see the flash of grief the cut of his features usually brought her.

For all he teased Romeo about it, he was the one who looked so much like their father. He also remembered that, for almost a year after the accident, she'd been unable to look upon his face fully or meet his eyes or speak a sentence in his direction. Her grief at losing her husband had been so great that it had choked her to speak of their father for a long while. On some dark days, he'd even wondered if she hated him for causing the accident, if she would ever forgive him.

"Romeo reminded me that I am unfair to you," she said, her eyes shining with a suspicious sheen. "Judging you for this affair, real or fake, as if you were some…jungle predator, when in truth, you have not looked this interested in anything in a long time."

Andrea gritted his teeth, feeling more than discomfited under her scrutiny. "I would prefer it if you didn't discuss my personal stuff with him. Or with me. Or at all. There are certain things a man cannot continue to discuss with his mother."

"So it *is* personal?"

He groaned out loud.

She laughed and the soft sound snagged at his chest. "I forgot, momentarily, that you're your father's son, Andrea. That you would never knowingly hurt another. As for when it comes to your…manly affairs and desires…remember what he—"

"Mama," he groaned, clasping her cheeks in return. "This is worse than when Papa and you gave me the sex talk. At least then, I was remunerated for sitting through it."

His mother blushed but relented, nevertheless, by going on her toes to kiss his cheek. "I want you to be happy, Andrea. In whatever form it takes. I am sorry I…neglected you all these years."

"*Cristo*, Mama," Andrea said, enfolding her in his arms, his throat tight and aching. She was so small and had always been mostly unaware of the world's schemes, but hid a spine of steel. Just like another woman he knew. "I am a grown man and it is my turn to look after you. As it is Romeo's right, too."

She nodded, hiding her tears in his suit jacket. "I will not push you, but if you truly like her so much, why not turn this into a more—"

"You nicked yourself in two spots while shaving," Romeo said, coming to his rescue, his eyes full of devilish humor.

"Mama's right. I haven't seen you drink a glass of wine that fast before, much less three, and now this. If it is this bad now, I cannot wait to see your condition once you two—"

Leaning away from his mother, Andrea pushed at Romeo's shoulder, hard enough that the wheelchair squeaked on the polished marble tiles. "*Basta!* You won't speak of her like that."

To the background of his mother's outraged gasp, Romeo not only recovered but also delivered a solid punch to Andrea's gut that he hadn't seen coming, and did so with a resounding cackle.

Eyes wide, his mother stared between them, and then shouted, *"Basta!"* just as Andrea decided to retaliate in kind. "You're behaving like dogs and I know your father and I have taught you better manners." At least she hadn't grabbed the tops of their ears and twisted them around like she used to do when they had been kids.

Whatever Andrea had been about to shout into Romeo's face died as a vision in pink appeared at the top of the steps of the circular balcony.

Her amber eyes widened, her pink mouth open on a gasp, Monica stared at Andrea's crooked jacket and Romeo's ruffled hair and Flora standing between them with her arms spread out like a referee at a particularly nasty soccer match. "What's going on?"

Andrea jerked his jacket down, his head feeling woozy as if he'd received a pounding to his head rather than to his gut. In a hot pink sleeveless dress that hugged her breasts and then flared out from under them, Monica looked like some lush, exotic flower at full bloom. The rich pink made her shoulders and neck gleam like burnished gold, while the upper swells of her breasts rose and fell with her shallow breaths. With each step she took down the stairs, the almost thigh-high slit bared the lean length of her thigh, her legs even longer than usual in gold-strapped stilettos that Andrea had to swallow and look away from, counting his breaths. Her dark, silky hair had been curled into long waves and they slithered over and away from her chest, as if beckoning him for a closer look.

She neared them and a subtle scent overlaid with her own hit his nostrils.

"What's happening?" she asked, slowly but definitely moving toward Romeo.

Andrea gritted his teeth, while his brother wriggled his brows in a childish taunt, meant for him.

Monica's hands went to Romeo's ruffled hair and in a smooth move, she pushed at the thick, wavy strands until they settled back into his designer haircut. Jealousy at the open affection clung to Andrea's throat like the thick brew Mama used to make them drink to ward off colds.

"The Valentini brothers forgot that they're full-grown men and instead decided to fight like ruffians." His mother took the younger woman's hand and pulled her close for a better look. "You look beautiful, *cara*. I know you're nervous about this whole...drama that you and Andrea are cooking up, but do not be, *si*? Anyone who talks to me and Romeo will know that we wish it were the truth."

Alarm flickered through her eyes but Monica nodded. Still not meeting his eyes. "Thank you. I want to be of help."

"You've always been more than that to me," his mother said, tapping Monica's cheek. Then she stepped back and gave her a once-over. "I would recommend a piece of jewelry with your outfit but I will leave that in Andrea's capable hands."

As he watched, Romeo pulled Monica to him and kissed her on the cheek—a little too close to the corner of her mouth for Andrea's liking, but he had already given his far too intrusive family too much ammunition against him. Then his brother whispered something in her ear that made her cheeks flush the same color as her dress.

A slow, thunderous beat seemed to take up in his blood as his mother and Romeo left the lounge, intending to arrive at the gala separately from him and Monica. Finally, when Monica set that liquid gaze on him, something he couldn't recognize shimmered there. Her slender arms spread in a welcoming stance, she asked, "What do you think? Will I do as Andrea Valentini's fiancée?"

"What did Romeo say to you?" he bit out, instead of acknowledging her question.

Her expression shuttered and her chin rose with that willful streak he was coming to recognize and like. Although not so much at this particular minute. "That's between me and your brother."

Cristo, no wonder his family was teasing him like they did. He behaved like a hormone-ridden, angsty teenager around her. And he should have known she'd clam up when he demanded an answer to such an inane question.

In nearly two years of working intimately for him and with him, she had never cowered or bent at his criticisms or his demands or his perfectionist, workaholic tendencies. She didn't engage in an argument, but always brought him around to her point of view in the end. Slowly, but surely, as she was driving him out of his mind now.

Sighing, he said, "Mama is right. We need jewelry for you."

He didn't wait to see if she followed him, leading the way to his father's old study. Like his mother had rightly guessed, he'd already had a jewelry showroom that he knew Chiara had always liked send him some pieces in advance.

Now he regretted not asking Romeo to look through the selection and eliminate the worst options. He knew nothing of the current trends in jewelry—design and fashion had always been Romeo's field of expertise—nor of Monica's tastes. But there were at least a dozen pieces for her to pick from.

He turned to find her looking around with wide eyes. The study was a remnant from his father's time and while Mama constantly asked him to redo it, he hadn't found the heart to erase memories of his father.

"This is different from your study at work. Or upstairs," she said, not meeting his eyes. "It's so full of…character and charm."

Beyond the smooth, silky skin of her shoulders, he saw the tightness with which she held herself. And Andrea suspected he had hurt her by not complimenting her, even after she'd specifically asked it of him. A part of him found it maddening that he couldn't give her a simple compliment that she could appreciate, but a bigger part of him was almost resentful of her for reducing him to such peevish behavior.

"It was Papa's," he said, gentling his tone. "He was an avid reader and a fan of woodworking. Many of the pieces are his."

She nodded, her long neck tilting forward to look at the pieces up close. "He was very talented."

"Si."

"But this one…" She bent and leaned close and Andrea didn't look away fast enough to miss the delectable sight of how the silk moved over the swell of her buttocks.

She touched the one he had carved of a wood nymph from a dark wood that Romeo had acquired from some trader a couple of years after Papa's death. In turn, Andrea had put a sketchbook into his brother's hands, determined to provoke him from the deep, dangerous fugue state Romeo had slipped into. It was the first step they had both taken to carve their way back to each other and to life itself.

While Andrea had worked on that particular piece during the nights Romeo had sketched, he hadn't taken it up again since. Not until this past year. He had had very little time for woodwork, after he'd taken over the company full-time, especially when all his risks and strategies had exploded it beyond even his own vision.

Or was that another lie he had told himself?

Maybe because it was the one thing where he and his father had seen eye to eye, had understood each other, had met each other without the usual frustration and animosity that had colored their relationship when he'd turned eighteen and his ambitions and vision for life had veered completely away from his father's dreams for him.

"This is yours," she said, awe in her tone.

"How do you know that?" he said, his voice sharp from the sudden, overwhelming flush of pleasure that bathed him. When she didn't answer, he said, "Answer me."

She turned, but her arms crisscrossed over her belly in a defensive posture he hated. "The style is different from the others. Also similar to the almost finished one, the mermaid that you keep hidden away in your drawer at work. The detail in such a tiny piece is…magnificent."

"You went snooping?"

She stood ramrod, her eyes going wide. "Of course not. I was just curious if you had—" now she was blushing again "—liked it."

"What do you mean?"

Her lush mouth puffed out in a frustrated exhale. "I was snooping, *si*. Fire me for my sins."

"I have worse punishments in mind if you don't give me the answers I want, Ms. D'Souza."

A lick of heat dawned through her yellow eyes, making them burn bright and hot. An answering heat punched through Andrea, knowing that she understood him, knowing that her mind had gone there just as his did.

"That would have frightened me a few months ago, Mr. Valentini. Now whatever you deal out..." She swallowed, the pulse at her neck thrashing at her own boldness. "I'm more than willing and ready."

He cursed. "Tell me, *per piacere*."

Even his "please" was apparently not enough. Her gaze searched his, looking for reassurance, he thought. Finally, she sighed and gave in. "I asked Romeo what you might appreciate for your birthday last year and he told me about your hobby. That dark African wood..." Her words came out rushed now. "I found a dealer online and had it shipped. But it was so expensive that I could only afford a small piece. For weeks after, I was curious to see if you'd worked on it. Even then, I didn't snoop on purpose. I... You gave me the locker combination one night eight months ago in the middle of the Japanese buyout and it was there. Not fully formed and yet already incredibly beautiful in the promise emerging. I couldn't help going back to check on its progress."

"Why?" he asked, floored by her admission. He had assumed the gift had been Romeo's doing.

"Why what?"

"Why did you ask Romeo?"

"Am I not allowed to gift you a small thing, Andrea?" Her tone was soft, whisper-thin, but the thrust of her question so deep and precise that he found himself floundering.

"Why didn't you just contribute to the staff pool?" he said, sounding churlish to his own ears.

"I… I wanted to give you something meaningful. Do you remember how Flora had been sick for weeks with that cough and we worried it might be pneumonia?"

"*Si.* You stayed with her and nursed her through four nights. Through the worst. Romeo said you slept in that armchair."

She shook her head. "That was nothing. You… You were so worried about her and I wanted to—" she licked her lips again "—make you feel better, I guess. Obviously, I couldn't afford any of the good stuff like your favorite liquor or cuff links or a tie. But when Romeo told me you used to woodwork quite a bit… I was surprised and went researching."

"*Grazie* for the gift," he said, staring at her in spiraling consternation. "It distracted me from…everything."

Resentful bastard that he was, he didn't tell her that it had done so much more. It had brought him back to his hobby again. To the thing he had shared with his father and loved. Even to a part of himself that he had lost. He had worked on two more pieces since then and even commissioned a woodworking shed to be built on his property. Something that had remained only a dream for his father.

Her throat moved on a swallow as she nodded. "I'm glad. When I saw the finished piece, I realized Romeo hadn't been exaggerating out of brotherly love."

He laughed at that, as she intended him to. And he wondered how much she must have managed his moods, his uneven temper in the throes of a project or his demands and his criticism, without his noticing it for so many months. "As you probably know by now, he is the very opposite. More along the lines of my critic and my mirror," he said, meeting her eyes again.

Her teeth dug into her lower lip, her eyes flaring with understanding. "I appreciate that he looks out for me. But he also knows I need to make my own decisions, right or wrong. Even the stupid ones."

Luckily for them both, his watch beeped before he could pick up the gauntlet she threw down and pounce on her right there in what had been his father's study. "We will be late. Take a look and pick what you want," he said gruffly.

Dutifully, she sauntered toward the dark mahogany desk where everything from necklaces to diamond studs were lying open in dark green velvet cases. She gasped. "I… These are real diamonds and sapphires and…emeralds. I can't pick one out of these. If you really think I need jewelry, I have some costume jewelry pieces in my—"

"That won't do for my fiancée," he said, taking her wrist in his hand and tugging her forward when she staggered back. "And you promised to accept a gift or two from Mama, remember?"

"Yes. But these aren't from your mother. These are from you. And way too expensive."

He sighed. "Do not turn this into a fight."

"Do not order me around, then."

When he turned to face her, she gripped the desk and stayed where she was. Her beauty hit him with the force of a tsunami. "This will never work if you won't accept gifts from me. Or if you jump every time I touch you."

"I didn't jump. I just… I've never been so aware of another person's…nearness. I'm trying, Andrea."

As if to prove her point, she covered the distance between them until a flying lock of her hair hit his chest. This close, he could see the yellow-amber flecks in her big eyes. Could see the tiny beads of moisture over her upper lip.

"Let's make a deal. If you grant me what I ask for," she said sweetly, "I'll pick a piece and be the most obedient fiancée you could ever want."

Every muscle turned flint-hard in his body. “What do you want, *bella*?”

“One of your sculptures.”

“What?” he repeated, as if he was hard of hearing.

“If you promise me one of your sculptures, then I’ll accept one piece of jewelry tonight. I won’t even try to return it.”

“That’s the most ridiculous negotiation I’ve ever witnessed.”

“I don’t care what you think,” she said, setting her mouth into that mulish set. “I want what I want.”

“Give me one good reason why.”

“Those are beautiful and they’re a piece of you. A piece of Andrea Valentini that only a few know. A piece I will cherish for a long time, whatever and wherever this farce leaves us.”

With that simple request, she reminded Andrea exactly who she was and who she would always be. Of how a fundamental part of her makeup meant she’d always see the world in terms of emotions he could not afford. She was already asking for pieces of him that he was loath to part with and soon, she’d ask for something he couldn’t give.

Cristo, she was far too innocent and good for the likes of him. She had no idea what an affair with him would cost her. And as much as he hated to admit it, he was…*fond* of her in a way that precluded ruining his relationship with her by adding sex to it.

Suddenly, he hated the very idea of having to parade her in front of guests and friends and family, letting them stare her up and down as if she was a prime cut of meat. He hated the idea of anyone destroying that fragile, deep-rooted sense of kindness and generosity with which she greeted the world.

"Bene," he said, turning her around to face the necklaces with a hand on her shoulder. "It is a done deal. You'll have one sculpture of my choice. Now, choose something."

Leaning forward, she bumped her side into his front, pointing to the farthest one in the top corner. He should have guessed that it would be her choice, given it was the most delicate and smallest of the lot. He almost pointed out to her that it was the most expensive one, given its intricate flower and leaf-like work with platinum and tiny high-carat diamonds by one of the most exclusive jewelry designers in all of Italy. He'd only been able to acquire it because the designer was a friend of Romeo's.

"Turn around," he ordered briskly, once he had the delicate thing in hand.

When she tugged her hair away from the nape of her neck, he noticed the expanse of smooth, silky flesh exposed by the plunging cut of the dress in the back. Instant goose bumps rose on her flesh and the most overwhelming impulse to run his mouth down the line of her spine rode him hard.

Hands shaking, as if he had been whittling away at wood for hours, he clipped the necklace at her nape. Then without meeting her eyes, he checked his watch and barked out that they were late, thanks to her arguments.

Determined not to feel her hurt as she tried to keep up behind him, he turned himself into one of those sculptures he carved. He wanted her too much to keep this in his control and she… *Madre mio*, she was made for a different kind of man.

CHAPTER EIGHT

IT HAD BECOME astoundingly clear to Monica over the ever-stretching evening that she was a complete disaster on her first outing as Andrea Valentini's fiancée.

Beginning with the moment they had entered the huge ballroom, when she had immediately drawn the eyes of every guest. Which was bad enough, because, in her determination to help Andrea out of this mess, she'd forgotten how much she disliked being the center of attention. And being Andrea Valentini's fiancée meant all the eyes of the Milanese high society would be on her.

When she'd frozen at the top of the steps to the huge ballroom, Andrea had gently rubbed her hip with his fingers, his expression patiently inquiring. It was the patience, as if he were afraid that she might fall apart, that had her straightening her spine. Especially when she knew he was not happy with her.

He hadn't liked it that she knew about his hobby earlier or that she'd demanded a piece of his art. She'd known that he was an intensely private man but she hadn't thought she'd come up against a boundary that soon. He'd been quiet all through the drive to the gala, barely even meeting her eyes. So the downfall of the evening had begun even before they had arrived.

Then, with each step they took, she sensed something

off in the large room with its high domed ceiling and crystal chandeliers. Once people began to flock toward them and Andrea began introducing her, she got it. Everyone was dressed in very somber navy blues and beiges and even browns. The only splash of color she'd seen other than her own was a dark purple belt on one of the navy blue dresses.

Why hadn't he asked her to change when she'd shown up in the garish pink thing from the freebie closet at the Valentini design studio? Why hadn't he told her that the charity gala was a sober affair?

She looked like a weed—wild, overgrown, forced to bloom an unnatural color by fertilizer—among the rows and rows of perfectly manicured prize flowers. That had thrown her off completely. Even then, she might not have cared, could have simply told herself that no one would expect poise or sophistication of the gauche, awkward American Andrea had saddled himself with. Only, after the awkward dance where she hadn't been able to shed the embarrassment and had more than once trampled on his feet and slammed into him with her full body, Andrea had begun progressively freezing her out. To which she had reacted by spilling champagne over herself. After that, she'd barely held off tears.

The worst part, Monica told herself, rubbing at the already spreading stain of champagne from near her boob, was that Andrea had spent the rest of the evening with his ex. She'd have preferred if somehow Mrs. Rossi had been responsible for Monica's various faux pas through the evening. But all the woman had done, having been seated at the same table as her and Andrea, had been to answer his questions about a mutual friend's wedding. Their conversation had progressed from there naturally. Clearly, Mrs.

Rossi had learned from her mistake and was trying to correct it, even at this stage.

Not that anyone would blink an eyelash if Andrea announced tomorrow morning that a connection had been reignited with his ex and he was dumping the little mouse. So here she was, emerging from the restroom, where she had tried her best to get rid of the stain and only ended up smearing it across the fabric, to find Andrea dancing with Mrs. Rossi.

Monica stilled, the flash of Andrea's genuine smile piercing her skin like a thorn even across the ballroom. Whatever embarrassment she had felt through the evening weighed nothing in comparison to the hurt she felt at seeing him happy with his ex.

She wondered if whatever attraction he'd admitted to feeling for her had already passed under the weight of something older, deeper and more real. And she knew that she had to get away before she made an even bigger fool of herself.

Andrea barely waited for the lift car to open as he stepped into his penthouse. He'd never been so angry with Romeo before, not even when they had constantly fought in their younger years—so badly that Papa had to threaten them with dire punishments.

To calmly and quietly send Monica away from the gala, without even telling Andrea…it was a miracle he hadn't lost his temper. All he'd wanted was to run after her, but somehow, he'd kept his common sense. The annual charity gala was to honor his father, to raise funds to donate to a children's charity that had been close to Papa's heart.

It would have been the height of distaste for Andrea to leave the guests. So he had bidden his time. For a while, a very short while, he'd even forgotten about her absence thanks to an interesting conversation with Chiara, who had made a smart turnaround and admitted that she'd considered him an easy prize and persuaded her father to add her as a clause.

It had been both refreshing and unsurprising to know that after all these years Chiara hadn't lost her ambition or her ability to see through to his mood. Just when he'd spent almost five minutes without thinking of his fleeing assistant, she'd dipped her head toward him and whispered, "I don't remember seeing you this out of sorts even when I announced my engagement."

He had nothing to say to that because *he was*, over a slip of a woman who kept surprising him at every turn.

He scanned the expansive lounge that gave a three-sixty-degree view of the living room, dining space and the kitchenette, and beyond it the glittering lights of Milan, to find it empty. Monica's pink dress was lying on the plush leather sofa under the glare of a tall designer lamp. Then he saw her, his assistant slash fake fiancée, on the floor, on her knees, her white teeth gritted tight.

Her long, wavy hair hung in a thick, loose braid down her back. Andrea had the most insane fantasy of wrapping that thick braid around his hand while he… As if aware of his filthy thoughts, she turned around.

"What the hell are you doing on the floor?" he asked, barely restraining his temper.

"Andrea…what are you doing here?" Her eyes were wide in her face and a little red-rimmed.

The passing thought that she might have been crying only made his answer sharper. "Seeing as this is *my penthouse*, my private space, that is my question, *sì*?"

"Fair enough," she said, and shied her gaze away. When

she tugged a thread and bit it off, he realized she'd been sewing the hem. Then, with infinite care, she folded the dress into a garment bag and pushed to her feet.

He stared.

She was wearing a white dress shirt, *his shirt*, the cuffs folded to her elbows but still falling down to cover her fingers. Since she was almost as tall as he was, the edges fell to her thighs and *Dios mio*, her legs went on and on. With a few buttons undone, he could see the silky swath of her neck and chest and all he wanted was to touch and kiss and lick her.

Picking up the bag, she walked toward him. "I never meant to invade your privacy. I thought Romeo was sending me to his friend's place. If you can call a cab, I'll get out of your way."

"Not before you tell me why it was so important that you leave the gala. Are you already regretting making all those promises to me?"

He sounded so irate that he could see her mouth tremble, then stiffen to a taut line. "I wanted to leave before I embarrassed you even more."

It was the last thing he'd expected her to say. And he could see the truth of it in her face. Why was it that suddenly they were on two different wavelengths? Why the hell was this so…hard? "I never said that you embarrassed me."

"It was only a matter of time. Two minutes in, I knew it was the most ridiculous plan. We should have never…" She swallowed and met his gaze. "Will you call a cab for me, please?"

"And where will you go dressed in my shirt, looking like you do, *bella*? Crying into Romeo's arms again? You reach for him even as you tell me you can take me on."

Frustration and something more danced across her face.

"Fine, he's become a safety net. I'll sleep on the sofa here and before you're up, I'll be gone. Then—"

"Why are you upset, Monica? Why leave without telling me?"

"I told you, I didn't—"

"And I have told you that I wasn't embarrassed by you and—"

"How the hell would I know that?"

"You know me well enough to know I would tell you if you were embarrassing me, *bella*."

"Would you? Andrea, I trod on your feet during the dance and I slammed into you twice so hard it's a miracle I didn't take us both to the floor for everyone to laugh at. And then I dropped a glass of champagne on myself during the silent bidding and there was the fact that I looked like a tacky weed among your guests and my God, why didn't you tell me the gala was to honor your father and—"

He pressed his hand to her mouth and felt her warm exhale. "Tacky weed? What has that got to do with the fact that it was to honor my father and—"

She shoved his hand aside but he refused to let her go. "I dressed like I was the main act at a carnival. Didn't you see how I stood out among the others? I never thought you a liar, of all things."

"I did notice how you stood out, *si*," he said, taking the garment bag from her and throwing it aside. "How does that make me a liar?"

"Because you're pretending now as if nothing was wrong," she said, pink cresting her cheeks. "You could barely look at me the entire time we were dancing and then the rest of the dinner, you were deep in conversation with your… Mrs. Rossi. You know, it's not too late."

"Not too late for what?"

"You could claim that this was all a misunderstanding and you realized that you and she have…reconnected. It was clear that you are…"

"We are what?"

"You will make me say it? Make me sound even more foolish?"

"*Si.* I do," he said, unrelenting.

"You enjoyed her company so much that you ignored 'your fiancée.' You could barely look at me after you two struck up a conversation. What was I going to do? Sit there with a stained dress and let everyone see how miserable and jealous I felt?"

Admission of jealousy would have sent him running if it had been anyone else. But with her… Andrea wanted to understand it. "So instead of confronting me about it, or demanding that I pay attention, you hid behind Romeo? Did you think for a second how it would look that my fiancée ran away from me?"

"Demand your attention?" she said, eyes wide, as if it was such an alien concept that most of Andrea's anger melted away.

"Is that so shocking?"

"When you would barely look at me, yes."

Andrea cursed. "I know I'm closed off enough to make a lover feel ignored. And I take full responsibility for our crossed signals tonight. But you know me, Monica. You know I'm not so fickle as to change my mind about you or to lose myself in Chiara all of a sudden. So explain to me why it is so hard for you to demand attention when it is your right."

"You want to know? Really?"

Some hard shell that had formed around his heart broke open at her shocked tone. Did she expect so little from him, for herself? He ran a hand over her cheek, feeling that intense protective urge again. “Yes, *bella*.”

“I’m not used to…attention,” she said, her mouth pinched. “All my life, I’ve done my best to deflect it, to keep away wandering eyes and hands. When we walked into the ballroom, all those eyes on me…it was like my worst nightmare come true. I desperately didn’t want to disappoint you and then I went and did exactly that because I was so anxious with all the attention.”

“Why didn’t you tell me that?”

“It took me four years and a near-lethal rash and a botched wedding to admit that I… I’m attracted to you. But before we left your house, you…didn’t like that I encroached on your personal life.”

Andrea rubbed a hand over his jaw, knowing she was right. Guilt settled like a hard weight on his chest. “I’m not used to sharing personal stuff.”

“I know that. But you barely even paid me a compliment, although I know now it’s because I dressed like—”

“I didn’t compliment you because you rendered me speechless. I avoided looking at you because I wanted nothing more than to take you to the floor, as you put it, and have my wicked way with you, right there for the entire world to see. As for standing out, you would have stood out if you had gone there wearing what you are in now, *bella*. There was not a person there that doubted why the ruthless mogul, Andrea Valentini, was suddenly, secretly engaged to a woman out of nowhere. No one who saw you this evening could doubt how much I want you.”

“Oh…” she said, pink tingeing her cheeks. “You really liked me in that dress? It wasn’t too much?”

“However you dress, whatever you say, you are never too much, *bella*.”

"This event, going out as your…fiancée…felt like a safe way to put myself out there, to try something new. But it was hard. And then when I learned that the gala is to support a foundation that was very dear to your father… I wondered why even Flora didn't tell me to change."

"Because, like me, Mama found nothing wrong with how you dressed. Chiara might have turned her snotty nose up at you but that's because she knows she can't carry that color."

A frown marred her brow and Andrea knew there was more. A thread of tenderness wrapped tight around his chest at how little she expected of the world while still meeting it with all the generosity she could muster. "Mrs. Rossi… You genuinely seemed to enjoy her company. I won't stand in the way of something real and good and—"

"My overwhelming reaction when you walked in this evening looking like you do and my jealousy about how close you are to Romeo… It made me angry with myself." He thrust a hand through his hair, knowing she deserved more. Vulnerability, he could not do, but honesty, he could. "I'm not used to being out of control and I don't share what's in my head easily."

"But you and—"

He clasped her cheek then, forcing her to look at him, hating that he had caused her so many doubts. "Chiara knew me well enough to see I was having a tantrum and teased me about it."

"Teased you? About what?"

"That, uncharacteristically, I was denying myself something I really wanted, that I suddenly possessed an overdeveloped sense of honor."

Her yellow eyes met his, her breath a sudden rasp in the quiet. "Honor… Ah, yes. Because you pity me. You think I'm not strong enough to handle you. Or she's wrong and you just don't want this at all." She stood close enough that he could smell the faint scent of vanilla and sweat, could see the drops of perspiration on that bow-shaped upper lip. "All I asked Romeo was to—"

Andrea tugged her to him suddenly enough that her chest slammed into his. His own breath punched out of him at the delicious press of her soft curves. "You should have told me you wanted to leave. Not him."

Her gaze searched his, some new understanding dawning there. "You don't like it when I ask you for things."

It was close enough to the uncomfortable truth and yet he couldn't back down. "That's not—"

"Maybe because you think I'll ask for too much or because—" she tilted her chin up, her openly wanting gaze hitting him square in the gut "—you're afraid you can't truly give me what I need. Maybe this is not about me at all."

"The little mouse is turning into a cat with claws?"

She shrugged and the shirt fell off, revealing one smooth brown shoulder. "Or I'm realizing that I should stop pursuing men who think I'm not good enough for—"

"I will give you what you want, *bella*," he whispered, his words thick with desire. "Anything you want. Ask me, Monica."

She didn't say anything for so long that Andrea thought she'd lost her nerve. Then she exhaled and her hands came up to clasp his cheeks and she brought that luscious mouth to his. That first soft press of her lips against his drained away all the anger he'd felt at her leaving and all the resolve he'd shored up the entire evening to resist her.

Yes, this would only be a fling, but she knew the score and who the hell was he to decide what she could or could not handle?

He had behaved like a donkey's ass all evening—ignoring her, cursing himself for the possessiveness he felt—but the moment he had realized she had left, he'd known it was useless to try to resist this heat between them. He wanted her too much.

Her kiss was gentle and exploratory, as if she still didn't believe that he wouldn't push her away. When Andrea pulled his head back, she followed with a protest, lips clinging to his, fingers digging deep into his shoulders to keep him tethered to her. A chuckle emerged from his chest but she swallowed that, her mouth opening wider, her tongue swiping at his with tentative but wanton strokes. Her fingers went to the nape of his neck, the tips digging into his hair and pulling, and when she pressed herself flush against his body and moaned, every little lie he'd told himself collapsed.

Wrapping his arm around her waist, Andrea tugged her to him. A soft *oof* escaped her mouth as he circled her nape and tilted her mouth just so for his liking. *Dio mio*, she was sweet like the thickest of honeys and responded like quicksilver. When was the last time he'd known such pure, sweet passion, the last time he had even allowed a woman to touch him with such abandon, the last time he'd truly looked for a connection and not just easy sex?

"More, please, Andrea. More," she whispered against his lips.

He ravished her mouth, desire licking through him like an inferno, as she responded to every stroke and lick and nip without backing down, demanding in that breathy little voice that he not stop. When he sucked on the tip of her tongue, her nails dug into his nape, egging him on. He didn't remember the last time a kiss had revved him up this fast; didn't remember when it had become the end rather than the means.

He could have gone on kissing her for the rest of the night, if that was all they could have. He felt dizzy like he used to when he'd beaten a previous speed or taken to a new racetrack and broken records.

Slowly, he pulled back, their breaths choppy and fast around them. Pupils blown wide enough to eat up the unique yellow, Monica clung to him.

Andrea kept his hand around her neck, loving the way she burrowed into his touch, loving how she molded herself against him like a climbing vine, loving how she trembled from head to toe. Finally, she looked up, and a lazy smile stretched her swollen lips. Without looking at him, she rubbed the pad of her thumb against his lower lip, the touch exploring and gentle.

Andrea opened his mouth and sucked the digit in. Her rough rasp sent his blood pooling south. He released her finger with a pop.

"That was…" She blinked, pulled back and searched his gaze. "That was the best kiss I've ever had," she said, chin risen almost belligerently.

"If you're looking for disagreement," he said, his hands stroking over the planes of her back, loving how she pushed toward him, seeking more, "you will not find it here. Tell me, *bella*, did you get what you wanted?"

She nodded. Then, leaning forward, she pressed her cheek against his and rubbed, like a cat. Her skin was like the softest velvet against his rough jaw, and slowly, as if in beat to his drugged pulse, she brought her mouth to his ear and said, "Yes, but I'm greedy, Andrea. I want more."

"Spell it out for me."

"I want to go to bed with you. I want to touch you as I've wanted to for three weeks. I want to see if reality can stand up to my feverish, delirious dreams of you. I want to explore this between you and me and I want so much pleasure that I—"

His hands on her hips, Andrea picked her up and she instantly wrapped her arms around his back. He kissed her roughly, deeply, even as he maneuvered through the lounge to his bedroom. He bit her lip and when she jerked against him, nudging her sweet core against his thick shaft, he told her in filthy words all the stuff he'd wanted to do to her the moment he'd seen her in the dress earlier that evening; all the things he'd thought when she'd slammed into him during the dance; all the possessiveness that had swirled through him when she'd danced with a colleague who had a reputation for wandering hands.

CHAPTER NINE

MONICA WOULD HAVE floated on the fluffy clouds of sensation from his kiss for the rest of the night, if not for Andrea gently lowering her to what felt like another cloud. It was his bed, she realized, her heart fluttering in her chest like a hummingbird's wings. Then there was a sudden explosion of light and she scrunched her eyes shut, fighting it and the urge to hide herself.

"Monica?"

From his soft tone, she knew that he'd seen her momentary hesitation. His hands rubbed over her arms, gentling her. "It can just be a kiss."

God, what a coward she was.

She opened her eyes to find him looking down at her. Her breath hung suspended in her chest at the sight of him like this, with her, for her. Out of the periphery of her vision, she took in the vast bedroom with all-glass walls on two sides, giving a delicious peek out into the night glitter of Milan. And inside, she was aware of the sheer luxury of the silk sheets under her hands, the vaulted ceilings and the airiness of the space. But all of it was a background hum to the main attraction, the man whose attention she held now.

This was not the Andrea Valentini that the world got to see, with his hair all mussed, and his thin, sculpted mouth just a little puffed up from her kisses, and his dark, dark eyes betraying his desire. This was the Andrea she'd conjured in her dreams and for a second, Monica felt a frantic pulse of panic thrash through her that she couldn't handle him in reality, that she might not be enough to hold his attention for more than… Which made her even more desperate to grab this moment and enjoy it to the fullest. She shooed away all those niggles and, leaning back onto her elbows, drank him in, letting her senses fill her up with him.

He was a feast to her eyes with scruff on his cheeks, his shirt unbuttoned enough for her to see the shadow of taut olive-colored skin stretched tight over his chest. Unlike Francesco, who had been very proud of his gym body and his waxed chest and oiled muscles, Andrea was lean and taut. There was an effortlessness to his masculinity, a raw, innate confidence that established him as a natural leader.

"Any more doubts, *bella*?" he asked, a twinkle in his eyes. But he wasn't laughing at her; she knew that, too.

"Nope. Nada. Zilch," Monica replied, sitting back up. Reaching him, she unbuttoned his shirt all the way and pushed it back onto his shoulders. His chest was covered in a smattering of hair. Fingers trembling, she traced the contours of his torso, from the corded column of his throat to the hard pectorals, all the while loving the graze of his hair against her palm. Just touching him made desire beat louder in her veins, and she never wanted to stop. Never had she felt this kind of desire to make a man crave her as much as she did him.

When she reached his leather belt, she hesitated, but slowly pushed on, undoing it first. His fingers arrested her. Bringing her hand to his mouth, Andrea pressed a kiss to her wrist. "My turn." And then he tugged the lapels of her shirt up in his hands and tore them apart until the few buttons she had managed flew off and pinged on the cold marble floor.

"Will you let me do what I want with you, *bella*?"

"You don't have to test me anymore," she said, watching him with greed.

He grinned then and bent over her, licking the shell of her ear. "When I found that you'd left the party without telling me, I was so angry with you. All I could think of on the ride over here was how I would torment you for leaving."

Startled by the possessive edge of his words, Monica looked up. The intensity of his gaze only made her skin feel tighter. She rubbed her thighs together but didn't find even a bit of relief. "You're not going to scare me off. Do to me what you will. Just...tell me what I can do, too, please. I want to please you, Andrea."

If he heard the doubts in her voice, he didn't mock her for them. Bending, he pushed the shirt off her shoulders and took her mouth with a rough need she understood very well. Then he took her hand and brought it to his crotch.

A needy gasp escaped her mouth as she felt the hard length of his shaft against her palm. She instantly cupped him, driven by an instinct that told her everything about this encounter was going to turn her inside out, change her, ravish her.

But God, she was so ready for it, for him. "You are already blowing my mind, *bella*. I've been walking around with an erection most of the evening, like some uncontrollable adolescent."

"I'm sorry for doubting you," she said, clinging to his lips, breathing shallow.

"I'm sorry for making you doubt my desire for you," he returned. "Do you trust me?"

"Yes. More than anyone in the world."

His gaze gleamed with satisfaction. *"Bene."*

When she thought he'd release her, he pulled her hands behind her, his scruffy cheek rubbing against her own. "Is that okay?" he whispered at her ear.

She was so lost in those dark eyes and his heated whispers that it took her a second to figure out he'd tied her hands behind her with the ripped shirt. Breath shallowing, she wriggled her wrists to find it was a very loose knot. The action made her thrust up her chest, and the sudden swamping heat on her skin told her she was bare to his intense eyes except for her lacy thong. Her nipples instantly puckered and goose bumps rose on her flesh. She let out a groan, unable to catch it.

"*Cristo, bella.* You're beautiful," he said in simple words, but his tone said so much more that for the first time in her life, Monica loved being in her own skin. "Every inch of you is...gloriously made."

And then he shocked her yet again by bending down and rubbing his scruff against her nipple. Arching her spine, Monica fell into the rough slide with a deep groan. One hand on her upper back, he held her still for his tender assault that continued to her other breast, her belly and then back up. Just when she thought she might grow hoarse with begging, he used his fingers and his lips and oh, God... his teeth.

Nipping and licking and suckling, he turned her into a writhing mass of sensation and pleasure. And then he moved down with his deliciously rough stubble and his wicked fingers and his decadent lips.

His filthy curse when he ripped the thong off her pinged over her skin; his scruff at her inner thigh made her writhe. The dig of his teeth at the fold where her hip met her thigh made her sob. His rough inhale at the top of her pubic bone, telling her that her scent was divine… She thrashed wildly to get rid of the knot. "Shh…*bella*, you said you would trust me, *si*?"

His pupils were blown and with his nostrils flaring and his mouth damp, she knew this was an Andrea that she would never forget. She nodded.

He pinched her nipple between his fingers and said, "Good girl."

A wealth of dampness bloomed between her thighs. And slowly, holding her gaze, he dipped his finger into her core and let out another filthy curse. Then he laved her wetness over her folds, tracing them with as much care as a cartographer charting new territory. "I want to taste you, Monica. Will you let me?"

Fresh tingles broke out against her skin as she stared at him. "I've never…" She flushed and tried again. "No one's ever done that and I…"

"If you don't want me to—"

"No, I do. I… You don't understand, that is, I'm not saying this well and…"

He waited, with infinite patience it seemed, while his palms dragged all over her trembling flesh as if he couldn't stop touching her. At least, that was what she told herself. And that gave her enough courage to see this through without mentioning what else was new for her. "I want to do everything with you."

"Good girl," he whispered again and with his words and kisses and caresses, he built her up into a frenzy all over again. Monica lost count of the times she thought she would splinter apart only for him to take away his hands and kiss her softly, tenderly, until she was not standing any longer at the edge. Over and over.

"Please, Andrea, I can't take this anymore. Please, make

me come," she said, sounding both angry and begging. Her skin felt hot and damp, and she needed release so badly that she was close to sobbing. After all this time, after all the men who had called her frigid and boring and worse names, here she was, ready to sell her soul for an orgasm.

"Since you asked so well, *mia cara*." His hands on her hips, he pushed her up the bed.

Monica slithered over the sheets, every inch of her eager to do his bidding. Then he was kissing her belly again and lower and lower, his hands pushing her knees apart scandalously wide.

Her thigh muscles trembled violently when he finally, finally, bent his head and licked at her folds. The shock of that quick, rough swipe had her arching her hips off the bed, chasing his mouth shamelessly. And he did it again and again, setting a rhythm to which her entire pulse seemed to beat. "I need words, *bella*. I need to know what you need more of, where you want me deeper and longer," came his command in such gravelly tones that even that fueled her ascent.

So Monica told him, more voluble than she'd ever been when it came to intimacy; more abandoned than she'd ever been with another person; more demanding and brazen and alive and selfish than she'd ever been her entire life.

She told him she could take another finger after he thrust two inside her; she told him she was seeing stars when he hit some wildly responsive spot deep inside her, and she told him that she was *so, so* close that she couldn't think or talk or maybe even breathe. She told him she'd never felt like this with another man and she told him that all she could see and feel and know was his mouth and his fingers and his breath whispering over her folds.

His fingers pumped with a delicious rhythm that pushed

her on and on, and his lips drew on her clit with a subtle tug…and her climax broke through, thrashing her about into so many jagged pieces.

Tears pooled and spilled at the acute, unbearable ripples jerking through her pelvis and down even as her hips still chased that wicked mouth with a mindless greed. Finally, his mouth stilled. She was desperate to touch him as he kissed a soft trail up her body, praising her, telling her how much he wanted to feel her fall apart around his cock, and she fell back against the bed, feeling wrung out and yet already thrumming with fresh need.

She slowly came back to herself as he undid the knot at her wrists, and it felt like she'd returned not quite the same. Which was ridiculous because it was one orgasm—albeit, yes, the kind that she'd heard friends and colleagues rave about. Her throat felt raw with all the screaming she'd done, and her limbs felt as if they were filled of thick honey, and her heart still hadn't returned to its normal pace.

When Andrea climbed up over into the bed, she instantly turned her face into the sheets, loath to reveal how much the orgasm had knocked out of her, physically and emotionally. God, he'd think her an idiot of the first order if he saw her tears. She pressed her face into the sweat-damp sheets, wiping away the wetness, feeling a sudden, strange shyness.

She rifled through one thing after the other that came to her lips, second-and third-guessing what she should say to break the building awkwardness, how she could speak to sound more confident and less…turned inside out.

"Are you okay, *cara*?" he inquired softly, one hand rifling through her hair with a tenderness she wouldn't have expected of him in a thousand years.

"More than okay," she said, sounding half-feverish, half-delirious. She couldn't blurt out how much she liked that he was still touching her.

It took her a few seconds, wrapped as she was in her own head, to realize that behind her Andrea had stilled. Except for those two fingers that moved over the scar on her waist with a compulsiveness that betrayed his usual indifference to most things.

"You really don't like that scar," she said, her tease sounding raspy.

"I don't like what it reminds me of," he said and then exhaled roughly.

Something about his tone made her desperate to see his expression. She jerked back on the bed, slipping and sliding on the now cooling sheets, to get a better look at him. Whatever teasing words she'd thought up disappeared because this intimacy was a punch to her gut. As much as the knowledge that he'd blasted through her defenses on more than one level.

Heat rushed to her cheeks as she met that dark gaze, the scene of just moments ago replaying in Technicolor in her mind. How she'd screamed; how she'd begged when he'd slowed down the pace; how she'd clamped her thighs around his head…and now the sight of those thin, sculpted lips that had woven such wicked pleasure through her.

"I know you know this, but she feels no lingering trauma from it," she said. Mentioning his mother when she was naked should have felt awkward. But it didn't. But then their relationship, if she could call it that, so far hadn't followed any rules or conventions.

He took a long while to answer, his brows furrowed, his fingers still dancing over the scar. When he finally spoke, his mouth was flat with tension. "And you think that's all that matters? That *she* is unhurt and trauma-free?"

Monica stilled, a cavern of longing opening up inside her.

He cared about her, in his own grumpy you're-another-nuisance-I-have-to-look-after way. She had known that even before the whole episode with Francesco. But to hear it in his words, delivered with that grumpiness, made her chest expand like some secret hidden chamber had been opened. She covered his hand with hers. "I'm unhurt, too, Andrea. And here, with you. Like this," she said, feeling the need to stretch and work loose the tightness in certain places. "And I know you will call me silly and pathetic and even twisted, maybe, but I met you and Flora and Romeo that day because of that accident, and you gave me a new life, and friends and almost-family, when I had nothing. And even without gaining all that, I would—"

"You would save Mama, I know, *bella.* You have little regard for your own safety."

"Not true," she said, inching closer and closer, pushing his shirt off his shoulders. "I know what I want and how I want it and I'm finally, thanks to you, beginning to flex my claws." She rubbed the tip of her nose against his with a giggle, and that he allowed this…was a gift, too. "I just don't stomp about, declaring and announcing and demanding that the world bend to my will and my wishes, that's all."

"Ahh…but in your case, I would make the bending to my wishes so worth it."

"Then what are you waiting for?" she whispered, finally taking his mouth like she wanted to, reaching for this man who seemed to have somehow tunneled deep into her heart without her knowledge.

He was an explosion in her mouth as she poured every ounce of need she felt into it. Her kiss lacked finesse but was filled with a new frenzy she didn't hide. He grunted into her mouth when she bit his lower lip, knowing already that he liked it a little rough, and she smiled, joy beating like a live pulse through her.

She gave in to all the overwhelming impulses, turned and stretched out like a lazy cat, and heard another rewarding grunt as her breasts rubbed against his bare chest. Flexing her newfound freedom, she sank into the stretch, while attached to him from chest to feet. The press of his thick shaft against her lower belly fanned out into a thousand flickers of fresh want and a near-painful ache where his fingers had been.

Leaning forward, she kissed his chin, and the sharp slashes of his cheekbones, and his thick brows and the scar that stretched out from his right temple to his mouth and lower. She trailed her mouth down to his throat and the notch there, across his chest and back up. Insatiable when it came to touching him, she registered the catch and release of his breath when she moved her mouth to the slab of his abdomen, those grunts and curses that flew from his mouth like punctuation marks to his pleasure. And it drove her on as she undid the trousers and pushed them down his hips. When his cock plopped into her palm, she pressed her thighs together and rubbed in a wanton gesture that did nothing to assuage her need.

She stroked him, slowly at first, marveling at the texture and shape and weight of him, and imagining how he would feel moving inside her; how he would submerge her in sensation; how he would own every inch of her dreams and wants.

His grunts and commands finally came to her past the deafening beat in her ears, and she squeezed him as he ordered her to, rubbed her thumb over the soft head, and when pre-cum pooled at the tip, she bent her head and licked at it without his command. It was strange and musky-tasting, and Monica needed another taste so she dipped her head again and closed her lips around his length.

It was uncomfortable at first, his girth stretching her mouth, but God, the rough, guttural grunts that fell from his mouth, and his fingers tugging at her scalp as if he was trying his best not to push her down and the instinctive thrust of his hips upward until he hit the roof of her mouth… It was the most daring and rewarding thing she'd ever done in her life.

She released him for a breath and took him in again, this time actually sucking a little more of him inside her mouth and laughing when he cursed, which turned into a hum when he filled her, which resulted in him telling her that she was such a "good girl" and *Cristo*, who knew her innocent countenance could carry such filthy spirit, and Monica wanted to stay in that moment forever and ever.

Two seconds later, she was on her back and heard the rip of a condom wrapper and he was lodged between her legs. Monica squeezed her inner thighs and her core muscles tight as if she could forever keep his hardness there, just there, where she needed it so desperately. One hand in her scalp tugged her head back, his lips playing and nibbling at her nipples, his hard hips bearing her down into the bed, and all that feverish longing she thought had been satiated came flooding back into her body.

Monica pressed up into him, arching into his touch when his lips moved up her neck, biting and licking and nipping, as if he meant to leave marks on her for days to come.

"I need you. Are you ready for me, *bella*?" he asked, and she nodded, feeling frantic and frenzied enough to burst out of her skin.

"Words, Monica," he said, his own breaths rough now, his thick shaft rubbing against her drenched folds. "Give me words and I will give you everything you crave, *bella*, and a little more that you won't ask for."

"I want you, Andrea," she whispered, pushing her face into his throat with a craven possessiveness she shouldn't feel, breathing the words into his skin, wishing she could keep the furor she felt from creeping into her tone and not caring at the same time. She bit his neck and pulled that pulse between her lips like he had done to her, and she felt the rewarding pressure of his body increase. "Like I've never wanted anything else in the world." It was her truth and she felt a freedom in releasing it to this man who had broken through all her known and unknown defenses.

She could feel his smile in his kiss and even that sliver of arrogance only heightened her feel of him, her experience of everything he gave her. She gasped as he pushed her knee into her chest and then he was there, testing her readiness again with his fingers, probing slowly before he moved inside her with one smooth thrust until he was lodged all the way inside.

"*Cristo, cara.* You will be the death of me," he murmured, hard and still around and inside her, his hands gripping her hips.

A pinch of pain speared through her pelvis, freezing her for a second. She dug her stubby nails into his shoulders with a stubborn possessiveness, holding his rising body as her anchor until it passed. And it passed soon, thank God, submerged by a host of other, new sensations. Quickly enough that she could marvel at the feeling of utter fullness of having him inside her. Fast enough that she could feel those thick tendrils of pleasure uncurl all over again as Andrea pulled out, almost all the way, and thrust back in. If he wasn't holding her captive with his lean, powerful frame, she'd have flown off the bed at the force of his thrust.

Monica bit her lip to stifle the moan that wanted to escape. His teeth dug into her shoulder and his free hand pinched her nipple and he was stroking in and out of her as if they'd never been apart at all, and it was such a symphony of sensations that she thought she might pass out for a second at all the different layers.

"Monica, speak, *bella*," he said, twisting his hips in some strange dance that stirred that spot inside her again. Every time he did it, pleasure unfurled in a thousand new filaments, as if she was lighting up from inside out. "Tell me you're okay."

She cleared her throat, but still her words came out as if from a deep, dark tunnel where words didn't matter. Only sensations and pleasure and a strange sense of…belonging. One instance of good sex and God, she was ready to build a damned nest. "You ask for the impossible even here. Expecting me to talk right now is…unfair."

"Shall we push you off again, *bella*?"

Monica hid her face in his throat and whispered, "I don't know if I can. Just please, don't stop what you're doing. Andrea…don't stop."

His mouth found hers and Monica lost herself in the kiss and in the rough slide of his hair-roughened chest over her sensitized breasts. Then, somehow, he notched his thumb at her clit and every time he stroked in and out of her, he hit that spot inside her and soon, she was climbing that mindless cliff again, desperate for release.

Her orgasm broke through her like a shock wave, out of nowhere, and Monica screamed at the near-violent intensity of it.

She heard his filthy curse as her muscles milked his shaft and soon, there was a new intensity to his thrusts. Monica closed her eyes and her awareness hit a new plane with the sounds of his body thrusting into her, and his guttural grunts and the scent of his sweat and cologne. When she opened her mouth, she could taste his sweat, and then he was shuddering and shaking and she wrapped her arms around him as he pinned her hips into the bed with his and gave a hoarse shout.

Their breaths were rough and harsh-sounding in the sudden silence, the air scented with sex, and he was a delicious weight on top of her, and Monica knew she would not forget this moment if she lived to be a hundred.

CHAPTER TEN

WHEN ANDREA WOKE from the likes of a deep sleep he hadn't known in years, the light in the room was so bright that he had to blink a few times. One glance at his watch told him it was past ten-thirty in the morning.

With a groan, he fell back against the bedsheets, a strange lethargy stealing over his body and his head. With a languorous laziness he rarely indulged in, he reached out with his arm before he turned to his side, only to find the bed empty and cold. Which meant she had been up for hours.

He'd appreciated that in his assistant, but not so much in his lover. He also could just imagine those feathery brows of hers tying into a tiny frown, while she hesitated to ask him how she would know which role she was playing on a given morning. A silly grin stole over his face.

Whatever dissonance he had expected didn't come, and Andrea decided not to overthink it. If last night was anything to go by, their chemistry was off the charts and he knew very well it was the kind one didn't come by often.

What was wrong with enjoying it? With exploring the undeniable heat between them? Who said they couldn't part as he did with his other lovers? Yes, Monica was different, but she had gotten over her engagement with that rascal, hadn't she? Even better, she'd openly admitted to wanting Andrea, to dreaming of him.

It wasn't like she didn't know the ways of the world. More important was the fact that she knew *him.* Better than most women, better than even his family maybe.

And yet, there was something that had niggled at the back of his mind last night when his body had been sated. The surfeit of pleasure had numbed his thinking cells for a while. But it was something he'd wanted to ask her at the peak of his explosive climax.

Two minutes after he'd untangled himself from her so that he didn't crush her and inquired if she was okay, she'd disappeared into the bathroom, claiming she needed it. Laughing, he'd put it down to her shyness and then wondered at when he'd last laughed after sex. Usually, he was angry with himself for giving in to the temptation of sex when he had nothing else to offer, even though he made it clear up front to his partners, and then he itched to leave to avoid awkwardness.

It wasn't the way he'd been once. He'd had more than his share of lovers and girlfriends as a handsome, vibrant race-car driver with the world at his feet, but he had liked companionship, too. He had liked spending time with his then current girlfriend, or Chiara later, liked the connection and laughter it brought into his life.

Having grown up with parents who kissed each other at the drop of a hat and danced in the kitchen at the slightest chance and expressed their affection in that easy, simple way, had made Romeo and him grow up with the same need to form deep connections.

After the accident, everything had changed. Or rather, he'd forced himself to change, to survive. But now, for the first time in years, he found himself wanting more than just a quick screw as some kind of stress relief. He wanted lazy mornings and long, glorious nights with Monica, and he decided he would enjoy every bit of it, as long as it lasted. He would treat her well, that was a given, but he would also indulge himself.

Once they had to break the engagement, which would be many months down the line, he would go back to his usual punishingly rigorous schedule at work again. With his body satiated and his mind resolved to the plan, thick sleep had claimed him. He had no idea how long she'd been gone because he had drifted off into sleep soon, still wearing a smile on his face.

He'd woken up in the hours of dawn to use the bathroom and found her at the edge of the bed, dressed in his shirt again, scrunched into a tight ball with her knees tucked into her chest, as if she meant to occupy the smallest space possible on the bed.

What she had shared with him struck him hard enough that Andrea found himself sitting at the foot of the bed, watching her sleep. She'd grown up in an orphanage first and then foster homes, had fended off wandering eyes and arms, had always dressed to minimize her looks and not to draw unwanted attention… Something he didn't want to feel or examine cracked open in his chest.

All the softer emotions that he had turned off, like tenderness and caring about anyone other than Mama and Romeo, cauterized for so long that he simply didn't feel them anymore, now pushed through like tiny new buds. He refused to let them send him into any kind of panic, though. At heart and by nurture, he had always been a man who cared about the people who revolved around his life, especially the ones who had less security, less privilege, in their lives. This…concern was that, that was all. As much as he chastised her for that sense of obligation she was forever mentioning, he felt it toward her, too.

How could he not, for the woman who had saved his mother's life? He and Romeo had nearly shattered at Papa's loss, so he could not even imagine their state if Mama had been hurt.

So yes, he would always "care" a little about this particular woman. Maybe even after they burnt out this chemistry.

When he had gotten back to bed, he had dragged her to the middle of it, to find her toes and fingers icy cold. The moment he turned her to face him, she came awake with a start and instantly stiffened, her arm coming up to block him. His heart had twisted in his chest, and his throat had felt thick with raw anger. Startled yellow eyes met his, fear slipping through the deep flush of sleep. "It's me, *bella.* You're safe," he'd said, running his hands through her long hair, kissing her temple.

In the next blink, she whispered something he couldn't catch, her body softened and with a tentativeness that tugged at his heart, she burrowed into him all the way. Her trust was a gift more precious than any he'd ever wanted or received.

With her face pushed up into his throat, her feet tucked between his legs and her curves tightly pressed against his hard muscles, all her stretching and wriggling had turned him rock hard. Hands stroking her back, Andrea had kissed her, urging her to wake up. It took all of five seconds for their kiss to turn voracious, their hands seeking and stroking, and when he touched her folds, she'd almost flinched. When he'd inquired, she'd admitted she was sore and two seconds later, drifted off into sleep again.

With that niggle narrowed down to a crystal-clear realization, Andrea shot out of the bed now. Pulling on sweatpants, he marched into the lounge to find her on the open terrace, her black agenda open in front of her on the table along with a cup of coffee and a bowl of fruit.

Dressed in a peach-colored sleeveless blouse with a V-neck and dark skinny jeans that looked like they'd been made to showcase her long legs, and her hair in a French braid, she looked like the prim and proper assistant she'd been for nearly three years. But he knew what lay underneath that simplicity and shyness, and he liked it way too much that he alone knew that.

"How long have you been awake?"

Monica startled so badly at that voice that she almost spilled the coffee on herself. At the last second, she let the cup slide onto the table and take the brunt of it. Only after she'd wiped the stickiness off her fingers and her heart resumed a relatively normal pace—she needed new normals around this man—did she turn her head.

Andrea was standing at the entrance to the terrace, dressed in loose sweatpants that hung low on his hips. His hair was a mess, his mouth was still swollen and there were deep, crescent-shaped marks right below his shoulder, thanks to her nails.

She flushed at the sight of him—with mortification but also with a visceral kind of satisfaction. Who knew she could be so possessive? Had all her instincts been lying dormant just waiting for the right man? What else would he unearth and unleash within her?

"Good morning," she finally managed, getting up from her seat. "You're out of the coffee beans you like but I ordered a different brand. I know you don't like change but you'll love this blend. I'll have a cup of coffee and your omelet ready, if you want to wash up and get dressed." With each word she uttered, he straightened from his relaxed pose and something she couldn't decipher dawned in his eyes. "I have also had the contracts sent over here from the legal department so that I can take a look at this new round of changes Mr. Brunetti's company is insisting on. I moved your appointment with Mr. Makiko to Tuesday, since you're visiting the manufacturing plant on Monday," she said, reading out the bullet points she'd marked on the agenda. "All the funds from yesterday's gala have been cleared and routed to the charity foundation's accountant. I have also had all your calls rerouted to me since I'll be taking over as your assistant again. Your temp is returning to the accounts department."

"Is that all?"

She shrugged and went to move past him. His fingers locked around her wrist, arresting her.

Monica shivered at the scent of his sun-warmed skin and the warmth from his bare chest and God, did he have to look so delicious first thing in the morning? Selfish wanton she was, she wished he would tug her closer so that she could soak in all of that heat from his body and kiss her senseless.

But he didn't do any of it. Instead, he released her once she stopped moving, his black-as-night gaze examining her face with an intensity she wasn't sure she could withstand without betraying herself.

Already, just the sight of him, disheveled and rough, had her body remembering the achy soreness she'd felt when she'd woken up, tangled around him. For long moments she'd stayed like that, her breath crashing through her as if she were a thief, intent on stealing something that didn't belong to her. He had been in such deep sleep that even when she'd untangled herself from him, he hadn't shaken.

Pushing herself up on her elbow, Monica had stared at him to her heart's content, tracing the scar on his face, the deep, jagged patchwork of scars she'd missed on his hip last night. In the end, her desperate need as she lay there for close to half an hour, watching him like some sort of love-sick fool, had made the decision for her. She wasn't going to cling to him or make any demands or even act like they'd done all the intimate things they'd done together. She would give him no reason for complaint, nor behave with even a whiff of lover-like expectations.

That was the only way this could work, the only way she could have him. So she'd done what she'd always done, put her head down and gone back to work, creating minimum ripples from him. She'd have even left the penthouse and given him space, if she could be sure her face wouldn't betray her night's activities to Romeo and Flora as if it were a high-def plasma television.

"Where did you get the clothes?" Andrea asked, startling her out of her reverie.

"I called the villa hoping to get Shania, Romeo's physio. Instead, I got Flora," she said, flushing.

His mouth twitched. "And?"

Monica sighed. "She made me give her a list of things I needed, packed all the things she made me buy at that boutique when she learned of our plans and told me she'd order two sets of toiletries, for here—" she moved her hand to indicate the penthouse "—and the villa because you don't know your own schedule and I want to be wherever you are, right?" By the time she had finished the retelling, his grin had deepened and Monica wanted to thump him for laughing at her embarrassment. "You know how Flora gets when she decides on something. I barely got in two words."

"Mama knowing about us bothers you. Why?"

"I don't want her to think I'm taking advantage of the situation, of you."

He laughed then, throwing his head back, drawing her attention to the column of his throat and his bobbing Adam's apple and his lean chest. Mortification swirling through her, Monica let out a filthy curse and instantly felt wrong for doing it.

Andrea's laughter doubled, and he had to bend down with his hands on his knees to balance himself. This time, when she went to pass him, muttering to herself, he not only stopped her again, but also lifted her in his arms, ignoring her rabbit-like squeal, walked into the lounge and sat down with her in his lap.

One arm wound around his neck, Monica drew in sharp breaths. An intense ribbon of longing held her in a choke-hold as she stared at the deep grooves around his mouth. His eyes danced with mirth and she thought he had never looked more heartbreakingly gorgeous.

"I'm glad to provide entertainment for you. Maybe I should also add *clown* to all the roles I perform for you."

"Don't tempt me about performing for me, *bella*," he said, nuzzling under her jaw and drawing a straight line to her earlobe with his teeth. She shivered anew. "I might throw a list of bullet points for your agenda. Especially since I'm feeling deprived after waking up alone. You should have stayed in bed."

Monica arched into his touch, her nipples peaking painfully as his mouth drifted lower, tugging the V-neck of the blouse as far as it would allow. She hummed at the back of her throat, an action she didn't know she was capable of, begging him wordlessly to do more. His scruff was rougher than the previous night, and pleasure jolted down to her sex when he pushed her blouse and bra roughly down and rubbed it against her nipple.

It was decadent, wanton and felt so filthily divine that she thought she might come apart at the seams.

Moaning, writhing on his lap, she sank her fingers into his hair, keeping him there. He licked at the needy knot before drawing it into his mouth. Monica jerked at the swift pool of dampness that one action caused and God, if he continued, she would come just like that and… He stopped.

Then he was tugging her bra and blouse back into place while she trembled with unmet need. "You're dangerous, *bella*. That wasn't what I had in mind for this morning."

"Then why did you start it?" she asked, unable to keep her peevishness out of her tone. "You…you…"

Brow risen, Andrea watched her with a keen interest, the earlier amusement returning to his eyes.

She struggled to get off his lap but his arms were steel bands around her. "I'm beginning to think you find this all hilarious," she said, anger and something more beating at her. "Me, I mean."

"I find you…sweet and naive, *bella*," he said, the humor vanishing from his eyes. "But it doesn't mean I'm laughing at you."

The tenderness in his voice could undo her so easily. Monica nodded without looking at him. This time when she tried to stand, he let her go, and she wished she hadn't.

God, she was a contrary fool.

Instead of running away or clinging to him, she chose the middle ground and settled on the coffee table in front of him, her legs on the outside of his, pathetic enough to want that little bit of closeness.

Hand under her chin, Andrea lifted her head. His dark eyes searched hers, challenging her to hold his gaze. "Now, tell me what this morning is all about."

She wished she could lie or fob him off with some flirty remark, or have the guts to grab him and kiss the hell out of him like she wanted to. But she was who she was and Andrea wasn't someone she could deter when he set his mind to something. "I…didn't want to be a nuisance to you. And I didn't want you to think I was expecting anything. Work had piled up anyway so I thought I should just…make myself useful."

He nodded, looking thoughtful. "This doesn't have to be awkward, Monica. We're consenting adults who trust each other, *si*?"

"I just… I panicked because I didn't know how to behave in this context and—"

"Because you've never done this before?" he cut in.

"No," she said, this time managing the fake flirty smile. "I haven't had a red-hot affair with my boss before."

"No, you've never had sex before."

Her gaze met his and her silence offered its own answer without her permission. Suddenly, she understood the intent behind his frown before. If he called her pathetic again… she might get actually mad and stomp out of there. "I think that's my business."

He leaned forward, trapping her between his thighs before she could pull away again. "I agree, *bella*. I only wish you'd told me so—"

"So you could find another reason to put me off? I don't know about you but I truly enjoyed what happened last night, Andrea. And I have zero regrets. Maybe this is about you and your—"

He caught her mouth in a devastating kiss that would have taken her out at the knees if she hadn't been sitting. There was none of the gentleness from last night, no exploration, no building to something more. Only rough, hard possession, making her words a lie, making her tingle from head to toe, telling her in no uncertain terms that this was a two-way obsession. At least for now.

His tongue plundered her mouth; his teeth nipped her lips as if in punishment for her doubts and God, his hands stroked over her hips and her back and sank into her hair and tugged her neat little braid until she tilted her head up in complete surrender. "I have plans for this braid and you." His words sent pulses of damp desire arrowing down to her core. Like a bow, he pulled her body taut and tight under his hold, ready to splinter at one tug. And she didn't mind one bit.

All her life, she'd hidden in the margins, making safe, defensive choices, always toeing the line of security but now, she was more than willing to let it all unravel at his hands.

His mouth left a wet, hot trail down her blouse, and then he bit the curve of her breast. "Still believe I didn't enjoy last night?"

Hands splayed on his thighs, she scooted closer and closer until somehow, she was on his lap and his erection was notched right where she needed it. She cursed herself for wearing skin-tight jeans. "Let's leave it at that, then."

Slowly, he released his hold and pulled back. This time, Monica couldn't help it, she ran her thumb over his lower lip and farther down until she could trace the marks she'd left on his skin. God, she loved touching him like this, loved knowing what he liked, just…knowing him at this intimate level.

"You were engaged to that scoundrel, *cara mia*. I'm trying to understand what was going on and if I need to find him and thrash him."

"I know how…it looks and I want to share some things with you. But what if it makes you laugh at me?"

His mouth flattened with quick anger and she felt stupid for projecting her own insecurities at him. "I'm not him, *bella*."

"I know that. I didn't mean to..."

"It's okay," Andrea said, covering her mouth with one finger. "You're from such a different background than me. And so young and..." He shook his head as if he couldn't be *that* honest with her. "I would never laugh at anything you've done to survive in this world, ever. In fact, I think you are a marvel, *bella*, to retain that spirit of yours after such a start in life."

Every word of his took down some unknown brick wall she'd built around herself, made her feel seen. And until now, she hadn't known how much she needed someone to see it, someone to tell her that she had survived it all without losing parts of herself. And that it was this man who had her trust, filled her with a giddy kind of joy, with a rightness that she felt down to her marrow.

Monica leaned into his chest and wrapped her arms around him, tears beckoning at the backs of her eyes again. And then while she hid her face in his throat, she talked, because she'd always wanted to talk to someone about it all and who better than this man who somehow made her brave enough and bold enough to reach for her deepest desires.

"When I was growing up, I... My body developed too soon," she said, the past swirling through her mind like a movie. "By fourteen, I was as tall as I am now and I had this face and these breasts and these legs but no one to help me understand why I seemed to draw the worst kind of attention from boys and men. Maybe if I had continued to live with Father D'Souza, he would have explained it to me, but he wasn't allowed to have children older than eleven."

Andrea was stiff beneath her, his fingers cradling her scalp, his other hand stroking down her body as if he meant to make the telling easier. "Father D'Souza?"

"I was left as an infant on the steps of his church. He's

like a…father to me, the only family I've known. When I was old enough, I decided I would take his last name."

"That is the man you visit every year in New York."

She smiled, remembering how cranky Andrea had been last year when she'd been gone for three weeks. "Yes. He worries about me and I worry about him. He's seventy-three now and I like to see him at least once a year. My aptitude for languages… He recognized it first, encouraged me to take courses at the community college. He was also the one who urged me to go on a vacation the first time I came here, helped me with the funds even. Now he keeps asking me if I'll ever move back."

"What do you say to that?"

Monica hid her grin. She didn't miss the stiffness of Andrea's tone when he asked that. "I tell him that I'm building a good life here, that I have friends and a grumpy boss who will probably hound me across the pond if I take off for too long. He was worried that first year, after the accident." She instantly regretted going there as Andrea's hand stilled, but pushed on. "But now he knows about all of you. Romeo and he have an ongoing online chess game, even."

"Send a donation to the orphanage in Papa's name," he said, that ring of command back in his voice.

Monica hid her smile in his chest. As his personal assistant, and sometimes Flora's companion at these events, she knew how many charities Valentini Luxury Goods supported. But this particular donation…meant a lot to her. Even bracing herself for him to laugh at her, she kissed his cheek and whispered her thanks.

"I'm sorry for interrupting you. Tell me more about… you."

She refused to examine why it was so easy to pick up where she had left off, why it felt so good to tell him things she'd never admitted to anyone, even Romeo, who had become a true friend.

Was it the protectiveness that Andrea gave off? Or just simple, abiding trust in him? Or was it the fact that he was the man who had helped her push through the armor she'd built around her own sexuality? Or was it all of it?

"It didn't take me long to realize that my looks, my own body, was a curse. I shied away from anything that remotely touched on my femininity or my sexuality. There was another guy when I was eighteen. He wasn't unkind, but I couldn't get out of my head. When push came to shove, I…backed out. I realized I wasn't really into it. With Francesco, we…kissed and did other stuff. I tried so hard but I just couldn't go all the way. He was frustrated and I was frustrated. I wanted him and me to work so much. I had this perfect life in my head and he suited it to a tee. He said we had all our lives and it was another reason why I fell for him. I thought he was so sweet to wait, ready to try again. When I reached him after he dumped me—" Andrea's arms tightened around her waist "—he said I was a shiny package but the contents were useless or something like that. That I was like a cold, hollow sculpture, useful only for showing off."

"He needs to be taught a lesson," Andrea bit out.

"He's taught me one thing, though, and I'm grateful for that."

"Forgive me if I don't ask you what that is, *bella*. You're far too forgiving and generous to attribute any good thing to him."

Monica clasped his cheek, feeling the most insane urge to hug him, which was definitely not a sexual urge. A part of her marveled that she could touch him freely like this, could talk to him so openly, while the other part of her was wary to flex her newfound role.

She settled for a soft kiss on his lips, pouring out all these new sensations fluttering through her as if a thousand butterflies had been released. Gratitude and more fluttered on her lips but she didn't dare try to put it into words. She wasn't sure what would come out.

"What was that for?" he asked, raising his brows.

For a man who rarely showed emotion or liked it in others, he was very good at reading her and her kisses. She shrugged and before it could get awkward—or was it her own wariness at this kind of intimacy?—she stood up and checked her watch. "We do have a few matters to get through today."

"What a strict assistant you are, *bella*. It is Saturday."

"And you have worked every Saturday since I joined the company."

"Today I feel like goofing off. I will spend the day in bed with my fake fiancée and explore her very real passion. There are a few things I didn't get to try last night. So, if you can see yourself out for the weekend and call her in, *por favor*. I'm eager to get started."

How had Monica not known that it was possible to blush and smile at the same time? Where had he hidden this flirty, roguish side of him?

He was already larger than life but to see this real side of him… What woman could stand a chance against him? She was beginning to feel like she was on a ride that only went up and around, making her dizzy. Biting her lower lip, she took a step away from the sitting lounge. "Your fake fiancée is busy today."

"Busy with what?" he said, standing up, every inch the arrogant CEO who wanted the world arranged just so at his command.

"She's going to a pizza-and gelato-making class."

"With whom?" he prompted, coming unerringly to the point.

Monica considered evading for one moment, and then sighed. "Romeo. We made the date weeks ago. I can't cancel it because you've decided you want to…stay in bed. The chef is like a genius and his classes take months to get in and the gelato is to die for. After the last few weeks…it's the one fun thing I've been looking forward to."

"I would never want to stand in the way of your fun, Monica," he said, taking a step in her direction. "Only, you will go with me instead of my brother. He hogs too much of your time anyway."

"I like spending time with him. And I'm not ditching him just so…" Her words fell away as he began stalking her across the open layout, a wicked twinkle in his eyes.

"Just so I can indulge us both, so I can taste you again? Just so I can give you a bullet-pointed agenda for the day's activities and see how fast we can get through them all? Your efficiency does drive me wild, *bella*."

She blushed and he was laughing and Monica thought she might burst apart at the seams. Desire and anticipation, yes, but this easy joy… God, it was like magic, vibrating through her every cell. "You really want to take the Saturday off and make gelato with me?" she asked, disbelief punctuating her words.

"With you, yes," he said, catching her. And then his mouth was on hers and Monica forgot about mergers and charity funds and gelato, and maybe even the reason for breathing.

CHAPTER ELEVEN

LIFE MOVED AT an insane pace for Monica over the next two months as Andrea's novelty fiancée. And she definitely was a novelty, she realized with increasing wariness.

For his family, because Andrea seemed to play the role of a possessive, protective fiancé with an easy aplomb they hadn't expected. More than once, she'd seen a shadow pass across Flora's eyes but the older woman, sweet as ever, never gave voice to whatever doubts she had. Thankfully, neither did she ask Monica much about their "fake relationship," treating her with the same kindness as always, and that was enough for her.

For his friends, colleagues and extended family, all of whom orbited Andrea for some sort of help, she was the "poor orphaned American woman" who had caught Andrea's fancy. *Temporarily* was implied but not said. Most of them, though, were smart enough to play nice with her since she did have his ear. The smart ones even understood that she not only knew every big business matter that passed his desk but that he also trusted her.

More than once, their casual attitude toward using his wealth and reach for their own benefit, as if he owed them that due to his meteoric success, rankled Monica. There were one or two people who wanted his friendship for no other reason than that he was a dynamic, witty person to be around. But Andrea did not allow that closeness.

One of them was her earlier boss, the CFO for Valentini Luxury Goods. While he trusted Maria, Andrea kept it purely professional with her, even though Maria had known him for years.

For the rest of the world and the media, she was a novelty because, once they had decided to believe Andrea's version, their affair was nothing short of a fairy tale coming true.

Having never spent a moment as the center of attention at any stage of her life, Monica struggled with it at every party and gala and public event, where she was cast as the beautiful American upstart of unknown origins, the woman who had stolen the gorgeous, powerful bachelor that all of Milan adored. Wherever she went, on Andrea's arm or with Flora and Romeo, she was besieged with questions about their relationship, as if they wanted to decipher how she had landed the uncatchable Andrea Valentini.

But for every second that she cringed at the invasive questions, flinched at camera flashes going off in their faces and tried to hide behind Andrea's broad frame like a scared rabbit, she enjoyed the glimpse she was getting into how fun and charming and utterly seductive he could be.

Romeo kept reminding her that the fake engagement suited his brother, that she was good for him, that he hadn't seen Andrea this lively and fun in a long time. Monica tried not to let it go to her head, though there was more than a grain of truth to Romeo's assessment. Hijacking her gelato-making date had been only the start.

She blushed profusely even now, remembering how Andrea had surprised her that evening when they had arrived at the world-class restaurant kitchen. It had been only them and the chef. All the other participants had been highly compensated to attend a different session, because Andrea Valentini wanted to learn how to make gelato with his media-shy fiancée in private, and the world had better arrange itself accordingly. For once, his high-handedness and his refusal to parade them in front of an audience had worked out for her.

It had been one of the best evenings of her life. From the sheer pleasure of spending hours in Andrea's company—his lips and hands constantly touching her in a hundred little ways, as if he couldn't help himself—to how he'd distracted her with whispered promises that her tiny batch of gelato had turned out awful while his had been mouthwateringly perfect, and the end of the night where they had barely made it back to his penthouse, full of delicious pizza and gelato and wine, and he had taken her against the wall just barely inside the elevator.

Even then, he'd first made sure she wasn't still sore, with his fingers. When it had been clear she was just as eager as him, he had picked her up, held her against the wall, pulled her sundress up and thrust into her with one hard stroke that had had her banging her head against the wall.

It had been fervent, frantic, near-frenzied, how they'd clawed at each other.

And in the weeks since that night, their frenzy had nowhere near calmed. Not hers, and definitely not his.

Monica almost wished their fake relationship only centered around the very real passion and chemistry that seemed to imbue every touch and caress. Then she could have firmly told her increasingly invested heart to stay out of the whole matter. She wanted to believe that at some point in her life, she would have met a man who would have disabused her of her hang-ups and fears about her body and her sexuality. Because she'd weaved them all into place to protect herself against a harsh world. She wanted to convince herself that that man just happened to be her boss, whom she'd trusted beyond any other man she'd ever met.

Andrea, at every turn, proved all the things she tried to tell herself to be lies.

It wasn't just the phenomenal sex or the incendiary chemistry between them that made Monica feel as if her life was simultaneously rushing fast like a river rapid and grounding to a halt like the rich earth under.

Because there were moments where it seemed, impossibly, marvelously, that he cared about her, that he enjoyed her company as much as her body and her kisses and her wild, deep need for him that drove him to his own edge.

That, however, was a slippery slope of wishful thinking because she wanted to truly live her life this time, take each day as it came with Andrea, however many she got, instead of making it fit into some childhood template of a dream life.

What she really wanted was to take initiative in their personal life. Not that she had a problem with following whatever Andrea decided—in the two months of their roller-coaster, fake and yet somehow real relationship, she had done more fun, adventurous things, had laughed more, had explored her own sexuality at his patient hands, had understood her own needs and wishes better than ever before.

She had lived in these two months more than she had her entire life. And she wanted to believe that it was the same for him, too.

He did seem livelier and more relaxed, more prone to spontaneity and taking time off work, since she'd resumed working for him. Still, wary reluctance was a knot in her belly anytime she wanted to cross a line that really wasn't there. So when that particular day approached that Andrea would not work, Monica ensured his schedule was clear and made plans to make herself scarce.

It was the day more than a decade ago when they had lost their father. Everyone, even at work, knew that Andrea disappeared that day. Not even Romeo or Flora knew where he went or how he spent it. As his new assistant two years ago, Monica herself had been witness to the change in his demeanor even a week ahead of that day each year, of how the shadow of grief ravaged him.

But…a small part of her desperately wanted to talk to him this time. To spend it with him, even if in utter silence. To provide a little solace and companionship to him on a day when he retreated from the world, and even his family.

She was still mulling over how she could do it without crossing a boundary when Andrea entered and closed the door to the office behind him. Monica looked away from her screen and rubbed at her gritty-feeling eyes.

It was eight in the evening on a Wednesday and the glittering lights of Milan's financial district shone through the floor-to-ceiling glass walls of Andrea's office.

They had been going through the final corrections that the legal department had sent on the merger with Mr. Brunetti's company since six in the morning. Not only was Monica bone tired after being up until two for a dinner with Andrea's business associates, but she was also worried about him.

All day, words had formed and dusted away on her lips as she waited to see signs of his mood spiraling or retreating. Instead, he had been on a high the past two days. Mr. Brunetti had finally agreed to most of Andrea's terms for the merger, and they had been working hard and playing harder. He'd been relentlessly demanding in bed, and Monica had begun to wonder if sex could be used as a way to blunt painful reminders of grief. Not that she minded one bit being used like that…

A file plopped onto the coffee table in front of her.

"You missed two pages of corrections again," Andrea said, planting himself onto the table.

Embarrassment flushed her cheeks as Monica opened the file, found the pages he was referring to. "I'm sorry, there's no excuse." Foolish, useless tears formed a lump in her throat. How could she have missed it? God, she prided herself on her work and this was unacceptable. "I'll look through these and get the new changes entered immediately. You'll have them ASAP."

When she made to get up, he leaned forward, his legs straddling hers and locking her in place. "That's two times you made a mistake today. And two times in the three and a half years since you started working at this company."

Monica looked up to find his eyes full of that sardonic humor. And that spark touched her heart as if it were a warm tendril wrapping around the chamber, cocooning her from the world. Slowly, she straightened her spine, when all she wanted to do was to lean into his warm body and let him envelop her. "That's two times too many for my liking," she said, flipping through the file. "I don't know how it happened but I promise you that it won't happen again, and—"

"It happened because I've been working you too hard," Andrea said, taking the file from her hands. He leaned in where she had pulled back and rubbed the pad of his thumb under her eyes. "You look exhausted, *cara.* Why didn't you tell me you needed a break?"

"*You* didn't take one," she said, drawing a finger across the gaunt brackets around his mouth. God, how she loved touching him like this, as if he was hers to do so. And what was she going to do when this merger was all signed off on? When his interest in her and the necessity of this fake relationship began to dwindle? How would she keep her hands to herself and her thoughts free of him? How would she sit across from him in this same office and pretend like she didn't want more of him?

Her thoughts looped in the same way, even as she tried to detach herself from them, detach herself from this growing feeling that pervaded every one of her waking and sleeping moments.

"You have double standards here," she said, smiling to make the complaint seem shallow. "Even Romeo agrees that you never slow down, despite preaching it to him."

"My fiancée and my brother are going behind my back and discussing me?"

"We're too afraid to say it to your face," she said, wondering when he'd begun to drop the fake part from her title. She tried so hard to not read anything into it.

"I have spent years training my body and my head to survive on little sleep and rest. For you, though, it has been long nights and long days, *si*?" His gaze encompassed her entire body, from her hair in a loose bun to her tight dress shirt and her black trousers, lighting every inch of her on slow, deep fire. "I should have realized I'm making too many demands on you. Which is something Mama and Romeo have been hounding me about."

"I like spending time with you. At work or outside of it. I mean, yes, I could do a little less of all the socializing and networking dinners as your fiancée but all the rest, I like it, Andrea. I like what we do together," she said, and then blushed so hard that she had no doubt her cheeks must look like tomatoes.

"I like how intensely you admit that, *bella*," he said with a grin and caught her mouth in a whisper-kiss that made her heart thud against her rib cage. He tasted of coffee and mint and like decadent want, his mouth drawing her deeper with each nip and stroke.

She kept waiting to see if the raw need she felt for him would dial down or change with each kiss and caress. But it hadn't. It didn't. If anything, now she craved him like a drug that she needed to function fully in the world. His kisses and his teasing and his carnal demands in bed… She reveled in every moment, yes, but now they were tinged with a deeper emotion, carried more weight with each passing day.

Like every single time, their kiss rose to a fever pitch soon, tinged with a desperate need on both their sides, racing toward more. Maybe because it had been a whole thirty-six hours since they had made love. They had been so busy last night that they had fallen into exhausted sleep as soon as they had returned to his penthouse.

She protested with a mewl when Andrea pulled away, even as her fingers were locked against his nape, holding him to her. Her eyes closed as he swept his mouth over her jaw and that sensitive spot where her neck met her shoulder. Shamelessly, she thrust herself into his touch, and had the even better reward of hearing his laughter.

Finally, he pulled back from her again, and she was glad to see his own pupils blown up with desire and more. There was always a little more that tinged his desire, too, but she could never be sure if it was only what she *wanted* to see.

His mouth trailed upward and landed at her temple, his rough fingers circling her nape with a possessive protectiveness that she'd longed for her whole life. "Go home, take a shower, catch some sleep and then I want you to take a couple of days off. There's a little mountain resort within two hours that the chauffeur will drive you to. I'll join you tomorrow night."

"No," she said, something close to panic rising within her. They couldn't go off this weekend, of all weekends. When he realized what it was, he would hate her. "I need to finalize these documents and—"

"I've been pursuing this merger for more than two years. Brunetti has thrown every obstacle in its way and we have resolved them all to our satisfaction. Signing on the dotted line can wait for a few days."

"It's not just work I'm worried about."

"Whatever is on the social calendar, cancel it. Why the resistance, *bella*?" He drew back, as if to search her face for some hidden meaning. Something she'd never heard before underlined his words when he spoke. "Aren't you the one forever nagging me to take it slow for just a little bit?"

Her cheeks heated at that word. "No, nothing on the social calendar. I already cleared the rest of your week, beginning tomorrow. I knew you wouldn't want to work on Friday and…"

"What's Friday?"

"It's the…twenty-third of September. You…usually don't work that day."

He reared back from her so fast that it was like whiplash. He had forgotten the significance of the date, she realized with a belated sort of horror, and that was exactly what was reflected in his face now.

He looked horrified that he had forgotten. And fast on the heels of that came guilt that filled his eyes.

Monica stood up, wanting to follow him, some knot of fear and guilt trapped in her throat making it hard to breathe. He walked away from the sitting lounge, his moments lacking that economic grace that made him a pleasure to watch. When he reached his desk, he rubbed a hand over his face, his shoulders tight with tension.

"Andrea, it's a small oversight. We've been busy with this merger and you—"

"I do not need you to assuage my guilt, Monica," he said, without turning around. But she saw his reflection in the windows and how he rubbed the heels of his palms against his eyes. It was a rare gesture of vulnerability that he never showed the world, not even his family. And definitely not her.

Monica, he'd called her. Not *bella* or *cara mia*. And in that particular tone that he rarely used anymore. She swallowed the sliver of hurt it invoked. This wasn't about her or their relationship. But somehow, she couldn't swallow that lie. "I'd never tell you to feel one way or another, Andrea. Just as you can't tell me to not care about you."

Her words landed in between them, creating a minefield she couldn't cross without it exploding in her face.

"I do not need your care. Definitely not in this and not in any area of my personal life. I thought you understood that."

She nodded even though he couldn't see her and rallied herself into acting as if the vast room wasn't suddenly swathed in tension. Gathering her files and folders, she started stuffing them into her laptop bag. "What you suggested earlier is a good idea. A weekend at the resort, I mean. I'll make arrangements for your stay. Anything that comes up, I can manage easily."

"What a thoughtful assistant and lover you are, *bella*, easily shifting from one role to the other, not making any demands in either," he said now, turning around, his mouth wreathed in a cynical twist he rarely showed her anymore. It was almost as if the Andrea from those beginning years of their acquaintance was back, and she was nothing but one of his dutiful sheep.

"I'm thinking of you," she said, a reckless kind of boldness sweeping through her. "I know you don't let anyone, not even Flora or Romeo, do that, but I do. And I won't apologize for it."

"And yet, you're not insisting on accompanying me on the trip."

"Not this time, no," she said, each step she took toward him feeling like an obstacle course she was jumping over. "I have a feeling anything I suggest will only rile you up right now."

"What a good little rule follower you are, always weighing your risks."

His words landed like a punch to her gut, given they carried so much truth in them. That he would taunt her for what she thought was her weakness…hurt on so many levels. "You're…not in a good place now and I have no problem being your target," she said, anger coming to her aid. "But don't presume to know how I feel or what I want."

"Tell me what you want, then," he said, the words full of some craven demand. "Tell me what the perfect assistant, perfect lover, perfect fake fiancée, Monica D'Souza, truly wants."

"I want to go to the chalet with you. I want to be with you and give you the space to talk about anything and everything. I want to give you companionable silence. I want to go to bed with you. I want you to tell me about that awful day. I want you to not struggle with your grief alone. I want to hear about what kind of man your father was, in your own words, because I know he must have been amazing to have raised you and Romeo to be who you are. I want to watch over you as you do for everyone that comes into your sphere. I want you to be not alone because every moment you are, I'll be thinking of you."

His gaze lost the dark humor, icing her out. His chin

reared down as if she'd attacked him instead of offering a short respite from his grief and his guilt. "I don't need to talk about it, *bella*. There's no big emotional resolution I'll achieve by talking about how I drove Papa into crashing our car. There's no big breakthrough I'll get by talking about how Romeo almost died because of my selfishness. There's nothing you can do that will change that day and what it stole from me. Or what it turned me into," he said, turning away. "You're one of a kind, *bella*, I'll give you that. But you cannot change me. And if you're beginning to think that…"

"Oh, don't worry, Andrea. That kind of arrogance has never been my strength. As for wanting to change you or claim you…even I'm not that naive. But—"

"I think you should leave. Before I say something I cannot take back."

Monica had known this was coming, this clearly drawn line in the sand that would shove her back beyond that boundary. Her entire life had been about lines like this that told her she was wanted only if it was convenient, only if she behaved well, only if a foster family was faring well financially, only if she behaved perfectly, only, only, only…

Something that had been forever yoked to that fear, that she might have a family or love if only she stayed behind that line and didn't ask much, splintered. Suddenly, it felt as if she had been set free from a huge weight and it was both terrifying and liberating.

With that came a kind of recklessness, even as she dutifully walked back to the other side of the line. She had a question to ask. And it flew from her mouth like a bullet. "Are you angry that for the first time in a decade, you were so happy with your own life that you forgot the relentless grief you carry as some kind of shroud? Or are you angry that it is our fake relationship that made you forget? Or is it that you have decided you cannot be happy at all?"

His shoulders tightened enough for her to know that her question had landed exactly as she'd intended it to. But she didn't wait for his answer because Andrea Valentini was an honorable man and she didn't want to make a liar out of him. Though there was little satisfaction in knowing she was right.

Her heart felt heavy in her chest as she walked out of his office and closed the door, even as every inch of her wanted to stay, wanted to be strong enough to withstand his misdirected anger and guilt and hold his hand through the pain that came later.

CHAPTER TWELVE

It was a full two days before Monica returned to his family home, a huge bunch of wild lilies clutched in her hand. The moment she saw him, wariness turned the corners of her lush mouth down.

Andrea had spent the anniversary of his father's death mulling over the questions she had posed for him and chastising himself for being hard on the one person who had dared only to think of him. He still didn't know what to think or how to process the fact that he had forgotten that date this year.

For years, it had stood out like a black mark against his very soul on the calendar, reacquainting him with guilt and grief and raw pain that he took on as punishment. He spent it drinking, replaying the argument with Papa, regrets piling up until he couldn't breathe. For days, he would be unable to face Mama or Romeo for fear of seeing their hatred or resentment or even grief. He had never allowed himself the luxury of grieving with them, of reflecting on what they'd all lost that day. He'd forced himself to be alone, both as punishment and repentance.

And yet this year, all that had changed.

She had changed it, even as he had taunted her that their relationship didn't matter in the scheme of things. Not a minute after she'd left, he'd regretted his callous words. Still, he was cowardly enough not to want to face her even though her hurt weighed on him like another shroud. He didn't have an answer for her question and was ruthless enough to know that he wouldn't give it to her even if he had it.

Instead, he had turned up at his family home two mornings later, so that it wouldn't look like he was seeking her out. Neither did he miss it that she had drawn him here on that day when he'd stayed away for so long. Only she wasn't there and instead of the heavy silence he'd braced himself for, he'd heard laughter, the kind that surged up from one's belly, like a cleansing fire.

He had shocked Mama and Romeo in the middle of watching those home videos Papa had made out of every tiny occasion, their laughter ringing around Romeo's high-tech studio lounge.

Transfixed by the sight of the laughing man in the grainy video on the screen, Andrea had folded himself down onto the sofa, a little distance away from them. Papa had come alive for those videos, dancing with Mama while he or Romeo held the camera precariously, playing with them, teasing them…

They had watched those videos for hours, laughing and shouting and reminiscing and at the end, Andrea had found his eyes wet and his head achy and his heart somehow lighter and yet heavy, too. Mama had buried her face in his chest and sobbed silently, even as she hurried to reassure him that she loved him with all her heart. That whatever his father had dreamed of for him and Romeo for the future, he had fulfilled it a thousand times over and wouldn't he forgive himself, too?

And Andrea had realized what a fool he'd been all these years. How unnecessarily he'd suffered through his grief alone. On the heels of the first came another realization. He didn't want that life anymore, where he punished himself, where he struggled alone, where he hid himself from his family. It was the exact opposite of what Papa had wanted for his firstborn.

Beneath all of it was the gnawing realization that two days had passed since their argument and Monica still hadn't returned. Only Romeo's admission that she'd told him she was fine and needed space had stopped him from calling the *chief commissario* of the police to look for her.

The third morning, she walked into his home, her pale pink sundress rumpled—had she slept in it?—and an expensive bunch of wild lilies, her favorite flowers, in hand. Her mouth instantly drew down when she spied him prowling the garden around the patio. Her hair in a messy braid, her eyes wearing that haunted look he'd seen once before—the very sight of her made emotions surge through him. Gritting his teeth, he sought control, trying to find some rationality out of the thorny knots.

He had worried over her safety. He had…hated sleeping by himself and had repeatedly reached out an arm, desperate for her warm body across his bed. He had…missed her with a longing he couldn't kill or define. And with each hour that had passed, he had become more determined to come up with a plan that would both satisfy his needs and prune the buds of things he didn't want to feel or nurture.

Seeing her, hearing his heart thud in his chest and his body tighten with desire, told him this was the change he sought in his life.

Turning their fake engagement into a real one was a simple and brilliant solution. Monica would have what she'd wanted all her life—family, security and a promise of a long, solid future. If she wished, they could even have children.

He would have her in his bed, and when passion waned

as it eventually would, they would have a stable partnership built on loyalty and friendship and mutual care. It wouldn't be the soulless business merger with Chiara, but neither would it be the great love story his parents had shared that had left his mother shattered. It would be something in between, something that suited him and Monica.

She knew him, maybe better than anyone, and she would understand what a reach this was for him, would know how far he was willing to go for her. *Just her.*

With each second, the idea held more and more appeal. She would be his. Her loyalty, her generosity, her affection, her passion, her days and nights, all of them would be his. The very thought sent a staccato of urgent need beating through him.

"Where the hell have you been?" he asked as she skated a wide arc around him to reach his mother and Romeo, who were breakfasting on the patio.

She kissed Mama's cheek and then wrapped her arms around Romeo from behind, smiled when he whispered something in her ear and then planted a sound kiss on his scruffy cheek.

Bitter jealousy ran rivulets through Andrea, tying his stomach in tight knots, and he swore to himself that he would have that easy affection from her, too. He'd never been a patient man and now that he knew what he wanted, he wanted it sealed and done now. He wanted her acceptance now. He wanted to tell his mother to plan the wedding so that they could have it as soon as possible. Then he would whisk her away on a short honeymoon—with this merger going through, he could afford at least a weekend. And then he would punish her, in the best way he knew, for this stubborn act. For cutting him off for two whole days, for being unavailable to him when he'd been desperate for her. He would give her so much pleasure that she'd never even think of parting from him again.

After what felt like an eternity, she turned to him, her chin lifting at that stubborn angle that both infuriated him and fascinated him no end. "Good morning to you. too, Andrea. I have been staying with a friend, taking a break as you ordered me to."

He walked toward the breakfast table, not liking the reminder that she had sought his brother for help, yet again. To avoid him specifically. "You switched off your phone."

"I wasn't working and you told me to steer clear of you." Her eyes held his, and at whatever she saw there, she sighed. "Romeo knew I was fine."

"What about what you owe me?" he bit out, not hiding his frustration, and her eyes widened. "Was that your little petty punishment because I behaved like an ass? Because it worked."

Whatever anger and defiance she'd drummed up seemed to drain out of her at his admission. Her hand shook as she lifted the carafe and poured a cup of coffee, added a spoon of cream, stirred it in and handed it to him. Even now, she catered to his wishes and unspoken needs first and damned if he knew how to feel about it.

He was shocked enough to grumpily say, "I don't need your peace offering." But the scent of her was already working on him, making his body buzz.

"I know you worry over me, and you think I'm some naive lamb out in the jungle. If I try really hard—" her mouth twitched "—I can even appreciate where your concern stems from. But it's not necessary."

"I disagree."

She thrust the coffee cup into his hand and went back to the table. Loath as he was to have this spat in front of his mother and Romeo, he settled down at the table. They'd been pestering him about their "little fight" for days now and this way, they would understand his intentions and he wouldn't have to reassure them that he wasn't hurting their little lamb.

"What's with the flowers?" he asked after taking a few sips of his coffee. Already, his day felt better, in his control, with her seated across from him and his plan cementing in his mind.

She ran a finger over one fragile petal, shying her gaze away from his before she said, "Birthday flowers from Francesco."

Silence fell over the table. Even Mama's look for Monica was full of soft chastisement.

"That's the friend you've been staying with?" Andrea bit out, jealousy clinging to his throat like a thousand tiny pinpricks. "Did you run to him the minute we fought?"

Her head jerked up, her gaze blazing with fire. *Cristo*, why was he saying all the wrong things? "If you really think that—"

"I don't." He rubbed a hand over his face, wondering what the hell was wrong with him.

"I stayed with that waitress friend of Romeo's," she said, cutting his brother a cheeky grin. That grin should be his, as should the light in her eyes. "We went to the lakefront in Navigli, and Francesco was there with some friends. He came over, ordered expensive wine, remembered all of a sudden that it was my birthday and bought the flowers from one of those expensive shops. He was trying to show off his elevated life status and it was easier to accept them than argue with him."

Another regret to add to his mounting pile, Andrea thought.

It had been her birthday and he'd sent her off to spend it with strangers, by herself. And that scoundrel knew that little detail about her and he hadn't. For the first time in his life, Andrea wished he could redo the whole past few days all over again.

Mama broke the spiraling tension between them. "Four years and you didn't tell us the same day is your birthday, Monica? We would have celebrated it with you!"

Monica shook her head, dislodging a thick strand of hair from her braid. Andrea felt the most overwhelming urge to tuck it behind her ear and pull her into his lap until she poured down all the reasons for her swollen eyes and pinched mouth. If it wasn't just him, that is.

"I know how hard that day is for you all. As for my birthday, I don't think it's even real. It was the day Father D'Souza found me on the front steps of the church. We simply decided that would be my birthday."

"Giovanni would have been delighted to know that the anniversary of his death could be marked with celebrating such a lovely person like you, *cara mia*," his mother said, her words trembling, but her mouth stretching into a wide smile.

"We will celebrate it tonight," Andrea said, and his mother and Romeo added their excitement.

Monica stared at him, her hand stilling on her own coffee cup. Anger flashed in her eyes and yet, she pushed it away with the sort of control he'd never seen her possess.

Andrea sat back in his chair and watched her, his gut tight with some strange sort of premonition. There was something different about her, he realized, even though she'd only been gone two days. Like a wall of newly erected defense between her and him. Like she wasn't being herself.

When she looked at him, her gaze was calm. It was not the

Monica he had known for almost four years, the woman who wore all her emotions like bright colored signals on her face. "Is it okay if I excuse myself, Flora? I want to shower and maybe catch up on some sleep. I'm afraid I don't feel good."

When his mother nodded, she stood up and left without so much as blinking in his direction. Effectively dismissing him, which was novel in itself.

Bemusement and something more sang through Andrea's veins. He'd never seen her anger or her armor before and he didn't like it one bit employed against him. Especially the latter.

He followed her slender frame up the stairs with his hungry gaze. Disappointment curdled through him when she chose to go to the room she had convalesced in, instead of his suite where they'd been staying for the past two months.

"I believe the Americans call it being in the doghouse," Romeo supplied softly, unhelpful as ever.

"It was her birthday and you forced her to spend it with a stranger. You better make it up to her, Andrea," his mother said, casting a shrewd glance at him. "If, however, you're bored with her, it might be better to tell her. I do hope you know that I will not be picking sides."

"Hardly, Mama," Andrea said, reaching for her hand and giving it a squeeze. "For once, you're going to be not only impressed with how I plan to make it up to her, but thoroughly ecstatic."

Her eyes widened and even Romeo looked stunned for once. Andrea kissed her cheek and left for his own shower, ignoring his brother's rapid-fire questions. He'd let her sleep a little and then he'd make it up to her.

Monica came awake slowly, and instantly sought her cell phone to check the time. Instead, she found the electronic alarm clock that rested near Andrea's bed winking at her, the red digits showing it was just past six. Frowning, she sat up in the vast bed, the luxury cotton duvet clinging to her bare legs, the all too familiar navy furnishings and that cozy scent of wood shavings making her body react as if it were a scent specifically designed to comfort and arouse her in equal measures.

"Feeling better after your nap?"

She turned to find Andrea sitting at his woodworking desk, torso bare and whittling away at a small slab of dark ebony wood in front of him. For a few moments, she simply watched his fingers use tiny tools with the same precision he used against her intimate folds. Heat flushed within her at remembered pleasure.

He wasn't even looking at her yet somehow knew the exact moment she'd woken up. Closing her tired eyes, she told herself to stop reading meaning into the silliest things. Especially now, in a vulnerable state after the phone call she'd received this morning from one of the two friends she'd made at the orphanage about Father D'Souza.

It was not good news and yet, somehow it felt like if it had to happen, it had happened at the right time. Somehow, even in his ill health, the kind father was looking out for her well-being.

Pressing the heels of her thumbs into her eyes, Monica willed the roiling panic to abate. She knew what she had to do. All weekend she'd wondered how she could shore up her defenses against him, how to finish this thing between them with dignity instead of letting the coming end consume her.

Fate had handed her a way out and now, all she had to do was act on it. And yet, there had been something different about him this morning. He'd shown more emotion—yes, it was masked by jealousy, but it had been there. Even a sense of urgency. It had taken all her willpower to run from him, though she knew she needed the reprieve.

The bed dipped at her side the same moment a wall of warmth rubbed up against her arm. She felt his fingers on her cheek, the abrasive pad of his thumb tracing her jawline. Her breath came in deep, eager pants, the scent of his sweat and soap making her nearly delirious with desire and longing. "Monica? I was an ass to you in the office, *bella*. Forgive me." He whispered the words into her temple, one arm coming up behind her to hold her loosely.

Monica leaned her side into his chest, automatically seeking whatever he would give. "Forgiven," she whispered, hiding her face in his neck. God, he smelled delicious, and she wanted to burrow under his skin.

His fingers encircled the nape of her neck, the tips digging into her scalp, and she pushed into the touch, needing that rough, fierce claiming of his. Her nipples drew into tight, painful points under her flimsy tank top at first contact with his hard chest.

She rubbed herself against him, like an animal in heat, and licked at the hollow of his throat. Usually, she didn't even do that much. In two months of their relationship, it was always Andrea who initiated touching, kissing and playing. The few times that they had sex without any foreplay, it was because they'd engaged in it indirectly for hours on a hectic workday or at a party with little, intimate touches or sitting across from each other at his mother's table while Romeo called them lust birds.

Always, it was he who reached for her and always, Monica was more than willing and ready for him. But today he gently but firmly pushed her away and she felt a sudden flash of anger. She'd spent two months making sure she never asked him for more than he was willing to give, never even going near the boundary he kept around himself. Except two days ago. And now again…

Turning stiff in his arms, she tried to jerk away and off the bed.

He didn't let her. His fingers trapped her wrists and tugged—with that ever-present gentleness he always showed her—until she was prostrate against the headboard and she had no choice but to look up at him.

"I have something important to say to you," he said, bringing her palm to his cheek and rubbing against it. He was kneeling between her thighs, and her world was reduced to this gorgeous, possessive man and his gloriously warm body. How was she supposed to walk away from this?

"I'm not in the mood for talking."

"You're always in the mood for talking, *bella*."

"Well, not right now. I want something else. And if you won't give it to me, I…"

He raised a brow. His mouth twitched but there was an unnerving intensity to his gaze that she'd never seen, that arrested the juvenile taunt she'd have thrown at him. Flushing with heat and something more, she said, "If you don't want to give me what I want, just say so."

"When did I ever deny you anything you asked for, *bella*? Truly asked for?"

Dismay curled through her as his gaze held hers. He was right. Even that day in his office, she'd given him a rhetorical answer with a lot of "woulds." She hadn't demanded to go with him. But it was also only true because she'd never made any demands of him. And today, on the day when she had to make the hardest decision of her life, she did want something from him. She wanted *him*.

She scooted closer to him. Pushing him back onto his haunches, she straddled him until his shaft was pure torment against her core. "I want to have sex, Andrea. Now. I need you inside me. Please," she added, her gaze flitting between his eyes.

"As you wish, *bella*," he said, catching her mouth in a brutally tender kiss. She was on her back on her next breath and he rocked his erection into her core, his tongue plunging into her mouth with the same erotic insistence.

Monica clung to him like a rag doll as he got rid of her tank top, leaving her in her silk panties. Then his mouth drew a line down her neck, between her breasts, and he played with them just how she liked, kneading and cupping, his tongue and teeth leaving marks on her. With a loud groan, she tugged at his hair roughly when he wouldn't touch her where she needed it and finally, finally, his tongue circled her nipple and his lips drew the tight knot into his warm mouth and Monica bucked off the bed.

His rough stubble against the sensitive nipple made her shout his name in a brazen demand that she'd have blushed at any other time. But more than just desire beat through her. Was it brushed with a stroke of grief and pain at what she was losing? Was it loss if she never had it in the first place?

Urgency beat through her veins, a desperate need to bottle everything from this moment so that it would last her a lifetime. And for the first time in their relationship, she didn't want to passively wait for him.

When his fingers dipped into her folds and stroked her clit in those mind-numbing circles she liked, it took her everything to jackknife herself into a sitting position and push at his chest. "I want to touch you," she announced.

He catered to her with a wicked smile and shifted to lean back against the headboard, lacing his hands behind his head. Licking her lips, Monica tugged at his sweatpants and he lifted his hips until they got rid of them. Then holding his gaze, she wrapped her fingers around his cock.

Arousal thrummed through her as if it were his fingers touching her intimately, instead of the opposite. He was all thick hardness wrapped in soft, velvet-like skin here, the exact opposite of the man he was everywhere else. Already, she could see the tightness around his mouth, hear the rough grunts of his breaths, feel the infinitesimal thrust of his hips when she stroked her fist all the way to the base and then up, until she was squeezing the soft head. "Monica, look at me," he said, his words a gravelly whisper that slid along her skin like pings of electricity. "You don't have to do everything today, *bella*."

"I want to, Andrea. I want to taste you and suck…" Here, she blushed beetroot red, no doubt. "And do all that stuff that men want their lovers to do. I want you to…come inside my mouth, or on my face or wherever you want to. I want to make your filthiest fantasies come true. I want to be everything you need."

His hands circled her nape, bringing her up to him so his mouth could take hers in a rough, hard kiss that told stories of his actual wishes. "We have time for you to do all this, *bella*. And you're already everything I want."

Tears pooled in her eyes as those simple words speared through her with the force of a silken thrust. Those were the words she wanted to hear, but in a different context. Her stupid, stupid heart. "I want to do it now," she said on a thready whisper.

Leaning down, she licked at the soft head and before he could recover with a curse and a grunt, she opened her mouth and sucked him in. He was salty and musky and he stretched her mouth too wide but God, the sounds he made, the filthy curses that fell from his lips, the "good girl, just like that," he kept saying, made the little discomfort worth every inch of it.

Monica followed his instructions to the letter, and could feel his body draw tighter, his hips thrust up when he lost control, his erection hitting the roof of her mouth, his need to go deeper and harder, his thighs rock hard against her nails.

His fingers tightened in her scalp, rougher than ever before, a breath before he was pushing her back into the mattress and with one rough stroke that almost pushed her off the bed, he entered her.

The sensation of being claimed by him like this… It was the most connected she'd felt to her body, to the world around her, and yet somehow, utterly divine, as if her soul couldn't remain untouched. A lone tear escaped her and fled into the bedsheets.

"I was rough. *Cristo*, did I hurt you?"

Monica licked her lower lip and shook her head. "No. It was…perfect. As it always is. But I want more, please. I want you to move. I want you to make me forget. I want…so much, Andrea, and it feels like I will never have enough of you." She looked away, scared that she had said too much, betrayed her innermost feelings somehow, even though she hadn't even articulated them for herself yet. She braced for him to push off or withdraw or even to just finish what she'd demanded he give her without acknowledging her mindless words.

But as always, Andrea surprised her.

Whatever he saw in her face, or heard in her words, he gave her more than she asked for this time. Hands under her hips, he pulled her up until she was in his lap, straddling him, entrenching him even deeper inside her.

Throwing her head back, wrapping her arms around his

neck, Monica let out a deep groan. "God, it feels like you're everywhere inside me like this."

"Look at me, *cara mia*," he said against her mouth, and she complied.

Fire burned in his gaze as he trailed tiny butterfly kisses over her face.

And then he was thrusting up into her and Monica knew she'd never forget this moment. Sex in this position was different, raw, on a visceral level. They were joined head to pelvis and she felt as if she was enveloped in this gorgeous, generous man's very essence. With every upward thrust of his, she bore down until they found a rhythm that reverberated with their heartbeats. Her breasts pushed against his chest and when he dragged her hand to her clit and said, "Come for me, *bella*," she felt a new, wild, wanton heat thrash through her.

Touching herself while he watched her dialed up her pleasure another notch. It was filthy and awakening and when her fingers wandered down and touched the place where he thrust in and out of her, he let out the filthiest curse of all, and as his gaze told her he was almost there, Monica fell apart. Her orgasm ripped through her out of the blue, with the force of a wave pulling her under, and then there was nothing but swimming through the hazy pleasure of it while Andrea's thrusts became rougher and wilder and his body pressed her down into the bed when his own climax claimed him.

Their breaths were a rough, harsh symphony in the sudden silence, their bodies damp and sweaty. And then when he pulled back and kissed her temple and whispered, "Marry me, Monica," it felt like fate had dealt her the cruelest hand one more time. Only this time, it was couched in the shape of her deepest, darkest want.

CHAPTER THIRTEEN

SHE SAID NOTHING in reply for so long that Andrea began to wonder if she'd heard him at all. Through the long, hot shower he carried her to, through the sudden foray into the kitchen in their robes when her stomach growled violently, through their return to his bedroom—giggling, after Flora had found them in the kitchen and watched them with red streaking her own cheeks—to feeding each other bits of cheese and figs and grapes and washing it down with wine. Through another bout of sex after Monica had demanded to know one of his fantasies and he had bent her over the arm of the couch while they watched each other in the full-length mirror. He began to wonder if he had said it at all.

Even wondering that, Andrea had fallen into a sort of blissful sleep, wrapped around her, after two days of emotional turmoil. When he suddenly startled awake, dawn was streaking the sky with fingers of pink, and the side where Monica slept was not only empty but cold, too. Again.

He shot to his feet, pulled on his sweatpants and followed her voice into the closet to find her packing her suitcase with her cell phone clutched to her ear.

He lasted two minutes before he grabbed the phone, ended the call without checking who it was and threw it behind him until it clanged against the floor with a loud thud. "Why are you packing?"

"You brute! That was my phone."

Hands on his hips, he gathered all the patience he could find within himself. There was a strange flutter in his chest, like a panicked bird beating its wings. "Why are you packing, Monica?"

"I have to leave," she said, shying away from his gaze, folding a sweater.

Shocked beyond reason, he grabbed her wrist, gentling his hold as he always did, and pulled her behind him back to the bedroom. He turned all the lights on and was struck by the sight of her anew. Deep shadows cradled her eyes as she wrapped her arms around herself. She looked as if she hadn't slept a wink. Andrea ran a hand over his face, willing his anger to cool, his spiraling emotions to plateau.

"Leave for where, *bella*? And why are you packing at dawn, like some thief stealing away before morning hits?"

"I wasn't going to leave without saying goodbye. The airline called about my ticket and I thought I might as well finish packing."

"Again, why are you leaving? To where?" he said, knowing that he sounded like a desperate child and not caring.

"A friend told me that Father D'Souza has developed pneumonia. He has no one to look after him. I need to do that. I want to. For once in my life, I'm in a position to give my time and energy to him. I can't leave him alone in this condition."

Relief shuddered through him, even though Andrea felt awful for the old man. This was a solvable problem. This was within his control. "I will have a nurse by his side within the hour. He will not be alone," he said, immediately reaching for his phone.

"Yes, but that would be a stranger. Not someone he knows."

"*Bene.* You can go in a couple of weeks, then. I'll even accompany you. You can spend a couple of days with him, making sure he has everything he needs and we can make a trip out of it. You always tell me how much you love New York in winter. It could even be our honeymoon trip."

Her shoulders sagged but her head jerked up. Her gaze widened. She swayed where she stood like a leaf in a storm. "You're joking."

"Twice in a row about something like this? You know me better than that, *bella*," he said, grabbing her hand. He felt this…strange, almost desperate, overwhelming need to touch her, to hold her, to anchor her to him in every way possible. He didn't question the urge.

Seating himself at the edge of the bed, he pulled her to him. And something in him calmed when she came without the protest he was expecting and buried her face in his chest. She was trembling, he realized, and tightened his hold. Her arms went around his waist, as if she was intending to vine herself around him for days to come and yet, she was planning the opposite. Lifting her chin, he kissed her and all the urgency of the past few days came rushing back. A thread of something curled within him, roping tighter and tighter around his chest.

When he pulled away, she mewled in protest. He dug his fingers into her hair and pulled her head until she was looking into his eyes. "Tomorrow. We will get married tomorrow. Mama won't like it but she'll be too happy to—"

"Why do you want to marry me?" she said, eyes wide and emotions slamming through them one after the other. There was hope and excitement but also doubt and confusion and some new inner resolve he didn't know how to break.

At least he had an answer ready for this. "I like having you in my life. I like that I can trust you in every way and I like that you and I share the kind of passion that one doesn't come by often. I like knowing that I can give you the kind of security and family that you've always wanted and dreamed of. Is that not so?"

Tears filled her eyes and overflew, the tip of her nose turning adorably red. She swiped at the tears slowly, her gaze never leaving his. "I did. I do. But I… I want to be by Father D'Souza's side as soon as possible."

"That's not an answer, Monica."

"I can't think of this now, Andrea, and—"

He nodded. "We will fly with you to New York in a couple of days, then. Mama and Romeo and I. We can marry in that church with the father's blessing."

Her mouth fell on a gasp, and a smile cut through the tears. "You're serious."

"Of course, I am."

A groan seemed to wrench out of her and she mumbled, "You're making this so hard," while drenching his chest in fresh tears. Then with a deep breath, she stood, stepped back from the circle of his arms, the line of her shoulders stiffening. "You didn't like my disappearing on you for two whole days, did you?"

"No. But—"

"Marrying me is about efficiency for you. About keeping things in control. About compromise, *si*?"

"I have no need to marry you, *bella*. So what am I compromising on?"

"It's giving me just enough without truly letting me in," she said with an empty laugh and scrubbing at her cheeks. Even watery, her eyes shone with that resolve he'd never seen in her before. "My dreams are not the same as they were three years ago, a year ago or even three months ago when you saved me from Francesco."

"So you don't believe in marriage and family and security anymore?" he asked, unable to keep the taunt out of his voice.

"I do, and you have no idea how tempting your offer is. I'd have your trust and your fidelity and the security you offer and Flora's love and Romeo's companionship. I'd belong to you, like I've never been anyone's. But all of those things can't make up for the one thing I need. You have changed me, Andrea. Being with you these two months... It's unlike anything I'll ever live through again. It's taught me so much about myself."

"You talk as if you're..." His heart gave a swift kick against his rib cage as realization landed. He stood. "You're ending this. You came back yesterday with this intention set. You asked me to make love to you as some sort of wretched goodbye. All night, you laughed and talked and kissed me...with this in mind."

"I don't want to, but I have to. Before it gets ugly and I start clinging to you. Before you push me away again. Before I do something that violates that boundary around yourself. Before my heart shatters into so many pieces at your feet. But more than anything, I need to understand what this is."

Every thought and word that came to Andrea was ugly in its shape and full of a bitter jealously. And after those came something worse. He felt as if he were in that floundering car again, yelling at his father to steer into the skid, yelling at Romeo to sit back, yelling and yelling and yelling until he could no more and the oncoming tree loomed larger and larger and fear shone in Papa's eyes and he was shouting, too, telling him that he loved him, asking him to look after his mother and Romeo, telling him that...and then there had been nothing.

Not sounds. Not sights. Not the tears in his father's eyes, or his moving lips, or his fingers' death-like hold on Andrea's hand. Nothing but wretched darkness consuming him. And when he'd woken up days later, the world had been painfully colorful, so bright and yet so empty that he had wished himself to be swallowed up back into that darkness.

He had vowed to himself that he would never feel like that again. Never feel such love again that it left him searching for the dark. And yet, here he was, losing his foothold on reality again, losing something he had never wanted at all.

"Andrea, please try to understand," she said, reaching for his hand.

He jerked away from her, his action now one of self-preservation. Somehow, he made himself look at her. The large lamp behind her limned the contours of her face and body with loving care and he wondered at how empty this space would feel without her.

"I don't," he said, reaching for some composure. It didn't matter that he could see the pain in her eyes, in her entire body. All he could focus on was the sinking sensation in the pit of his stomach. "But it is your life and as you made it clear over the weekend, you owe me nothing."

"Is that what you truly think?" she asked, anger etching itself into her words. She looked impossibly, achingly beautiful then, her emotions making her bolder and taller and making her shine brighter than he'd ever seen her before. As if her very conviction was a light inside her. "If I told you I'm in love with you, would you still marry me? If I told you it hurt to be sent away from you, it hurt to not reach for you and offer solace, it nearly ripped me apart to know that you might never feel the same about me as I do you, would you still marry me? If I told you I'd settle for nothing less than love, would you still be ready to marry me?"

He would've been less shocked if she'd slapped him across the face out of nowhere. "You've imagined yourself in love before, Monica, and look how that turned out." The moment the words poured out of his mouth, he wanted to snatch them back. *Cristo*, what was the matter with him? Why did he always say the worst things when it came to her? Why did he hurt her when it was the last thing he wanted to do?

And he had his answer as surely as she let out a humorless chuckle. It was the very thing he'd always been determined not to feel, the very thing that was making him lash out at her, the very thing that was turning him inside out at the thought of losing her. But he could not give in, could not take that risk.

Her arms went around her middle, as if he had attacked her but she'd also expected it. It shamed him that she knew him better than he knew himself, that he had proved her right. "This is why I need to leave. I can't be near you, much less marry you when I feel this way. When I don't know if this is just me reaching for security again. When I don't know if these feelings that make me so angry at you can be trusted, when this constant knot of fear sits in my throat, warning me that I shouldn't ask for more, I shouldn't crave more, I shouldn't demand more than you give. I don't want to be in a relationship with that fear in my heart. I never should be in one unless I know I can ask for whatever I deserve. It's not fair to me. It's not…" She gasped in a pained breath. "I don't want to live in that fear. I don't want to love you with that niggling whisper in my heart. So I have to leave. I have to say goodbye to the best thing that has ever happened to me. I have to let go, even though I don't want to, and hope that in the future, I will know a love that doesn't come with conditions. I have to start believing that I deserve that kind of love. And *you* made me realize that, Andrea. Even if you can't offer it."

She came to him then and went on her toes and kissed his cheek and pressed her cheek to his chest, her arms going around him again, as if he was both the storm and the port and she was caught in the middle.

Andrea couldn't bear it. Couldn't bear to smell her and hold her, and touch her and kiss her, all the while knowing that she was leaving him, alone and adrift in the snow again.

He pushed her away from him and left the suite, wanting to be swallowed up by darkness again.

Andrea hadn't imagined, in his darkest nightmares, that he would feel her loss so keenly every single day.

Of course, the fact that Monica had run his life like a well-engineered machine, always anticipating his needs and meeting them before he even verbalized them, made it impossible for him not to miss her.

But it wasn't just his work life. It was the way she'd made him laugh; the way she'd dragged him along to every new experience that she was determined to have; the way she'd sit quietly with her knitting while he worked on his sculptures; the way she'd seemed to bring him back to the man he'd been once before.

Ever since the accident, he had drawn a boundary around himself; had reduced his life to a single dimension—work—and let everything else about him die a slow death. But that had never been what Papa had wanted. He had never asked Andrea to turn himself into a machine.

He had only asked him to be careful with his racing, to dial down the unnecessary risks he had begun to take, the highs he had started chasing, to think of others before himself. And yet, as punishment, Andrea had turned himself into another version Papa would have hated, too.

He would have told him that life was to be lived, with the ones you love, that one's heart was for more than just beating and pumping blood. He had shown him and Romeo by making their family name stand for so much, by loving their mother so well that to this day, that love was a shining light in her smile.

How could Andrea be anything less? What was left of his life without Monica? How was this empty darkness better than the light and laughter she had brought him?

The merger was done, production had started on the new plant and yet he felt no surge of pride or sense of satisfaction. All he wanted was to hear her voice one more time, see her and hold her.

He knew Romeo was in touch with her, but he refused to ask his brother about how she was faring. It was bad enough neither his mother nor Romeo would meet his eyes or say a word to his face. For all that she'd said she wouldn't take sides, Mama's displeasure was clear.

But as weeks piled into a month, what little pride he had hung on to had dissolved. For a few hours he decided he would fly to New York, to offer support to her while she tended to the man who had shown her kindness and love, without imposing any conditions. He wouldn't ask for anything, demand anything.

But then her face swam into his vision, her eyes full of anguish when he'd straight out told her that she'd believed herself in love before. *Cristo*, he'd been cruel to taunt her for what she thought was her weakness. Still, she'd behaved so bravely, *his fierce little mouse*, walking away from him, *from them*, from the golden future he'd painted using her darkest fear against her, to get clarity, to know herself, even as she'd told him she was in love with him.

I don't want to love you with that niggling whisper in my heart.

How could he then be any less brave? How could he chase her to New York and steal that time and space she'd asked for? How could he browbeat her into saying yes to him and then wonder for the rest of his life if she truly loved him?

Suddenly, he understood the anguish of the dilemma she'd faced.

If he truly loved her, which he realized he did painfully with each passing day that he didn't see her or touch her or kiss her or hold her, he would give her the space to figure it out.

He would let her be, let her know herself, see herself as he saw her, the vulnerable yet fierce, the generous but bold, the gentle but brave, creature that she was. He would wait and hope that when she did have that clarity that she would come back to him and give him just one more chance.

Just one chance and he would lay the world at her feet.

Every cell inside him revolted at the idea of waiting, of leaving the decision in her hands—at least for now. He balked at the idea of not chasing her down to wherever she was in the world and seducing her and kissing her and bending her to his will, at the idea of not making her say that she loved him all over again. He was not a man used to inaction, to letting others dictate his happiness and yet there was another thing he was coming to recognize—his happiness was with her.

In her kisses and embraces and her soft smiles.

It was the pain and uncertainty and the anguish that came with loving her, the very thing he'd wanted to avoid. But then he'd remember the sweetness of her kisses, her shy boldness when she was under him and looked up at him with those yellow eyes, and the soft, slow way she'd stroke his lips when he laughed, as if she wanted to bottle the sound. The easy, effortless way she had loved him, even when he hadn't been able to appreciate it. And he knew that it was all worth it. That without this pain, they would always be unsure of each other. That now, he could live with nothing but her unconditional surrender, and his own in return.

The waiting made each day that much longer, that much more unbearable. Whatever they saw in his face now melted Mama's and Romeo's silent admonishments.

Then suddenly, as he sat working on a wooden piece in his new shed that gave him little pleasure without her company, it came to him. He would give her the one thing, *the only thing*, she'd ever asked of him and hope that she'd understand his message.

That everything that was his, his mind, body and heart, were all hers, if only she'd demand it of him.

CHAPTER FOURTEEN

IT HAD BEEN three weeks since Monica had returned to Italy and joined Valentini Luxury Goods again as an executive assistant. Only instead of assisting the CEO, she was now working for the Executive Head of Design, which was Romeo. Working for him at his studio, where he allowed no one, and staying at his girlfriend's place, hadn't made Monica any less worried about running into Andrea. Or any less eager.

It felt unnecessarily sneaky, though, and Romeo wasn't happy about it. She didn't blame him. But the good friend he was, he also understood that she had needed to do this.

She'd spent two months looking after Father D'Souza and when he had not only recovered but also returned to his work at the orphanage as if he were a spring chicken instead of a seventy-three-year-old man, Monica had found herself not only heart-sick but at a loose end, as well. As much as she loved Father D'Souza and was glad to see him restored to his full self, her life wasn't in New York.

The new friends and family she'd made were all across the ocean. Even as she'd nursed Father D'Souza with full devotion, her mind, heart and soul had remained behind with *him*. Thinking of Andrea, remembering the look in his eyes when he'd asked her if she was ending it, the shock that seemed to reverberate through him when she'd proclaimed that she loved him, she hadn't been able to sleep or eat or function in any kind of normal way.

All she could think of was whether she'd made the wrong decision, if she'd thrown away a lifetime's worth of belonging and happiness by confusing her feelings. Not for one moment could she stop imagining what life would have been like if she'd said yes.

Would they have been married already? Would she have shown him all her favorite spots in New York? Would she have settled into married life as well as she'd settled into being his fake fiancée? Would there have been a day where she woke up and realized that she was simply another cog in his life, like everything else that was convenient and easy and suitable?

Would she have been happy knowing she loved him and he would never love her back?

When the last question came, she inevitably fell into the thinking she'd been right to leave, though it provided no solace.

But one thing had become clear.

She had to be strong enough to return to Italy because her friends and life were there. She was still connected to Flora and Romeo, still connected in some way to Andrea. She had to reclaim her life, her strength, in this way. She might even have to face a future where Andrea would move on with another woman and would simply have to hope that someday she might move on, too. Though at this point in time, it was impossible to think of a moment or a day when she wouldn't love Andrea with a soul-deep need. At least that much had become clear to her across oceans and two months of time.

So she'd returned to Italy, asking Romeo to help her find a job and start afresh. As much of a businessman as his brother, Romeo had said he was loath to let talent like hers go off to another company, especially with her familiarity of the company culture and organizational systems. Her first instinct had been to beg him to find her something else, but she knew she couldn't avoid Andrea forever, either.

She couldn't run and hide and avoid life, as she'd done for so many years.

And yesterday, another mundane, lifeless day in a number of them, it seemed, a small cardboard box had been sitting on her desk in Romeo's studio, looking a little worse for the wear. She realized why when she looked at the different stamps. The little package was addressed to her and had been sent to the orphanage, but must have missed her by days. Father D'Souza must have received it and forwarded it to her here.

Hands trembling, breath whistling through her as if she'd run a marathon, Monica pulled at the tape and the numerous layers of bubble wrap around the object. She was sobbing by the time she got the last one off and the little dark mermaid danced in her hand.

Through her blurry vision, she ran her fingers over the delicate contours of sculpture, marveled at his craft with wonder in her heart. And then she was unfurling the small note, torn out of his notepad, and read:

Ask me, bella. For whatever you want.

Her knees giving out under her, Monica had fallen to the floor, clutching the little mermaid to her chest, her heart expanding so big that it might explode out of her. He'd given her what she'd asked for. He'd always give her what she asked for, if only she was brave enough to ask for it.

So here she was at his family home, in the bedroom suite she'd shared with him, knowing that Romeo was out and Flora would be at her friend's anniversary party, wondering if her sudden burst of bravery had, after all, been a foolish idea. She didn't even know if he would be home tonight. But she'd wanted to surprise him and had even thought up an excuse in case he was in a frightful mood.

She was staring at the pieces on his desk, shocked at seeing several new ones, her throat full of that sticky pain she felt whenever she thought of him, when a voice said behind her, "Should I call the *polizia* on you, Ms. D'Souza?"

Monica whirled so fast that her head felt dizzy.

Andrea stood against his closed bedroom door, eyes alive with an unholy shine that sent a thrum of awareness through her. It was the look he got when he wanted to tease her, or torment her extra for her climax, or when he wanted sex. Basically, all the times when he wanted her, saw the real her, the American orphan that no one wanted.

He looked like he hadn't shaved in a couple of days but otherwise, he looked as magnetic and gorgeous as he had ever been. His dress shirt hung open to reveal the rough hair on his chest that she loved to touch, and the black trousers he wore emphasized the lean power of his thighs.

Meeting his gaze, though… She felt like every bit of oxygen had been sucked from the room and she was almost lightheaded from the impact.

"You look like hell," he said, walking toward her, barely giving her time to recover or react in any way.

She tucked a strand of her hair behind her ear, fervently wishing she'd washed it and worn something other than faded sweatpants and the thick, chunky sweater made out of Italian wool—the one thing she had stolen from him. But she'd been acting on instinct, urged on by a reckless kind of desperation. She'd needed to see him.

The closer he came, though, the less panicky and anxious she felt. Almost as if she couldn't be anything less near this man than her whole self, this man who had taught her that she deserved everything she ever wanted in life—including his love. Straightening her shoulders, she lifted her chin. "I haven't been doing well." When he scowled, she sighed and added, "Emotionally, I mean."

"But you're well enough to come into my home and rifle through my things? What were you planning to steal?"

"I'm not stealing anything. There are a couple of things I left and they're mine," she bluffed.

"Like what?"

"Like the necklace you picked for me."

"Why do you want it when you didn't want me?"

Outrage erupted from her mouth like an indignant squeak. "I never said I didn't want you. I never even said I was ending it. You did. I just wanted some space. I needed to know that what I felt for you was different from what I felt for Francesco. For that I needed to grow up, understand my own needs and wants first. In the end, it turned out to be right."

He was closer now and she could smell that delicious scent of his and feel that warmth of his body, and her knees nearly buckled.

"What turned out to be right, *bella*?" he said with an infinite tenderness, and this close, Monica could see that he had not fared any better than her at all. There was a gaunt, downright pinched, look to his features as if something dark had etched itself permanently onto them. Her loss, she wanted to think, though it didn't really give her solace. He looked ravaged, reduced, less of that vibrant, energetic man she knew and adored. "What did your little experiment prove, except that it made us both miserable?"

She swallowed at the rough rasp of his voice as he asked that, as if he, too, was making an effort to speak past the pain. And this new, brave, not-delusional version of her knew, in her gut, that he *was* in pain. That he had missed her as much as she'd missed him or even more. Because when Andrea Valentini gave something, he gave it with his whole heart. And that gave her the courage to say all that was in her own. "It proved that I am in love with you, that these feelings I have for you—" she rubbed at her chest, feeling actual pain there "—are so real that you're all I think of and see and feel even when I'm not near you. It proved that what I thought I felt for Francesco was nothing more than a cheap imitation of the real thing. What I feel for you, Andrea, it makes me braver, stronger, makes me know myself like I never did before. It makes me want the best for myself. So it also proved that I'd have been miserable to marry you without having your love."

"If I talk about my grief about Papa, if I tell you of myself at my worst moment, then, *bella*?"

"I already know you blame yourself for that accident. That for months after, you wouldn't look at Flora. That you and Romeo nearly lost each other all over again. I know that it has only driven you to be a better man, a man your father would have been proud of. Whatever you think is your worst, Andrea, I only love even more."

"And yet instead of facing me, you return to Italy, work for my brother right under my nose? What is that, *bella*?"

It took her a moment, looking around the shifting light in the room—suddenly they were cocooned in a thick darkness—to realize he had gotten even closer. With his arm on the wall behind her head, he had caged her in, and yet it felt so natural that if they were in a room together, any room, it was impossible that they would stay apart. Something about his tone made her tilt her chin up and look into his eyes. He had known she was back, that she was working for Romeo. The little flicker of hope in her heart turned into a bright, glowing flame. "It was *your* idea that I work for Romeo. Your idea that I stay with his girlfriend. Even my return ticket, you arranged it through him."

"Si."

"Why? So that I can feel even more indebted to you? So that you can flex your power over me?"

"Is that what you truly think, Monica?" he said, his breath warm on her cheek.

She turned and their mouths were so close that she could feel the weight and depth of his lips crashing over hers. She wanted to touch him and kiss him so badly that she was trembling with the need. And the truth was plainly written in his gaze if only she was brave enough to see it. "You… You wanted me to have that safe space. You wanted me to prove to myself that I'm strong enough to come back and face you. You wanted me to have the security of knowing that Romeo and Flora are not lost to me. That you're not lost to me, even outside of our relationship."

"Si."

A sob threatened to burst through her chest. Monica bunched her fists against his chest, the sensation of his skin against her fingers nearly burning her. "Why? Why do all that for me? Why?"

"You have a pretty logical brain, *bella*. Why don't you follow through?"

"I can follow the logic, yes," she said, smiling through her tears. "But I need to hear you say it, Andrea. All my life, I was desperate to belong somewhere, to be wanted. So desperate that somewhere came to mean anywhere. But not anymore. With you, I need so much more. With you, I want the entire world. I want…" She pressed her hand to his chest and felt the thundering beat of his heart. "I want… your words, because I know you don't give them lightly."

He smiled then and she could see his heart in it. "Flexing your claws again?"

"With you, yes. Since I know you love them," she said, gaining back some of her own spirit.

His gray gaze held hers then, his hands taking hers. He opened his mouth and closed it a couple of times, as if words couldn't encompass what he felt. God, she had always understood him best, better than anyone.

Finally, when he spoke, his words were low and soft and full of his love. "My heart, my body, my everything, is yours, Monica. I'm so sorry it took me so long to see what I have in you, to realize how much I already needed you. You didn't just change me, *bella*, you brought me back to life. You completed me even before I knew what that meant."

When Monica had imagined this moment, and she had over the past few weeks with a feverish, desperate urgency, she was laughing and screaming with joy. But reality was different. Even hearing those words from him only brought into keener contrast all the doubts and ache she'd suffered, all the anguish of wondering if he'd ever choose this between them, if he'd ever choose *her*.

"To wait for you to come to me, to hope that you would see you belong with me and I with you…has been the hardest thing I've ever done in life. I will give you words and actions and promises and presents, if only you give me one chance, *bella*. I will give you all of myself."

And then she could hold off no longer. She pressed her mouth to his, half sobbing, half yelling and the shape and taste of him started a riot in her body. He clamped her hard to him, his fingers digging almost painfully into her hips as he devoured her mouth. It was a hard, rough, possessive kind of kiss and it was exactly what she needed.

He bit her lower lip, licked the hurt and repeated the rough caresses over and over again. Shaking and gasping, Monica clung to him, rubbing herself against his body. "I need to be inside you, *bella*," he whispered, his words taking on a guttural slant, his urgency in every touch.

"Yes, now, please," she said.

He pushed her sweatpants down roughly and she kicked them off, and when he lifted her, she wrapped her legs around his waist. Pressing her back against the wall, he thrust inside her and Monica banged her head into the wall and he cursed and cradled her head, but the jarring pain of it only made the pleasure in her lower belly even more white-hot.

But she didn't want to miss an inch of this, so she clasped his cheek and looked at him and when he said, "Say it again," she shouted the words instead.

"I love you, Andrea!" She repeated his name again and again, on each silken thrust, and soon, she burst like a star in the sky and he was following her.

And even though she'd come to accept that the future was uncertain, Monica knew she'd never regret a moment spent with him. Not when it was true that he loved her, too.

It felt like hours but it was only minutes later, after they had both washed up and she was in his lap in his armchair, that Andrea was able to hear his heart's muted whispers again.

It was only now, when he could physically touch her and feel her weight in his arms, that he felt like his world was all right again. Her cheek pressed to his heart, Monica burrowed into him as if she never wanted to leave again.

"Tell me, Andrea. I know your heart but still, I want to hear it. Please."

He tilted her chin up and looking into those beautiful yellow eyes, Andrea saw his future. "I'm in love with you, *bella.* I knew it even as you shouted it at me. I knew as I walked away from you. But I couldn't face it. All I could see was pain and loss ahead, even as I was already losing you. So young as you are, what you did was right for both of us. It was only after losing you that I could see why it was so easy for me to jump into a compromise of a marriage. You were right. I was cheating you. And I was cheating myself."

"You still want to marry me, then?" she asked, her voice small and fragile, and he felt as if she could turn him inside out.

"*Si.* More than anything in the world. I want to have you all to myself first. Then I want to have a family with you, if that's what you want. And I want to love you every day for the rest of our lives. You changed me even before you were my fake fiancée, *bella.* And I can't wait to see what else life holds for us."

Then she was crying and whispering, "Yes, I'll marry you," and Andrea kissed her and tasted her tears and her pain and her love and vowed to himself that she'd never doubt herself or his love ever again.

* * * * *

MILLS & BOON®

Coming next month

HUSBAND FOR THE HOLIDAYS
Dani Collins

In so many ways, this was her dream come true. Could she really complain if it wasn't exactly perfect? "Yes. I will marry you, Konstantin."

"Good." He slid the cool ring onto her finger, then looped his arms behind her.

Eloise's hands were on his lapels, quivering with pleasure at having this right to touch him.

She looked up at him, expecting him to kiss her, but he only caressed the edge of her jaw with his bent finger.

He dipped his head into her throat and nuzzled his lips against her skin.

She gasped and shivered. Her nipples stung and her knees grew weak.

His breath pooled near her ear, fanning the arousal taking hold in her. This was surreal. Too perfect. Like a Christmas miracle. Not that she believed in such things, but maybe it was?

Continue reading
HUSBAND FOR THE HOLIDAYS
Dani Collins

Available next month
millsandboon.co.uk